SEE WHAT HAPPENS
WHEN YOU LISTEN TO ME?

"Only good things." He smiled at her. "Now, are you going to thank me properly?"

"I said 'thank you.' That's considered in some cultures as thanking you properly."

"I was hoping for a little more than that."

She studied him for a long moment before she nodded.

"All right." She scooted down a bit on the bed, pulled her gown up high on her thighs, and relaxed back into the mattress. "If you could make it quick before the food gets here, that would be great."

Gwenvael felt a small twitch beneath his eye. He often got something similar right on his eyelid but only when he had to deal with his father. Apparently a new one had developed that belonged only to Lady Dagmar. "That's not what I meant."

"I hope you're not expecting me to get on my knees because I don't think the healer—"

"No!" *Good gods, this woman!* "That's not what I meant, either."

"That's always what men mean when they ask to be thanked properly."

"Your world frightens me. I want us to be clear on that." He leaned over and grabbed her waist, lifting her until her back again rested on the propped-up pillows.

"I'm unclear as to what you want, then."

"A kiss," he said, pulling her dress back down to her ankles. "A simple kiss."

BOOK YOUR PLACE ON OUR WEBSITE AND MAKE THE READING CONNECTION!

We've created a customized website just for our very special readers, where you can get the inside scoop on everything that's going on with Zebra, Pinnacle and Kensington books.

When you come online, you'll have the exciting opportunity to:

- View covers of upcoming books

- Read sample chapters

- Learn about our future publishing schedule (listed by publication month *and author*)

- Find out when your favorite authors will be visiting a city near you

- Search for and order backlist books from our online catalog

- Check out author bios and background information

- Send e-mail to your favorite authors

- Meet the Kensington staff online

- Join us in weekly chats with authors, readers and other guests

- Get writing guidelines

- AND MUCH MORE!

**Visit our website at
http://www.kensingtonbooks.com**

WHAT A DRAGON SHOULD KNOW

G.A. AIKEN

ZEBRA BOOKS
Kensington Publishing Corp.
http://www.kensingtonbooks.com

ZEBRA BOOKS are published by

Kensington Publishing Corp.
119 West 40th Street
New York, NY 10018

All Kensington titles, imprints, and distributed lines are available at special quantity discounts for bulk purchases for sales promotion, premiums, fund-raising, educational, or institutional use.

Special book excerpts or customized printings can also be created to fit specific needs. For details, write or phone the office of the Kensington Special Sales Manager: Attn. Special Sales Department. Kensington Publishing Corp., 119 West 40th Street, New York, NY 10018. Phone: 1-800-221-2647.

ISBN-13: 978-1-4201-3298-4
ISBN-10: 1-4201-3298-9

First Printing: September 2009
10 9 8 7 6 5 4

Printed in the United States of America

To Kate Duffy. You have always been brave enough to let me off the leash—even when you had no idea where I might be headed or what I might maul along the way—and for that I am truly grateful.

To Doug Lindquist. Although you are gone, your guidance, encouragement, and suggestions to "slow down, breathe, and stop panicking" still help me every time I sit down to write. You are very much missed, my friend, but you and your words are forever with me. Thank you, Doug—for everything.

Dear Reader:

As a former instigating, tattletale baby sister, I've been looking forward to writing the story of the instigating, tattletale younger brother of Fearghus the Destroyer and Briec the Mighty.

But I can't say that it was easy writing Gwenvael the Handsome's story because I knew he needed a heroine who could do much more than challenge him in the bedroom. To keep a more than two-hundred-year-old dragon entertained for another six hundred years when most of that dragon's days were spent plotting and planning "shenanigans" and "hijinks," I needed a heroine who absolutely *lived* for "shenanigans" and "hijinks." And that heroine is Dagmar Reinholdt, The Beast of the Northlands.

And although it may not have been easy writing this book, it was fun. How could it not be, with two scheming troublemakers at the helm?

Also, even though my books can be read as stand-alones, in the world of dragon politics there are often quite a few players, so I want to suggest you read Fearghus's book, *Dragon Actually*, and Briec's story, *About a Dragon*, to get yourself up to speed on the Dragon Kin.

Now, after that brief aside, I invite you to enter the world of my Dragon Kin—where the dragons are much saner than the humans surrounding them could ever hope to be.

—G.A. Aiken

Chapter 1

It wasn't the first time he'd run for his life. And it most likely would not be the last. In the past few decades, though, he'd mostly run from angry fathers who'd found him where they felt he should not be. Or he'd run from town guards—sent by angry fathers who'd found him where they felt he should not be.

But this day, Gwenvael ran from his own kin. Not that this was in any way new to him either, but it had been a while since he'd been forced to.

Also true was that he should have kept his mouth shut. Yet it had been a legitimate question. As always, though, his kin blew everything out of proportion and took out their misplaced rage on him.

Why did they just not admit they were jealous? For he was Gwenvael the Handsome. Third-born son and fourth-born offspring of the Dragon Queen, Former Captain of the Dragon Queen's Northern Armies, and most-loved male throughout the Dark Plain regions, Gwenvael was always magnificent, magnanimous, and loving.

And his kin hated him because of that.

Besides, who knew that a queen would be so sensitive? Even a human one.

All he did was ask a simple question—"Are you supposed to be that large at only seven months with child?" A simple question that led to tears, unattractive snorting noises, and thrown weaponry. It seemed the human queen may have lost her ability to run quickly, but her throwing arm was still true. *Nearly took my damn ear off.*

Now the queen's consort—also known as Gwenvael's eldest brother and future Dragon King of the Southlands, Fearghus— felt the need to chase him down like a rabbit.

That's why Gwenvael ran. Because if Fearghus the Destroyer *destroyed* Gwenvael's beautiful face, the big bastard would never face retribution for it. Because, as always, he'd be forgiven his violent transgressions while Gwenvael was never forgiven his more sensual ones.

Found naked with a few of his grandfather's kitchen maids? His father's claw right to the back of the head. Suggest that when his mother was in human form she may want to stay away from things that brought out the largeness of her ass? His father's claw right to the back of the head. Set up a small eightieth birthday party for his youngest brother Éibhear that involved a few of the local brothel girls? His *mother*'s claw right to the back of the head.

Fearghus, however, had hacked off the tip of Gwenvael's poor tail more than a century ago and still he had not been punished. While the spiked tip most dragons used as a weapon floated in a river somewhere, Gwenvael dragged around a stump.

Thankfully, he'd found other uses for his tragically lame, disfigured tail. Uses most females appreciated quite a lot.

Gwenvael dashed around a corner, heading toward the stables and out the back entrance. It was then he saw sweet Izzy, daughter of the delicious Talaith and Gwenvael's idiot brother Briec.

Izzy was not Gwenvael's niece by blood, her true father a Southland human who'd died many years ago in battle before Talaith and Briec had ever met or mated. But Izzy was still family and he adored her as she adored him. Or, at least that was what he thought until she slammed into him as he charged by, sending Gwenvael flying into one of the stable doors. He kept forgetting exactly how strong his human niece was. Her mother may be a small dainty witch trained to kill on command, but Izzy was a bit of a bruiser—and enjoyed that about herself immensely.

Izzy stood over him and yelled out, "Got him!"

"Iseabail!" he cried, devastated. "My love! My adoring niece! How could you?"

"You shouldn't have hurt her feelings! It was mean." She shook her finger at him. "Don't be mean!"

Izzy. Sweet, beautiful, but eternally strange Izzy. Her loyalty to the queen was never to be questioned. Even now she trained with the troops daily, hoping to be sent off to war so she could prove her loyalty with blood. Why anyone felt the need to do that was beyond Gwenvael. He didn't like to bleed or be harmed in any way. He liked all his bits and pieces exactly where they were and in the correct working order. As he was forced to tell his father more than once, "I said I'd *fight* for my mother's throne. I never said I'd die for it." Then he'd add, simply to annoy the old bastard into one of his frothy temper tantrums, "Don't you think I'm too pretty to die?"

"I thought you loved me!" Gwenvael yelled at Izzy.

"Not when you're mean!" Her goodness was so sincere that the thought of fireballing her from his existence for this betrayal only went through his mind once . . . maybe twice.

Big, abusive hands grabbed Gwenvael by the hair and proceeded to drag him away from the stables.

"Let me go, you big bastard!"

"You're going back in there, you son of a bitch," Fearghus growled out. "You're going back in there and you're going to apologize if it's the last thing you *ever* do."

"I have nothing to apologize for."

To prove he disagreed on that point, Fearghus stopped long

enough so that he could stomp his big foot against Gwenvael's stomach.

"Ow!"

"You made her cry. No one makes her cry."

They were going through the Great Hall of the Garbhán Isle castle now. At one time this had been a place of horror, the seat of power for Lorcan the Butcher. Now it belonged to the woman who was Lorcan's bastard sister and the one who'd taken his head.

"I can walk on my own," he told Fearghus when he realized the whiny lizard had no intention of stopping any time soon. And although Gwenvael could shift to his natural—and exquisite—dragon form in his bid to get away, he'd only unnecessarily harm the humans who lived here. Something he was loath to do. He liked humans. . . . Well, he liked female humans. The males he could do with or without.

"I'm not chasing you anymore," Fearghus said while dragging Gwenvael up those hard stone stairs. When Gwenvael began to kick and try to yank himself away from Fearghus's grasp there was second-oldest Briec grabbing his legs and assisting Fearghus.

"You betraying bastard!"

"What are we doing with him?" Briec asked eagerly. "Are we throwing him out a window? Let's throw him out a window! Or off the roof!"

"We're going to take him to Annwyl."

"Won't our mother notice if he no longer has his head?"

"She'll notice," Fearghus answered, ignoring Gwenvael's struggles. "The question becomes 'will she care?'"

Now in front of the queen's bedchamber, Fearghus kicked the door open and, together with Briec, tossed poor Gwenvael into the room. The door slammed shut, and Gwenvael realized that his brothers had left him to the tender mercies of the Queen of Dark Plains. Also referred to as the Blood Queen of Dark

Plains, the Taker of Heads, the Mad Bitch of Garbhán Isle, and the much pithier Annwyl the Bloody. For some reason the human queen was known to have a wee bit of a temper.

Steeling himself, Gwenvael looked up at fair Queen Annwyl and said, "My lovely and sweet Annwyl. My soul aches for you. My heart pines for you. Tell me you'll forgive me for my hasty, foolish words and that our love will never diminish."

She stared at him a long moment and then, to Gwenvael's ultimate horror, burst into more tears.

He knew then he'd never forgive his brothers for this.

They called her The Beast of Reinholdt. Or The Beast, for short.

She didn't appreciate it, especially since her name was actually Dagmar, but she tolerated it. In her world there were worse things than being given a name she didn't think she deserved.

All right . . . perhaps she deserved the name a *little*.

Closing her book, Dagmar sighed. She knew she couldn't spend all day in her room hiding, no matter how much she wanted to. She knew she had to face her father and tell him what she'd done. The fact that she'd done it for the good of her father's territory and his people would mean little to The Reinholdt, the mightiest warlord in the Northlands. But she'd learned to ignore her father's "moments," as she liked to call them, early on in life if the end result meant getting what she wanted.

Placing the book aside, she stood and donned one of her grey wool dresses. She tugged it into place and then wrapped a plain leather girdle around her hips. She slid the small dagger she used for menial cutting into the girdle and then tied a grey kerchief around her head, her long braid reaching down her back.

Before giving herself a cursory glance in the full-length mirror beside her bed, Dagmar carefully placed her spectacles on her nose. She didn't need them to read, but she needed them for everything else. All those years ago, it had been the monk, dear Brother Ragnar, who gave Dagmar her first pair of spectacles when he noticed how often she squinted any time she looked more than a few inches past her nose. He made the pair himself and she'd been wearing them ever since.

One quick look in the mirror proved nothing truly horrible with her ensemble, so she stepped from her room and allowed her dog to race out in front of her. Dagmar locked her door and double-checked to make sure it was securely locked, before proceeding down the stone halls of her father's fortress. She'd been born here and had never gone farther than into the closest town. She knew she would die behind these walls one day, unless she could convince her father to give her a small house in the surrounding woods outside the gates. Tragically, she'd have to wait at least another ten years before she was firmly in the "spinster" category.

In the Northlands, females didn't stray far from their kinsmen until they were handed off to their husbands. After three failed attempts at marriage, she doubted any man foolish enough would come along willing to risk his neck among the Reinholdt Clan just to get into her bed. Which, when she was honest with herself—and when wasn't she?—she found very much a relief.

Some things came naturally to those of her sex. Being accommodating, loving, charming, and endearing—she knew many women who naturally possessed these gifts. Dagmar, however, possessed none of these traits—although she could pretend she had them for short periods of time. If pretending got her what she wanted, then why not?

Because Dagmar knew there were worse things in this

world than pretending to be a caring, demure woman. For instance, actually *being* a caring, demure woman. The Northlands were a rough, hard land and not for the meek of heart or weak of spirit. To actually care, or to actually *be* as weak as the Northmen expected their women to be was an excellent way to die young.

Dagmar's intention was to live to be a hundred. At least.

Intently studying the papers in her hands allowed Dagmar to ignore everything that went on around her. The violent fights, the drunken kinsmen littering the floor, the writhing bodies in dark shadows.

Another early morning in the Reinholdt Fortress.

She'd taught herself a long time ago to simply block out all of the extraneous activity that did nothing but distract her from what was important.

An easy enough skill with her dog, Canute, walking boldly beside her, keeping watch and protecting her. She'd raised him from birth and now he was her loyal companion. He was one of the many battle dogs she'd bred and trained for her father since she was nine winters old, but Canute was hers and no other's. For the last three years, he'd protected her like Canute's father had protected her. Viciously. So viciously, no one else could get near her. She adored it.

Dagmar was well aware it was strange for a woman to be responsible for the dogs that a warlord like her father would use during battle, but he'd been unable to ignore the way she had with canines. But most especially, he couldn't ignore the fact that she'd trained every battle dog within his province to respond only to her voice, her command. She'd only been a month shy of her tenth birthday when she'd plotted, planned, and executed her first victory. She clearly remembered standing in front of her father, every vicious, uncontrollable battle dog standing in front, beside, or behind her at attention and waiting for orders. Squinting up at her father, for even then her long-distance sight had been failing, Dagmar softly explained, "I am sorry your trainer lost his arm, Father. Perhaps you need someone who can handle these animals a bit better, with kindness rather than brutality."

"You're just a girl," he'd snarled back, gesturing at her with that trainer's torn and blood-drenched arm. "What do you know of war and battle?"

"I know nothing," she very nearly whispered, her eyes downcast. "But I do know dogs."

"Show me then. Show me what you know."

Lifting her gaze to meet her father's, she'd pointed at one dog, then motioned to one of the guards. Only one of the eighteen dogs charged over and tore into the guard that had once referred to her as "that ugly girl."

Her father watched the dog do what he'd been trained to do, not at all concerned with the guard screaming for help.

"Very good," he'd finally said, but she'd known the test wasn't over.

"Thank you."

"Now call him back."

They both knew this to be the true challenge because the Reinholdt battle dogs could often be uncontrollable once the bloodlust got them. Many of them were often put down by their own handlers at the end of battle.

So, still keeping her father's gaze, Dagmar again raised her fingers, gave a short whistle, and motioned with her hand. The dog had dropped his screaming, crying, and bleeding prey immediately, trotting back to her side and sitting in the spot he'd left. His tongue hanging out, blood on his muzzle, he'd stared at Dagmar, waiting for her next command.

At the time, her father had only grunted, walking off with the trainer's arm still in tow as it left a bloody trail behind him. Yet by the time her sixteenth winter passed, Dagmar had complete control of the kennels and any dog—working or pet—on her father's lands.

Stopping abruptly when Canute did, Dagmar waited until a chalice flew past her head and into the wall beside her. Another fight between one of her brothers and his wife.

Not even bothering to look, she stepped over the rolling and dented chalice on the floor and headed to the Main Hall. Her father sat at the main dining table; several of her brothers sat near or across from him as did their wives, but the chair next to him was vacant because it was Dagmar's chair. Something she knew annoyed her sister-in-law Kikka, who sat glaring at her from across the table.

As she walked in and took her seat, her father shoveled food into his mouth as if afraid the thick porridge would try and make a run for it. As always, she ignored the sight of her father feeding.

In her world, there were worse things than bad table manners.

"Father."

Her father grunted. He'd never been a talkative man, but he especially had little to say to his only daughter. After twelve sturdy sons from three different wives—two had run away and Dagmar's mother had passed away during childbirth—he never expected a daughter. And he never expected a daughter like her. When drunk, he often bemoaned the fact that she hadn't been born a man. He could do more with her if she was useful, rather than something he simply had to protect.

It should hurt her that after all this time her father still didn't recognize what she did for his fiefdom. How much she contributed, including the defenses she'd designed, the dogs she'd trained to save the lives of his men during battle, or the important truces she'd help to arrange. But why waste time being hurt? It wouldn't change anything and would only take precious time out of her day.

Dagmar reached for a loaf of bread and tore it apart. "The new batch of puppies looks very promising, Father. Very strong. Powerful." She tore the half of bread in her hands once more and gave Canute a portion.

Her father grunted again, but instead of waiting for an answer she didn't expect, Dagmar dug into the hot porridge one of the servants placed before her. Their mornings together, when he wasn't off defending his lands, were often like this. In fact, she'd become so very used to the silence or occasional grunt that when her father suddenly did speak to her, Dagmar nearly choked on her food.

"Pardon?" she said, once she'd swallowed.

"I said what message did you send out a few days ago with my seal on it?"

Dammit. "You allow me to use your seal and sign your name to almost all correspondence. So you'll have to be more specific, Fa—"

"Cut to it," he snarled.

So she would. "I sent a message to Annwyl of the Dark Plains."

He stared at her for so long, she knew he had no idea who she meant. "All right."

Without another word, he stood and picked up his favorite battle ax. Mornings were for battle training in the Northlands, when the two suns were in the sky but the air was still at its coldest. As her father walked out of the Main Hall, Kikka put down her spoon and loudly asked, "Isn't Annwyl of Dark Plains also called the Mad Bitch of Garbhán Isle?"

Dagmar had only a moment to look coldly across the table at her worthless sister-in-law when The Reinholdt stormed back in, Dagmar's brothers suddenly disappearing in the face of their father's rage.

The blade of The Reinholdt's ax slammed into the dining table, the sound of cracking wood scattering the remaining servants. Before Dagmar could speak a word, her father yelled, *"You sent a message to that crazy bitch?"*

Gwenvael stared at the Queen of Dark Plains and worried. She seemed so weak. Weaker than he'd ever seen her before. And pale, which didn't fit a warrior queen who spent most of her time outdoors with her troops, killing all those in her way. Her skin had always been golden brown from the sun. Not as brown as Talaith and Izzy, but they were from the deserts of Alsandair where everyone was born in varying shades of brown. Annwyl was not.

Yet these last few months, as her belly grew larger and her twins more active inside her, Annwyl had seemed to have none of the glow of other first-time human mothers he'd seen throughout his travels. Instead, she looked drawn and tired.

"What is it, Annwyl?"

At least she'd finally stopped crying, but now she stood at the window and silently stared down into the courtyard.

"What's wrong, my queen? You're not your usual self."

She smiled. "I'm not your queen."

"You are when I'm here. And as your loyal and most loving of subjects, I just want to help."

"I know you do."

"So what is it, Annwyl? What is it that has you so worried that I'd bet five gold pieces you haven't even told Fearghus." When she turned farther away from him, he sat down in one of the sturdy straight-back chairs and held his hand out to Annwyl—he wasn't fool enough to approach her again when she was in a mood. Not with those damn swords no more than arm's length from her. "Come tell Gwenvael what you cannot tell my dear—but not nearly as handsome or charming— brother."

After a long moment, Annwyl took Gwenvael's hand and

allowed him to place her on his lap. He stroked her back while she dug into the pocket of her gown. She handed over the piece of parchment, and Gwenvael immediately looked at the wax seal still stuck to part of it. He didn't bother immediately reading the letter itself because he'd found that *who* letters came from mattered almost as much, if not more, than what was actually stated inside.

"Whose seal is this? I don't recognize it."

Annwyl let out a sigh. "The Reinholdt."

"The Reinholdt?" He frowned in thought; then his body jolted. "Good gods! That madman from the north?"

"The very one."

"Honestly . . ." He glanced again at the letter. "I didn't know anyone in the Reinholdt Clan could write."

Dagmar patiently waited while her father ranted. He must have had another sleepless night, because he lasted longer than usual. Although she was impressed by two things when her father got like this toward her. Not once had he ever touched her in anger or with violence and not once had he ever made his screaming fits personal. While more than one of her sisters-in-law called her "plain bitch" or "ugly sow" when wittier words had failed them, her father always kept it about his issue. And his issue was usually that Dagmar had overstepped her bounds.

Usually . . . she had.

When her father finally stopped long enough for her to speak, she said, "I think you underestimate what Queen Annwyl can do for us."

"Besides bring her love of blood to our door?"

"Father," she soothed, "you can't listen to rumor." She smiled. "That's my job."

"Ohhh, you have a job now?" Kikka asked sweetly, all smiles.

And, all smiles herself, Dagmar asked her, "I didn't know Eymund bought you a new dress. It's beautiful!"

Her brother Eymund, who'd been conspicuously absent upon their father's return, walked back into the Main Hall. "What? What new dress?" He glared at his young wife. "New dress?"

Kikka's glare was almost worth every moment of having to deal with The Reinholdt.

Dagmar turned back to her father and raised her voice to be heard over her brother's yelling. "Now, Father, I do understand your concerns. But we cannot ignore the kind of ally Queen Annwyl would make. It is believed she has near a hundred legions at her disposal. All of them trained and ready."

Her father rested his big fists on the table, and Dagmar knew she was no longer talking to the frightening warlord feared throughout the Northlands, but Sigmar Reinholdt. The man who cared greatly for his people and his kinsmen. "It's Jökull you're worried about. Isn't it?" he asked, not looking at her.

"With good reason. We can no longer ignore your brother."

"I ain't been ignoring him!"

"He's increasing his troops, buying them apparently. Your men are clearly preparing for a siege. I want to help and Queen Annwyl allows me that."

"I don't need your help, little miss."

"No. You need hers. And I see no shame in it."

Her father cleared his throat, glanced around, and muttered, "You know this ain't ya fault."

Unfortunately, she didn't know that. But when she didn't reply to his statement, her father took a large breath and slowly let it out. "What are we giving her?"

"Information." They could afford to give her little else.

"You and that bloody information."

"It's what I barter in." She leaned forward, looking him right in the eyes—one of the few unafraid to do so. "I need you to trust me on this."

He snorted and stared down at the table, Dagmar patiently waiting.

When he finally grabbed hold of his ax handle, yanking the weapon from the table, she knew she'd won—or at least gotten a short-term reprieve.

"Don't push your luck with me, little miss," he grumbled.

Of course she would. She was so good at it.

As her father walked out, a servant rushed in. "My lady, Brother Ragnar approaches."

She nodded and stood, her appetite long having left.

"Look all"—Kikka sneered, her husband still ranting about "all the bloody coin you spend!"—"another male who won't be bedding our little Dagmar."

"And then there's you, sister." Dagmar leaned down and finished on a whisper, "Who will apparently fuck anything."

Heading toward the doors and her respite from idiocy, Dagmar heard her brother snap, "What did she say? What are you doing?"

Gwenvael skimmed the note quickly. "The Reinholdt wants *you*—they're very clear on that 'you'—to come to his territory to save the lives of your unborn children. You know, personally, I don't appreciate him trying to order my lovely queen about, but what really bothers me—"

"Is that the barbarians already know I'm having twins?" At Gwenvael's nod, she added, "And if they know that, they might already know I'm no longer as fierce as I once was."

"You won't be expecting forever, Annwyl. And once

the twins are here, you'll be as violently cruel and madly bloodthirsty as you always were."

"Now you're just trying to make me feel better."

"Is it working?"

"A little." She closed her eyes, and he knew she was in pain, the "twinges," as she called them, happening more and more lately. She took a cleansing breath and went on. "But even if I wanted to go to the Northlands myself, Fearghus will never let that happen. And Morfyd! Gods, the whining." Gwenvael's older sister, a powerful Dragonwitch and healer, could wear the scales off a fast-moving snake when she was in a mood. "Besides, someone I thought adored me told me I was too *fat* to travel."

"That is not what I said, although I love how all of you willfully misinterpret me. And how quick we are to forget I did notice that your breasts had grown even fuller and more lovely. If that's possible."

Annwyl laughed and shook her head. "Not even a modicum of shame."

"Not even a teaspoonful. Now, we both know you can't travel, so what would you like me to do? Want me to write them back for you? I think we both have to admit that I have a way with the written word that you do not, my lovely."

"This is very true." She turned a bit on his lap so that she looked directly at him. "But I thought perhaps you could go in my stead."

"Me? Go back to the Northlands?" he scoffed. "I'd rather eat bark."

"Do you think I like asking you to take this risk? Especially with the reputation you left behind?" She raised a brow. "Ruiner."

"You know, they weren't virgins," he argued as he'd been arguing for decades. "They stumbled upon *me* at the lake. Took advantage of *me*. They used their tails in a manner I found enticing, and I did what I had to do to survive the horrors of war."

"Is it true you, and you alone, is specifically mentioned *in* the truce?"

"As long as I keep my distance from Lightning females—you may also know the Lightnings as the Horde dragons, my beautiful majesty"—he gave her his most appealing smile but she only stared at him, so he continued—"I can go into the Northlands for short periods of time."

"Then I need you to go. But to be quite honest you're the only one I can send."

The admission surprised him. "I am?"

"I can't send Morfyd. She's female, and the Lightnings would snag her faster than you can lure a local girl to your bed."

"What a lovely analogy. Thank you."

"Besides, your sister is needed here because she's the only one who can stop Fearghus from killing his own parents."

Gwenvael barely stopped his angry frown, determined to keep the conversation as light as possible. "I see Mother still refuses to believe your babes are Fearghus's."

"I don't know what she believes, and I don't care. She hasn't been here in six months since she was first told and that's fine by me." Gwenvael knew that to be a lie. That fight had been the ugliest he'd seen among his kin, and though all of Fearghus's siblings had stood by him and Annwyl that day, the whole thing had hurt Annwyl more than anyone wanted to admit.

"I can't send Keita," she went on, "because she'll have all the men turning on each other and won't even remember why I sent her. Besides, when is she ever here for me to ask?"

Gwenvael couldn't argue with her on that. His younger sister was more like him than anyone in their family. Only a couple of decades apart, they'd always been close and understood each other well. Yet he'd noticed that over the past few years, Keita had been spending almost all her time as far from

Devenallt Mountain and Dark Plains as she could manage. She had her own cave but was rarely in it, and when she did return home, things often became uncomfortable between her and their mother. When he thought about it, Gwenvael couldn't remember a time when mother and daughter had gotten along, making family get-togethers quite intense. Then again, Gwenvael lived for that sort of tension and often found perverse pleasure in making it worse.

"Of course there's Briec, but—" Annwyl looked for words but couldn't seem to find anything to say about the arrogant, silver-haired dragon, and ended with, "Do I really need to ex- pound on Briec?"

"Not to me."

"And Éibhear is still too much a babe. Besides, to be quite blunt, you're the most politically savvy of the entire bunch."

Gwenvael smiled, shocked and truly flattered by her state- ment. "Do you mean that?"

"Of course I do. I'm not blind. And one should always know the strengths and weaknesses of the allies they have surrounding them. My father used to say that . . . you know, before he went off and destroyed something or someone."

She chewed on her thumbnail, a habit she'd developed over the last few months as her stress level grew. "In the end, I'm sure you're the only one who can truly do this."

"And I'm sure you're quite correct on that point, but what do I get out of it?"

Annwyl dropped her hand into her lap. "Get out of it?"

"Aye. What is my reward for doing this task you've set for me?"

"What do you want?"

Grinning, Gwenvael craned his neck forward a bit and, using his thumb and forefinger, gently pulled the bodice of her dress forward.

"Stop that!" She slapped at his hands and laughed.

"Come now. I'm just asking for a moment to immerse myself in the lush garden of your bosom."

"The lush garden of my . . ." Annwyl shook her head. "You're not immersing yourself in any part of me, Lord Gwenvael."

"Now, now. I'm only asking for a chance to play with them a bit." He stuck his nose in her cleavage and Annwyl laughed and pushed at his head.

"Gwenvael! Stop it!"

The front door slammed open and Fearghus stalked in. "What the hell's going—" Black smoke billowed from Fearghus's nostrils. "Get your nose out of there."

Taking his sweet time, Gwenvael looked up into Fearghus's raging face. "Oh. Hello, brother. What are you doing here?"

Dagmar smiled warmly when the gates opened and several monks came in, two pulling a large cart weighed down with books. Books brought for her.

"Brother Ragnar." She briefly bowed her head in respect.

"My Lady Dagmar. It's so good to see you, my dear."

Brother Ragnar, a longtime monk of the mysterious and rarely seen Order of the Warhammer, had been bringing books to Dagmar since she was ten. It was the one thing about her father's fortress and the surrounding towns that kept her sane—non-warring travelers who always had information she found of use. Brother Ragnar was definitely her favorite of all their regular visitors, but she'd met and talked with many—most of them monks or scholars—over the years, learning much about a world she'd never seen. They brought her books, news, and gossip that she often used to help her father and her people, but it was Brother Ragnar who'd actually tutored her in reading, writing, and negotiation skills.

He'd taught her much from the beginning, suggesting ways she could get what she wanted from her kinsmen without ever appearing as if she were trying. "Why be a battering ram, my dear, when you can simply knock on the door and be let in?"

He'd been right, of course. Like he always was.

Dagmar took his right arm since his left hand held onto his traveling stick. She never could see much of his face because of the cowl he always wore but doubted he was extremely old based on the sound and strength of his voice. And although he'd been wounded badly, his body broken and weak, he hadn't lost his spirit. The eyes that gazed at her from the darkness of his cowl were a vivid blue with strange flecks of silver throughout the iris and were always bright and lively.

The Order forced Brother Ragnar, even with his body broken, to walk everywhere although she'd offered more than once to purchase him a horse. But it came down to the sacrifices monks of every order were forced to make, which Dagmar would never understand—wasn't life difficult and painful enough without adding more misery to it?

"I'm so glad to see you, Brother." She squeezed his gloved hand. "You're looking well."

"It's still pleasant out. Although I don't look forward to winter." Winter in the Northlands was a hard time for all of them, and only the most hearty—or stupid—trekked through the winter storms to reach the Reinholdt lands.

"Well, you're here now. And we have much to discuss."

"Yes, we do." He gestured to the cart. "And I've brought you some wonderful new books I think you'll enjoy."

She glanced in to the cart and smiled. "You bring me the best presents."

Placing Brother Ragnar's hand on her arm, she led him and his comrades to the Main Hall for warm wine and food. "So, Brother . . . any more on my uncle?"

"Much, I'm afraid. I don't like it, Dagmar. I don't like it one bit."

"Nor will I, I'm sure."

"Did you send a message to the Southland queen as I suggested?"

"I did, but my father was not exactly pleased."

"She is a woman," he teased. "Her weakness is obvious."

"But her reputation, Brother . . ."

"I know. She is quite insane, but she has near a hundred legions at her disposal, my lady. Imagine what even one legion could do to help your father."

"But if she is completely insane as everyone says, will she understand what danger she's in?"

"My lady, most Southland monarchs are quite mad. But they are always surrounded by the most reliable and clever minds of our age. Queen Annwyl will be no different." He squeezed her hand gently. "No worries, my lady. If the queen does not come herself, I have no doubt she'll only send her most respected representative in her stead."

Chapter 2

How long should a dragon of my stature be expected to survive without a warm, willing pussy at my disposal?

For days he'd been traveling through the cold and unforgiving Northlands over Oceans of Despair and Forests of Death and Rivers of Bile. He didn't call them these names out of caprice. He called them that because that's what most of them were named in some form or another.

And after so many days of constant travel through what he was now convinced was a form of hell, he was still without a woman. He tired of men; he wanted to see females. He wanted to smell their hair and taste their skin and lose himself in their bodies. He sure as hell didn't want to see one more angry, snarling, unattractive Northland male.

Such were the thoughts racing through his head when Gwenvael came in sight of the mighty Reinholdt fortress. More useless, worthless Northland men with their worthless codes and rules. He briefly debated shifting to human but decided against it. He needed the advantage with The Reinholdt and his warrior son The Beast.

Decision made, Gwenvael landed in front of the Reinholdt fortress gates in all his dragon glory.

Clawed feet slammed into the ground, shaking the fortress walls; gold wings stretched far from his body, the slow, even movements stirring up much dirt and air. Then Gwenvael leaned back his head and unleashed a line of flame into the sky.

When he tired of that, he looked down at the humans staring up at him. "Go on," he offered magnanimously. "Feel free to piss on yourselves and cower helplessly."

Gods, sometimes his generosity overwhelmed him.

Dagmar picked up a book from the floor and quickly flipped through the pages. So focused on her work, she didn't realize anything might be amiss until Canute got to his feet and snarled at the door. She was already looking in that direction when one of her brothers walked in with nary a knock. Typical rude Reinholdt male behavior, but Canute charged him anyway. Dagmar stopped her pet with a simple, "No."

The dog was already in midair, teeth bared, but he automatically jerked back, hit the ground, and hastily rolled over. He snarled and snapped a little for show before coming back to Dagmar's side.

"What is it?"

Her brother Fridmar, third born to The Reinholdt, leaned

casually against the doorway and ate an apple. In between bites he mumbled, "Dragon outside."

"Yes, well, I'll get right . . . wait." She looked away from her work. "Pardon?"

"Dragon," he said calmly. "Outside the gates. Eymund called an attack, but Da told me to get you first."

Dagmar carefully placed the quill on the desk and slowly turned in the chair, placing her arm on the back of it. "A dragon? Are you sure?"

"It's big, scaly, and has wings. What the hell else could it be?" She would have perhaps been less annoyed if he hadn't made that reply with bits of apple flying out of his mouth.

"Well what kind?"

Her brother frowned. "Kind? It's a dragon, I said."

It amazed her she had the patience for this anymore, but what she'd learned early on and what her sisters-in-law could never seem to grasp—her brothers and father moved no faster than was absolutely necessary. Yelling at them, screaming . . . waste of one's time. So Dagmar plodded along until she got what she needed. She called it the "water against rock" method. "There are different kinds of dragons, brother. There's purple. Blue. Forest green."

"Forest . . ." He shook his head. "Right. Whatever. It's yellow."

"Yellow?" Dagmar tapped her finger against the desk, being as plodding as her kinsmen and loving the fact they had the nerve to hate when she was. "They don't have yellow dragons, brother. Do you mean gold?"

"Yes. Fine. Gold then."

Dagmar blinked. "A Gold? This far north?" She desperately tried to remember what she'd learned about dragons over the years, which hadn't been much. It wasn't that she hadn't believed they existed, but she had doubted they had much to do with humans. Why would they?

The Horde dragons of the north lived deep in the highest mountains, keeping mostly to themselves. Their colors were distinct but simple, ranging from deep dark purples to near white, and they held the power of lightning within them. Like her Northland kinsmen, they were mostly warriors and pit fighters.

The Southland dragons came in an array of colors and had their own queen. Fire was their internal power, and they were often scholars and teachers.

"Who cares how far it's come?"

"You should. Father should. Why else would a Gold come this far and risk clashing with the Horde dragons? It's my understanding they're sworn enemies." She eyed her brother. "And why does Father want me out there? You do know it's a myth what they say about virgin sacrifices and dragons, yes?"

"Of course I know that," he snapped in such a way that Dagmar knew he believed the myth to be true. "And after them three marriages, you ain't much of a virgin yourself, now is ya?"

"Those last two barely counted."

"Look, woman"—Fridmar tossed his apple core onto her floor and Dagmar gasped in outrage—"that dragon outside demanded to see Da, and Da demanded to see you."

"It demanded?" She widened her eyes and blinked at her brother. Her "surprised look" she called it. "You're letting a dragon *demand* things of The Reinholdt? Where's your bravery? Your honor?"

"Would you shut up?" A small tick began in her brother's jaw. "You get mad when we start killing without . . . without . . ." His face twisted up a bit as he thought really hard. It pained her to watch her kin try to think. It honestly physically hurt. "What's that word?" he finally asked.

"Provocation?"

"Yeah. Right. You get mad when we start killing without that 'prov' word, and now you're mad cause we haven't killed it yet."

"I'm not mad you haven't . . . there's a difference between . . ." She shook her head. "Forget it."

"Where the hell is she?" Valdís—second-born son to The Reinholdt and most nervous ninny—stormed into Dagmar's room. "What's going on? Why are you still sitting here? Father has summoned you."

"And I don't jump at every demand. Go find out what he wants first."

"What who wants?"

"The dragon." She motioned both away with her hands. "Go and find out."

Without another thought toward her brothers, Dagmar went back to her work.

Sigmar Reinholdt, Protector of the Reinholdt Lands and People, Warlord of the Northwest Properties, Eighteenth Born to Dechard Reinholdt, Killer of Dechard Reinholdt, and Sire of The Beast turned to face his male offspring.

"She said what now?"

One of his sons—don't ask him the name, because he really couldn't remember and didn't care enough to try—shrugged. "She said to ask the dragon what he wants."

"And you let her get away with that?"

"You know how she is, Da. Besides, she looked real busy."

"Busy doing what?"

One son glanced at another son whose name Sigmar couldn't remember.

"Well?" he pushed when they didn't answer quickly enough.

"Readin' . . . I think."

"Readin'? You couldn't pull her away from reading some bloomin' book?"

"You know how she is," he repeated.

'Twas quite true. They all knew how she was. After so many

bloody sons, Sigmar had held out hope for a daughter. A sweet, tame thing who would bring a solid marriage connection to the Reinholdts and then perhaps a few granddaughters. But he'd gotten Dagmar. The Beast. Cruelly named by his long-dead nephew, but she'd been living up to that moniker ever since. Yet she always seemed the tamest of them all.

Sigmar grabbed his second oldest by the collar and yanked him close. "You take your scrawny ass back to her room and you tell her to get her royal self out here . . . *now!*"

"I'm here." Dagmar glanced at her brother. "I somehow knew Valdís wouldn't get it right."

Seconds away from asking who the hell Valdís was—and then realizing it was the son whose collar he still held in his hand—Sigmar snarled and snapped at his daughter, "Dragon. Outside."

"Yes. I've heard." Always calm that Dagmar. Always controlled and unruffled. Like a crow watching from the top of a building, knowing it was too far up to reach with a bow and arrow. "He's a little far north if he's a Gold. But if he hasn't attacked yet, I'd say he has a purpose here."

"That Blood Queen you're so interested in—she sent him."

His daughter's eyes widened, and she glanced at the door, then back at him. It was, in many years, the first truly startled reaction he'd gotten out of the little miss.

"The Blood Queen sent him? Are you sure?"

"I'm sure. He said, real clear like, 'I was sent by Queen Annwyl of the Southlands. I'm here to see The Reinholdt or The Beast.' Then he added something like, 'Feel free to piss on yourselves.' I decided it was best not to ask him more questions on that."

She chuckled. "He's used to the dragonfear from the Southlanders."

"I don't care what kind of fear you call it. Ain't no Northland man going to—"

"I know. I know. No Northland man will show fear." She dismissed the Code, by which all Northland men lived, with a wave of her hand. "What's important now is whether he can bargain on her behalf."

"You want us to bargain with a lizard?"

"They're not lizards, Father. They're extraordinary creatures who were here long before any human was crawling on this earth. They are warriors and scholars and—"

"He has long hair like a woman," one of Sigmar's sons blathered—which son, however, still could be anyone's guess.

The girl closed her eyes and sighed. Deeply. She did that sometimes when around the men of her family. "To avoid all of this, I'll simply go ask him why he's here and what he wants." She made it sound simple enough, stepping past her brothers and heading for the door, but Sigmar caught her upper arm, yanked her back.

"You ain't going out there."

"Then why did you call me here?"

"To tell me what you been up to so I can handle that Gold."

Her lips pursed a bit, and she stared at him. He knew that expression better than any other. She wouldn't tell him anything now because she wanted to be the one to talk to that giant lizard standing outside their gates. The Beast believed herself a politician. She didn't understand that was the work of men. She handled correspondence and such well enough—especially since she was one of the few of them who could read and write really well—but it was up to the men to manage these things face to face, over a keg of ale with a wench or two for entertainment. Dagmar simply failed to learn this, and he worried what would happen when she found a worthy husband who wouldn't allow any of the nonsense Sigmar let her get away with.

Knowing well there was no point in fighting her when she got that particular expression on her face, Sigmar relented the smallest bit. "You'll wait behind the guards until you're asked for. Understand?"

"If we absolutely must waste time . . ."

"We must." He glanced down at the canine that never left her side. Canute, she'd named him. Strange how he could remember the dog's name . . . "And you'd best find a safe place for him. He'll look like a tasty morsel to that thing outside."

"Yes, Father."

"And don't annoy me anymore today."

"I won't, Father."

And they both knew she was lying.

Chapter 3

Dagmar glanced down at her gown again and checked to make sure her head scarf was on properly before readjusting the spectacles balanced on her nose.

A dragon. A real dragon here, at her father's fortress and she was about to meet him. Not even another Northlander, but a Southland dragon. A scholar, a teacher, an intellectual.

Reason help her, but Dagmar realized she was so excited about this, she was almost . . . dare she say . . . giddy?

She wondered how old this dragon was. He could be six or seven hundred years old! Because of course the mightiest queen of Dark Plains would only send the most learned of scholars, the most experienced of delegates to represent her in the halls of The Reinholdt.

Dagmar cringed when she heard her father speak to the dragon.

"I be Sigmar," he told the dragon, and Dagmar barely

stopped herself from yelling over the gates a more proper and dignified greeting.

"So you asked for me, Reinholdt?"

What a voice! Deep and low, and it lightly rattled the windows from its timbre alone, because he did not yell. He sounded calm and quite . . . respectable.

"No. I asked for your Annwyl," her father practically snapped back.

Dagmar began to tap her fist against her leg.

"Well," the dragon replied smoothly, "she's indisposed at the moment, so she sent me as her emissary."

"A dragon emissary for a human?"

Dagmar gritted her teeth in frustration. What exactly was the old bastard doing? Why was he asking rude questions? Questions that could be asked and answered over dinner when the dragon was more relaxed. She knew for a fact that one of the local herders had cows grazing in the east fields—enough to feed a dragon, she was sure.

Honestly, was this her father's idea of good politics? No wonder she had to fight so hard to prevent war between the Reinholdts and the surrounding fiefdoms. Because her kinsmen were rude idiots!

"Again, Reinholdt, you wanted to see me or someone from Dark Plains?" the dragon pushed. It was obvious his patience was running out. Well, obvious to anyone with sense.

"Nay. Not me, dragon. The Beast made that request."

The Beast? Her father was introducing her as The Beast?

If she thought she could get away with killing them all and razing the land they all stood upon—she'd do it in less than a heartbeat.

"And may I meet The Beast?" the dragon countered.

Dagmar stepped forward, but Valdís grabbed the back of her dress and held her in place.

"Off!" she ordered.

"You'll wait," he snarled.

"You sure about that, dragon?" her father asked, and she knew now he was toying with the creature. And he had the nerve to wonder where she got her attitude from.

"Yes," the dragon grumbled. "I am."

Her father must have motioned for her, because her brother released her gown and the soldiers protecting the front of the fortress moved out of her way. Dagmar walked outside, across the courtyard, and through the main gates. Her father's guards formed two lines, allowing her to pass. Dagmar walked up to the magnificent being. He glinted gold in the dull light of the two suns, each scale shiny and bright. He was like a bit of a sun himself, bringing a small amount of light to her world. His wings stretched out from his body. They, too, were covered in scales, but the wings seemed somehow weightless and fine, like the most exquisite metal ever created. The tip of each wing had a sharp, gold talon, and there were gold talons on each claw. Two bright white horns sat atop his head and long, shiny gold hair fell across his back and down his body, brushing gently against the ground. Beautiful gold eyes focused on her as soon as she stepped closer to him.

She'd had her greeting all ready for him. The words— a *proper* greeting for so important a diplomat—on her lips, but she couldn't speak. Not once she saw him.

In all her thirty years nothing so beautiful had ever crossed her path.

When Dagmar feared she'd embarrass herself by her silence, she finally found her voice and opened her mouth to speak. But the words stopped in her throat again.

Only this time they stopped . . . because he was laughing. At her.

It wasn't mere laughter either. Not a muffled sound behind his claw. Nor a brief snort of disbelief. These were things she experienced on a daily basis and had grown quite used to. No.

This overgrown . . . *child* was rolling around on the ground like he'd never seen anything more amusing than she. Massive dragon legs and arms flailed while his guffaws echoed over the courtyard and around the countryside.

Some scaly lizard was laughing at her! The only daughter of The Reinholdt! And he was having this moment on Reinholdt land, no less!

Any awe and admiration Dagmar had were wiped clean in that moment, and she felt that distinct coldness she hid so well from outsiders. It swept through her like ice from an avalanche. The men behind her began to murmur amongst themselves, feet shuffled, and her father cleared his throat. A few times. It wasn't the dragon that made them uncomfortable. Not directly anyway.

Dagmar waited until his laughter turned into chuckles. "Are you done?" she asked, keeping her voice even.

"Sorry, uh . . . Beast." It snorted out another laugh.

"Dagmar will do. Dagmar Reinholdt. Thirteenth child of The Reinholdt and his only daughter. I asked your queen here," she continued, "because I have news that may save her life and the lives of her unborn whelps."

The dragon's expression of humor quickly changed to a scowl. Apparently it did not appreciate the term she'd used, but she was past caring. All her dreams of building an allegiance with the Blood Queen faded as soon as that woman sent this *idiot* to represent her. No, Dagmar would have to find other allegiances for her father. The Blood Queen of Dark Plains simply would not do.

"Tell *me*, sweet Dagmar," it sneered, rolling back to its belly and lifting its head a bit. "And I'll tell her."

Dagmar remained silent for one very long moment, then answered simply, "No."

The dragon blinked in surprise and abruptly pushed itself up a bit so that its snout was barely inches from her nose. Its gold eyes were locked on hers, and she wondered how she ever saw them as pretty. They were as ugly as the rest of the dragon. Ugly and mocking and absolutely useless.

"What do you mean, no?" it demanded.

"I mean, you've insulted me. You've insulted my kinsmen. And you've insulted The Reinholdt. So you can return to your bitch queen and you can watch her die."

Confident she'd made her point, Dagmar Reinholdt turned on her heel and walked away from it. But she did stop a few feet away and glanced over her shoulder.

"Now that, dragon"—she happily sneered back, mocking the creature's tone—"*that's* funny."

Without another word, she returned to her father's fortress. But before she disappeared into its mighty embrace, she heard her father ask, "You are a bit of a dumb bastard, aren't ya, dragon?"

And it was times like these when she truly did appreciate her father's coarseness.

A woman! The Beast was a woman! Why didn't anyone tell him that? Why did everyone keep claiming he was a man? If Gwenvael had known, he would have handled the whole thing quite differently.

But he hadn't known and his first reaction at seeing her . . . well, it had not been his finest moment. Even he'd admit that. Yet how was that his fault when everyone kept telling him that The Beast was some mighty giant warrior spit up from one of hell's many pits?

Pacing restlessly in the abandoned cave he found high in the Mountains of Sorrow—a rather fitting name at the moment—Gwenvael tore at his mind trying to figure out how to fix this.

His first thought, naturally, was to seduce the woman. She

had that look of a spinster, didn't she? A bitter, unhappy virgin who didn't trust men enough to allow them in her bed. In the past, he'd had great success with women like that. And yet . . .

He sighed, rubbed his eyes.

And yet this one didn't seem like that at all, did she?

She was plain, that was true enough. But not hideous. He didn't feel the need to scream and run away at first sight of her. And she had those eyes—steel grey and cold as the top of this mountain. Eyes like hers could go a long way if managed correctly, but she wore a drab, grey dress that did nothing for her. No adornments on it, no low-cut bodice, teasing of her bosom. Nor was there a painfully high and prim collar up to her chin so that one demanded to know what she was hiding. The girdle was a boring brown leather, when a silver weave would have been much nicer. The eating dagger she had tucked into it was nice enough, but so? The boots on her small feet were grey fur as well. And she wore that head scarf tied over her hair as if she were about to go off and scrub a kitchen.

No, it wasn't looks that had gained her a name like The Beast. She wasn't ugly, but she wasn't such a gorgeous animal that men were devoured in her bed.

Nor was she a raving lunatic, which one would think a woman named The Beast by Northmen would be.

The coldness in those eyes ran through her entire body. Without a thought to what a powerful dragon could do if angered, she'd kept the information about Annwyl to herself. To be honest, Gwenvael wasn't even sure the Reinholdt men knew what she held.

The Reinholdt himself seemed to be completely clueless unless he had a war ax in his hands. Surprisingly short for a Northlander, The Reinholdt made up for it with width—his shoulders and chest disturbingly large, his muscles near busting from his clothes. Yet beyond his appearance, the stumpy Northlander reminded Gwenvael a bit of his own father,

Bercelak the Great. His father was never as happy as when he was killing someone or something in battle—politics absolutely bored the older Black dragon.

Gwenvael scratched his head. Yes, yes, he could read the old Reinholdt well enough. But it was the girl . . . dammit! She was the key. He knew it! It wasn't merely the knowledge she had about Annwyl either. There was something else about that girl . . . woman . . . whatever. Really, if he didn't know better, he'd swear she was a dragon with those damn cold eyes and features. She had a young face, but those eyes were filled with ageless knowledge that she used for her own selfish gains.

Not that he couldn't admire that a bit since he did the same.

He had to go back. He knew he did. And he realized now that going back just to take her and seduce her would not work. Not with her. She wouldn't swoon at a mere look from his human self. She wouldn't be entranced by the extraordinary beauty of his face or the exquisiteness of his human body. Nor would she be intimidated by threats and yelling.

He'd have to go a different way, but first he'd have to get in and see her. To go back in his true form would be useless. He'd have to be human and . . .

Gwenvael smiled, the etiquette of the Northland rulers and its people coming back to him in a sudden flash. *Yes, yes. That would work.* The woman he'd faced today knew her etiquette, kept her own council, and played by the rules. At least . . . she did as far as everyone else was concerned.

It would only buy him a night, but that would be enough.

He'd make it enough, because he wouldn't fail Annwyl on this. Not this. She'd nearly broken his heart when she sent him off, kissing his cheek and holding him for a long time in a hug before telling him, "Don't listen to the others. I know you'll be amazing in the north. Just be careful and watch your back, Gwenvael."

That's when Gwenvael knew she had more faith in him

than any of his own blood. She was entrusting him with her life and the lives of her babes. And if he had to go so far north that he entered the forbidden Ice Lands himself, he'd do it. He wouldn't let any harm come to Annwyl.

He walked to the mouth of the cave and stood there a moment, staring down at the countryside below, until that scent he knew so well tore into his nostrils. He should have caught it sooner, but he'd been deep in his thoughts and now he only had a moment to use the shadows around him. A gift from the blood of his loving Grandfather Ailean, Gwenvael's scales changed colors until he became one with the cave shadows surrounding him.

Right on time too, as they came into view seconds later. Four of them, all big, bold . . . and purple.

Lightning dragons. Also called the Horde dragons. He'd fought their kind for the first time during a war nearly a century ago. They were barbarians but mighty warriors, and he had the permanent scars to prove it.

These days, some would say the Lightnings lived in peace with the dragons of the Southlands, but that wasn't remotely true. There was a truce, but it was a delicate one, easily broken at any moment. All that kept a new war from starting was the fact that the Lightnings were broken up into fiefdoms, similar to the way the Northland humans were. They didn't consider themselves monarchs but warlords. They were often so busy fighting each other, they rarely had the energy or time to take on the armies of the Southland Dragon Queen.

Still, Gwenvael had moved carefully through the territories leading to his Northland destination. Olgeir the Wastrel controlled the Outerplains—the borderlands between the north and the south—as well as the territory overlapping the Reinholdt lands, and he'd never bothered to hide his outright hatred of Queen Rhiannon. He kept the truce, but not happily. And Gwenvael didn't doubt for a minute what Olgeir would do if he caught one of Rhiannon's male offsprings on his territory. Especially the one the Horde males referred to as "The Ruiner."

The Lightnings moved past the cave, but one stopped, hovering in front of the entrance.

Gwenvael didn't move or make a sound. He certainly didn't charge the bastard. He wasn't here to fight and he wasn't a fool who thought he could take on a Lightning scout party and come out still intact.

The Lightning sniffed the air and inched a bit closer. As Gwenvael could smell the lightning inside the barbarian, the barbarian could scent the fire in Gwenvael.

So Gwenvael slowly lowered himself into a crouch, readying his body and flame to attack.

The Lightning was mere inches from entering the cave when Gwenvael heard the caw of a crow overhead. The Northlands were simply inundated with crows, it seemed. And, at the moment, Gwenvael had never been so grateful, as the crow's shit unceremoniously landed on the Lightning's snout.

The dragon's eyes crossed as he tried to see it and he snarled. "Why you little mother—"

"Come on, you idiot!" another voice yelled farther ahead. *"Move!"*

Wiping the shit from his face, the Lightning followed after his comrades.

Letting out a sigh, Gwenvael stood at the very edge of the cave and looked up at the crows overhead. There had to be hundreds of them making good use of the limbs and vines that protruded from the mountain's rock face.

"Thank you for that," he offered kindly. And in answer, another crow unloaded itself, and Gwenvael hastily stepped back. "Oy, you tiny bastards! Watch the hair!"

When all those damn birds began to laugh at him, he was not pleased.

Chapter 4

Dagmar exited the library that only she ever went into and that only she ever maintained with Canute faithfully by her side. His paws silently padded against the stone floor as he kept pace with her.

It was time for training, and she didn't like to be late. But she wasn't exactly shocked when her father fell into step beside her, smartly staying on the opposite side of Canute.

"Well, that went well," he grumbled. Her father had never been one for wasted words or preamble.

"Come to gloat?" she asked.

"No. Come to find out what you're planning."

Dagmar kept her gaze straight ahead and her expression purposely blank. "What makes you think I'm planning anything?"

"You're still breathing, ain't ya? Never known a day when you ain't planning something. Plotting is what they call it."

For once Dagmar didn't have to step around people as they moved through the Main Hall; people automatically moved out of the way of The Reinholdt and anyone who happened to be with him.

"I'm not planning anything," she assured him. "But don't be surprised when it comes back in another day or two."

"'It?' Don't you mean 'him'?"

"It. Him. Whatever."

"And he'll come back to what? Tear the place down?"

"Doubtful. He won't want to harm the one who holds the information."

"Always so sure, you are. Always so damn sure you're right."

With a shrug, she left her father by the doors leaving the Main Hall. "When have I ever been wrong?" she smugly asked.

Dagmar walked through the courtyard and around to the side near one of several barracks. She passed groups of men training hard to be the warriors her father expected. The Reinholdt had no patience for weakness or complaints of injuries. You fought and you fought well every time or dying in battle would be the least of your problems.

As she walked by, like every day when she walked by, she was completely ignored. Nothing new there.

Cutting through the training grounds and past some of the barracks, Dagmar headed to the large training area that was hers and hers alone. To get to it, she had to enter the vast building constructed under her direction. It housed all The Reinholdt's battle dogs, and she never had to limit access to only the trainers chosen by her because few of her father's warriors were idiotic enough to enter here and risk that even one of her dogs was loose.

As soon as Dagmar entered, the dogs still in their runs began to greet her with barks and howls. Using voice commands only, she eased her dogs' excitement and walked through the back exit and toward the training ring. Johann, her assistant, was already working the young pups that would soon be two-hundred-pound warrior dogs. He'd been a good choice on her part. Like her, Johann preferred the company of dogs to the company of humans.

"How goes it, Johann?"

"Well, my lady."

Dagmar gave the hand signal for Canute to lie down and stay outside the ring until she returned to him. Closing and locking the gate behind her, she patiently waited for Johann to finish. He had the dogs lying down, waiting for his next signal. They wouldn't move until instructed to do so. They were the most obedient dogs one could find in the Northlands. And also the most obedient and the most bloodthirsty because of her training methods. Only the companion animals of the Kyvich witches—giant wolflike beasts with horns—were more feared than Dagmar's dogs. She prided herself on that fact.

As she waited on Johann, she pulled her list from her pocket and studied her remaining tasks for the day. But it wasn't the words on the page that had her attention, it was that damn dragon.

Could that have gone any worse? She'd always doubted the Blood Queen would come herself, but Dagmar never thought the crazed monarch would send an actual dragon to represent her. Yet did she send one of the Southland Elders Brother Ragnar had told her about last time he'd visited? No! Instead she'd sent that . . . that . . . swine! He'd laughed at her. *Laughed!* Loudly. In front of her kinsmen.

That had been the worst part, in truth. That her brothers had heard it all—which meant her sisters-in-law had heard it all.

Johann made the dogs wait a few more seconds before he released them. When he did, they ran to Dagmar and began jumping on her, barking at her. They were chatty today. Excited. She smiled and petted them all.

She loved her dogs. With them, she never had to be anything but what she was. They never judged her or expected anything from her, and the plainness of her face meant nothing to them.

The dragon's rudeness from earlier already forgotten, Dagmar crouched down and the dogs proceeded to lick her face and neck while trying to push each other out of the way. She was about to get them back into training formation when she heard Canute's angry bark from the other side of the gate. He didn't like it when she left him, but she didn't dare bring him in the ring while the other dogs were around. But when he wouldn't stop barking, she signaled for the other dogs to stay and walked over to the gate.

Putting her feet between the lower slats, Dagmar pulled herself up, leaned over the fence . . . and looked straight into gold eyes.

He was staring up at her, looking guilty, with his hand around the back of Canute's neck.

"What are you doing to my dog?" she asked.

"Nothing?"

"Why are you saying that like a question?"

"I wasn't?"

"Yes, you were. And unhand him."

He had a handsome face, whoever he was. Even when he gave a little pout at her order. He looked down at the dog again and then, with a shrug, unclamped his hand. Canute charged back and started growling and barking again.

"Quiet," she softly ordered.

Canute stopped barking, but he didn't stop the growling.

"What do you want?" she asked the stranger, curious as to whom he was. He couldn't be from the Northlands. His skin was too golden from exposure to the suns, and the gold hair that reached past his knees was loose and wild around his face. The Northland men didn't wear their hair that long or free from their single braid except when they slept.

He slowly stood . . . and he kept standing until he towered over her more than her brothers did and that said something. Unlike their father, The Reinholdt's sons were all tall, strapping men. But this one was unreasonably tall. And big. Large, powerful muscles rippled under his chain-mail shirt and leggings, the pale-red surcoat tight across his chest.

Oddly, he stared at her in such a way as to make her feel . . . but no. No man looked at Dagmar like that. Yet there was something so undeniably familiar about him—had she met him before? Long ago?

While she tried to remember where she'd seen or met him, he grinned.

And it was that grin she recognized. That damn mocking, rude grin. Even without the elongated muzzle or sharp fangs, she'd recognized that rude grin!

"You," she said flatly.

His brow went up in surprise. "Very good. Most humans never put the two together."

"I thought I made myself clear earlier."

"Yes, but I have needs."

She blinked, keeping her expression blank. *He has needs? What did that even mean?*

"Your needs are not my concern."

"But are you not lady of this house?"

He did have a point. Without a new wife for her father, etiquette demanded the task fall to Dagmar.

"And as lady of the house, isn't it your job to care for your visitor?"

"Except I asked you to leave."

"I did leave. Then I came back. As I'm sure you knew I would." He rested his elbow on the gate, his chin in his palm. "I'm hungry."

The way he said that . . . *honestly!* Dagmar simply didn't know what to make of this dragon.

He glanced over her shoulder. "Think I can have one of those?"

Dagmar looked behind her and saw her dogs snarling and snapping in their direction while poor Johann stood around, completely baffled. For once the dogs ignored his commands, and he had no idea why.

"Have one?" she asked, also baffled.

"Aye. I'm hungry and—"

Her head snapped around and she slapped her hand over his

mouth. "If you say what I think you're about to say," she warned softly, "I'll be forced to have you killed. So stop speaking."

She felt it. Against her hand. That damn smile again. She ignored the feeling of another being's flesh against her own. It had been so long that it felt disconcertingly strange to her.

She pulled her hand away and blatantly wiped her palm against her dress. "Leave."

"Why?"

"Because the mere sight of you frightens my dogs."

He leaned in closer to her. "And what does the mere sight of me do to *you*?"

She stared up at him and stated flatly, "Besides disgust me, you mean?"

His smug smile fell. "Sorry?"

"Disgust. Although you can hardly be surprised. You come to my father's stronghold disguised as a human when in fact that's nothing but a lie. But I wonder how many unsuspecting females fell for that insipid charm you believe yourself to have only to later realize they'd done nothing but bed a giant slimy lizard. So you, as human, disgust me." She sneered a bit. "Now aren't you glad you asked?"

Actually . . . no he wasn't glad. How rude! She was rude! Gwenvael liked mean women, but he didn't much like rude ones. Slimy? He was *not* slimy!

And if she wanted to play this way, fine.

He leaned in closer, studying her face. He could tell by the way her entire body tightened at his approach that she wasn't remotely comfortable with him getting so close. He knew he could use that to his advantage if necessary. "What *are* those things on your face?"

Beyond a tiny little tic in her cheek, the rest of her face

remained remarkably blank. "What exactly are you talking about?"

Gwenvael's head tilted to the side a bit, not sure what else she thought he could mean. "The glass." He went to poke one, but she slapped his hand away.

"They're my spectacles."

"Do you mean like a 'spectacle of bad'? Or a 'spectacle of horror'?"

"No," she replied flatly. "They're so I can see."

"Are you blind?" He waved his hands in front of her face. *"Can you see me?"* he shouted, causing all those delicious-looking dogs to bark and snarl louder.

That constantly cold façade abruptly dropped as she again, but more viciously, slapped his hands away. "I am not blind. Nor am I deaf!"

"No need to get testy."

"I don't get testy."

"Except around me."

"Perhaps you bring out the worst in people, which is not anything one should be proud of."

"You haven't met my family. We're proud of the oddest things."

Her lip curled. "There are more of you?"

"None quite like me. I'm unbearably unique and, dare I say, adorable. But I do have kin." He shrugged. "I'm so very sorry about earlier," he lied. "And I'm hoping you'll help me."

There went that flat expression again. She had this constant expression of being unimpressed. By anything, everything. Yet he was beginning to find it kind of . . . cute. And annoyingly intriguing.

"I'm sure you'd rather I help you, but I delight in the fact that I won't."

That was her delighted expression? *Eeesh.*

Gwenvael pulled back a bit. "And why wouldn't you help me even after I apologized? So sweetly too!"

"One, because you didn't really mean that apology, and two . . . I really don't like you."

"Everyone likes me. I'm loveable. Even those who start out hating me end up liking me."

"Then they're fools. Because I don't like you, and I won't like you."

"I'm sure you'll change your mind."

"I don't change my mind."

Gwenvael frowned a bit. "Ever?"

"Once . . . but then I realized I was right the first time, so I never bothered to change my mind again."

She was not going to be easy, this one. Yet she wasn't resisting him as much as simply not responding to him. No matter how he taunted her, she refused to rise to the occasion. He couldn't be more irritated by that!

"Fine," he snapped. "I'll talk to your father then. See if he can convince you to act like a true and proper hostess."

"You do that."

Gwenvael continued to stand there, staring down at her, until she was forced to ask, "Well . . . ?"

"Don't know where he is."

"Find him."

"A proper hostess would show me the way."

"A proper hostess wouldn't have your kind in her home."

"That was mean."

"Yes."

"So you're not going to help me?"

"No."

"Why?"

"I already explained this. I don't like you. True, I don't like most people, but I especially dislike you. I could start my own religion based on how much I dislike you."

Out of ideas on how to handle this wench, Gwenvael went with one of his tried and true methods. He sniffed . . . and then he sniffed again.

The Beast blinked, her expression confused, but then her eyes widened in horror when she saw that first tear fall.

"Wait . . . are . . . are you . . . *crying*?"

It was a skill he'd taught himself when he was barely ten years old. With brothers like his, he needed it in order to get his mother to protect her favorite son as much as possible. He rarely used the technique now, but he was desperate.

"You're so mean to me," he complained around his tears.

"Yes, but—"

"Why won't you help me?" he wailed.

"All right. All right." She held her hands up. "I'll take you to my father."

He sniffed more tears away. "You promise?"

"Do I . . ." She sighed and stepped down from the fence. She didn't jump down, nor did she step down daintily. It was a carefully, plotted step. He bet she took lots of careful steps in her life.

She came out of the gate and closed it behind her. "Canute, here." The tasty morsel that had almost been Gwenvael's afternoon meal immediately went to her side, his yellow dog eyes watching Gwenvael closely.

"And you," she said to Gwenvael. "Come along."

Gwenvael watched her walk away. Her clothes were bulky and plain. He couldn't make out a bit of her body, and he couldn't help but wonder what she looked like under all that. Was she thin like a rail, or did she have some curves? Were her breasts big handfuls or things to be tweaked? Was her ass flat, or would he be able to grip it tight while he rode her? Did she moan, or was she a screamer?

She stopped and glared at him over her shoulder. "Well . . . Are you coming?"

And she didn't seem to appreciate it much when he started laughing at her again.

Chapter 5

As soon as they stepped within the main courtyard, Dagmar felt every eye on them. People stopped in their work; the soldiers and warriors stopped in their training. And the women . . . Dagmar was surprised fainting wasn't involved. She knew she heard sighing. Deep, longing sighs. When a servant girl carrying a large basket of bread to the soldiers' dining hall walked into a wall because she was busy staring at the dragon pretending to be human, Dagmar could only roll her eyes.

"Are those men naked?"

Dagmar squinted across the courtyard toward one of the many training rings and nodded. "Yes."

"Why?"

"Learn to fight in this cold naked, chances are you'll be able to fight no matter what you're wearing."

"Are there a lot of naked fights among the Northland men? Is that something they enjoy doing?"

His teasing tone almost made her laugh. "If it is something they enjoy, I assure you not one will admit it."

"I thought you would have asked me questions by now."

"What would I ask you about?"

"About Queen Annwyl. About her affiliation with dragons. Or even ask me about my name."

"It's no concern of mine."

"That's a lie. And my name is Gwenvael the Handsome."

"Fascinating. And I know my place, Lord Gwenvael. I know my role."

"Oh, come on. You can ask me something."

"All right." She glanced at his chest. "That crest on your surcoat."

"What about it?"

"I've read that the nation it represented was destroyed more than five hundred years ago."

He stopped walking and scrutinized the crest. "Damn," he said after a few moments. "I hate that."

"Kill them yourself, did you?"

"I'm not that old, thank you very much. And I think it was one of my uncles. But it's so awkward."

"Is it?"

"Imagine standing there, having a very nice chat with some human royal and then he gets a good look at your crest. His face gets all pale and sweaty, and you suddenly realize— gods, I wiped out the entire male line of your family, didn't I? That's awkward."

"I imagine so."

They began to walk again, and, not remotely surprising to Dagmar, he asked, "So how did you get the name Beast?"

Dagmar stopped at the large front door that would lead into the Main Hall. She lowered her eyes, kept her voice soft. Wounded. "The wife of one of my brothers nicknamed me that because I am plain. She wanted to hurt me, and she did."

A long and large finger slid under her chin, tipping up her face. She kept her eyes averted, did her best to look nearly destroyed by it all. She'd lost count of all the stories she'd made up over the years about how she'd obtained her nickname. She didn't lie about it simply for amusement but because the truth was something she would never share with anyone. The guilt of her actions from that day and the subsequent outcome was still fresh even after all this time.

Yet molding the story to fit whoever asked was an indulgent form of entertainment on her part and had gained her either pity or fear, depending on what she needed. She kept the tales simple and unadorned, avoiding possible traps should her memory fail her at a later date.

"My sweet, sweet Dagmar," he said softly, seductively. "That would have been almost perfect—if you could have just managed the tear."

Dagmar made sure she only appeared confused, rather than annoyed. "Sorry, my lord?"

"You have to learn to cry. Otherwise the whole thing falls apart at the end. Just that single tear works wonders. Right here." He drew his finger down her cheek and Dagmar immediately pulled her head back.

The Gold smiled. "Now that's the real you. Look at those eyes. If they were knives, they'd cut me to ribbons."

"I'm sure I don't know what you mean, my lord."

"Of course you don't. You're just a silly woman. Without a brain in your head." He walked around her and she felt a hand swipe across her ass. She jumped, and he had the nerve to look startled. "Come on then, silly woman. Introduce me to the more important men."

Gwenvael followed the lying Lady Dagmar—did she truly expect him to believe that story?—into the Reinholdt fortress. It wasn't as miserable as he expected, but he'd seen uninhabited caves that were a lot more warm and friendly.

The first floor of the building was mostly one big room with a sizable pit fire in front of rows and rows of dining tables with several boars roasting over it. There was a small group of women sitting at a table chatting, and if they saw the man asleep under their table, they made no mention of him. Dogs that didn't look at all like the ones The Beast was breeding for battle ran free around the hall, eating whatever was left on the floor.

By the time Gwenvael and Dagmar reached the center of the room, all activity stopped and every eye focused on them.

A large human carrying a pint of ale in his hand stepped in front of them, his suspicious gaze locked on Gwenvael.

"Dagmar."

"Brother."

"Who is this?"

"This is Lord Gwenvael. I'm taking him to see Father."

The Northlander examined Gwenvael closely before saying, "He must be from the south. So brown."

"I prefer golden," Gwenvael corrected. "It's a tragic curse really since I live in a part of the world where the two suns actually come out during the day and don't cower behind clouds, afraid to be seen by the scary Northmen."

When Dagmar's brother only stared at him, Gwenvael glanced down at the female. She was smirking, and he knew he'd been right. Any intelligence in this group had gone to the woman.

"Lord Gwenvael, this is my brother and oldest son to The Reinholdt, Eymund. And I don't think he understood your joke."

That was sadly true. He didn't. "Lord Eymund."

The Northlander grunted, but kept staring. Gwenvael had no idea if this was an unspoken challenge so he said, "The men of the north are very handsome. Especially you."

It took a while for his statement to get through the immense skull surrounding that excessively slow brain, but when it did Eymund eyed him intently.

"Uh . . . what?"

"If you'll excuse us, brother"—Dagmar motioned for Gwenvael to move toward the end of the massive hall— "we're going to see Father."

When they reached a plain wood door, she knocked.

"In."

She pushed the thick door open and ushered Gwenvael in, signaling for that tasty morsel of dog to stay behind. After closing the door behind them, she walked to her father's desk. She kept her hands folded in front of her and her demeanor as nonthreatening as possible.

"Father, there's someone here to see you."

The Reinholdt lifted his gaze from the maps in front of him, glanced at Gwenvael, and immediately went back to his maps. "Don't know him."

"I know. But you've met him."

"I have?"

"He's the dragon from this morning."

Grey eyes similar to his daughter's slowly lifted, and the widely built man leaned over in his chair, looking around Dagmar to see Gwenvael.

"You havin' me on?" he asked his daughter.

"Because I'm known for my rich and well-developed sense of humor?"

Actually, the dry way she said it, Gwenvael thought she was extremely funny.

"Good point," her father said. "But still . . ."

"I know it's hard to believe. But it's him."

The Reinholdt let out a soul-weary sigh and sat back in his chair. "Yeah, so . . . What's he doin' 'ere?"

"He asked to meet with you."

"Last I remember, we weren't tellin' him nothin'."

"True. But I had little choice but to bring him here. He asked for shelter and as an outsider alone I had to give it to him at least for the night as per Northland etiquette law, which he's obviously studied."

"Ya act like he's some starving woodsman who fell at your feet. He's a bloody dragon."

"True. But it was hard to turn him away when he cried."

Eyes now wide, the warlord again leaned over and gaped at Gwenvael. *"Cried?"* That one word dripped in distaste.

"Yes, Father. There were definite tears. A touch of sobbing."

"I'm very sensitive," Gwenvael tossed in.

"Sensitive?" And he said it like he'd never heard the word before. "He's . . . *sensitive*?"

Dagmar nodded. "Very sensitive and has a tendency to cry. So . . . I'll just leave you two to it."

"Get your skinny ass back here," the warlord harshly demanded before she'd taken more than three steps. Gwenvael didn't immediately jump to the woman's defense as he would with most women. His instincts told him she didn't need his help, and he knew for a fact she wasn't like most women.

She raised a brow at her father and he raised one right back.

"When you put it so nicely, Father . . ."

"Cheeky cow," he mumbled before returning his attention back to Gwenvael. "So what do you want?"

Putting his hand over his chest, Gwenvael softly replied, "Warm food, a soft bed, and a good night's sleep. That is all I ask."

The warlord gave something that a few partially blind beings might consider a smile. "What ya hoping for? In the mornin' she'll change her mind? She won't. Tell ya that right now."

"Can't you beat it out of her?"

He heard it, though she desperately tried to hide it—a little cough trying to cover a laugh.

"We don't do that here," The Reinholdt told him. "We leave that to you Southlanders. We prize our women in the Northlands."

"Ohhhh! You mean like cattle!"

Her father cut her such a look that Dagmar wondered if the dragon cared for his head at all. Or did he want it mounted on her father's bedroom wall with the two fifteen-hundred-pound bears he'd slaughtered the winter before?

"Lord Gwenvael, I'm sure you're not trying to insult my father. Again."

"Trying? As in effort? No."

All right, she had to at least admit it to herself . . . He was funny. And had no concept of personal safety.

Not only that, but what was he doing bringing up how handsome the men in the north were—although she knew that lie for what it was—and admitting to the crying with her father right there. He was no fool, this dragon. He understood the ways of the north quite well. So what in the name of reason was he doing?

She didn't know, but she couldn't wait to find out.

"As it is our way, Father, we should let him stay the night."

"Fine."

"And can I join all of you for dinner?" the dragon kindly asked, blinking those big golden eyes.

"Dinner?" Her father looked at her. He was so confused right now, it was almost endearing.

"Aye. I'd love to chat with the great Reinholdt over dinner. As well as the delightful Lady Dagmar."

"Well . . . I guess."

"And those fine strapping, handsome sons of yours! They're all not taken, are they?"

The snort was past her nose before she could stop it, but when she saw her father start to rise from his chair, she held up her hand.

"It's all right, Father." She leaned in and whispered loudly, "I'll keep an eye on him."

"You do that."

Her father settled back in his chair, and Dagmar motioned to the door. "My Lord Gwenvael. I'll show you to your room."

Chapter 6

She led Gwenvael up to the second floor in another part of the building. The Main Hall may have been one mammoth room that could accommodate a small army, but behind that was an eight-story-high section that housed a substantial amount of sons, wives, and offspring.

"You'll stay here." Dagmar stepped into the room and waited for him to enter. "There are fresh linens, and the furs have been aired."

He walked around the room. *It could be worse, I guess.*

"If you need anything—"

"A bath. Please." Gwenvael sat down on the end of the bed. The day had caught up with him and he was tired.

"Well, there's a lake." She walked to the window, looked out. "And I believe it might rain tonight if you want to stand outside."

Gwenvael dropped his head into his hands.

"Is something wrong?" she asked.

"By all that's holy, tell me you have a tub!"

When she didn't answer, he looked up to find her hand over her mouth and her shoulders shaking as she laughed at him.

"Woman, don't make me cry again. Because this time I promise you mucus."

She laughed a little more freely now. "Reason's defender, please no more of the crying."

Gwenvael rubbed his tired eyes, yawned. "Reason's

defender? I haven't heard that expression since the time of Aoibhell."

"You've heard of Aoibhell? So you have read a book."

"I've read at least two, but I actually knew her."

"You knew Aoibhell the Learned? The philosopher?" She stepped closer. "You?"

"Don't you mean Aoibhell the Heretic?" Arms behind him, palms flat against the bed, Gwenvael stretched his legs out in front of him. She was close enough that if he wanted to, he could run his foot up the inside of her leg. Well . . . He did want to, but he feared what might be waiting inside her skirt to snap his toes off. "Do you really not have a tub?"

"I have a tub. And heretic was an unfair title. So what was she like?"

"Like?" He shrugged. "She was nice enough. But she debated about absolutely everything. Do you really not believe in the gods?"

Dagmar kept her hands loosely clasped in front of her. To all outward appearances she seemed the perfect royal spinster daughter. Demure, well spoken, knowledgeable of etiquette, and just smart enough to hold conversation with those around her. But he already knew better. Only the brilliant and the brave followed Aoibhell's teachings. To openly dispute others' beliefs in the gods was risking a lot.

"There is nothing in Aoibhell's teachings to suggest gods do not exist. But like her, I don't worship them."

Gwenvael smiled, remembering the passionate discussion he'd had with Aoibhell the Learned about the gods and her belief that reason and logic were all that was necessary to successfully and happily get through life. And it wasn't that Gwenvael had disagreed with her at the time, but he could tell she liked to argue.

"Don't you worry you'll need a god one day?"

"No. They can't be relied upon. One is better off standing

on her feet, relying on herself rather than falling on her knees praying to gods who will not listen."

He chuckled. "She would have liked you."

"Would she?"

"She liked thinkers. 'Those who think beyond their day-to-day cage,' she'd say."

"You really have met her. I've only read that phrase in some letters of hers a friend gave to me. Never in her books. Were you there when she passed?"

"No." He winced at the memory. "We stopped speaking when she caught me in bed with one of her daughters. She was so mad. Came after me with a pitchfork."

Her demure pose ended when her hands rested haughtily on her hips. "You defiled her daughter?"

"I didn't defile anyone. Her daughter was a young widow. I was merely helping her back into life."

"How altruistic of you."

He grinned. "I thought so." Gwenvael dropped his arms out at his sides and fell back on the bed. "Tub! Or I start stomping my feet and crying."

"Please do. My father looked moments from throwing you out anyway."

"He did, didn't he?"

"A good crying fit should toss him right over the edge."

"That would be a shame now, wouldn't it?"

"Would it?"

"It would. Annwyl's a powerful queen. An alliance with her would be wise."

"*You* can broker an alliance for the queen?" she asked carefully.

"Of course."

"So the Blood Queen sends you as an emissary and you think it's a good idea to laugh at the Only Daughter of The Reinholdt in front of his sons and troops?"

Gwenvael flinched. She got a direct hit with that one.

He forced himself to sit back up. "All right. I'll admit that was not my best moment. I know this. But you need to understand that for the entire *long* trip here I kept hearing about The Beast. The Beast, The Beast, The Beast! The scary, frightening Beast. The size of a bear with the cunning battle skills and fangs of a jungle cat. And then you walk out. And you're . . . you're . . ."

"Plain, boring, and fangless?"

"I was going to say dainty."

"'Dainty'? Me?"

He couldn't help but smile. "Compared to the women I know, you're as dainty as an air fairy." He gestured at her body. "Look at you. Your feet are small, your hands delicate, your neck long and lithe, and there's not a scar on you. Not that I have a problem with scars. They can be quite alluring. But it's been a while since I've seen a woman who didn't have at least a few." He pointed at her spectacles. "And being nearly blind only makes you appear more innocent and vulnerable."

"I am *not* nearly blind. And it is believed in the north that a woman who has scars other than those from her typical daily chores, does not have a male in her life who takes very good care of her."

"And the women I know don't need a man to take care of them."

"That doesn't repulse you? Women like that?"

"Hardly. But my brothers keep finding them first and then they won't let them go. Even for a night."

Her lips began to bow into a smile, but she managed to stop before it got out of hand. "I do have a tub you can use. I'll have it moved in here. It might take a bit, though. It's heavy."

"Don't bother. I'll just come to your room."

It was only a smirk, but it was lethal. "Oh, will you?"

"Don't you trust me, my innocent Lady Dagmar?"

That cold gaze scrutinized him for a long time. "I trust no

one," she finally admitted with what Gwenvael instinctively knew to be complete honesty. Complete honesty he doubted she practiced most days.

"My room is five doors down, on the right," she said. "I have to tend to my dogs now that you've frightened the life from them, so it will be empty until after tonight's dinner."

"Thank you, Lady Dagmar."

She walked back across the room and pulled open the door. That thing she called a dog stood there, waiting for her. His head lowered and he bared his fangs at Gwenvael.

"Canute. Out." She never raised her voice, and apparently she didn't have to because the dog stopped immediately.

"That reminds me," he said, standing up. He knew if he lay back down, he wouldn't get up again for hours.

"And what is that?"

He took a long look at the dog before smiling at Dagmar. "I'm starving. Anything to . . . snack on before dinner?"

Her eyes narrowed and she made a quick motion with her hands. The dog immediately walked off. "I'll have some cheese and bread sent up to you."

"Cheese and bread? Don't you have anything with a little more mea—"

"Cheese and bread, Southlander. Be happy you're getting that. And stay away from my dogs."

She walked out, and Gwenvael yelled after her, "Someone is not taking very good care of me!"

Chapter 7

"We have a problem."

Briec glanced up from the book he was reading and into the face of Brastias, general of Annwyl's armies and one of the few male humans Briec could tolerate.

Closing his book, he asked, "What did Gwenvael do now? Do I need to contact my mother? Are we already in war, or is it simply heading our way?"

Brastias, whose scarred face looked grim at the best of times, smiled. "Any time I start a conversation that way, all of you ask me the same questions."

"My brother starts trouble the way horses shit when they walk. And we all know that."

"It's nothing like that, I'm afraid. And you might prefer that it were a problem with Gwenvael instead."

"What's wrong?"

"You need to see. Telling you will reveal nothing."

Brastias led him out to the training fields. As Annwyl's armies had grown, so had the multiple areas used specifically for training. The one Brastias took him to was the one they used for the new trainees. Briec's daughter was one of those trainees. She spent most days with her training unit, but came and went from the castle as she felt the need. And although her mother—his dear, sweet, *quiet* Talaith—waited impatiently for Izzy to lose all interest in being a warrior, Briec feared that day would never come, for Izzy talked and dreamed constantly of being in battle, of being a warrior.

Yet every time Briec saw his Izzy she had a new bruise or cut or some part of her was swollen to twice its normal size. When she did join them all for dinner, she'd come in with a scowl that could terrify the gods, limping or with her arm in a splint or bandages wrapped around a nasty head wound. While eating she'd fall asleep at the table, and Talaith and Briec would take her to her room so she could sleep in her own bed. By morning she was gone, back out with her unit for more training, more bruises, more pain.

To say it drove his Talaith mad would be a grave under-statement. For sixteen years she'd done all she could to pro-tect a daughter she'd never held in her arms. Izzy had been brutally taken from her by those who worshipped a goddess hell-bent on revenge. They'd used Izzy's life as the yoke that kept Talaith in line, training her to one day kill on order. When mother and daughter finally met, all was wonderful. Until Izzy decided she wanted to be part of Annwyl's army. After so many years of trying to protect her daughter, of doing things she'd never be proud of to keep her daughter safe, Talaith now had to worry her precious and only child would be killed on the battlefield. It was a concern any parent of warriors might have, but Talaith simply refused to accept that this was what Izzy wanted. At least for now.

Talaith clung to the hope that Izzy, who had a tendency to walk into walls or trip over her own large feet, would bore of this like she seemed to bore of most things. And although he'd never admit it out loud, part of him hoped the same thing. Izzy may not be his by blood, but she was his daughter in every other way. He didn't want to see her harmed or put at risk any more than her mother did. In truth, Talaith and Izzy were the few beings he had any tolerance for. Even when they annoyed him, it never entered his head to blast them with flame and dust the remaining ashes from his life. There were few about whom he could say the same.

Briec leaned against the wood fence surrounding the arena, briefly regarding the other army officers and some of Annwyl's Elite Guard standing around with him. "Now what?"

Brastias rested his arms against the top of the fence and let out a sigh before he began. "When we took Izzy in, it was with the understanding that if she failed, she'd have to go. Not only for her safety, but for the safety of those in battle with her."

"Of course. I'll not have my daughter in danger because she has some pipe dream of being a warrior."

"Aye," Brastias mumbled. "Pipe dream."

Briec flinched a bit. "How bad is she?"

"You need to see."

Brastias motioned to one of the trainers and that man called out, "Iseabail, Daughter of Talaith, come forward and fight!"

Briec could see where this was going. Brastias, weak human that he was, wanted Briec to be the one to break the news to Izzy that she still had much more training to do before she moved to the next level. Not good, because his daughter had little patience for the normal way of things and she wanted to be a soldier in Annwyl's army *now*.

Izzy stepped into the training area. She had more bruises on her face, and her lip had been split open. But none of that took away from the beauty she'd gotten from her mother. Although at only seventeen winters she was still all legs, having not really filled out yet. And she was still getting taller. Right now, she was as tall as Annwyl, able to look the six-foot-tall human queen directly in the eye. But in a few more years, Izzy would blossom, rounding out a bit to resemble her mother even more only with light brown eyes and lighter brown hair.

Already, though, the unworthy local boys had been looking closely at Briec's daughter. A little too closely. And those who had tried to move past mere looking, Briec, Fearghus, and Gwenvael took great delight in slapping around until they learned that anything *but* looking at his daughter could get a man killed.

Weighed down with a short sword and the full-length metal shields Annwyl's army favored for close in battles, Izzy glanced around the arena. She wasn't looking for anyone, he'd guess, but her mind had wandered. Izzy's mind wandered a lot, it seemed.

Izzy spotted him and her grin grew wide. "Daddy!" she squealed and waved excitedly with the hand holding the sword. She almost hit herself in the head with it too, and had apparently forgotten she'd seen Briec only that morning near the stables.

He smiled back at her. "Hello, little one."

"Are you here to watch?"

"I am."

She scrunched up her nose nervously and said, "Oh. Well, remember . . . I'm still learning!" And she gave him that hopeful look that tore his heart out.

He nodded at her and muttered to Brastias, "It's only been seven months. Perhaps, you could give her another—"

"You have to see." Brastias motioned to the trainer, who motioned to a huge bear of a man. A man Briec recognized from battles they'd been in together. This was no fellow trainee, but one of Annwyl's favored warriors, whom she affectionately referred to as "Slaughter-Bear."

Briec felt his anger grow, wondering why they were trying to push his daughter out. Most trainees had until they were twenty-one winters to prove they were worthy of any more time and training before they were sent packing. "This is cruel, Brastias. I won't allow—"

"You have to see," Brastias said again. "Go!" he yelled at the two combatants, and Izzy smiled and nodded.

Briec did see then. He saw so clearly that he knew his

problem was worse than he could have imagined. Worse than he'd ever dreamed of. For the first time in his life he didn't know how he was going to handle something. Because he knew this would get dangerously ugly before it ever got better. And he knew there'd be no avoiding it. Not now.

Every warrior standing outside the training ring grimaced when they heard bone break and a cry of pain seconds before Annwyl's favored warrior flew into the fence, knocking part of it and himself completely out.

"Oh!" Izzy said, her teeth briefly gnawing her bottom lip. "Sorry, Captain, about your . . . uh . . . face." She grimaced and slowly peeked over at Brastias. "Sorry about that, General. I guess I forgot to back off . . . again."

Slowly, so slowly, Brastias looked at Briec. The expression on the man's face, the tic under his eye made it clear what Briec needed to do.

But how was a dragon, any dragon, supposed to tell the woman he loved that her only daughter, not yet eighteen, would be going off to war?

Dagmar made sure the last of her dogs were in their runs, fed, and cared for. It took some time to calm them down, the fear of the dragon lingering, but for being not even a year old, they'd done well. They hadn't backed down from the dragon at all. Good. She couldn't afford for the dogs to be cowering during battle.

After saying good night to Johann, Dagmar headed back to the fortress, Canute by her side. When she walked into the Main Hall, she wasn't exactly surprised to find her kin in the midst of a fight. It was a verbal altercation, not yet moving into a physical one. Although it most likely would. Her brothers needed very little reason to fight and as long as she stayed out of their way, she rarely got injured.

Yet the arguing stopped as soon as she walked in, her brothers immediately focusing on her.

Dagmar paused. "Yes?"

"He's in your room?" Eymund asked, leaning against one of the long dining tables.

"Yes. He wanted to take a bath."

"A bath?"

"Yes. In a tub. Not everyone feels the need to face the freezing cold water of the river."

"That's all well and good, but he shouldn't be in your room, sister."

In no mood for any of this, Dagmar walked off, tossing over her shoulder, "I know. He might be writhing all over my bed like a big cat or sniffing my shoes."

"Or having a hearty snack."

It was something in his tone that made Dagmar stop. "I sent up cheese and bread."

"That's not hearty. Not for *him*."

"Is it true?" Valdís rested his arm on Eymund's shoulder. "Da says he's that dragon from earlier only changed to look like a man. Can they really do that?"

"Yes. It's true."

"That must be from those gods you don't believe in."

His sarcasm unappreciated, she said, "I am not, once again, explaining my belief system to—" She stopped abruptly. They were all smiling. Her kinsmen didn't smile unless they were drunk or they'd killed something. They wouldn't kill the dragon, or even try, since he was under the protection of their father for the night. Then what had they done?

Dagmar glanced around the room, looking for something that might tell her what was going on. Something out of place or missing . . .

She scanned the room again, counting this time. "Where's that puppy from Tora's litter?" Unlike the rest of the puppies,

who were already in training, the too-small, scared little bundle
would become a house pet instead of battle dog. He'd feast on
scraps, play with children, and basically live a happy, if useless,
life.

"What puppy?" Eymund asked, trying to look appropriately innocent.

Dagmar glared at them all. "You bastards!" she nearly
yelled, lifting the gown of her skirt and tearing across the hall.
Her brothers' laughter followed her as she ran through the
back hallway to the stairs and up to the second floor.

She was panting by the time she reached her closed bedroom door, horrified she could actually feel a tiny bit of sweat
trickling down her back. She didn't *sweat*! And that her brothers made her exert herself in any way was something she'd be
getting retribution for at a later date. Yet for now . . .

Dagmar pushed her room door open, but the dragon was
not in the tub. Quickly surveying the area, she finally spotted
his wet, naked ass trying to wiggle under her bed.

"Come here, little one," he crooned seductively. "Just a
little closer, you yummy little thing you."

Disgusted, appalled, and angry beyond anything she could
ever remember before, Dagmar grabbed the naked bastard by
his ankle and yanked him out from under her bed, her outrage
temporarily providing the strength she needed to move such
a large, dog-eating son of a bitch.

"*Oy!*" he yelped before turning over and cradling that
frighteningly large weaponry he had between his legs. And,
if she weren't so upset, she might notice what an amazingly
gorgeous human body he had. Unlike her kinsmen who were
muscles on top of muscles, some of them appearing to have
been born without necks because the size of their shoulders
hid the evidence, the dragon at her feet was large but lean. No
fat, no oddly shaped, overdeveloped muscles. His thighs were

strong and powerful, his abdomen flat and tight, with an interesting but clear delineation between it and his hip bones.

Staring down at him, she realized her fingers twitched and her tongue rubbed the roof of her mouth, but she decided to ignore all that in favor of her anger.

He glared up at her. "I don't appreciate the stone burn against my balls, woman!"

"And I don't appreciate you going after one of my dogs—again!"

"Oh. That." He cleared his throat and gave a little shrug. "Someone opened the door and threw it in. I'd just assumed it was a little treat from you to me."

So the little barbarian did have a temper after all. At least when it came to her dogs. And her temper was in full swing as she raised her leg and brought her foot down over his cock.

He knew he had the area protected by his hands, but Gwenvael still curled on his side, grunting in pain as her foot slammed down on the area near his kidney instead.

"Stay away from my dogs, dragon! *All* of my dogs. From the smallest to the largest," she ordered, marching over him and over her bed to track down the little fur ball hiding on the other side. "Every dog in this fortress and on these lands belongs to *me*. You are not to touch them, speak to them, or go near them in any way."

She marched back over the bed and over him, with the puppy now in her arms. She petted him and crooned to him softly.

"It's a dog, little barbarian," he sighed with absolutely no pity. "And only a dog. Sometimes I use their bones to pick my teeth."

With a snarl, she leaned down and grabbed a handful of his wet hair, nearly yanking it from his head.

"Ow! Get off!" He slapped at her hands, trying to get the

unhinged female to release his precious and lovely hair. Women always spoke of how they loved when his hair draped across their bodies and how they loved to stroke it before they eventually started stroking him. The last thing he needed was some mad woman removing it.

She gave one more strong tug before she released him and stepped out of his reach. "Listen well, *creature*. Touch my dogs and I'll do to you what I do to the male dogs I decide not to breed!"

With fascination, Gwenvael watched Dagmar carefully and precisely rein in her sudden burst of temper. When those grey eyes locked on him again, they were as cold as ice.

"Now that we have that clear, I'll leave you to finish your bath, Lord Gwenvael."

She started out, then stopped. "One thing. The men of this land don't wear their long hair out. They have one plait down their back. It's custom and to keep the complaining of my siblings down, I'd appreciate if you'd abide by that."

"Of course."

She nodded and again started toward the door.

"Tragically," Gwenvael said to her back, enjoying how she stopped and her entire body tensed.

"Tragically . . . what?"

"My hair is so long and unmanageable . . . I'd never be able to braid it properly." He grinned. "Perhaps you can do it for me."

"I'll send a servant to take care of it for you."

"But as hostess of the house . . ."

She turned to face him. "As hostess of the house . . . what?"

"Shouldn't *you* tend to your guest?"

Her face showed nothing. Her demeanor didn't change one bit. But he knew he'd gotten to her because the puppy yelped in her arms and she had to loosen her grip before he stopped squirming.

"If you insist, my lord."

"Oh"—Gwenvael grinned—"I do insist!"

His groaning seemed awfully excessive and only added to the absurdity of her situation.

Really, she should only be doing this sort of thing for her husband or her kinsmen and only before they rode off into battle. She'd been putting warrior braids in her father's hair for years. And then when he returned from battle, she'd spend an hour at least trying to get any remaining blood and gore out of it that his "dip" in the river had not touched.

What she should *not* be doing was braiding the hair of this dragon. Even more appalling, he didn't simply want her to braid it.

After putting the puppy outside, he'd explained to her as if she were some servant girl, "First comb it for me, love. Carefully. Don't want you to pull any hairs out, simply get out the tangles." But he didn't stop there. "Then three hundred strokes of the brush—each side gets a hundred and then one hundred for the back."

After he'd explained all that, he'd relaxed in the chair with a fur casually tossed over his naked lap, appearing as if it could and would drop off at any second.

It briefly crossed Dagmar's mind to use the eating knife she kept tucked in her leather girdle to cut his throat, but that would not be in the best interest of her people. And, more importantly, *her*. So, instead, she took the ivory comb her father brought back from one of his raids and began to carefully untangle the dragon's hair. It reached to the floor, so this was no easy task.

Even worse, he never shut up.

Dagmar didn't know any being on the planet could talk as much as this one dragon. He talked and talked and then talked some more.

Perhaps she wouldn't have minded so much if he actually said something of interest. The spark of hope she'd had when he mentioned knowing Aoibhell was quickly extinguished. How had the great philosopher that Dagmar based most of her belief system on tolerated an entire dinner with this . . . this . . . dragon? He seemed only to manage inane babble about all the women he'd known, which apparently were many!

Eventually Dagmar exchanged the comb for her brush, and that's when the groaning started and, tragically, did not stop.

"That feels wonderful," he'd sighed out at one point. "Have you thought of doing this for a living? You're very good."

Dagmar kept silent and went through the first one hundred strokes. When she started on the second side, she didn't think the dragon would notice if she'd brushed fifty times or fifteen hundred. She was wrong.

"That was only seventy-five, love," he'd told her when she started to move to the back. "Another twenty-five and you'll be done with that. Then you can do the back."

Again, she considered killing him but thought better of it.

Three hundred strokes later, Dagmar slammed the brush down. Now to the task of braiding all this hair!

Dagmar began braiding it and was halfway down his back when she said, "It would help with the rest if you'd stand."

"All right."

He stood, and Dagmar was greeted with that naked ass. That magnificent naked ass, if she did say so herself. His front had been exquisite, but his back was . . . reason help her.

"Think you could wrap the fur around you completely?" She feared she may start petting his ass the way she'd petted the puppy's head.

"I could. But isn't your question more of a 'do I want to'?"

"You do know that I and my eating knife have access to much back here and—"

She didn't even have to finish before he quickly wrapped the fur completely around his hips.

"Thank you, my lord," she said sweetly.

"Welcome," he grumbled back.

It took her a bit, but eventually she finished braiding all that golden hair and tied a leather thong to the end. When Dagmar stood, her fingers ached from the task, and the dragon turned to find her flexing her fingers.

He reached for her hand. "Need help with that?"

"No," she told him, pulling her hand away before he could grasp it. "There are clothes for you—in your room. Evening meal is in another hour. Until then, stay away from the dogs."

"I will." He took a step toward her. "This has all been very kind of you, my lady. Thank you."

"You're welcome."

Another step. "Perhaps you could come to my room and help me dress."

She pressed one finger against his chest and the dragon stopped in midstride. "What *are* you doing?"

His smile was shameless. "What I always do."

"Well, don't do it with me."

"Are you sure? I'm known for my skills."

"And I'm sure that's the *only* skill you possess. But in the Northland, women, including the servant girls, are given proper respect. Do not think because of how their husbands may treat them that anyone, especially an outsider, may do the same."

"I have no plans to harm you, my lady."

"I'm sure you don't. But don't think because you're a dragon my brothers will show you any fear. So if you hope for your manhood to stay intact, you'd best watch your step."

His grin, the absolute beauty of it, lit up the room. "What are you trying to tell me, my lady?"

"I'm telling you to keep your cock in your pants and your hands to yourself." She walked to the door and pulled it open, a tense Canute jumping to his large feet, ready to defend her honor. "Take it as a friendly warning."

"Did you just tell me to keep my cock in my pants?"

Dagmar ignored him and walked out of the room, closing the door behind her. She was halfway down the hall when she turned right around and walked back. She knocked, and the dragon opened the door.

"It's my room you're in," she snarled.

His laughter made her jaw clench. "I was wondering when you were going to notice."

Chapter 8

She had no idea what he was doing, but she was absolutely fascinated.

True, he was ignoring her, but Dagmar had long been used to that sort of treatment. What she wasn't used to, however, was a man—or in this case a dragon male—ignoring her sisters-in-law. They weren't all beautiful. Several had features that made Dagmar quite grateful to simply be plain. Yet what they lacked in beauty, they made up for in eagerness. And Kikka—who'd replaced Eymund's beloved first wife when she was killed during a brazen raid by Jökull several years back—was eager *and* beautiful.

Yet Kikka's generously exposed bosom, her perfectly coiffed hair, and the scent she simply drowned herself in didn't seem to hold the dragon's attention as well as Eymund's habit of eating with his fingers.

"So have you been in many battles, Lord Gwenvael?" Kikka asked, making sure to lean over to give him a better view of her chest.

"A few out of necessity. But I'm not much of a swordsman." He turned in his chair and looked at Eymund. "But you must have quite the way with the sword. So strong."

Dagmar almost spit out her wine.

Carefully placing her chalice on the table, Dagmar glanced at her other brothers and father. They looked as uncomfortable as Eymund and as . . . panicked? Yes. It was definitely panic she saw among her kinsmen.

The truth of that did nothing but amaze her. They find out he's a dragon, and they barely blink an eye. No one said a word or showed a bit of interest when he sat down uninvited at the head table with her father, her four oldest brothers, their wives, and Dagmar.

Yet the idea he may be interested more in them than in one of their women had the lot ready to bolt from the room. The dragon knew it, too. He knew exactly what he was doing and seemed to be enjoying every moment of it.

Her father caught her eye and motioned to the dragon.

She shrugged, unsure of what he wanted. Her father had never offered her to a man except as a wife, and she doubted he'd start now.

But her father scowled harder and she could only guess that he wanted her to distract the dragon's attention from her brothers.

If she had to be bothered, she might as well make it worth her time.

"So, Lord Gwenvael . . . What exactly is your connection to Queen Annwyl?"

He gave her a lazy smile while continuing to stare at poor Eymund. "She's a very good friend of mine."

"Do you run errands thousands of leagues from your home for all your friends?"

"When they're Annwyl. It makes sense, though, don't you think? My kind can fly here in half the time it takes humans to ride across country on horseback."

"Very true. And yet you say that she's empowered you to bargain on her behalf. She's putting a lot of trust in you, especially since an alliance was never discussed in the missive we sent her."

"But why else would you want to see the queen herself, if not for a discussion on an alliance between the kingdoms? With all those defenses I saw on Reinholdt lands, I can't help but think perhaps you're in need of a good alliance."

"And I can't help but wonder what it is about Annwyl's unborn children that makes them such an important target."

"Don't you know?"

Holding her chalice between both her hands, Dagmar rested her elbows on the table. "All I know is who wants to cut her babes from her like a festering infection. Why is a question I have been unable to get an answer on."

He relaxed back in his chair with an air of nonchalance she didn't buy for one second. "Why should be of no concern to you, but I'm sure there's some . . . agreeable arrangement you and I can come to that would work for all involved."

"You and I? No, no." Dagmar gave a small, false laugh and placed her chalice back on the table. For a moment, a splendid moment, all he felt from her as they talked was heat and sex. This one loved the game as much as he, but these barbarians held her back. A shame, really. For he wondered what she

would really do if given free rein. "I would never handle negotiations of such great importance."

"What's this, sister-in-law?" the one who must have bathed
in whatever sickening scent she used—*Kikka, was it?*—cut
in. "Are you not the politician of your father's lands?"

Dagmar didn't move, her expression never changed, and
she did nothing that suggested the woman's words hit a nerve.
But for Gwenvael those cold, grey eyes always gave Lady
Dagmar away.

Did these females not know the dangerous animal they
played with? Did they really not see it? Or did their jealousy
of her make them blind to the risks they took?

Kikka placed one smooth, unmarred hand on his forearm.
"You see, Lord Gwenvael, our little Dagmar hopes the rules will
change one day and she'll be reigning warlord over everything
you see here. That when our great warriors ride into battle,
they'll be chanting 'The Beast' and not 'The Reinholdt.'"

Ahhh, not blind. Stupid.

The insipid women at the table laughed at Kikka's joke
until Kikka yelled out, pushing her chair back and stumbling
away from the table.

Eymund rolled his eyes. "What is wrong now?"

"One of those vicious beasts of hers bit me!"

Dagmar put her hand to her chest. "Oh, Kikka, I'm so
sorry." She glanced under the heavy wood table. "Come here,
little one. Come here." A dog large enough that Gwenvael
could ride it back to Dark Plains emerged from under the
table. "Now, Idu, I know you want to play with Canute, but
not tonight. Go outside now."

The large but older dog, based on her white muzzle and the
grey in her fur, eased out from under the table and sauntered
out of the hall.

"You put her under there on purpose!" Kikka accused, one
of the servants wiping away the blood from her ankle.

"And why would I do that?"

"You know that dog hates me."

"The dog hates you. I see. And therefore I put her under the table to attack when you said something she didn't like? That was the *dog's* grand scheme, eh?"

"No! I meant you . . . you know what I meant, dammit."

"Sit down," Eymund ordered. "You're making a bloody fool of yourself."

"But she—"

"Sit!"

Her face red from anger, her glare for Dagmar alone, Kikka pulled her chair back and sat down. She looked at Gwenvael and he knew what he saw in her eyes. A clear invitation. With the right word or look, she'd find a way to invite him to her room or to meet somewhere outside later tonight.

In answer, Gwenvael turned in his chair and focused on Eymund again. "Since your sister can't handle negotiations, I do hope *you* and *I* will work together on this. Very closely."

He so enjoyed the way the man froze any time Gwenvael did that. The human looked like that deer Gwenvael had come upon a few days ago in the forest. He wondered what would make Eymund scamper off completely.

Dagmar pushed her chair back and stood. "I'm off to bed, Father. Lord Gwenvael."

"Lady Dagmar," he said, but he kept his attention on Eymund—much to the man's horror. "So tell me, Eymund . . ." Gwenvael nibbled on a crunchy piece of fruit. "What are you planning to do . . . after dessert?"

Morfyd the White Witch tore off the dress she'd put on only moments before and grabbed for another. When did she get like this? This pathetic and . . . and . . . female? Honestly! Did she really need to put herself through any of this?

She pulled the red gown on and stared at herself in the mirror. She frowned. Her . . . in red. Were there not laws against that?

As she began to pull the dress off and try on another, her brother's voice echoed in her head.

She immediately stopped, feeling guilty as if she'd been caught red-handed, until she remembered he was in the Northlands. And, she reminded herself, he couldn't read her thoughts. But, like most dragons, they could communicate with each other using their minds alone. A true gift . . . unless you were hiding something and jumpy as a sparrow.

Are you there or not? her brother's voice demanded.

Don't bark at me! She rubbed her forehead, tried to calm down a bit. *What is it?*

Nothing. But I'm in the Reinholdt Fortress.

The dungeons?

Very funny.

She smiled and dropped down on the edge of her bed. Actually it was very funny.

I'm not in the dungeons. I'm in a room. Just finished dinner with the lot of them. Which was tedious, to say the least.

And what did they tell you? What do they know?

I'm still working on that.

You're still . . . Morfyd gritted her teeth together. *What did you do?*

Nothing.

Gwenvael!

Would you leave it to me? Why don't you trust me?

Are you really asking me that? She sighed. *I told her we should have never sent you.*

And thank you for the never-ending trust, sister.

Morfyd grimaced, realizing too late she should have kept that thought to herself.

Gwenvael, I'm sorry. Please—

But she already knew he was no longer there.

She hadn't meant to hurt him, but this was Gwenvael. She and Fearghus had tried to talk Annwyl out of sending Gwenvael as her emissary, but her friend had insisted.

Morfyd did know her brother would try, but still . . . This was Gwenvael!

"Is it Gwenvael again?"

Her body immediately tensed at the sudden intrusion until a familiar hand stroked down her back.

"I hurt his feelings," she said without turning around. "I didn't mean to."

Lips brushed against her cheek, the back of her neck. Teeth nibbled lightly at her ear. "I know. But sometimes he does ask for it."

Morfyd leaned back against the human male behind her. He'd come into her room the same way for the last few months—through her window. Their days may belong to the kingdoms they served, but their nights belonged to each other.

"He says we have no faith in him."

Sir Brastias, general to the entire Dark Plains armies, put his arms around Morfyd's body and held her close, his chin resting against her shoulder. "Faith and trust must be earned, Morfyd, and your brother plays too much for that to be the case. Besides, he can't poke at the bear and be surprised when it attacks."

"But he does care. In his own way. I know no one thinks he does, but he does. He really wants to help Annwyl. He's worried about her."

"We all are. She's not been looking well these last few weeks."

"I know. And I appreciate you making sure she's not

bothered with much." And for keeping their relationship a wonderful secret. Morfyd wished she could say it was only her worries for Brastias's physical health should her brothers find out that kept her from admitting the truth. But it was more than that. It was having to tell her mother that almost had her curling into a ball on her bed, afraid to move. Queen Rhiannon could be difficult at the best of times, and the gods knew she treated her sons vastly different from the way she treated her daughters.

"I try to protect her, but sometimes she searches me out." He smiled, a rare thing of utter beauty. She always felt like his smiles were a special gift just for her. "How much longer?"

"I don't know. It should be at least another two months. But even with twins . . . she shouldn't be this big yet."

"Are you terribly worried?"

"I'm worried." She rested her head against his. "I'm definitely worried."

"You're already doing the best that you can for her. She can't ask for more than that. None of us can."

"I know."

"She won't be at dinner tonight. Did anyone tell you?"

"No." She instantly became concerned. "Is she all right?"

"She's fine. Fearghus said she just wanted to lie in tonight. It sounds like few will be down in the Great Hall."

"All right."

"So I thought you and I could have dinner up here. Have our own lie in."

She turned her face toward his, let the feel of his kiss move through her.

"Were you going to wear that dress tonight at dinner?"

Her eyes fluttered open, and she realized he'd stopped kissing her. She hated when he stopped kissing her.

"This? Uh . . . I was just trying it on. I wasn't going to wear it."

"Let me see." He pulled away from her. "Go on. I want to see."

Feeling uncomfortable, she stood and slowly turned to face him. She should never wear red. Her mother had specifically told her she should never wear red. What had she been thinking?

"Back up a bit so I can see the whole dress."

She took several steps back. "Well?"

"Nice gown. You look amazing in red."

"I do?"

"Aye." His gaze swept her from head to foot and back again. "You do."

Morfyd felt her confidence grow under that gaze. Blossom. "Thank you."

He stretched out on the bed and let out a wonderfully contented sigh, his gaze never leaving hers. "It's a tragic shame you won't be wearing it for long, though."

Walking toward him, her fingers already sliding the sleeves of the dress off her shoulders, she said, "Aye, Brastias. A tragic shame."

Gwenvael shook his hair out of that stupid braid and began to pace his room.

"Of course," he muttered to himself, "don't send Gwenvael. He'll just muck it up. Useless, worthless Gwenvael."

From one of his three brothers, Morfyd's comment could and would have been dismissed. But from either Morfyd or his younger sister, Keita, it hurt. Deeply. For them to think he didn't take any of this seriously hurt. Annwyl meant the world to him, and he wouldn't risk her or the twins. So why did his family not see it? Was it because he refused to face every challenge as some grim test to the death? Should he constantly glower at every living thing like Fearghus? Or show nothing but constant disdain like Briec? Or perhaps be constantly wide-eyed and openly earnest like Éibhear? Could his kin only then take him seriously? How, after all these years, could they still not see?

And he refused to hear any longer that it was his "whoring" as his father loved to call it. None of his kin had been monks, though Morfyd was the closest to that ideal than any of the others.

Yet when it was all said and done, it was only Annwyl, a human he hadn't even known five years, much less two centuries or more, who seemed to understand his worth. Only she had any true faith in him.

Because of that, she would be the reason he would not fail.

A knock pulled him from his rather depressing thoughts— and the gods knew he hated being maudlin—and he walked across the room to open the thick, sturdy wooden door. When he thought about it, most things in the north seemed made of wood and sturdy. Even the people.

Gwenvael blinked down at the servant girl standing in the hallway.

"Aye?" When she frowned, he said, "Yes?"

"I . . . uh . . ." She looked him over and shivered a bit before she boldly walked into his room. "Is there something I can help you with, love?"

"I'm a gift," she said, already pulling off her dress. "A gift for you, my lord."

Her gaze devoured him. She wanted his cock, but he wasn't exactly surprised by that.

"Are you now? A gift from whom?"

"The Reinholdt, of course."

"I see." Gwenvael walked across the room and leaned his back against the wall by the window, his arms crossed over his chest. "And what kind of gift are you?"

Her dress fell to the floor, and she stood before him confident and beautifully naked.

His body stirred, but that wasn't surprising either. It *had* been awhile. Nearly a whole week! And yet—

Gwenvael abruptly pivoted toward the window and watched as Dagmar Reinholdt slipped out of the shadows beside one of the stables, walking away from the fortress gates. She was dressed warmly in a wool cape and gloves, a satchel over her shoulder.

Now where is she going?

He had to admit, he found the Lady Dagmar quite diverting. At dinner she seemed confused by what he was up to, but intrigued—and thoroughly entertained. The image of a cat with hidden claws always seemed to come to mind when he saw her. Especially when he watched those cold, grey eyes look around the room, taking everything in, processing, and sorting what she saw.

So what was a demure Only Daughter to a Northland warlord doing wandering about in the evening?

He had to know!

"My lord?"

Gwenvael scowled at the girl, and she stepped back. To be honest, he'd forgotten she was in the room.

He smoothed over the scowl with a perfectly acceptable smile. The kind he kept for elderly ladies and detestable small children. "Sorry, love. Can't tonight."

"What?"

He picked up her dress, pushed it into her arms, and as gently as possible shoved her toward the door.

"I do, however, really appreciate you stopping by. Very nice of you." He opened the door and pushed her out into the hall. "Tell Lord Sigmar thanks and, uh . . . nice tits."

Then he closed the door and locked it. He stripped off his clothes and walked to the window, throwing it open. By the time he slipped outside into the cold Northland night, he'd shifted to dragon, his claws digging into the stone walls. He then blended into his surroundings and went off after Dagmar Reinholdt.

Eymund and his brothers watched as the lovely Lagertha came tumbling into the hallway from the dragon's room, as the door was slammed shut and immediately bolted. She was naked but had her dress held up in front of her. She hadn't been in there three minutes. That wasn't even time enough for a good suck, in his estimation, much less a worthy fuck.

He motioned to her, and she ran over, her face red and her body shaking.

"That bastard tossed me out. *Me!*" There had been few men on Reinholdt lands who had not had their time in Lagertha's bed. She enjoyed a good ride and made no apologies for it. When they'd pointed out the dragon as he'd been heading back to his room, she'd practically tripped over her tongue with lust, and readily agreed to be his "gift."

"What did he say to you? Did he give you a reason?"

"No. He just wasn't interested."

Eymund looked at his brothers and they were equally as confused. How could the bastard, even a dragon pretending to be human, not be interested in free pussy? What male wasn't?

"Maybe he only likes his own kind," one of his brothers reasoned. "Can't say I'd be too comfortable bedding one of them dragon females, though."

"I don't think it's only because he wants a dragoness," said Valdís. "More like he only wants Eymund."

And that's what worried him. Usually it was Dagmar they felt the need to protect from strangers from the outside. But for once she seemed to be at no risk at all. "I'm going to see Father," Eymund said abruptly.

And off they all went to the pub.

* * *

Dagmar got herself comfortable on the roof of one of the army barracks. She had extra furs because she knew she'd get cold. Plus in her favorite satchel she had a bottle of wine, the dessert from the earlier evening's meal, and a chalice. With everything set into place, she crossed her legs and pulled her plain but comfortably warm skirt over her knees and feet. Then she waited for the entertainment to begin.

She didn't have to wait long.

Kikka tiptoed from the shadows, looking this way and that, making sure no one could see her. But she wore the expensive cape she'd insisted on buying. It was bright yellow and although dark out, there was enough light coming from the different buildings to make her stand out like a spot on one of the bloody suns.

Foolish girl.

Since she'd come to the Reinholdt Fortress to be Eymund's bride, Kikka had made it her business to bring Dagmar to heel. She didn't trust her, didn't like her, and felt threatened by her. Fair enough, since Dagmar felt the same way about her. The difference, however, was that Kikka was stupid. Dagmar wondered if there was a brain at all in her addled little head. While Kikka tried to sweet-talk Sigmar into sending Dagmar away and seduce her husband into pushing the issue, Dagmar had a lovely and growing list of all Kikka's lovers in the last five months, including locations, times, and positions.

True, she could have revealed Kikka's whoring ages ago, but why waste the power? More importantly, Kikka kept her brother happy with more brats while Sigmar worried less about the state of his sons' marriages and more about important things like Jökull.

And, she could admit to herself, while she sat up here on

the barrack roof, that Kikka did provide a form of entertainment Dagmar could not indulge in otherwise.

She enjoyed watching. It was a flaw, but she only used it against those who would try to take what she'd fought so hard for all these years. As long as Kikka remained ineffectual, her secrets were safe with Dagmar.

Kikka slipped into the stablemaster's room. Horses were so important in the Northlands, so revered by the warriors that the position of stablemaster paid incredibly well and often included a house on the grounds.

Thankfully this stablemaster's small house included lovely windows that he never closed the small wooden doors on. When he moved toward Kikka, his intentions clear, Dagmar reached into her satchel and pulled out the specially made spectacles Brother Ragnar had given her several years ago. Unlike the ones she wore on her face, these were much larger, needing both her hands to hold them. Nor did she wear them per se, but simply held them up to her eyes, the leather they were encased in allowing her a wonderful grip. While her regular spectacles were merely to see what she should normally see in front of her, these were so she could see much farther away . . . and in fascinating detail.

She grinned when she saw the stablemaster tear off Kikka's gown. How would the girl explain the state of her dress when she returned to the fortress? And she had to know by now that Eymund would realize another gown had been "accidentally" damaged. Her brother was stingy with his coin and Kikka's allure had worn off long ago. Much to Kikka's growing dismay, if Dagmar was guessing right. The servants told Dagmar of nasty arguments and her brother spending more and more time in the local pubs with his comrades and kinsmen—and bar wenches.

With Kikka's dress and shift torn open, the stablemaster, Valtemar, bent her over his arm and feasted on her absurdly large breasts. As Dagmar watched, enjoying herself thoroughly, she still grimaced a little at his performance.

"He is lacking technique, isn't he?"

Mortified and shocked all at the same time, Dagmar lowered the big spectacles to her lap and turned her head to the left. She blinked, looked behind her, then to her right.

"He has eagerness, but he also has a bit of . . . well . . . slobber."

Again, she looked to her left. But all she could see were the tops of other buildings close by, the tops of trees off in the distance. But even though she couldn't see anything beside her, she still felt . . .

Stretching out her hand, she hit something hard and smooth. Her hand slid down the surface, trying to understand what she was touching.

"That feels wonderful."

Dagmar snatched her hand back. "Show yourself, dragon."

The darkness shimmered and what was not there was now there. Gold scales, large wings tight against his body, talons, fangs. He was facing her, his back to the world behind him, his long tail with the clean blunt end swung lazily back and forth over the edge of the roof.

"Lady Dagmar. It is a beautiful night."

She didn't reply; she was too annoyed he'd found her. Too annoyed he'd seen her.

Fire surrounded the dragon, and Dagmar quickly turned her head, the heat of it feeling much too close for her comfort. Then, moments later, he sat down beside her. As human.

And naked.

Like he had in his bedroom, he placed his arms behind him to prop up his upper body, his palms flat against the roof slats. His long legs were bent at the knees, his ridiculously large feet planted firmly in front of him. But it was his sizable cock, lying lazily against his thigh that had the saliva in her mouth drying up immediately. *Mighty reason, if that's him flaccid . . .*

Forcing herself to look away, she asked, "Are you not chilly?"

"No."

She handed him one of her fur blankets. "Put this on anyway."

He chuckled, spreading the fur out over his lap. "Did you even peek?"

"I don't need to. I see naked men everyday."

"But none as superb as I." That was truth, but she'd not admit it out loud.

"Why are you here?"

"Came to see the sights. Just as you have." Dagmar didn't reply to his glib remark; instead she analyzed how bad this could get for her.

He could try to use this against her, but only if she allowed him to. Her father would not be pleased, but no matter which way she examined it, it all seemed to be worse for Kikka, which could easily distract attention from Dagmar. It was Kikka who was betraying Eymund. It was Kikka who was—

"You can stop."

Dagmar glanced at him. "I can stop what?"

"Trying to figure out how I'll use this against you."

"I wasn't—"

"Because I won't be."

Dagmar closed her mouth, stared straight ahead. "You won't?"

"No. Is that wine?" He leaned across her and grabbed the bottle.

"Why?"

"Why what?" He unhooked the top, took a long gulp—and choked. "Gods in the underworld! What is this?"

"My father's wine. It's not as smooth as the wines from the south."

"It's not as smooth as jagged glass." But he took another gulp anyway before handing it back to her. She started to reach for her chalice, but it seemed to be the kind of night where one drinks right from the bottle. So she did, taking several mouthfuls before she locked the top back into place.

"So you say you won't use this against me."

"I won't."

"And why is that? We both know there's something you want from me. Something I won't give. So why wouldn't you use this to bargain with?"

"For two reasons. One, that would make you an enemy. And I don't want you as an enemy. In fact, you're the last person in all the Northlands that I can afford to have as an enemy."

"You're right," she admitted.

"I know. Were I to use any of this, I'd get the truth, to be sure. But only part of it. Enough to make me go away, but not enough to really help me. Not enough to keep Queen Annwyl safe."

He was right. He was *exactly* right. "And the second reason?"

The dragon smiled. "I like to watch too. It would be hypocritical of me to use that against another."

"I do not watch for enjoyment. I merely need to be sure—"

"Don't"—he shook his head, his expression serious—"don't lie to me." He swung his arm out, encompassing the vast lands around them. "Lie to everyone. Tell them all that they want to hear while you get what you want. But don't lie to me."

"Why shouldn't I?"

"Because we understand each other too well, Dagmar, to bother with the smaller games."

She was confused by his directness. Confused and intrigued.

"So what are you suggesting, Lord Gwenvael?"

"Is that the dessert from tonight?"

She glanced at the rich dessert lying on a cloth beside her. For a moment, it seemed she didn't even remember bringing it. "Yes."

"Mind?" he asked while reaching over her and grabbing it. "It was really good. You have excellent cooks."

"We do."

He used his fingers to tear off a piece of the dessert and drop it into his mouth. He let out a sigh as the flavor burst against his tongue. "Just wonderful."

"What are you suggesting, dragon?"

He licked his lips and said, "I'm suggesting several things. But most importantly that we not see each other as combatants."

"But aren't we?"

"Only if we want nothing out of this." He licked delicious paste and dough from the tips of his fingers. "I'm not blind, Dagmar. These are serious defenses built on your father's lands. There are hidden pits filled with oil just waiting to be lit, constant patrols, the lovely spikes you have built into the ground, waiting for the right trigger to unleash them. And I know those are only the few I spotted."

"And your point?"

"There are basic defenses, and there are wartime defenses. Clearly war is coming here."

"War is here." She let out a breath, and in that moment, all pretenses, all illusions went away and Gwenvael knew he was talking to the true Dagmar Reinholdt. The one her kinsmen never saw and didn't want to see. And it was this Dagmar who was taking a chance on him.

"My father earned this land when he was only seventeen. Six of his brothers are loyal to him, three of them are dead, two side with Jökull, and then there's Jökull himself."

She pulled off a chunk of the dessert as he held it out for her. "Jökull is determined to get this land for himself. He and his armies raided the town and lands near the fortress a few years back. We were caught unprepared and . . . It was very bad. Eymund's first wife was there and she was killed. It's a great source of shame for him."

"Jökull killed her?"

"It depends who you ask. The Code which my father and kinsmen live by, says that blood- or marriage-related females are to be kept unharmed." She looked off, out at the lands. "The men of my family refuse to believe Jökull would stoop so low, would willingly break the Code. They prefer to believe her death was an accident."

"You don't believe that."

"I believe Jökull follows no code but his own."

"And you think he's planning to strike again."

"Whether he is or he isn't, it behooves us to be ready."

Gwenvael pulled off another piece of the dessert. "And an alliance with Annwyl would—"

She shook her head. "I cannot bargain with you over that alliance. You'll have to do that with my father."

"Charming as your kinsmen may be, Lady Dagmar"—he licked cream off his thumb—"it is you that I trust to handle anything that requires actual thought and reason."

She looked away abruptly, and he knew she was trying not to laugh.

"Allow me to handle your father, Lady Dagmar."

Her smirk illustrated her lack of faith in his skills. "If you think you can."

"I know I can."

Dagmar took another drink of wine and handed him the bottle.

"Interesting," he finally said.

"What is?"

He gestured toward the stablemaster's open windows with the wine bottle. "What he's doing to her."

Dagmar again lifted up to her eyes those large pieces of glass wrapped in leather. "Oh, my." She lowered the glasses, looked at him. "Isn't there some sort of proper preparation that's necessary for that sort of thing?" she asked.

"If you want *her* to enjoy it as well . . . yes."

"Then that's just rude." She brought the glasses back up. "He is all over the place, isn't he?"

"There is no finesse there. She'd be better off getting mauled by a bear."

Dagmar laughed while she kept watching. Something told him she didn't laugh nearly as much as she'd like to.

"Three gold pieces the mauling bear story is what she tells my brother happened to her."

"No, no. Three gold pieces that he believes it."

They watched until the bitter end, the dragon's comments nearly bringing her to tears of laughter. Even more rewarding was that she'd made him laugh as well. She'd never really been considered entertaining before and she could definitely see the allure of it.

When Kikka finally limped and tottered her way back to the fortress, Dagmar packed up the few things she'd brought with her and the dragon stepped off the roof, effortlessly shifting back to his natural form in midair.

"Come, Beast. I will take you back."

"Take me back?"

He landed on the roof of the barracks, surprising her with his lightness. In the morning the soldiers wouldn't be wondering what shook their building.

"Aye." He turned a bit and lowered himself. "Climb on."

Flying? He wanted to take her flying?

"I—"

"Come on. You know you want to try." He grinned and

showed all those fangs. It worried her more that she wasn't worried at all. "I promise I won't drop you."

"Comforting."

"Grab hold of my long, luxurious mane and hoist yourself up."

"I don't hoist, dragon."

"Grab hold then."

She put the strap of her satchel across her shoulders and grabbed onto his mane. She felt his tail slide under her rear and lift her. She gave a startled squeal.

"Just being helpful," he said before she could start stabbing at his tail with her eating knife. "Now tighten your thighs against my neck and hold on to my hair."

He stepped off the edge of the building and his wings extended from his back. The Northland winds caught him, lifting them up. He glided for a bit before moving his wings to take them higher. Dagmar stared out over the world, fascinated by what she saw. To look down on everything was amazing, to feel this free was addicting.

He flew her around the town and lands for nearly an hour. She had no idea why he stayed out that long, but she didn't complain. Why bother when she loved every second of it?

He brought her back to the fortress and she pointed out her window to him. He landed against the wall, his claws holding him in place. She clung to him, terrified she'd slip off his back and fall to her death straight below. But then his tail wrapped around her waist and lifted her up.

"Open your window."

She did, and the tail carried her inside. It didn't unwind from her waist until her feet touched the floor.

"I have to say, Lady Dagmar, that is the best time I've had in quite a while where I was not the one bedding a woman."

Dagmar placed her elbow on the windowsill, her chin

resting on her fist. "I know it was hard for you not to give him direction."

"It was! He was a mess."

She curled her lip in distaste. "And messy. If you understand the difference."

"I do."

"Think my sister-in-law enjoyed it?"

"How could she when she spent the whole time thinking about how she was fooling your brother?"

"How do you know she was thinking that?"

"I know. I've seen that look before."

She bet he had.

"In the morning, Lady Dagmar, I'll need you to trust me."

"That doesn't sound very good."

"It will. But you'll have to trust me."

She nodded, hoping that he would trust her as well—even though she most likely wouldn't deserve it.

He walked back toward his room, his steps light even as his talons tore into the stone face.

Canute growled behind her and Dagmar turned, raising her hand. Canute immediately sat. "Good boy."

Then she felt it, sliding across her ass, briefly sliding under her dress and between her legs. . . .

By the time she spun around, the tail was gone. She leaned out the window and Gwenvael said, "See you in the morning, Lady Dagmar," before he disappeared into his own room after a flash of flame and naked male taunted her.

She closed her window and put her hand to her chest. She seriously hoped she'd gauged him correctly. If not, she could end up no better off than that idiot Kikka.

Except that Dagmar had much more to lose than mere dignity.

Chapter 9

Olgeir the Wastrel of the Olgeirsson Horde spat into the ground beside his claws. He should be angry. They were on *his* territory. As one of the mighty Northland dragon warlords, his territories ranged from the Mountains of Suspicion in the High North Plains, to the River of Destruction in the west, straight out to the Vile Seas in the east. His territory stopped at the Outerplains, which marked the territorial lines between him and that dragon-bitch queen.

Although he dreamed of ruling all the Northlands, it was the thought of claiming that Southland bitch's territory that made him hard. He and several warlords had briefly banded together and declared war on Queen Rhiannon more than a century ago, but the lot of them couldn't stop bickering amongst themselves long enough to put up a decent defense, much less a proper offense. Attacking faster than anyone thought they would, those prissy Southlanders swarmed over the Northland borders and decimated some of the finest warriors Olgeir had ever known.

He'd tried to warn the other warlords. Tried to warn them about Rhiannon's consort. Bercelak the Vengeful was no pampered monarch who liked to play warrior. He was one of the Cadwaladr Clan, low-born lizards the Southland royals used like the humans used their battle dogs. Calling them to duty when the royals had a war or needed protecting, tossing them scraps, and locking them outside in the cold when there was peace. But none of that lot seemed to mind; instead they spent most of their lives going from one battle to another, even fighting with humans as human when the dragons were at peace. Yet among the Cadwaladr, it was Bercelak who had the most brutal reputation in all the dragon nations.

Olgeir still remembered what happened when one of Bercelak's warrior-sisters was captured by Northland warlords during a war several centuries ago, when Rhiannon's mother held the throne. Bercelak captured the eldest sons of the enemy warlords and tore their scales off, piece by piece. He sent the scales back, each batch wrapped up like a present, to the corresponding fathers. He included no written message, nor did the ones who brought the pieces back have anything to impart. But his message was clear . . . Either his sister was released—wings intact—or the warlords would be getting wings and limbs next as "gifts."

Bercelak still ruled by the current Dragon Queen's side, but he was older now. Those prissy sons of his went into battle the last go round. They fought well enough, but Olgeir didn't worry about them like he did their father—the Horde simply hadn't been prepared then. Yet he still had to beware of the Cadwaladrs. Last Olgeir had heard, they were fighting in the Western Mountains, but when he decided to strike, he had to make sure they were dealt with first.

And Olgeir would strike. He'd see that dragoness brought to heel and her land made his, if it was the last thing he did.

First, though, he had to deal with that treacherous son of his.

He had many sons, Olgeir did. Nineteen last count. But this one, his eighth born . . . he was the smartest of the lot. And could cause the most problems. He'd already turned at least two of his cousins to his cause, and Olgeir had no doubts at least one of his sons would follow the traitor. He was persuasive, that one, always plotting and planning to be warlord, as if Olgeir would simply hand it over to him.

Olgeir had always warned that idiot's mother he read too much, spent too much time with those mages and monks littering the countryside. Now he thought he was better than his father.

And, unfortunately for him, he'd have to learn the hard way he wasn't.

A strong claw closed over Olgeir's shoulder; one of his many nephews leaned in. "I just received word a Southland dragon was spotted over Reinholdt territories."

Olgeir's lip curled. "Anyone we know?"

"Not sure yet."

He motioned to three of his grandsons. "Send them to check it out."

"They may have to bring him down."

"So? We have what we need." *And she's perfect*, he inwardly sighed as he thought of the prize safely chained inside his mountain fortress.

His nephew sent off the three with their instructions and came back to his uncle. "And what about that lot?"

Olgeir looked at the ones caught traveling through his territories. It was because of them he was out here before the two suns rose. Their kind were rarely sighted this far from the brutal Ice Lands. But when they were seen—this time because of a tunnel cave-in—alarms went up. They were unstable, as most from the Ice Lands were, but mighty fighters in their own right. Even dragons had to be careful around them.

There were over forty of them, all standing tall and powerful, but they were nothing more than animals, the lot of them. Yet these animals had a higher purpose. A higher purpose he had no problem supporting.

"Take them to the tunnels near the bridge and send them on their way."

"You know where those tunnels lead, Uncle. Are you sure?"

Olgeir grinned, entertained by how every one of the beasts

had carved the goddess Arzhela's name into their chests with knives. They hadn't even bothered to wipe off the blood and some of the wounds weren't healing very well. But they were zealots, and that's what zealots did.

"Oh, I'm sure." He patted his nephew's shoulder. "Let them go to her. Let them honor their dead god."

He headed back to his den, his guards behind him. "If they kill *her*, half our battle is won."

Dagmar was well into the middle of an odd dream involving dessert cream and a dragon's tail when her bedroom door banged open. She sat up immediately, still caught between being awake and asleep when she yelled out, *"I did not lie!"*

Three of her brothers stood in her doorway staring at her. Which ones? She had no idea. All she could see were blurry outlines.

"What is it?" she demanded loudly over Canute's hysterical barking. "Canute!" The dog fell to a low, threatening growl while she reached over to the small table beside her bed, her hands trying to find her spectacles.

"Father needs you downstairs. Now." She recognized Valdís's voice, felt his hand press her spectacles into her palm.

"Why? What's wrong?"

"Just get dressed. We'll wait for you in the hall."

She didn't have time for a bath, so she had to make do with scrubbing up at the basin and hurriedly getting dressed. As soon as she tied the scarf over her hair, she walked into the hallway and immediately her brothers pushed her toward the stairs. The moment they entered through the door into the Main Hall, Dagmar sent Canute off for a break and a chance to play with the other dogs in the side yard. Once the dog disappeared through the doorway, Valdís grabbed her wrist and dragged her to her father's private rooms.

He pulled the door open and pushed her in. She immediately saw her father at the big table that took up most of the room. As usual it was covered in maps and missives from troops who were stationed at key points throughout the countryside.

On the opposite side of the table was Gwenvael. As soon as the door opened, he turned around with a huge grin and exclaimed, "Eymund!" Then he saw her and his expression crumbled. "Oh. Hello, Lady Dagmar."

"Lord Gwenvael. Valdís, would you have a servant bring me—" But her brothers were long gone, the door slamming behind them. Shaking her head, she walked over to the table. "You asked for me, Father?"

"Aye. Uh . . . Lord Gwenvael here needs that information you've got."

"No."

Her father pointed a finger at her. "Look—"

"I said I was sorry," Gwenvael cut in, expertly rolling his eyes like a small child.

"That's very big of you. And yet I am in no mood to be forgiving."

Her father slammed his hands against the table and stood.

Dagmar motioned him to the door. "May I talk to you outside for a moment, Father?"

She walked out into the hallway, her brothers—all twelve of them—nowhere to be found.

Waiting until her father stepped outside, she closed the door and faced him. "What is going on?"

"He needs to go."

"Why? He's been utterly polite and—"

"I don't want to make a big thing of this, girl, but he needs to go. Today. So just tell him what he wants to know."

Now it had begun, and she had only one chance to make this work with all involved. First—her father.

"And lose out on a perfect opportunity?" she asked, her

heart beating fast, although she knew her face showed her father nothing.

"What opportunity? What you think you'll get from him?"

"Father," she said, making sure to add a note of impatience, "if you're simply going to hand the information over to him anyway, give me ten minutes to see what I can get on my own. Where's the harm?"

"I don't know—"

"At the very least let Eymund try," she offered innocently. "Lord Gwenvael seems to like him."

"No!" Her father took a breath, fought for calm. She made sure to look appropriately bewildered, hours in front of her mirror practicing finally paying off. He motioned her toward the door. "Go. Talk to him. You got until I get myself a pint to get something out of him. After that you tell him everything and get him out of here."

"Yes, Father." She pushed open the door, walked in, and quietly shut it.

She sat in her father's chair on the other side of the table. The dragon, in chain mail and a surcoat, had his boot-shod feet up on the table.

He smiled at her. "Well?"

"We've got ten minutes."

"All right." He dropped his feet to the floor and placed his hands on top of the wood. They stared at each other across the distance. "So what do you want?"

"Five legions."

"Five?" he asked, incredulous. "Are you mad?"

"No. You want to save that precious queen of yours, don't you?"

"Ten army units. That seems fair."

"Don't insult me, Lord Gwenvael. Four legions."

"How do I know your information is worth even one army unit, much less four full legions?"

"It is."

He sat back in his chair. "If what you have to tell me is solid . . . perhaps one legion."

"One?"

"That's fifty-two-hundred men, Lady Dagmar."

Dagmar let out a sigh, tapped her fingers against the table until grudgingly answering, "Fine."

"Good. Now tell me what you know."

"Someone wants your queen dead."

Dagmar jumped when Gwenvael's head hit the table, his arms flying out at his sides. "Is that the *best* you have to tell me?" Reason help her, he did have a love of the dramatic.

His head lifted from the table, and he speared her with his glare. "I know this already. Everybody wants her dead. They've wanted her dead for years! Tell me I haven't wasted my time here!"

"Are you done? Because I'm not."

"Thank the gods for that." He impatiently gestured for her to continue.

"It's my understanding that a party from the Ice Lands is making its way south, toward Dark Plains."

"The Ice Lands? I didn't know anyone even lived there."

"They do. You think this terrain is harsh? It's nothing compared to there. The people there are strong, hearty, and very unfriendly. And the bigger problem for you is that most travel underground."

"Whatever for?"

"There are sudden, deadly ice storms that hit at any moment of any day in the Ice Lands—hence the name." He snorted, and she continued. "So the dwarves began digging tunnels. First just leading from mine to mine, clan to clan. But they quickly realized they could make money offering ways in and out of the territory for those other than dwarves."

"You're telling me someone's sent assassins underground? That's worth about twenty army units, my lady."

"They're not assassins. There are hundreds of cults in the Ice Lands. They live to serve the gods who, in my opinion, deserted them long ago. The ones coming for your queen worshipped Arzhela. In honor of her they want your queen's babes. They want their blood. As you well know, my lord, those hired to fight are vastly different from those who believe in a cause. They'll stop at nothing. Absolutely nothing to kill your queen and her unborn offspring."

All drama and humor left the dragon's face as he stared at her, knowing the truth of her words. He slumped back in his chair. "Are you sure this information is accurate?"

"My source is impeccable."

"Understood." He pushed his chair back from the table. "One legion."

"Excellent."

He stood and Dagmar knew she had to take her chance now. "There's something else."

Gwenvael looked down at her. "What?"

"The tunnels from the Ice Lands lead through the Northlands, into the south, until they reach the desert lands of Alsandair."

His face went blank, his jaw slack. "I don't . . . what?"

"If they took the right tunnel, they could come up in the middle of your Main Hall and you wouldn't know it until they speared you clean, tore her apart, and took her babes." She sat back in her chair. "None of you know about the tunnels, do you?"

"I don't understand. If those tunnels exist, how come none of your kinsmen—"

"To bring a full army through there would be impossible. The dwarves made sure of that. Plus its use wasn't for Northlanders but for those from the Ice Lands who rarely call for war against anyone but each other. Most Northlanders don't even know the tunnels exist. And the few who do are not keen on the idea of battling anything underground. Tunnels are always risky."

"But *you* know this information."

"I have learned friends."

"You said if they take the right tunnels. I need to know which tunnels those are—I need to know all the tunnels."

Dagmar's toes curled in her boots. "I could get you that information." She took a breath. "For a price."

He rolled his eyes. "Fine. Two legions. Total."

"No."

"We're not back to five, are we?"

"No. One legion, for my father. As you promised."

"Then I don't understand—"

"I know who can help you, who can give you the information."

"All right."

"All you need to do . . . is take me with you."

Gwenvael stared at her a long moment, her back straight, her eyes looking intently at him through those bits of glass. "You want to run away with me?"

It hadn't been the first time a woman had asked him, begged him even, to take her away from her life. But Dagmar only laughed. "By all reason! Of course I'm not asking to run away with you!"

"Then what are you asking me for?"

"The one who can give us the information is no more than a day's ride from here. Even less if we're flying. I go with you and help you get this information, and before you say it, you will need me to help you get this information. Then you bring me back." She snapped her fingers. "Even better you can take me to Gestur's."

"Who the hell is Gestur?"

"He's my uncle. Loyal to my father."

"And why would you want to go there?"

"I have my reasons. Besides, he's planning to come out here anyway in another month or so. I could return with him. It would be my own little holiday away."

"Before you start enjoying your holiday, your father will never let you go. All that Northman Code to contend with."

"My father barely remembers my name. He refers to me as girl or little miss."

"I thought those were terms of endearment."

"Does he look endearing to you? But if you insist, it can be part of the deal that includes the legion and supplies—"

"What supplies?"

"The supplies you promised."

"I never promised you any supplies."

"You meant to."

"I did not." She was enjoying this entirely too much! He could see it by the little smirk on her face. She knew he needed the information on those bloody tunnels and she had no problem extorting him over it.

The world should be glad she hadn't been born a man. She'd be emperor by now.

"I'm not doing this."

"Why not?"

"Because you're up to something."

"A few hours of freedom are all I ask, Lord Gwenvael. Is that really too much?"

Damn her.

"You swear you'll really help me."

"On my life as a Reinholdt, anything I can do to help your queen, I will."

"Fine." He lowered his head, took several breaths, and when he looked at her again, he saw her through tears.

She reared back a bit. "What *are* you doing?"

Gwenvael didn't have time to warn her before her father came storming in, the simple fact the warlord hadn't bathed in at least two days giving him away to Gwenvael's poor nostrils. "What the hell's going on?" Sigmar demanded, a pint in his hand.

Sniffing dramatically, Gwenvael gazed across the desk at Dagmar. Without even a twitch, she immediately stood and walked to her father's side. "Give us a moment, won't you, Lord Gwenvael?"

"Of course," he choked out, impressing even himself by the little added sob at the end.

Dagmar took her father out into the hallway again. She wanted to jump up and down and clap her hands, but that would definitely work against her. Instead she said, "Sorry about that. He's very upset."

"By all the war gods—what did you say to him?"

"It's not what I said, Father, but what I couldn't. I know there's more information from Brother Petur. You remember him, yes?" Good gods, why did she pull that man's name out of her ass?

Perhaps because her father didn't find Petur remotely threatening. He belonged to an order that preached tolerance over war. Unlike Brother Ragnar's Order of the Warhammer or her other favorite, Order of the Burning Sword.

"Can't you show him on a map how to get to that idiot's convent?"

"It's not a convent, Father; that's for women." And how many times had she wished he'd sent her to one? "It's a monastery. And I gave him the directions there, but he wants me to go with him."

"Not in my life, girl. I'm not letting you out of here with that . . . that . . . *weeper*."

"Come now, why not? Surely you're not worried about my chastity." She laughed, even as delicious visions of dessert cream and a liberty-taking dragon tail swam into her head.

"What do you mean 'why not?' He can't protect you. He'll be too busy sobbing like a bloody girl while you're captured by some other warlord!"

"Keep your voice down! And his size alone will protect me." Her father grunted, which gave her hope she could convince him. "How about we do this? I go with him today, which will take a few hours, and then he can take me to Gestur's. He's barely two hours on foot from that monastery. I can bring the messages that you have for him and be back on safe Reinholdt ground before nightfall."

Her father's eyes narrowed. "You seem to have it all worked out."

She shrugged. "It's been ages since the cousins have been here. And Gestur can bring me back next month when he travels here."

"Next month?" Her father looked at her strangely and she had no idea what his expression meant. "I don't like it. And you still ain't given me much of a reason to send you."

"A legion."

"What?"

"As I told you, he wants to protect Annwyl the Bloody. He's promised us a legion of her troops."

"And you believe him?"

"I do. That's fifty-two-hundred men, Father."

"Southlanders," he sneered.

"Human targets, I say. Keep Jökull busy until you can tear the skin from his bones."

A rare smile crossed her father's face. "Like your mother sometimes, you are. You've got a vengeful streak." Her father's compliments were rare and strange, but she took them eagerly nonetheless.

"I do. And if helping the weeper gets us what we need . . . It's a small price to pay. For once, Father, please trust me."

"I always trust you're up to something, little miss." But he was no longer fighting her and they both knew it. "But you're sure, though? About being alone with him? You sure you'll be safe with him—he's still a male and I seen how your sisters-in-law have been watching him."

She eased the door open a bit, and her father looked in to see Gwenvael blowing his nose into a cloth and continuing to make choking noises. Dagmar raised her brow. "Unless I suddenly turn into Eymund . . . I'm relatively certain I'll be just fine."

Chapter 10

"My lady? My lady, please wake up."

Morfyd opened her eyes. "What is it, Taffia?"

"You'd best hurry, my lady. The guards have called out warning that your mother approaches."

"I'll be down in a bit. The suns have barely risen." Then she turned and buried her head into a warm, hard chest.

"My lady, if you do not go down to meet her, she will come up here."

"Mhhm."

Yes, yes. Her mother coming up to her room, seeing her cuddled up to Brastias . . .

Morfyd jolted awake, her entire body tensing as she sat up. "Good gods! She's here? Why is my mother here?"

"I don't know, my lady. But she approaches and will land soon."

Scrambling out of bed, Morfyd pointed to her wardrobe. "Get my robes, Taffia. Hurry!" She saw Brastias watching her. "Don't look at me like that."

"Like what?"

She sighed impatiently, pouring water into the bowl on her basin. "I can't tell her. Not yet."

"Then when? When will you tell any of them?"

"Do you like having your arms and legs? Because my brothers will ensure that you do not. And my father—" She shuddered at the thought. Bercelak the Great had torn the wings off a young dragon once who'd stopped by her parents' cave nearly every day for an entire moon cycle to prove his love to Morfyd. Her father had been incensed. "You've only turned forty!" he'd yelled, shaking her poor suitor's wings while blood flew around the chamber. "You're a child!"

"How long will you keep using your family as an excuse?" Brastias asked softly.

She glanced at him over her shoulder and realized he'd already gotten out of bed and was nearly dressed, heading toward the window.

"It's not that easy," she told his back while he pulled his shirt on.

"It's easy enough for the rest of your kin."

"You can't compare us to what Fearghus and Briec—"

"I'd better go." He pushed the window open and easily climbed through it and out onto the tiny ledge. She had no idea how he managed to do it every night and morning, but she'd be eternally grateful that he did.

"Brastias, wait."

He pivoted toward her on the balls of his feet, those large feet the only things that kept him from falling, if not to his death then definitely to a broken body part or two.

"I love you," he said. Then he was gone.

Morfyd had no idea how long she stood there, gazing at the

spot he'd been standing in like some kind of lovesick child. He loved her? He'd not said it before now, and she knew he wouldn't have said it unless he meant it. And, tragically, she loved him as well. Could either of them be more foolish?

Taffia tugged at her elbow. "My lady? Your mother."

"Yes, yes."

To say she was in no mood to see her mother would be an understatement, but she had no choice. Quickly donning her witches' robes, Morfyd dashed down to the first floor, through the Great Hall, and out into the courtyard. They'd expanded the size of the courtyard nearly two years ago to accommodate the comings and goings of dragons, and most of the humans were quite used to them now. But none were used to the Dragon Queen. Her mere presence brought out the dragon-fear in nearly all the humans who served Annwyl.

Morfyd watched as her mother landed. Beside and behind her were the loyal dragon guards who protected the Dragon Queen with their very lives. Not an easy task when her mother insisted on shifting to human and demanding of all that could hear, "So where's the whore?"

Briefly closing her eyes, trying to rein in her rarely shown temper, Morfyd said, "Stop calling her that."

"Well, that's what she is, isn't she? The whore who betrayed my son?"

"Why do you refuse to believe she carries Fearghus's babes?"

"Because it's impossible."

"Of all beings, Mother, you should know that anything is possible once the gods are involved."

A panicked scream sounded and Morfyd stomped her foot at the sight of one of Rhiannon's guards holding a stableboy in his mouth.

Frustrated, Morfyd snapped, "Mother!"

Her mother huffed impatiently. "Fine. Fine. Put him down, Cairns."

"But my queen"—the dragon guard whined around a mouthful of screaming human—"I'm hungry."

"Then go to the clearing and get a cow or something. But put him down!"

The human, rudely spit out, rolled across the courtyard grounds. Morfyd signaled to Taffia, and her trusted assistant went to care for the poor boy.

"Now where is she?" her mother snapped. "Where is the whore of Garbhán Isle?"

"I can't believe you're still not talking to me."

"And I can't believe you wouldn't bring my dog." Dagmar waited until Gwenvael settled in a clearing no more than a league or so from their destination—if she was guessing correctly—before she slid off his back. She tried to walk away, but her legs wouldn't hold her steady and she had to grab onto the dragon's neck to keep from falling to her knees.

"Gods!" Gwenvael growled, ignoring her discomfort. "Are we here again?"

"Yes! We are here again. You saw how upset he was!"

"Woman, he's a dog! And I am not a beast of burden to carry your pets around."

"He's more than a pet. He's my companion and protects me."

"I'll protect you now."

"And somehow that gives me so little ease."

The dragon moved away and Dagmar stumbled, almost falling. But his tail landed against her ass, keeping her upright . . . and taking liberties!

"Oh!" She planted her feet firmly, reached back, and slapped at his exploring tail. "Stop molesting me with that thing!"

"I'm not. I was merely helping you stand."

She gritted her teeth. "Then why is it between my legs?"

"You moved."

Feeling her strength return right along with her annoyance, Dagmar stepped back and raised her foot, slamming it down on the tip.

"Ow! Evil barbarian viper!" He rose on his hind legs, his front claws grasping his tail. "You are aware this is attached to me?"

"Yes. That's how I knew it was taking liberties!"

Gwenvael put the tip in his mouth, sucking it as she might suck on her finger after slamming it in a door. They scowled at each other, neither speaking. Then his gaze drifted and he said, "I know that city."

Dagmar looked out over the ridge, exhaled. "The great city of Spikenhammer. I've always wanted to come here. They have the most amazing library that you'll find anywhere in the Northlands."

"Spikenhammer," he sneered. "Could that name be more obvious?" The dragon abruptly dropped his tail and frowned. "Wait. I don't understand. I thought we were going to a monastery."

"Why would I go to a monastery?" She pointed at the big city she'd always heard about but had never been to. "We're going there."

"But you told your father—"

"I lied. He never would have let me come here, with or without him." She headed down the ridge, eager to reach the city. "We have a bit of walking, so you'd best hurry."

"What else have you lied about?" he yelled after her.

Dagmar laughed. "You'll have to be much more specific than that, I'm afraid."

The guards told him his mother had arrived, but he would have been able to tell without the notification. He could hear the yelling throughout the castle.

He stepped into the Great Hall and saw the two females standing toe to toe. Because neither female would let the other finish a sentence, Fearghus had no idea exactly *what* they were arguing about, but it was definitely heated and poor Morfyd was caught in the middle as always, trying desperately to calm the situation.

His mother towered over the other yelling female, but that didn't make the smaller one back down—and she wouldn't. Fearghus had learned that about her shortly after meeting her, and, at the moment, he appreciated it.

And while the two females argued, no one noticed him as he crouched down next to the chair of the woman he loved.

"What did I miss?" he murmured, his lips brushing against Annwyl's cheek.

"Not sure. I walked in, your mother took one look at me, and it simply blew up from there. They talk over each other, so I'm not sure what they are saying. But Talaith does seem quite angry," Annwyl said.

Fearghus chuckled, enjoying the way his brother's mate, Talaith, practically dared his mother to turn her into a ball of flame. "I'm glad she's handling it. I wouldn't be nearly as nice."

"Let your mother say what she wants about me, Fearghus. I don't care." It was true, Annwyl didn't care. Not like she used to. Not like the Annwyl he remembered, who, Gwenvael once said, "would fight her own shadow if she thought it was getting a little haughty."

But his mate, his consort, was tired. At twenty-nine winters, she shouldn't be so tired. Even heavy with twins, she shouldn't be *this* tired. Circles under her eyes, lines around her mouth. She wasn't aging, so much as . . . He didn't know. He didn't know what was wrong. And it terrified him.

"Why don't you go to bed?" He motioned to one of the servants standing around, watching the sideshow. "I'll be up in a bit and we'll nap together."

"Your mother is here for a reason. I should find out why." She looked down at her hands resting on the table. They were strong, capable hands that had many scars and had done much damage over the years. "But I just don't care, Fearghus."

"And you shouldn't. I'll handle it. So will Morfyd." He kissed her forehead, stepped back, and helped her out of the chair. Handing her off to the servant, he said, "Take her to our room and make sure she has everything she needs. Then return here. Make sure you close the door to our room when you leave."

A smile teased Annwyl's lips. "That was awfully specific, Fearghus."

"You like when I'm specific. Now go."

Leaning against the table, he first watched Annwyl make her slow, laborious way up the stairs. When she disappeared down the hall, he turned his attention to his mother and Talaith.

"What did I miss?" Briec asked, stepping up beside Fearghus.

"The arrival of our mother."

"Talaith's in a fine spitting rage . . . Mother call Annwyl a whore again?"

"Don't know." Fearghus glanced at his brother. "What happened to your face?" The gash went from his cheek down under his chin, and his bare chest and black leggings were covered in dirt and blood.

"My daughter."

Fearghus flinched. "By the dark gods—you didn't get in the training ring with her, did you?"

"I had to make sure Brastias was right before I ever talk to her mother."

"And?"

Briec smirked. "I'm sure."

"I could have told you that myself." He handed his brother a rag lying on the table. "Blood's dripping."

Pressing the rag to his face, Briec said, "I heard from Gwenvael this morning."

"And?"

"There's a cult from the Ice Lands coming for Annwyl."

"The Ice Lands?" He'd heard people lived there but could never imagine anyone surviving that horrible terrain. "Shouldn't be too hard to spot then. We'll alert our troops near the Outerplains—"

"He thinks they may be traveling underground."

Wonderful. Fearghus exhaled and briefly closed his eyes. "Has luck deserted us completely?"

"No. But nothing's ever easy. Not for us. Don't worry, though. We'll take care of it."

"We will?"

"Gwenvael had a suggestion; I agreed it was good, so we set Éibhear to do the rest."

"Why Éibhear?"

"Father never hits him."

"Gwenvael's grand plan involves Father?"

"Don't worry about it. We've got it under control."

Fearghus doubted it, but he was in no mood to argue and was simply grateful his siblings had stood behind him and Annwyl during all this. They were an annoying lot, but they were his.

The servant appeared again at the bottom of the stairs, indicating he'd done what Fearghus bid. Knowing Annwyl was resting and out of hearing range, he straightened, motioned his brother back a bit, and swung his fist overhead, bringing it down on the table. The table splintered and buckled where his fist landed. Both Rhiannon and Talaith jerked back from one another, Talaith with her dagger now in hand and Rhiannon with a spell on her lips.

"You come here," he said to his mother, keeping his voice low and barely controlled, "and call my mate a whore, and then you're upset you don't get a polite welcome?"

"I didn't call her a whore." When everyone simply stared at her, Rhiannon clarified, "I didn't call her a whore to her face . . . today."

"Then what's going on?"

Rhiannon's hands landed on her waist and her foot tapped against the floor. If she were in dragon form, it would be one of her talons. "I simply didn't understand why neither of these two idiots didn't contact me sooner?"

Talaith slipped her dagger back into the sheath tied to her thigh. "Contact you so you could call her a whore to her face?"

"I called her a whore when I thought she'd bedded another."

Fearghus walked toward his mother. "And now?"

"And now I know differently."

He couldn't help but be a little suspicious. "What? Just like that?"

"Aye. Just like that."

No, something was wrong. He looked from one witch to another, the three at different levels of skill—Talaith centuries behind the other two but catching up quickly—and he knew they were hiding something.

"What aren't you telling me?"

Rhiannon stroked his cheek and gave him a soft smile. In this moment, she wasn't the frightening Dragon Queen who ruled with an iron tail. She was his mother. He saw it in her eyes, felt it in her touch. "My son, there is nothing to worry about. We're simply going to try to find a way to get her energy back up so she's not dragging for the next few weeks."

His mother was lying to him. He knew it, deep in his bones. Yet he couldn't push further, because he wasn't ready to hear the truth. Not now. Because he knew she wasn't lying to hurt him—she was lying to protect him.

"All right?" she asked softly.

He nodded. "All right."

Talaith looked up at Briec, her eyes narrowing on the open wound that wouldn't stop bleeding. "What happened to your face?"

Briec stared at her a long moment before calmly replying, "Nothing."

And Talaith didn't seem remotely convinced.

"A little tired, are we? Feet sore?"

Dagmar gritted her teeth and answered, "I'm fine."

She wasn't fine. She was in agony. Her feet were not sore—they *hurt*! She could *feel* sores developing with every step she took. Her muscles had begun to scream in protest as well. And her forehead burned from the low-hanging two suns above her, the clouds that always hid them not providing nearly as much cover as she always believed they did.

Dagmar had always thought her occasional brisk walks around her father's fortress had kept her in shape. However, the laborers kept the even, tiled grounds clean. The main road to Spikenhammer, tragically, was riddled with rocks and deep indents she didn't see until her foot encountered one. Nor was the road one, straight path, but instead a winding route that went up and down hills, which also meant the city wasn't nearly as close as her eyes and those inaccurate maps had led her to believe. For more than three hours they'd been on this road with no apparent end in sight and the dragon seemed more than comfortable continuing.

"Sure you don't want me to fly? I can swoop us right in there so your tiny royal feet won't have to touch this dirty, mean-spirited ground a moment more."

His sarcasm certainly had gone up a notch since he'd discovered she'd lied to him. But, to her surprise, he hadn't insisted they return to her father's lands immediately. It was strange being around someone whose behavior she couldn't easily predict. She'd always relied heavily on that particular skill.

"And get us shot down in the process?" she asked. "Spikenhammer does not allow your kind beyond its gates."

"It may not allow dragons, but I can assure you dragons are in there somewhere. We're everywhere."

Dagmar stopped walking, disturbed and fascinated by his statement. "Even on my father's lands?"

"You had me there."

"You don't count." She dismissed him with a wave of her hand. "And no, no. There couldn't have been. I would have noticed. Unlike those who are fooled by the Magick of gods, I am not. I would have noticed," she said again, desperately trying to convince herself more than him.

"How?" He pointed at the crest on his surcoat. "True, you knew of this army, but do you know every crest of every army that's been destroyed over the centuries?"

"Because of course the Horde dragons must be as vile a gang of liars as the Southland dragons."

"Just admit it. You've probably had Lightnings in and out of your fortress and never knew. Some soldiers passing through, trying not to look too tall or always in their cloaks to hide their purple hair. There's no shame in not noticing. We've been fooling you humans for eons. Why should we change now? For instance—"

"Ahhhhh!" Dagmar fell forward, her foot stuck in one of those infernal holes in the ground, her arms stretching out before her to brace her fall. Her hands slammed into hard, unforgiving Northland ground, her tender palms torn open by the jagged rocks and bits of glass, stone, and other trash littering the area. Her breath left her in one big "woosh!" and her spectacles flew off her face.

Of everything, the loss of her spectacles worried her the most.

She reached out, her eyes squinting, trying to find the small round frames she'd come to depend on so much. When she got home, she would beg Brother Ragnar for several new pairs.

"No one's ever taught you to fall, I see."

Exhausted, in pain, and afraid she'd broken the only things that could help her see clearly, Dagmar glared at the dragon beside her. He'd crouched down next to her, so his form only blurred at the edges. "No, Lord Gwenvael, no one has ever taught me to fall."

"You need some help?" he asked.

"I need my spectacles."

He reached in front of her and took hold of something. "Is this the only pair you have?"

Panic swept through her. "They're broken?"

"No. Just asking. When you're on the road, things have a tendency to break or get stolen or simply lost. If this is your only pair—"

"It is my only pair at the moment, but I hardly have time to worry about getting a new pair now, do I?"

"You're being awfully snappy."

Gritting her teeth together so hard she feared she'd break them into little pieces, Dagmar reached out for her spectacles, hoping to snatch them from his hand. He easily held his hand up, out of her way.

"Give them to me."

"No. You'll get blood on them. Your palms are bleeding." He glanced around, the other people on the road walking around the pair as if they were simply dead animals in their way. "Here. Let's get off this road." He reached for her and she raised her hand, expecting him to take it. He didn't. He simply pushed her arm aside and picked her up by the waist.

"I don't need to be carried."

"Obviously you do, you poor, weak, clumsy thing."

Gwenvael took her deep into the surrounding forest and set her down against a large old tree, her back against its trunk. "Look up at me."

She did, and he carefully placed the spectacles on her face, making sure they fit perfectly behind her ears. "There. Better?"

She blinked, the world around her back in focus. "You have no idea."

"Actually I do. When I was ninety-eight, my brother shoved me into a volcano."

He told her the strangest, most violent stories about his family. And what did that have to do with *anything*?

"Please tell me there's more to that story."

"There is. As you can imagine, lava doesn't do much damage to my kind. Although"—he leaned in a bit and lowered his voice—"it is great for torturing the Lightnings and the Sand Dragons."

"I'll keep that in mind."

"Do. You never know when you'll need that kind of information. Anyway," he slowly and carefully moved her hand and wrist, side to side, up and down, watching her closely as he kept talking, "the lava did sting a bit but nothing that would really bother me. But I didn't close my eyes fast enough. Some splashed in. My sight was blurry for weeks. Finally my mother took me to a healer after I stood in the middle of her Court and cried out, 'Will no one help the blind one? Will no one love me now that I'm blind?'"

Dagmar twisted her lips to prevent any laughter from sneaking out. She wanted to stay angry at him.

"I'm sure you were relieved to have your eyes fixed."

"I was. But I must admit it was great fun reaching up to my brothers, feeling their faces, and saying, 'Is this you, Briec? I . . . I really don't know.'" He laughed. "And if Briec wasn't such a right bastard, he would have felt really bad for me. Instead he slammed my head against whatever was available."

He checked each finger and knuckle. "Good. Nothing seems broken there." He moved down her body and tugged up the hem of her dress. He pulled off her boot and smiled. "Wool socks?"

"They're warm."

"A royal wearing socks?"

"I'm not a royal, we don't have royals in the Northlands. And vanity versus keeping all my toes during our winters . . . guess which wins?"

"Fair enough." He pulled off her socks, and both of them cringed. "You need a healer, Lady Dagmar."

Looking away from the sores covering her feet, Dagmar was forced to agree. "Unfortunately . . . I believe I do."

Rhiannon walked quickly down the steps and around a corner to another clearing she could take off from. She sent out a thought for her guards to meet her, giving her a few moments alone with her daughter.

"I can't believe you hadn't contacted me before now."

"You made it clear you didn't believe her. What was the point of contacting you?"

She swung on her daughter, her forefinger pointed in her hatchling's face. "I only had to see her to know. Has it been like this all this time?"

"No. The last month or so." Morfyd threw her hands up. "Talaith and I have tried everything. But it's like she's—"

"Being drained. From the inside out."

"Exactly." Morfyd rubbed her forehead. "Perhaps we should take her to Devenallt Mountain. There we can—"

"No."

"Why not?"

"She won't be safe there."

"Since when?"

"Since the Elders have decided to focus their attention on Annwyl's twins. I thought they'd outright reject them, but they haven't—and that makes me more nervous."

"Why? What could they do?"

"This situation is utterly new, which gives them free rein, for we have no laws about it. And unless we're in the middle of a war, I share rule with the Elders."

"You don't mean the Elders, Mother. You mean Eanruig."

Elder Eanruig. It had been long since Rhiannon had an enemy so annoying and backstabbing as the bloodline-obsessed Eanruig. He'd thought her hatchlings had been tainted by Bercelak's low-born family connections, which meant that now his head was positively spinning with the thought of the dragon bloodline being tainted by a human.

"Leave him to me, Morfyd." She tossed off the robe her daughter had made her wear among the humans and shifted to her natural form. She shook out her wings, tossed back her hair. She simply didn't understand how her children could spend day after day trapped in these human bodies. A few hours maybe—but days? "Annwyl is safer here with you. You and Talaith keep doing what you can. I'll see what I can do from my end."

The royal guards stood behind her now, ready to return home.

"Any word from Keita?" her daughter suddenly asked.

Rhiannon's youngest daughter and most prominent pain in the ass, Keita the Red Viper Dragon of Despair and Death, was rarely in contact with her mother, which Morfyd knew well enough. But Morfyd also knew Rhiannon always seemed to have a good idea where her offspring were at any given time and when she might be needed by them, whether they called for her or not. It was no different with Keita, although she never seemed to need her mother or want her assistance.

Keita wasn't merely independent; she was belligerent, and always sure Rhiannon was nothing more than a meddling old dragoness bent on making her perfectly useless life miserable. There seemed to be so much misplaced rage in that hatchling, although Rhiannon often felt she was the only one who ever saw it. To Keita's siblings and Bercelak, Keita was the most fun-loving and carefree of them all, looking for pleasure wherever she could find it.

Yet Rhiannon knew differently. She saw Keita exactly as she was and treated her exactly as she deserved.

So, taking Morfyd's question literally, Rhiannon answered, "Not since she told me to fuck off, no."

"Oh, Mother—"

Rhiannon dismissed the conversation about her youngest daughter with a flick of her talons. "Gwenvael?" she inquired. Her son could be annoying, but he was never as antagonistic as Keita.

"In the Northlands," Morfyd reluctantly explained. "Getting more . . . information."

"And whose brilliant idea was it to send the Whore of the South into the Northlands alone?"

"Annwyl's."

"And that's when you should have known that something *must* be wrong with her."

"Mother!"

"What? I still didn't call her a whore!"

Juicy blisters were lanced and the contents cleaned out, a salve smoothed into the sores. Torn palms were carefully cleaned out and blood wiped away, a different salve then put on top. The wounds on her feet and palms were wrapped in clean linen, and a concoction practically forced down her throat would help with pain and make sure there was no fever or infection later that night.

Then, after much arguing and haggling over payment—he'd forgotten about the Northlanders' love of a good haggle—Gwenvael finally managed to get the difficult Lady Dagmar into a nice bed at the Stomping Horse Inn. Yet even with her hands and feet wrapped, she'd been more than ready to go off on her "little chores," as he liked to call them simply because it annoyed her so much. Yet, he wouldn't hear of it. Not when they'd had to go the more traditional route for her healing.

It had been ages since he'd seen someone insist that only the use of herbs could help them. His sister and Talaith always threw in additional spells and such to empower the speed of the healing process, but Dagmar had been adamant that that wouldn't work for her.

"Because I don't worship the gods," she'd explained. "Magick from witches or priestesses or whatever never works on me. One tutor I had actually told me that the gods themselves would have to get directly involved for Magick of any kind to assist me."

Since he and the healer doubted the gods would directly help with Dagmar's swollen ankle and ready-to-burst blisters, Dagmar had to rely on drinking some vile-looking concoction and resting for the remainder of the night.

"Go out wandering tonight on those feet and you'll be right back here in the morning," the healer had warned.

Although she'd still argued, Gwenvael finally dumped her off in a bed at the inn and went out to get her something to keep up her spirits. When he returned with the puppy he found in someone's yard, he thought she'd be happy.

"You stole someone's puppy?" she'd accused.

"Dragons don't steal. We simply take what we want. It's not like that little girl needs him more than you do."

She'd pointed at the door, looking haughtier than ever, even with her hands and feet bandaged. "Return him."

"But—"

"Now!"

He grudgingly had, not appreciating the way she'd dismissed him, and proceeded to pick up a few more things. When he returned for the second time, he'd found her not sleeping but working with quill and ink and parchment. Annoyed, he pulled the quill from her hand.

"I'm not done."

"You are." He took the parchment and the ink, placing them on an empty chest at the foot of the bed. "The healer wanted you resting."

"No. She didn't want me wandering around. She didn't say anything about me writing."

"Don't argue with me. I'm in a very bad mood because of you."

"Who told you to steal a child's pet?"

"Don't make me cover your face with a pillow until you see my side of things."

"Isn't that called murder?"

"In some parts of the world." He sat down on the bed. "Although you were completely ungrateful about that damn puppy, I got you other gifts." He pulled out the sack he'd brought in with him.

"I'd really prefer something to eat."

"Food will be up in a few minutes or so. Until then, ungrateful wench, I got you this." He placed the book he'd purchased on her lap so she wouldn't try and hold it in her hands. "I was told it's relatively new, so I'm hoping you haven't read it yet."

She studied the cover. *"Jani: The life and loves of a local tavern girl."* Dagmar let out a breath. "No. I can say with all honesty I haven't read this one."

"Good." He went back into the bag and pulled out the next few items.

"I already have boots."

"These are better boots. Better for when you'll be doing a lot of walking. You don't want those blisters back, do you?"

"And the socks?"

"Just as warm as wool but less rough against the skin. Wealthy soldiers-for-hire use them all the time when they're traveling from battle to battle."

Her fingertips rubbed along the leather of the boots. "Thank you. This was very sweet."

"You're welcome. Besides, I didn't want to go through another round of boil lancing."

"Blisters," she snapped. "They were blisters not boils."

"Blisters. Boils. Does it matter?" He glanced down at her feet. "How's the ankle?"

"Better. The swelling has gone down considerably."

"See what happens when you listen to me? Only good things." He smiled at her. "Now, are you going to thank me properly?"

"I said 'thank you.' That's considered in some cultures as thanking you properly."

"I was hoping for a little more than that."

She studied him a long moment before she nodded.

"All right." She scooted down a bit on the bed, pulled her gown up high on her thighs, and relaxed back into the mattress. "If you could make it quick before the food gets here, that would be great."

Gwenvael felt a small twitch beneath his eye. He often got something similar right on his eyelid but only when he had to deal with his father. Apparently a new one had developed that belonged only to Lady Dagmar. "That's not what I meant."

"I hope you're not expecting me to get on my knees, because I don't think the healer—"

"No!" *Good gods, this woman!* "That's not what I meant, either."

"That's always what men mean when they ask to be thanked properly."

"Your world frightens me. I want us to be clear on that." He leaned over and grabbed her waist, lifting her until her back again rested on the propped-up pillows.

"I'm unclear as to what you want, then."

"A kiss," he said, pulling her dress back down to her ankles. "A simple kiss."

"Whatever for?"

"Because that's what I want as a thank you." And because he was certain a kiss from this obviously cold fish was just what he needed so he could stop thinking about her and focus on what was important.

"What exactly are you expecting?"

"Sorry?"

"What I mean is, is there some particular response you need for me to have in order for you to be pleased? Should I faint or merely moan at the contact? Perhaps I could shake a little, which wouldn't be hard because I am so hungry right now."

"Can't you simply act like you always do when you're kissed?"

"I'm guessing you're used to much more dramatic responses than you'll ever get from me."

"Ah-ha!" He pointed a finger at her. "You're a virgin."

"Ah-ha!" She pointed her finger back. "No, I'm not." She suddenly blinked rapidly and pulled off her spectacles with one hand while using her thumb and forefinger of her other hand to rub her eyes. "I have been, in point of fact, married three times."

"You were? What happened?"

She put her spectacles back on. "The first insulted my father at the after-wedding first meal, although my husband did manage to drunkenly initiate me into womanhood the night before. By midday he'd been pulled into pieces by four of my father's war horses, much to the audience's drunken delight. The second wisely had his way with me right after the ceremony in one of the stables, but then insulted one of my brother's wives at the celebration feast. He lost his head right there during the stuffed pig presentation. And the third, poor thing, he barely got through the ceremony, shaking and quivering like a lamb. Then he excused himself right after the commitment and I never saw him again. Not that I could blame him. Father insisted I have the marriage dissolved, so I did."

Dagmar rested her hands on her lap, palms up. "Now," she said, "aren't you glad you asked?"

She did love telling those stories. They were all true, every word. She simply chose what to leave in or take out depending on her audience.

For instance, her father didn't attack Dagmar's first husband until The Reinholdt saw her face the day after her wedding. She'd tried to stay in her room, tried to hide what she'd woken up with after only one night with her husband. It wasn't that Dagmar hadn't been willing; she simply didn't have the kind of responses her husband had been expecting.

Yet her servant at the time, a much older woman who'd also tended Dagmar's mother, insisted Dagmar attend the after-wedding first meal as etiquette dictated. Dagmar would never forget the look on her father's face when he saw her. Or the way her brothers leaped over the table to get their hands on her still-drunk husband. And they only waited until mid-afternoon to set their horses in motion because, according to her father, "We want the bastard to be nice and sober when them horses start moving."

No, that part of the story was for no one else but her because at the time it had meant the world to her.

"I am glad I asked," the dragon finally said. "It makes me feel much better about the legion Annwyl is sending to your father."

"It does?"

"Aye. How a male treats his female kin shows me what kind of male he truly is. My father cleaved a dragon in half when he found out the bastard had been telling all his friends he'd been bedding my baby sister—which he had. But still, he shouldn't have bragged about it as he did, so my father used the dragon's own battle ax on him. Cut through him from the top of his head, straight through, splitting him into two distinct pieces. Keita mostly beds human males now. Dragon males avoid her."

"Shocking."

"Weak. If you're too afraid to fight for what you want." He smiled. "Now . . . Can I have that kiss?"

"If after all that talk of dismembering and cleaving in half you still want to kiss me, then be my guest."

He moved up on the bed until his hands rested on either side of her waist.

"Come on now, dear," he said in a high-pitched, elderly woman voice that made her laugh, "pucker up for me."

She did, closing her eyes and pursing her lips like a fish. She heard him chuckle and then felt his breath against her mouth seconds before she felt his lips. They pressed against hers, firm and warm. Strangely gentle and almost unbearably sweet. With her eyes still shut, Dagmar relaxed her mouth and Gwenvael tipped his head to the side, his mouth slanting over hers. He didn't rush her or push her, didn't try to force his tongue into her mouth or push her back on the bed. Instead the tip of his tongue gently lapped at her lips. First the top lip, then the bottom, then between the two. The movement was slow and teasing.

Dagmar was well aware that Gwenvael the Handsome had

kissed many before her. He would ease his way into her mouth the way he'd done with others. But she had no patience for this particular game of his and simply opened up. Perhaps once he got in, he'd leave her be and she could go back to finishing the message she needed sent to her father the following morning.

Gwenvael's tongue sunk deep into her mouth and Dagmar placed her hands against his shoulders, ready to push him away. She didn't want to start gagging, and she was already a bit bored, and she needed to get back to her . . . to her . . . uh . . .

Wait. What had she been doing before?

At the moment, she couldn't remember any of it, nor could she care as her fingers tightened against Gwenvael's shoulders, his chain mail harsh against the tips.

The dragon groaned, the sound of it rippling through her. His tongue tangled with hers and Dagmar's body responded to it. Her nipples hardened, her thighs tensed, and the walls of her sex clenched over and over, demanding something slide inside for it to grab hold of.

She would have been disgusted by her weakness if the dragon's gentle teasing hadn't also turned more urgent, more demanding. His hand slid around the back of her neck, holding her in place, the fingers squeezing and releasing the muscles there. His body moved in closer, his free hand gripping her hip.

Dagmar had to have more. She released her grip on one shoulder and dropped her hand to his lap. She whimpered when she felt the hard cock beneath her hand. Even through the chain mail, she knew it was large and powerful. Built to make a woman promise anything if she could only play with it for a night or so. She stroked her hand against him and the dragon shuddered. She liked that, so she did it again. Now he whimpered and moaned while he still kissed her. Her hand continued to stroke him, over and over again, developing a rhythm he seemed to be enjoying immensely.

The dragon's human form tensed, and then suddenly he was scrambling away from her, stumbling across the small room until he landed in the only chair they had.

He stared at her as if terrified. His eyes wide, his breath coming in short, hard pants, while his body trembled the tiniest bit.

The way he scrutinized her made Dagmar uncomfortable and she looked away, wincing when she tried to close her hand. She glanced down and saw that the bandage on her right hand had come off. She reached for the linen wrap lying on the bed as a brisk knock on the door told her dinner had arrived.

Gwenvael answered the door and let the servant girl in. She placed the food down, blue eyes flicking back and forth between the pair. She couldn't seem to give them their food and get out of there fast enough.

"Eat," Gwenvael ordered her. "I'll get you more ointment for your hand."

Before she had the chance to tell him that wasn't necessary, he was already gone.

"Where are you going?"

Éibhear the Blue, youngest son to Queen Rhiannon and Bercelak the Great, cringed when he heard that voice behind him.

That voice. That damn voice!

"To see my father."

"Can I come?"

"No."

"Why not?"

He stopped. "Shouldn't you be training?"

"I was. But my commander told me I could take off the rest of the day."

That was probably because no one in her unit would fight

against her anymore. In less than a year, the spoiled brat had become a one-woman wrecking team.

"Well, go find something else to do."

"I'd rather go see Grandfather."

Éibhear flinched. "Don't call him that."

"Why not? He is my grandfather."

Exactly the problem. Iseabail, Daughter of Talaith, wasn't blood, but she'd been accepted by his parents and siblings as Briec's daughter. And, in the process, they'd turned her into nothing more than a spoiled little brat . . . and his niece.

His annoying, spoiled, never-stopped-talking niece.

"Your mother doesn't want you flying."

"She doesn't want me doing anything." He could hear the frustration in her voice, understood it himself. At ninety-one winters he'd been in few battles. Most of them sudden skirmishes that had involved mostly human troops—very easily killed, those humans—and very few dragons. Like Izzy, he was ready for more. Ready to earn his name. Although he'd always enjoyed being Éibhear the Blue, he was ready to be something a little more substantial. Éibhear the Benevolent perhaps. Or Éibhear the Strong.

He had big plans for his future, and they didn't involve some brat who thought she was a warrior. He still couldn't believe her unit commanders wanted to send her into combat. She'd only just turned seventeen, and, more importantly, Éibhear saw how the men in the troops—and several of the women—looked at her. She'd be at great risk out there alone, without any kin to watch out for her. To care for her. To hold her close and smell her hair and lick that delicious-looking scar on her neck . . .

"Dammit!"

"What?" She stood in front of him now, never letting him ignore her—no matter how hard he may try. No one had a right to be that pretty with a severely bruised eye and a just-healing busted nose.

He simply needed to remember that she was his niece. Exactly right. His niece!

His nubile, firm-breasted, perfect-ass niece!

"What's wrong, Éibhear?"

"Nothing. I've got to go."

"Oh, come on." She grabbed his arm. "Take me with you. I promise I'll be quiet and won't braid your hair."

"No." He tried to pull his arm away, but the girl did have a grip on her. Sometimes, when he was alone, he could still feel the grip she'd had on his tail once, many months ago. It was one of those memories that woke him up in the middle of the night—sweating.

"Pleeeeeeeeeeaaaaaasssssssseeeee!"

"No!" He yanked his arm away. "Go play with your friends."

Light brown eyes looked up at him through those damn long lashes, her full lips lifting slightly at the corners. "But . . . I'd rather play with you."

Snarling, Éibhear pushed past her, stomping off to a clearing so he could shift and take flight in peace!

"I didn't mean it the way it sounded," she yelled after him. And he might have believed her, if only she hadn't been laughing when she said it.

Dagmar stretched, waking up yet again. She'd been napping off and on for the last few hours. Each time she woke up she was still alone and her body was still reacting to that kiss. If he'd come back to her, she knew she would have taken him into her bed like so many women had done before her. But so far the dragon hadn't come back.

No, he'd probably found someone else. Someone fuller in

the hips and prettier in the face. Though that was probably best for both of them.

Dagmar moved her right hand, waiting for the searing pain she'd been experiencing since she'd rubbed her palm on his leggings. But there was no pain. Nor was she able to move her hand very well. She blinked, bringing her hand closer to her face so she could see. It had been properly bandaged again, and she could now feel the fresh ointment underneath.

Squinting, Dagmar looked around the room and saw Gwenvael sitting in the only chair, staring out the only window.

"Gwenvael?"

"It's me. You're safe."

"Are you . . . is everything . . . I was just—"

"Go to sleep, Dagmar. I'll wake you when the two suns rise. Until then"—the blur that was Gwenvael turned his head to look at her—"go to sleep."

It was something in his voice, a seriousness she'd never heard from him before, that had her nodding and turning onto her side, away from him.

"Good night, Dagmar."

"Good night," she whispered.

Had he been with another? Her instincts told her no, but she could be wrong, trying to turn her hopes into truth. Would she blame him if he had?

Who was she kidding? Of course she would!

Damn her. Damn her and her festering feet!

Several of the bar wenches in the pub had made it perfectly clear he'd have a warm, *welcoming* bed to stay in this night, if he so wished. But for some unknown reason, he'd turned them all down and returned to The Liar. She wasn't a liar simply because she lied whenever it suited her. She was a liar because she'd been pretending she was something she was not.

Cold? That woman was not cold, no matter what she wanted the world to believe. Dagmar Reinholdt was contained. A quiet volcano waiting to go off.

And why should that bother him, one may ask? Because his response to her disturbed him. Between that kiss and a few strokes of her small, bandaged hand over his chain-mail leggings, he'd almost come like he'd never come before.

Even now he could still feel her touching him. And the thought of what direct contact would do to him had caused an ugly buzzing in his head he couldn't seem to stop.

And that was her hand, mate. Imagine what that sweet pussy of hers would do to you.

He needed his mind to shut up now. If he started thinking about *that* he'd be doomed. They both would.

Gwenvael glared across the room at her sleeping form. *Gods, what have I gotten myself into?*

Chapter 11

He knew it made no sense for them to be in a dress shop. He may have only had an hour or so of sleep, but he was clear enough on that point. This was *Dagmar* after all. He couldn't imagine her willingly going into a dress shop unless her father had his war ax to her head.

And yet here he was, wandering around a dress shop in the early morn.

He grabbed a lovely detailed gown of bright pink and held it up for her to see. Dagmar's horrified expression was priceless.

"You must be joking."

He was. Overdone gowns would do nothing for her except make her feel uncomfortable. And it was her confidence that he found so enticing.

"What was that message you sent off earlier?" he asked, putting the dress back and continuing to look around.

"To my father."

"Sure that was wise?"

"If he didn't hear something soon, he would have come looking for me. It's best to let him know that I'm not yet at Gestur's but that I am safe. The alternative is your head looking dazzling hanging from my father's gates."

He turned to face her. "Why are we here?"

She didn't answer him, but smiled at a shop girl who came out from the back.

"Lady Dagmar!"

"Hello, Saamik."

To Gwenvael's surprise, the shop girl hugged Dagmar as if they were long-lost cousins.

"You're looking well," Dagmar told her.

"Thank you."

"Are you happy?"

"I am so happy, my lady." She gripped Dagmar's hand. "I don't know how to thank you for this. I have a small house now and a lady who takes care of Geoff during the day."

"I'm so glad to hear that." Dagmar stepped closer. "Think we can talk for a bit? In private?"

"Of course. Give me a few minutes."

The shop girl rushed off and Dagmar smirked at him.

"A shop girl?" he murmured low, once he was closer. "You're getting your information from a shop girl?"

"The wives and kinswomen of very important men come in here every day. And every day they spend hours getting fitted into new gowns." She smiled. "Wives know more than men ever think they do, Lord Gwenvael. And their servants know *everything*."

Dagmar sipped her tea and listened to Saamik closely.

Saamik had grown up on Reinholdt lands. Her parents and their parents and their parents's parents had all been born and raised in the same small area. Saamik had been destined for the same life, her future husband already picked out for her. When Dagmar had made the offer to get Saamik an apprenticeship at a dress shop, she never asked for anything. Never made Saamik promise anything for this gift. Instead they simply passed letters. Saamik knew how much Dagmar enjoyed gossip, and Dagmar filled Saamik in on the family and friends she had left behind.

It all worked out well, but Dagmar felt the need now to ask specific questions and she wouldn't feel comfortable doing that in a letter that could be read by others.

"You were right, my lady." Saamik stirred milk into her own tea. "Lord Jökull's troops are expanding. He's created truces with at least three other warlords to the west."

"A truce? Not an alliance?"

"No. He'll get no troops from them, but he won't be fighting them either."

"Where is he getting his troops?"

"Hiring them. By the boatload, I understand."

For once, Dagmar received no pleasure from being right. "I see."

"Lord Tryggvi," young Saamik glanced at Gwenvael—again—and explained, "he's the leader of these lands." She let out a breath, focused on Dagmar. "His sister says he's none too happy about all this."

"Would he be open to becoming allies to The Reinholdt?"

"Perhaps. It's hard to tell with him. He's not a pleasant man from what I've seen."

"Who among them are?" Dagmar reached for a sweet biscuit, but her hand found only an empty space on the small table. She gazed at the dragon, amazed. "You had to take the whole plate?"

"I wanted them."

"Are you a child?"

Saamik stood. "I have more, my lady." The girl's warm smile doing nothing but annoy Dagmar, so she felt quite deserved of the several biscuits she took when Saamik held out the tin.

"There's something else . . ." Saamik again took her seat. "But it's only a rumor. I know not if there's any truth to it."

"There's usually a little truth in every rumor, Saamik. You might as well tell me."

Saamik leaned forward, looking uncomfortable. "They say . . . well . . . They say he has a truce with dragons."

Dagmar snorted. Not because she didn't believe Saamik, but because her own dragon was so startled that the biscuit he'd been eating flipped from his fingers and pinged him in the forehead.

"I know, I know," Saamik went on. "It sounds ridiculous. I mean, they're animals, aren't they?"

"Yes," Dagmar readily agreed. "Yes, they are."

"How does he even communicate with them? They can't read or write. And I hear they understand our words the same way a dog does."

"All very true. I'm sure I could easily train one to do my bidding. Although they're not nearly as bright as my Canute. Their brains are quite slow. So it's very possible someone like my uncle Jökull can easily bend them to his will."

"Tragically, I think you're right, my lady."

A soft jingle sound from the store had Saamik jumping up. "I'll be right back. Let me see who this is."

"Of course." Dagmar tapped her finger against the table. This was much worse than she thought. Much worse. Saamik had provided a good starting point for Dagmar, but she needed Brother Ragnar's real knowledge to help her now.

"'Slow brains'?"

"Well," she answered absently, "we both know the truth of that, now don't we?"

He was out of his chair so fast, all Dagmar had the chance to do was squeak in surprise and protest before he yanked her out of the chair.

"Train us like dogs, eh?"

She batted at his hands, which seemed a waste of time, but when his fingers caught hold of her on her sides, under her arms, Dagmar let out a strangled giggle and began to fight. It wasn't pretty.

"Wait. Have we found a weakness on my lady?" he teased, his hands seemingly everywhere.

"No, you have not!"

"I think we have." His fingers moved up and down her sides, making Dagmar squeal like a child. Although even as a child, she was never one to squeal. Or laugh. Or giggle. A chuckle now and then, but that was the most she could manage on a good day.

It didn't help that Gwenvael seemed quite entertained at the moment, swinging her around like a tiny kitten while his fingers kept up the pressure.

He suddenly stopped and ordered, "Apologize."

"Never."

He began again, whirling her around. They were both laughing, Dagmar trying desperately to get his hands off her when she saw Saamik standing in the doorway. She knew Gwenvael saw her, too, when Dagmar's feet suddenly landed on the floor with a thump.

"I can come back, my lady," Saamik said, not even bothering to hide her smile.

"No, no. Don't be silly."

"Actually," Gwenvael cut in. "Five more minutes—ow!"

Bercelak the Great, Consort to the Dragon Queen, Dragonwarrior Supreme of the Old Guard, Supreme Commander of the Dragon Queen's Armies, and All Around Kicker of Ass of the Dragon Queen's Royal Brats, landed near the blood-covered battlefield. His youngest son, Éibhear, had accompanied him and hadn't shut up in hours.

He loved all his offspring. He truly did. But they each had personality traits that wore the edges off his nerves on his best day. This was not one of his best days. Far from it. Running errands for his queen and love was nothing new and normally he didn't mind.

Yet this particular errand galled him more than any of the others because he knew it was too dangerous a move. But would she listen? Of course not. Instead she followed the dictates of her idiot hatchlings. *His* idiot hatchlings.

But to involve the Cadwaladrs was foolish. Bercelak had always considered his kin a last resort.

If one wanted to raze an entire city to the ground—followed by one of his cousins saying, "Ohhh . . . didn't mean to do all that, now did I?"—then one called in the Cadwaladrs.

Originally Rhiannon had wanted him to put out a call to *all* his kin, but that was simply too horrifying a prospect because he knew, without one iota of doubt, they'd come. Instead, he promised to secure his more rational sister and brother. They'd been fighting in the west for months with most of their offspring plus quite a few others of the Cadwaladr bloodline. That would be more than enough to protect one human queen and his son's spawn.

"I don't understand," his youngest blathered on. "How am I supposed to become a great warrior if you won't send me into real battles?"

"You'll get there eventually. Just stop whining about it."

"I'm not whining. It's a fair question. You're holding me back."

"Is that what you think?"

"It's true, isn't it? Fearghus, Briec, *and* Gwenvael had all been sent off to fight long before they were in their nineties. Yet here I am, running errands and being treated like I'm newly hatched."

Éibhear really didn't understand, did he? He couldn't compare himself to his older and much more devious brothers. Unlike that lot, Éibhear *cared*. Not merely about himself, the acceptable selfish attitude of most dragons, but about everyone. He cared if humans were safe, if they were happy. If *dragons* were happy! When were dragons ever happy—at least in that ridiculous human sense of the word? And why would he care if they were or not?

"I just think it's unfair you're not giving me a chance like you gave the others. What makes them so bloody special?"

As Bercelak turned to his son, he sensed the air moving and vibrating behind him. Acting on instinct and more years of what his own father had considered "training" than he cared to think about, Bercelak shoved his son to the side as a dragon's broadsword—the length of a human soldier's battle lance, the width of a middle-aged tree trunk—landed in the spot Éibhear had stood.

His son's silver eyes widened, his gaze locked at where the tip of that mighty blade met Éibhear's claw prints.

"And that, *boy*, is the difference between you and your brothers," Bercelak snapped, fear for his youngest son making his words hard. "They would have seen that blade coming."

His son flinched at the truth of Bercelak's words as the sword was yanked from the ground.

Ghleanna the Decimator grinned at Bercelak. "Tsk, tsk, tsk, brother. Seems you haven't trained your offspring well enough. Father would be horribly disappointed, Bercelak the Black."

"That'll keep me up nights," he shot back.

"Aaaah. My baby brother is still as charming as the day he was hatched." She slid the blade back in the scabbard tied to her back before throwing herself into Bercelak's arms. "You old bastard. You never change."

"Nor you." He gave a brief but hard hug to his beloved sister before holding her at arm's length and motioning to the blood-covered field of battle that lay before them. "Is this all your work?"

"Not all mine." She turned and smiled. "Little Éibhear?" she asked with a huge laugh.

"I was." The pair hugged. "I'm much bigger now."

"That you are." Her arm around Éibhear's shoulder, her tail scratching the top of his head affectionately, Ghleanna asked, "Well, brother, what brings you out to the west? And don't pussyfoot; you know how much I hate that."

"It's a long story, and I'm tired. Got a cave we can—"

"Tents. We've been living among the human warriors."

Bercelak's head fell back against his shoulders and he sighed. "You're living as humans . . . again?"

"You know how it entertains us. But there's food, a warm place to sleep, and your family to help you, brother. Truly, what more could a dragon want?"

"A bloody cave."

"Growl, growl. Snarl, snarl." She motioned to him as she headed through the recent field of battle, her strong arm still around Éibhear. "Come on, Lord Angry."

Bercelak muttered under his breath and followed his sister down to the camp. Once a few feet away, father and son shifted to human and changed into the clothes they'd brought with them. Ghleanna slammed her broadsword and sheath into the ground beside several rows of dragon weapons. She shifted, grabbed clothes from a hanging line, and clothed herself.

They entered the camp and Bercelak immediately saw his older brother Addolgar wrestling with one of his six sons. One of Addolgar's seven daughters was trying to bring her father down, and doing a piss-poor job of it from what Bercelak could tell. Like most of the Cadwaladrs, his kin never seemed to know when they'd had enough hatchlings. Thirteen for Addolgar, eight for Ghleanna, and a horrifying eighteen for his sister Maelona. And Bercelak himself came from a group of fifteen, what Rhiannon's mother used to refer to as "Shalin's litter of offspring." An insult Shalin, Bercelak's much-loved and much-missed mother always took with a smile because she'd won the prize. She'd won Bercelak's father, Ailean.

Now, with only six offspring of his own, Bercelak was often pitied by his siblings. Yet that had been a conscious choice between him and Rhiannon. And if his kin knew how much trouble six royal pains in the ass could be, they'd pity him for other reasons.

"Ho, Addolgar!" Ghleanna stopped by the cooking fire and grabbed a well-roasted chicken. "Look who has come to call." She tossed the whole bird to Éibhear.

"Aw, thanks. I'm starving."

"I figured. Could hear that stomach of yours growling from here. Sounds like mountains shifting."

Addolgar knocked his son in the dirt and walked over to Bercelak. "Ho, brother!" They clasped hands and Addolgar smiled. Bercelak didn't glare, which he'd always considered similar to a smile.

Glancing over his shoulder, Addolgar asked, "Are you done?"

"Oh!" The young dragoness released her father and

dropped to the ground. Her human form was not very large and Bercelak guessed it must frustrate her. "This isn't over!" She stormed off and Addolgar laughed.

"Just like her mum, that one." Addolgar eyed his brother. "So, what brings you here, Queen's Consort?"

"That idiot son of mine and his human mate."

Addolgar crossed his arms over his chest. "Don't you have *two* hatchlings with that flaw now?"

Bercelak bared a fang while his siblings' laughter rang out through the camp.

"Where are we going now?" Gwenvael asked, looking around the alley they'd stepped into.

"To the Great Library." Dagmar closed the back door to the seamstress's shop behind her. "There's someone I need to find."

"Who?"

"A friend."

"Does he have a name?"

"Why wouldn't he?"

"You plan to tell me?"

"Why would you need to know?"

"Why *wouldn't* I need to know?"

Dagmar held her hands up to stop him and herself. "Reason knows, we could do this all day." Very true. He could ask her questions until her weak little eyes bled. "But we're wasting time. I have a grand library to visit, and you have to get back to your precious queen."

"True, but you still have information to provide me."

"Which you will get once I'm done here and you take me to Gestur's." She raised her skirts a bit and walked off, her haughtiness wrapped around her like her cloak.

"Snobby cow," he muttered, thinking she couldn't hear him. He quickly realized that what her eyes lacked, she'd made up for with her hearing when she spun on her heel, raised her middle and forefinger, and flicked him off before spinning back. She never missed a step and was out of the alley before Gwenvael realized it.

"And quite surly, too," he called after her.

Chapter 12

The Great Library of Spikenhammer was beyond Dagmar's imaginings, with its marble columns and floors, plus the rows and rows of exquisitely made floor-to-ceiling bookshelves. Nearly all the shelf space was filled with tomes from all over the Northlands, Southlands, and the west. The east was less represented since a vast and temperamental sea separated them.

"You all right?"

"Isn't this amazing?" she sighed.

Gwenvael shrugged. "It's just books."

"It's not just books, you cretin. It's knowledge."

"Not the knowledge you can use every day. You get that from talking to people. Chatting them up in the pubs and the market."

"Are you being contrary on purpose?"

"I didn't know I was being contrary. I thought we were having a discussion."

"Not really." She stepped away from him, her fingers gliding along the big marble tables that had oversized books open for anyone to peruse at their leisure. "If I'd been born a man . . . This would have been the dream life for me. All day, all night with nothing but books."

He shook his head. "You are such a liar."

Insulted he spat that out so quickly, she faced him. "I beg your pardon?"

"You want me to believe you'd be happy trapped here? With all these quiet, boring library monks and their vows of suffering? My Lady Dagmar, we both know that is *not* the life for you."

"Is that right? And what is?"

He took a step and was barely an inch or two from her body. "Plotting, planning, negotiating, and, very often, lying."

Dagmar opened her mouth to argue, but he stopped her with a raised hand. "I'm not talking about the kind of lying your sister-in-law does. She wouldn't know truth if it slammed into that recently abused ass of hers." Dagmar laughed but immediately stopped when one of the monks gave her a vicious warning glare. "I'm talking about the ability to successfully manage truth and facts to get what you need. Now that, my Lady Reason, is a gift."

"I have to say I've never been so beautifully insulted before."

He beamed. "And that's *my* gift."

They laughed together now, ignoring the glares of the monks until one of the much older ones stormed over and banged the flat of his hand against the marble table, startling them both.

"Perhaps," Gwenvael cheerfully explained to the monk, "you wouldn't be so tense, Brother, if you managed to get a good fu—"

Dagmar slammed her foot down on his instep before Gwenvael could finish that particular sentence and bowed her head at the monk. "Ever so sorry, Brother. We'll be quiet."

With a sniff, the monk stormed off, and Dagmar watched Gwenvael holding his foot and rubbing it. It was an odd physical position for such a large male to be in, but it fit him somehow.

"Do you mind not getting us thrown out of here until I get what I need?"

"What you need?" He dropped his foot to the floor. "You should have said something."

"Said something about what?"

His answer was to grab her hand and pull her deep into the stacks. "Where are we going?" she demanded. "I don't need any books at the moment."

"Neither do I," he growled before turning and pushing her back into a corner.

Dagmar's hands flew up and braced against his shoulders. "What do you think you're doing?"

"Helping you get what you need." Gwenvael took hold of her hands and pinned her arms behind her back, forcing her up onto her toes, her chest lifted and pressed against him. "And I'm seeing if I dreamed that damn kiss last night."

"But it's the library!" she managed to gasp before his mouth covered hers and suddenly Dagmar didn't give a flying flip where she was. Not when the sweetest lips ever were urging hers to part, to allow his tongue to slip inside.

She sighed deeply, his tongue gently caressing and teasing. She'd never had such a sweet, patient kiss before. At least not one that made her feel so damn needy.

He pulled his mouth away from hers, and Dagmar realized her tongue had nearly followed him.

"No. Not a dream."

Blessed reason . . . he's panting. Because of me!

He gave her small kisses on her mouth, her chin, down her neck. She groaned and allowed her body to lean into his.

"I should take you right here, Lady Dagmar," he whispered, his breath like silk against her ear. "Among all your precious books and boring monks. They'll hear you come," he taunted, "and they'll wish they were the ones in my place."

Dagmar bit her lip and thought about letting him take her to the floor right now. Or up against the stacks, books on alchemy and the other sciences shaking around them as he pounded into her with that gorgeous, massive—

"What do you think you're doing?"

Dagmar jumped as a walking stick slammed against Gwenvael's back.

"Oy!" the dragon snarled.

"You release her this instant, you hooligan!"

Gwenvael stared down at her. "Hooligan?" he mouthed and she had to look away.

The walking stick was brought down again, and Gwenvael released his hold on her. The dragon turned on the monk and snapped in a fabulous Northland brogue she had no idea he'd mastered, "What ya hittin' me for? She was the one tossin' it about. Just look at her."

They did look at her, and Dagmar took a moment to adjust her spectacles and her grey dress before she took her time raising her eyes to the monk's face. Her "puppy-dog expression," she liked to call it.

"Oh . . . Brother!" she cried out, placing her hand over her mouth and shaking.

The old monk raised his walking stick again, aiming for Gwenvael. "You!"

"All right, I'm leavin', I'm leavin'!" Several monks followed Gwenvael to the end of the row and he glanced back at her, giving her a quick wink and motioning toward the door before he disappeared.

The monk placed his arm around Dagmar's heaving shoulders. "You poor, wee thing."

"Brother, he was just so . . . just so . . . *forceful*!"

"I know, dear. You must be careful around brutes like him."

"I will, Brother," she replied bravely as the monk helped her toward the main desk, where she could hopefully get her questions answered. "I never want to experience that horror again."

* * *

Gwenvael let the monks force him out the massive doorway and onto the library steps.

"You're all stuck up bastards!" he yelled as the door slammed in his face. He grinned. "I am such a bastard."

He turned and realized he had everyone's attention. *"What?"* he demanded with the appropriate scowl, and they all scattered.

Grinning again, Gwenvael went down several steps and looked around. He saw a nice-looking inn not too far away and thought about taking Dagmar there for a quick meal before they were on their way.

Though what he really wanted to do was get a room and keep her in it for the remainder of the day and all of the night. What was it about that woman that made his knees weak?

He'd only met one other woman who had ever done that to him before and she'd been his first. An older sea dragoness named Catriona who taught him all the important basics about pleasuring a woman. But he'd been a babe then—no more than thirty—and he'd realized too late that he was one of many. She'd waited until Gwenvael was good and attached to her before she disappeared one morning, back into the sea she'd come from. It had been his dear grandfather Ailean who'd tracked him down at a local whorehouse, knee-deep in ale and pussy. It had been his grandfather who told him that one day he'd find someone meant only for him and him alone. . . .

Gods, what was wrong with him? He hadn't even bedded the little barbarian yet and he was having wistful memories of his grandfather explaining love to his drunken ass.

Obviously he was losing his sanity in this cold, unforgiving place. Dagmar was not and would never be the woman for him. Not for more than a night or so and he was sure he could make that happen without much trouble. He knew she wanted it as much as he did, and there was no reason to deny either of them the pleasure.

Tonight he'd have her, tomorrow he'd take her back to her precious people, and with valuable information in hand, he'd head back to his own. Aye, perfect plan.

Gwenvael took a deep breath—trying to calm his cock down before anyone noticed—and looked up at the sky. As always there were those low-hanging clouds that seemed to perpetually block the beauty of the two suns, but he really expected to see darker clouds since it smelled like a storm was . . .

Realizing too late he should have been paying closer attention to his surroundings rather than day-dreaming about tiny plotters, Gwenvael swung around just in time to see that warhammer as it smashed into his head.

Yrjan had worked in the Great Library since he was fourteen winters. His father realized quite early that Yrjan would never have the skills or strength of his brothers, and he got rid of him as soon as he could manage by giving him to the Order of the Knowledge—the only order dedicated solely to the libraries of the Northlands. Not that Yrjan minded joining the Order. He was actually quite grateful to his papa.

Normally, here in the Great Library he was safe from the kind of violence he had suffered every day at the hands of his own kinsmen as he'd always been an easy, weak target. The brothers of his order, the other librarians, were all quiet, learned men who spent their time helping others find books or learning something new themselves.

But now that violence had come into their quiet lives.

The poor woman who'd ended up trapped in the stacks with that horrid warrior. His type thought they could get anything they wanted by taking it—and often they could. But the brute underestimated Yrjan's order. They simply didn't allow that sort of thing to happen among their sacred books!

Yet there was nothing to do about it now. Instead he was asked to soothe the young woman's rattled nerves. Poor thing. She appeared so stricken by that animal!

She was a wee, plain thing and, like Yrjan and his order, most likely spent the majority of her time in the safety of books. She wore small, round spectacles, as did many of his library brethren, and the unadorned wardrobe of a true scholar. Yrjan was sure the brute had targeted her as he would a small deer or elk.

"You're quite safe now, my lady," he promised, putting a cup of hot tea in her hands. "I can call the city guards, if you'd like."

"No. Please don't. It's unnecessary. I'm fine."

He didn't blame her. The city guards were not much better than the warrior who'd mauled her, though his order did have some influence with them. But he wouldn't push if she'd prefer it.

"You can stay here as long as you'd like, my lady and—"

"Actually, Brother, I came here for a reason." She placed her untouched tea onto the table and looked at him. "I need your help, if possible."

"If it's in my power, I'll do what I can."

"I am in search of an order of monks."

He smiled, feeling confident. The different Northland and Southland orders of monks were among his several areas of expertise. "I actually know most of the orders. Which one do you search for?"

"The Order of the Warhammer?"

"Ahhh, yes. A great order. We have many of their books and documents in a special room. I'm sure I can get you permission to—"

"No, no, Brother. I need to get in contact with the Order

itself. I was told their monastery is near Spikenhammer and was hoping I could get directions."

Yrjan blinked in surprise and leaned back in his chair.

"Is something wrong?" she asked.

"My lady . . . the Order of the Warhammer no longer exists."

She frowned thoughtfully. "What are you talking about?"

"They were destroyed."

Her hand flew to her chest, her eyes widening in horror behind her spectacles. She looked absolutely devastated by the news. "No! That's not possible!"

"I'm sorry, my lady, but it's true. The books and papers we have are all that's left of them."

"And Brother Ragnar?"

He shook his head. "I've never heard of Brother Ragnar."

"You must have. He's one of the leaders of the Order."

"Brother Ölver was leader at the time of their destruction, my lady." She looked so distressed that Yrjan placed his hand on top of her gloved one. "Perhaps you have the name incorrect. There are many war-god based orders and I'm sure—"

Her eyes suddenly locked on his, and Yrjan felt a fear he'd not known since he left his father's house to join the Order.

"Do you have any of their robes or clothes? Anything they may have worn?"

"No. We assumed all that was destroyed—"

"When?" she growled.

"My lady?"

"When was the Order destroyed?"

Yrjan took a deep breath to calm his shaken nerves. "According to my readings, eighty-six to eighty-seven years ago during the winter of—"

He didn't get to finish as her small fist struck the table and she jumped up, her chair falling to the marble floor. Many of the other Brothers rushed into the reading room and watched as the weak female paced angrily before them.

"My lady, I'm sure there's—"

"Liar."

Yrjan was insulted until she bellowed, *"That bastard liar!"* and he knew she was not speaking of him.

"My lady, please!"

She stormed toward the exit, and when his Brothers blocked her way, she screamed, *"Move!"*

They did, scattering like ants.

Yrjan followed after her until she stormed out the main doors, slamming them behind her.

Shaking and panting, he went back to the reading room and the Brothers rushed to get him his own hot tea and some soothing herbs to calm his nerves.

Abstinence. A very good decision.

Dagmar stalked out of the Great Library. She stopped on the third step down and looked around. *Where has that idiot gone?*

By reason, she was angry. Angrier than she'd ever been in her life. Angrier than she knew it possible to be.

He'd lied to her. Not for a few days or over a particular issue, but full lies for two bloody decades!

Dagmar had never felt so betrayed. So hurt. Ragnar had hurt her as no other could.

A sudden attack of pure anxiety and panic swept through her and she ran down the steps and to the side of the enormous building. Slapping her hands against the stone wall, she leaned over and brought back up all those biscuits and tea Saamik had fed her.

Her bouts of panic rarely caught her this badly. Usually she could control it with deep breathing or by focusing on something else entirely. But she couldn't focus on anything else but this.

Who had she been dealing with all these years?

Her father's words came back to haunt her. "Always so sure you're right, little miss."

She had been sure. She had trusted Ragnar with her life and the life of her kinsmen every time she allowed him into her father's fortress.

Trembling, Dagmar rested back against the wall.

All right, she'd been a fool. She knew that now, but there was no use shaking and crying about it like a newborn pup. Ragnar must have wanted something from her; she needed to find out what.

Dagmar used a cloth from her satchel to wipe her mouth and headed back to the stairs. She sat down in the middle and waited. The dragon probably went for food. He was always hungry, it seemed. He'd be back and they could set off. Besides, a few minutes alone would help her get some control and figure out what to do next.

She'd allow absolutely no one to make a fool of her.

Chapter 13

Dagmar sat on the steps to the Great Library until the two suns went down. Gwenvael never returned.

When she saw the same man pass her twice, she knew she could no longer sit out there in the open and decided to return to the inn they'd been to the night before.

She set off, torn between worrying something horrible happened to Gwenvael and feeling sorry for herself, positive she'd been betrayed by another male and that he'd left her. She enjoyed feeling sorry for herself much more and focused on that instead.

Because of course he left her! Kisses meant nothing to someone like him when he could have, or hire, any woman he wanted. Dagmar was sure he was in some wench's bed, his commitment to her completely forgotten as he took the whore again and again and again.

Dagmar stopped for a moment. That was a visual she didn't need. Especially when the "whore" abruptly turned into her.

"Get a hold of yourself, idiot." She was in a bad situation. If he didn't return, how was she to get to her uncle Gestur's or home or anywhere else? And what did it mean to the alliance with Queen Annwyl? The whole thing kept getting worse and worse.

Especially when she glanced over her shoulder and saw someone back into the shadows so she wouldn't see.

Yes. Definitely getting worse.

Taking much quicker steps, Dagmar rushed back to the Stomping Horse Inn. She stepped inside and let out a sigh of relief. The place was quite busy and she felt safer in the well-lit inn with many around her, male and female.

"My lady, you've returned."

Dagmar smiled at the owner. "Yes. I was wondering if I could get a table."

"Anything for you." She'd tipped him well that morning and she was very glad she had. He forced a few men to move and gave their table to Dagmar. It was in the back, and she faced the door, hoping to see Gwenvael come in looking for her. The owner went out of his way to keep the local men away from her, but a few still stopped by, trying to chat her up.

Men were so strange. She knew they weren't enamored by her looks, but the colder and more off-putting she became, the more they swarmed. Willing local women all around, but they wanted the "cold bitch," as one dismissed male mumbled at her.

She stared hard at the door, willing it to open and bring in

Gwenvael. The chair on the other side of her small table scraped against the floor as it was pulled back and Dagmar let out an annoyed sigh.

"Go away."

"I think we need to talk."

Dagmar felt a fresh blade through her heart as she turned and looked deep into blue eyes with silver flecks through the iris. And until her hands, bent into claws, were going for his face, she had no idea she'd react so violently. But Ragnar simply grabbed her wrists and slammed them back to the table.

"Sit down," he calmly ordered.

"My lady?" The owner rushed over. "Are you all right?"

Ragnar raised a brow, and Dagmar forced herself to smile up at the owner. "Everything's fine. Thank you."

He nodded at her and glared at Ragnar.

When they were again alone, she snatched her hands back and snarled, "You lying bastard."

He wore no monk's robes this time, no cowl, but a simple black cape with the hood pulled right to his forehead—to hide the purple hair, she supposed.

"Do you think it was so easy for me to lie to you for the last twenty years? You, who were always so kind to me?"

"Then why did you? What did you want from me?"

"What I got."

She studied him closely. Reason help her, but he was beautiful. Those gorgeous eyes combined with sharp cheekbones, full lips, and an almost-but-not-quite-too-long nose would make any female stop and stare—and dream.

"He warned me your kind is everywhere," she said. "But I believed a Northlander would be too honorable. Bigger fool, I."

"If it had been safe, I would have told you the truth. Hearing stories about dragons is vastly different from realizing one is sitting across from you, drinking your wine."

"You know it wouldn't have mattered to me."

"No. I see now that it wouldn't have." His smile was affectionate. "Not to my reasoning, Dagmar."

"Your name, dragon. What is it?"

"Ragnar the Cunning, of the Olgeirsson Horde."

"Fitting." She gazed into his handsome face. "And why are you here now?"

"I have contacts at the Great Library. I would have preferred you not found out that way, though." He leaned back in his chair. "Why were you looking for me?"

"Trying to confirm a rumor about Jökull's truce with the Horde."

He chuckled. "Where did you hear that?"

"Is it true?"

"No. Although it's a brilliant rumor to start, don't you think?"

"You know the actions of every horde?"

"Don't need to. I only need to know your father's territory is on my father's territory—and Olgeir the Wastrel isn't making any truces with humans. He considers you more . . . well, like your kitchen dogs. Pets that amuse and take scraps off the floor, but have no other real purpose."

Dagmar rested her elbow on the table and her chin in her palm. "If I thought I could manage it—I'd kill you where you sit."

He gave her a surprisingly warm smile. "I've always had a great fondness for you, Dagmar. A very great fondness. If I could have protected you from being hurt, I would have."

"But you want something more. Don't you? That's why you're here now."

"Always quick."

"Just as I've been taught."

"Your Fire Breather. The Gold."

She felt her stomach tighten, not enjoying the mention of Gwenvael one bit. "Deserted me for the night, I suspect."

"You know he didn't. But he was foolish to bring you here.

Foolish to think he'd be ignored by my father's spies or that the truce between the Hordes and the Dragon Queen would keep him safe."

Dagmar let out a breath, struggled for calm. "You have him."

"No. I have no need of him. But my father's Horde has long memories and we're just as protective of our females as your kinsmen. Chances are he will not last the night . . . unless I help him."

"You mean for a price."

"A price I suspect you're willing to pay to get him back." He took her hand in his and studied it. "Has he seduced you too, Lady Dagmar? Like he has so many others? Has that cold heart you always professed to have been thawed by a Fire Breather?"

Dagmar would give him nothing he could feed on, nothing he could use again in years to come. But she couldn't deny to herself that she feared for Gwenvael's safety. She'd seen first-hand what her kinsmen did to those who'd involved themselves with the wrong woman or sullied a kinswoman's good name.

She knew that as she sat here across from the lying Horde dragon, Gwenvael suffered horribly at the hands of his enemies. She also knew hysteria would get her nowhere. If she kept calm, cold, and just as merciless, perhaps she could get them both out of this.

"At the moment, we're business partners. And that's all. You know me well enough, my lord. Know that when I want something, I'll do what I have to in order to get it." She leaned back in her chair and folded her hands primly on her lap. "We both know I need him alive if I hope to get what he promised me from that mad bitch queen. So what's your price? What do I need to do to get you to bring the Southlander to me—alive?"

"It's simple." His small smile turned wide and brilliant. "Help me start a war."

* * *

Gwenvael gritted his fangs and bit back a cry of pain as the blade of a dagger was forced under his scale and then lifted, tearing away the scale from its flesh anchor. But it was not removed completely. No. That was a weaker form of torture. Instead a small, jagged piece of metal was placed between scale and flesh and the scale pressed back into place. In minutes the flesh would seal again to the scale, enclosing the jagged metal inside. The pain of that would only get worse as the hours went on.

It was a very old form of torture but had been quite popular in his grandfather's day.

When the Lightnings had first dragged him into the city tunnels, he'd thought they wanted information from him. Information he'd never give, but he'd assumed they'd try. Yet for hours, they hadn't said a word to him. They hadn't asked him questions or demanded anything. They'd simply beaten him until he shifted to his dragon form, and then they'd chained him from a thick steel pipe. After that they kept hitting him, again and again. If he passed out, they woke him up with water or herbs and went back to beating him. When they paused from beating him, one of them would lift several of his scales and put the metal bits underneath.

A good portion of his body was covered now, and as he hung from the chains manacled to his wrists and ankles, all he felt was pain. Excruciating, nearly unbearable pain. And it would only get worse. That much he knew.

It had crossed his mind to call out to his kin, but he'd decided against it. It would take them days to get to him, and in that time they'd have started another war with the Lightnings. He wouldn't be responsible for that.

With the scales back in place, the hitting started again. Someone had very big fists and seemed to enjoy hitting Gwenvael's face with them. By the tenth hit, he slumped in his chains.

That's when he heard her voice for the first time. "Gwenvael," she sang. "Gwenvael. My dear, dear heart."

"He's out again. Give me some water."

"We're out."

"Then get some, you idiot."

A claw gripped his jaw and lifted his head. "Don't you worry, Fire Breather. We'll get you taken care of."

"It's time to fight, Gwenvael," the voice told him so sweetly. "It's time to live. You must come to me. Come to me as quick as you can."

Gwenvael nodded. "I will."

"You are awake then? Good. So we can—"

Snapping his mouth open, Gwenvael wrapped it around the Lightning's snout. He bit down, enjoying the screaming, and unleashed his flame. The Lightning's purple scales would protect him to a degree, but he couldn't breathe through flames the way Gwenvael's kind could. So he kept the flame strong, drowning the bastard in effect, letting him twitch and struggle.

He heard other screams, knew the Lightning's kinsmen would come to protect him, but they didn't and eventually the one in his maw went limp. Gwenvael released him, staring down at the half-seared face of his torturer.

"Gods, look at him."

Gwenvael raised his head. More Lightnings, their swords covered in blood, watched him.

"And look at this." One of them swiped up something in his claw and showed it to the other two.

"They're still doing that? Ragnar's going to have a fit when he finds out."

"We'll worry about that later. Let's get him down."

"Can you walk?" one of them asked, and Gwenvael nodded.

"Can you shift to human?"

He nodded again. If nothing else, he'd definitely try.

"All right then, lad. Come on."

Chapter 14

Dagmar saw Gwenvael being helped out of the tunnels by three other Horde dragons.

"My brother and cousins," Ragnar murmured.

She rushed to Gwenvael's side and lifted his head. "He needs a healer."

Gwenvael surprised her by shaking his head and pulling away from the three who held him. She wasn't sure where he'd found the strength. "No," he said.

"She's right, Fire Breather. I can see what they did to you," Ragnar added with a frown. "Let me help you."

"Help? From a Lightning? I think I've had all the help I can stand from you bastards." Gwenvael took her hand.

"Don't be foolish," Ragnar argued. "Let me help you."

"No. I'll find my own help."

"In the Northlands? Do you really think more of my kin aren't out looking for you? Or that our Dragonwitches will help your kind?"

Gwenvael tugged Dagmar away, stubbornly refusing to hear anything else Ragnar had to say.

She glanced back at the Horde dragons watching them, and Ragnar gave a small nod of his head. She looked away and let Gwenvael drag her through the now-quiet streets.

"Where are we going?" she finally managed to ask.

"Someplace safe. She calls to me and says I'll be safe."

"Who?"

Gwenvael grunted suddenly, stopping to bend over at the waist, his hands resting on his thighs. That's when she saw all the blood and bruises riddling his human body as they must have been riddling his dragon one. But there were not only bruises and open wounds. There was something else. Under his skin? She didn't know, couldn't be sure. But she knew he was in pain—real pain he was fighting hard not to show.

"What's wrong?" She gently rested her hands on his arm and he jumped back from her as if scalded. "Gwenvael, what is it?"

"Nothing. We have to go. She calls."

"Not until we take you to a healer."

"No human healer can help me." He pulled her around a dark corner. "When I shift, get on my back."

"You can't do this here. Everyone will see."

"They'll only see you and only if they look hard. If we move fast enough, we can do this."

"But Gwenvael—"

"Don't argue with me," he snapped, but then his voice calmed. "Please. Just do as I say."

She had no choice. "All right."

He walked away from her, and she watched as flames surrounded his body. When the flames died, he was dragon again.

"Now."

She rushed to his side and grabbed hold of his mane. His tail lifted her from behind, seating her on his back. His wings moved, and they were airborne.

A few people looked up, frowning at the sight of a woman apparently flying above the city, but by the time they blinked and looked again, she'd disappeared into the clouds.

Rhiannon flipped through another ancient tome she'd found buried in the back of the royal archives. This area was for the scholars, witches, and mages. Unlike many dragons she knew,

Rhiannon never cared much about learning for learning's sake. She was a scholar only because it was necessary to be one as a witch. To be quite honest, she found this sort of research deadly boring. Yet she didn't have much time and she knew it.

Annwyl's body was simply not made to carry the kind of offspring she was near giving birth to. For those, like Rhiannon, who could see the tendrils of Magick wherever they looked, the power surrounding Annwyl almost blinded the Dragonwitch. For someone like Rhiannon, an actual birth of this kind would have exhausted her human body, but her natural, Magick-infused defenses would have most likely kept her healthy. But Annwyl was a true human warrior. There was absolutely no Magick inside her. No otherworldly skills that had been kept dormant until now. Her gift was her rage. The power of it was like a sudden storm that could wipe out an entire village in a night.

In the end, it was this pureness of Annwyl's spirit and strong will that attracted those around her, from the lowliest peasant soldier to the heirs of Rhiannon's throne.

Yet knowing all that hadn't helped Rhiannon find a way to assist the human queen. She'd brought in the best and even the most controversial Dragonmages she knew of throughout the land. Even now, they researched and toiled in other caverns of the archives and library, trying to find a way to help Annwyl.

Rhiannon flipped to the last page and slammed the book shut. *Another useless piece of Centaur crap*, she thought, tossing the book into the pile on her left while her tail grabbed hold of another tome from the pile on her right.

"You're up late this eve, my queen."

As much as Rhiannon wanted to sigh and flop dramatically to the ground as Gwenvael always did when something bored him beyond all hope, she simply gave a small smile and answered, "Yes, yes, Elder Eanruig. Much to do."

"Right. Before the birth of those children." He walked

across the room to one of the shelves, his tail slithering along behind him. He'd never seemed to have much control over that thing. Not the way most of her kind did. She couldn't help but equate it to some lowly snake slithering across the ground, hoping to dine on whatever pile of shit it happened to find along the way. "We really must discuss what we'll do with them once they're born."

Rhiannon looked up, not liking the sound of that statement at all. "Do with them?"

"Yes." He grabbed something off the shelf and turned to face her, his tail scooting behind him. She was surprised it didn't rattle as it moved. "The Elders and Your Majesty must discuss where the offspring will be taken once they're born."

"Taken? Why would they be taken anywhere?"

"You can't seriously be considering allowing a human to raise them?"

"A human and my son, Elder Eanruig. And since the off-spring will be both human and dragon this only makes—"

"Your son, my queen, is hardly the type to raise anyone's offspring. Especially his own."

The metal tip of Rhiannon's tail that she sharpened at least once, if not twice, a day, scraped across the stone cavern floor. "I'm not sure as to your meaning, Elder."

He walked toward her. He was an old Gold dragon, his golden hair nearly white with age, his scales no longer bright and clear but dull and worn. Though the more she'd gotten to know this dragon, the less she believed age had anything to do with it. Bercelak's father was nearly nine-hundred years when he'd passed on and he'd been as beautiful then as he'd been when she'd first met him. He'd definitely aged, but he'd never lost his energy or his love of nearly everything. Eanruig the Scholarly, however, had none of that to lose. He lived his life in books and believed in the strict boundaries of bloodlines.

To him, her mother Queen Adienna had been perfect

simply because she'd mated someone of her equal. Rhiannon
lost that potential for perfection when she was Claimed by
Bercelak, a low-born dragon of the Cadwaladr Clan. A breed
of warrior dragon that fucked, fed, and fought. From when
she was a young hatchling, Rhiannon had heard the Cadwaladrs referred to as the battle dogs of the dragon royals.
And that was how Adienna had treated them. Wars in far-off
lands that needed no finesse or a ready truce? Send in the
Cadwaladrs! Need a siege to last until the final starving body
was dragged from the fortress ten years from now? Send in
the Cadwaladrs!

More importantly, though, the Cadwaladrs didn't mind.
As long as they could continue to fuck, feed, and fight,
they didn't care where you sent them or what you expected
them to do.

Yet what Eanruig forgot—what all the self-important
royals always forgot: never fuck with the Cadwaladrs' kin.
Their bloodline may not be royal, but they protected it as
any battle dog would protect its pups.

And Annwyl and Fearghus's offspring were Cadwaladr
bloodline.

The Elder she hated above all others now stood beside her,
smirking down at her.

"You know exactly what I mean, my queen. Your son has
betrayed his kind by Claiming this human girl and the gods
have cursed them with these . . . these . . . *aberrations*. Unfortunately, there is nothing we can do about that now, except take
control of the situation before it gets any worse. The Council
will decide the best way for those offspring to be raised." He
leaned in a bit closer, and Rhiannon fought her body's desire
to tear him apart, scale by gods-damn scale. "And I do hope
you didn't send that foolish hatchling of yours—Gwenvael, I
believe—into the north simply so he can start some minor war

and you can take control of the Council. I strongly suggest a move such as that would be very unwise."

Rhiannon was moments from slapping the smirk off Eanruig's smug face when a tail much larger and deadlier than her own slammed down between the two of them. The book in Eanruig's claws fell to the ground, startled from his grasp. Rhiannon couldn't hold back her smile as Bercelak's head slowly eased around from behind Eanruig.

"Lord Bercelak."

My, she did enjoy how weak the Elder's voice suddenly sounded.

"Elder Eanruig. Something I can help you with?"

"No, no. Just a small chat with our queen."

"Chat's over, prissy tail. Piss off."

Eanruig gave a small nod at Rhiannon. "My queen."

"Elder."

They watched as Eanruig slithered out of the archives.

When they knew he was gone, Bercelak turned back to her. "Why will you not unleash me on him?"

She wrapped her tail around his, tugging him closer. "Because I can't afford for you to kill him. He'd love his death to cause a civil war among my court. I won't let that happen. Now why are you here? You're supposed to be in the west."

"I was. And Addolgar and Ghleanna are coming, handpicking the squads that will come with them. They'll be leaving in the next day or two with Éibhear, but I wanted to be home with you tonight."

"You left Éibhear alone with them?"

"Ghleanna's taking care of him. Besides, it's time he learns he won't always have his mother around to coddle him."

"I don't coddle him. And Ghleanna's mean."

"I know." He brushed his claw across her cheek. "You look tired."

"I am. Eanruig took what energy I had left, right out of me."

"Then it is time you return to our chamber." He grabbed her claw in his and led her toward the exit. "We'll play 'Does my tail fit in here?'"

Rhiannon laughed. "I adore that game!"

Gwenvael heard her again, the voice soft and sweet in his head. So sweet, he could go to sleep simply listening to it. It lured him, and he no longer knew where he might be.

"Gwenvael," she said again. "Follow my voice. Come to me, Gwenvael."

He had the distinct feeling he wasn't going the right way, but his eyesight seemed to be failing, which couldn't be a good thing. Nor was he breathing too well. What made it worse was that he was thousands of leagues above the earth with a fragile human on his back.

Still that voice kept calling to him. "Gwenvael. Sweet, sweet Gwenvael."

Those bastard Lightnings had done more to him than he'd realized. He could feel poison moving through his body like warm water.

Dagmar. He needed to take Dagmar home, where she would be safe. Yet he couldn't ignore that voice.

"Gwenvael!"

Those weren't the same dulcet tones luring him into a false sense of security. It was much too screechy and panicked.

"What?" he asked Dagmar.

"Mountain."

"What?"

"Mountain! Mountain! Mountain!"

He swerved as the word Dagmar kept repeating made sense, the tip of his left wing grazing against the mountainside as he barely missed it.

Which mountains were these? If he could figure that

out, he'd know where they were and the direction to take to get her home.

"You need to set us down," she yelled over the roaring wind.

"When I get you home," he promised. "Any idea where that is?"

"How the hell would I know?"

"That's a bit of a problem. 'Cause right now I can't see too well. Maybe I can borrow those spectacles of yours."

"Blasted reason! Set us down then!"

"That would be a good idea, but . . ."

"But? But what?"

He didn't answer her, simply dodged to the left, lightning strikes grazing his wing.

"Someone's behind us!"

"I sensed that," he said. More Lightnings, but not the ones who'd helped him from the tunnels. Who were those Lightnings anyway? And why had they helped him?

And maybe he should worry about that later when he wasn't in the middle of a fight with a different set of Lightnings bent on killing him.

"I need you to hold on," he told Dagmar. "Don't let go."

"What do you mean 'don't let go'?"

Again, he didn't answer her, simply jerked around and raised himself up. Dagmar screamed in panic, and he unleashed his flame on those behind him. The Lightnings scrambled out of the way and Gwenvael moved forward, slamming himself into the closest one. Once he made contact, Gwenvael rolled against the other's body until he felt the sheath against his arm. He reached out and grasped the blade attached to the dragon's back. Yanking it free, he swung forward and then back. The blade, perfectly maintained and delightfully sharp, cut through the owner's neck

Lightning was released from another, and Gwenvael tucked his wings in. His body dropped and he was glad to hear

Dagmar's healthy scream again. That meant she hadn't fallen to her death yet. He was quite relieved.

The Lightnings moved in closer and Gwenvael's wings snapped out from his body, quickly lifting him. He let loose another round of flame and dove through it—fast enough, he hoped, to keep Dagmar unharmed—while arcing the sword up and across. The blade lodged into a Lightning's body and stayed there, but at least the damage had been done. He let go, and the sword and body fell to the ground below.

"Gwenvael!"

He moved based merely on the way her voice sounded, twisting to his side and reaching out. His claws wrapped around the shaft of a spear but not before it tore into his chest, just below his collarbone.

Gwenvael roared in pain and fury, the spear twisting in deeper. Keeping one claw gripped onto the spear, he used his other arm and snapped the shaft in the middle. The Lightning tried to drag the broken shaft from him; Gwenvael knew well enough that would be the end of him and Dagmar. So he used what strength he still possessed and yanked the shaft from the purple claws desperately clinging to it. Once he had it in his grasp, he turned the broken end out, lowered it, and brought it up again in one swift jab.

The shaft pierced the Lightning's soft underbelly, Gwenvael silently thanking the gods his challengers didn't have their battle armor on.

The Lightning bellowed in pain and grabbed hold of Gwenvael's shoulders. Desperate, Gwenvael twisted the broken shaft again and again, digging it in deeper until the Lightning dropped against him.

His strength gone, Gwenvael couldn't even push the big oaf away from him and together they plummeted to the ground. The Lightning on top, Gwenvael underneath him.

But he somehow heard it. As his eyesight went dark

and his brain struggled to think, he heard it. Screaming. A woman screaming.

Dagmar.

He was mere feet from the ground when he rolled over, the Lightning now beneath him. His tail lashed out, winding around her waist and lifting her seconds before they all crashed into the hard, unforgiving earth.

Brastias woke the second Morfyd's body jolted beside his. He reached for her but she was already scrambling across the bed.

"No, no, no, no," she kept chanting over and over.

"Morfyd?"

She stumbled naked to the door and pulled it open, standing there as if waiting for something. Knowing she must be freezing since she was often chilled in her human form, he grabbed a fur from the bed and moved in behind her, wrapping it around her.

"What is it, love? What's wrong?"

The door to Annwyl's room opened and Fearghus stalked into the hallway. For Morfyd's sake, Brastias would normally move out of sight, but the look on the dragon's face pinned him to the spot. The siblings stared at each other until Briec jogged up the stairs, stopping on the landing and gazing at his kin.

"Well?" Briec demanded.

Morfyd pulled away from Brastias, tugging the fur tight around her. "I don't know."

"How could you not know?"

"Don't bark at her." Fearghus went to his sister, pulled her into his arms. "I'm sure we'd all know if Gwenvael was . . ." He closed his eyes, kissed the top of his sister's head. "I'm sure he'll be fine."

"The pain, Fearghus. He was in so much pain."

"I know. I felt it too." He scowled at Briec in warning, and his younger brother walked over and patted his sister's shoulder.

"Don't worry. He's Gwenvael. He gets into trouble, he gets out of it."

"All right?" Fearghus asked softly.

"Aye." She stepped back, rubbed her forehead. "And now I've got Mother screeching in my head. I need some wine." She walked past her brothers and down the stairs.

Leaving Brastias there alone, forgotten . . . and naked.

Fearghus noticed him first. Brastias had only seen that glower on the dragon's face once before. When Annwyl had gone off to Devenallt Mountain for the first time and had told the dragon nothing. Brastias didn't like the glower then, and he hated it more now.

Briec's frown was much more threatening, somehow. Maybe because he looked so astounded as well as angry. Not a good combination. Startling anything that breathes fire was always a bad idea in Brastias's estimation.

"Our . . . sister?" Fearghus growled.

"Our baby sister?" Briec snarled.

"She's two-hundred-and-fifty-two-years old."

"Our *innocent* baby sister?" Briec went on, ignoring him.

Innocent? No. Probably best not to dispute them on that point.

Brastias shrugged. "I love her."

Briec shrugged back. "Then we're just going to have to kill you."

Talaith walked up the stairs, stopping in the same place Briec had. She studied the three of them before asking, "What's going on?"

"He's defiling our sister," both brothers said.

"Of course he is. And from what I understand, she's enjoying every second of it, so leave him be."

Briec glared at his mate. "You knew?"

Understanding he only had one chance, Brastias quickly cut in, "Did Briec mention he's ready to release Izzy for combat duty?"

The brothers went rigid. Fearghus's eyes wide, while Briec closed his own and cringed.

Talaith gaped at the three of them as her mind tried to understand his words. "They . . . you . . . uh . . ." She shook her head. "I'm sorry. What did you say?"

"You *bastard*," Briec whispered.

"You drove me to it."

"Briec?"

He let out a breath and faced Talaith. "I know you're not ready to hear this, Talaith, but—well, don't walk away!"

After Briec disappeared in pursuit of Talaith, Fearghus said, "Nicely played, human." He headed back to the rooms he shared with Annwyl. "But once Talaith is done giving Briec a brand new anus with her fist and we know whether Gwenvael is dead or not . . . we'll be back."

Brastias didn't doubt that for a moment.

It was his strange and invasive tail that had saved her life, holding Dagmar up and away as they crashed into the ground.

Even now with the two dragons nothing more than a big ball of bright purple and gold scales, Gwenvael's tail still held her tightly around the waist and she struggled to get it off. When she finally did, she fell a few inches, her rear slamming hard into the thick root of a tree.

She winced in pain but still managed to crawl over to Gwenvael. Up close, she could see his face and brushed the hair from his eyes. "Gwenvael?"

He didn't move and she wasn't even sure he was breathing. She gripped his claw with both hands, careful of his razor-sharp talons. "Gwenvael, please answer me."

Dagmar had no idea how long she stood there, holding on to Gwenvael. She knew she needed to do something, but for once she was at a loss. She couldn't move him, afraid to leave him alone for even a moment. She had no idea where they were and knew more dragons could be lying in wait anywhere.

There was a part of Dagmar that wished she hadn't left her home, still living safely under her father's protection, blissfully ignorant of the truth around her.

"There you are."

Startled, Dagmar dropped Gwenvael's claw and reached for her eating dagger. She whirled around to face the threat, prepared to protect Gwenvael with her life, when the dagger slipped from her hand and skipped depressingly along the ground, landing at the intruder's feet.

"Hhhm. Not much of a fighter then?" The woman in witches' robes picked the blade up and trudged over to Dagmar. "Shouldn't bring this out unless you really know what you're doing." She handed Dagmar the blade. "Because nothing could be worse than getting killed with your own weapon."

Dagmar gawked at the woman. "Who are you?"

"Esyld."

"Esyld who?"

She didn't answer Dagmar's question, but leaned over Gwenvael. "Poor thing. I was afraid he wouldn't make it this far, but he has much strength in him." She glanced at Dagmar. "And much passion to protect you."

"I'll ask you again. Who are you?"

"A friend. I'm only here to help. But we need to get both of you inside where it's safe."

She motioned Dagmar back, and raised her hands over Gwenvael.

"What are you doing?"

Again there was no answer, but the woman began to chant.

Flames rose over Gwenvael's body and then receded, leaving him human.

"Much easier to handle this way for me."

"How did you . . . ?"

The witch grabbed hold of Gwenvael's arm and leg and lifted his body onto her shoulder. "Come on then."

Even in his human form, Gwenvael was a mighty weight. No human witch her size could pick him up.

"You're a dragon."

"That I am."

"Your kind is everywhere," Dagmar couldn't help but sneer. "I never seem to know when I'm dealing with one."

"But you're learning," the female said with a laugh. "I can tell."

Chapter 15

Dagmar followed Esyld to a small house deep in a copse of trees. To be honest, it was a charming little place. Smoke puffed from a chimney, with an herb garden right out front and a stone walkway that led to the door. Large trees surrounded the house, the branches and leaves providing cover.

The dragoness had left the front door open and walked right in, Dagmar behind her.

The inside of the house was as comfortable and charming as the outside, although it had only one room. Dagmar could see herself happily living here alone. In truth, she knew she'd enjoy it and had hoped when she reached her fortieth winter or so she'd get a small place like this near her father's fortress. She knew her sisters-in-law would happily push that situation on their spouses.

Esyld carried Gwenvael to the long bed pressed against the wall. She lifted him off her shoulder and placed him down carefully. With a soft smile, she brushed his hair from his face. "He's grown up so handsome."

Dagmar's eyes narrowed. Who the hell was this? And why did she feel it was acceptable to touch him in such a way? "Are you going to tell me who you are or not?"

"I already did. Name's Esyld." And before Dagmar could argue, she pointed at Gwenvael. "See these?"

Dagmar crouched beside the bed, pushing her spectacles on top of her head so she could closely study how his skin puckered in several places.

Many places, in fact. All over his body.

"What is this?"

"A brutal torture."

Esyld pulled off her robes. She wore a simple blue gown beneath. It set off her red hair perfectly.

"You're not one of the Horde."

"No, I'm not." She knelt on the floor beside Dagmar. Her finger slightly hovered over one of the raised welts. "This is the old way of doing damage to a dragon. When in dragon form, your scales are forcibly pulled away from the flesh and small, jagged pieces of steel are slipped beneath. That process alone is quite painful. It's not easy to pry scale from flesh. You usually have to use a knife in between the seams."

"I never noticed . . . what I mean to say is . . ." Dagmar, tired of crouching, went on her knees and rubbed her eyes with her fists. Was she actually about to ask for more information on blasted dragon seams? "Forget I was trying to say anything."

"You'd have to look very closely to notice the seams. Now once the scale is released back into place, it heals shut, locking in the jagged piece of metal. The pain is quite excruciating," she said easily, almost cheerfully. "Even worse, the flesh underneath heals over it, intensifying the pain."

Dagmar's balled fists landed in her lap. "All that for vengeance?"

"They wanted him to suffer." She rested her arm on the bed. "It's doubtful they'd hoped to get any information from him. A royal he may be, but also a descendent of the Cadwaladr Clan. You can never get them to talk."

"He's . . ." Dagmar straightened her spine. "He's a royal?"

"Son of the Dragon Queen herself." Esyld regarded her intensely. "He never told you, did he?"

"He was quick to tell me about that time he woke up in a sewer in Kerezik. But his royal lineage . . . *That* never came up in conversation." And reason knew, he never *acted* like a royal.

The dragoness chuckled. "That's my Gwenvael."

And Dagmar felt it again. That strange feeling in the pit of her stomach any time Esyld asserted some kind of hold on Gwenvael. "Who are you?"

And yet *again* Dagmar received no answer with Esyld too busy clucking her tongue. "I see what's wrong," she said. "Those bastards added poison to the tips of the metal."

"They what?" Dagmar immediately placed her hand to Gwenvael's forehead. He felt cold. Not good when he was made of fire. "You have to do something."

"I will. I'll have to cut the pieces out. One by one. I made him human because it'll be easier that way. No scales to tear open again."

Annoyed the dragoness was just sitting there, Dagmar snapped, "Shouldn't you be moving with some purpose?"

"Why? He's not going anywhere."

"The poison?"

"Too late for that. It's already in his bloodstream."

Dagmar lifted her shaking hands and placed them against

her eyes. The calm, merciless sound of the woman's voice was driving her past reason. Past logic.

"Now, now, dear. No need to cry. I'm sure—*ack*!"

She didn't even let the female finish before she grabbed her by the back of the neck and slammed her head into the metal frame of the bed. For the first time in Dagmar's life, she knew what it felt like to be one of her brothers—and it was quite a heady sensation.

Esyld gripped her forehead. "Ow! *Are you mad?*"

Dagmar stood. "Now listen well to me, Esyld. You do what you must to make him better. Mix whatever potions necessary, call on whatever useless gods you're loyal to, sacrifice whatever animals those useless gods require—I don't care. But you make him well. Or I swear by all reason—"

"What?" The dragoness towered over Dagmar now. "You'll what, reason-lover? What does an obvious follower of Aoib-hell think she can possibly do to me?"

"I can make sure this will be your last quiet night in these woods. I'll make sure that every male—man, dragon, or otherwise—knows you live here. Alone. I'll make sure that hunting you becomes a sport they can't resist."

"And perhaps I'll just turn you into ash where you stand."

"Do you really think that'll stop me?" Dagmar smirked. "Really?"

After a moment of mutual glaring, the dragoness shook her head, her brow furrowed. "No. I believe it won't." She stepped away from Dagmar. "Who are you?"

She found it almost amusing the female had the nerve to ask. "I am Dagmar Reinholdt, Only Daughter of The Reinholdt."

"*You're* The Beast?"

"Some would say."

"I have to admit, you don't see it right off . . . until you look in those eyes." Rubbing her forehead and wincing,

Esyld went to a small table covered in dry herbs, half-burned ritual candles, several different daggers, and a wand. "I will say I appreciate how protective you are of him. He deserves that."

Not about to ask the same question yet again, Dagmar instead tried, "What's your connection to him?"

"Not what you think." She flashed Dagmar a smile over her shoulder. "He's my nephew."

"Nephew?"

"Aye." She brought a large bowl, a clean cloth, and a sharp dagger over to the bed. "My sister is Queen Rhiannon. When she came into power, I fled. I'm now called Esyld the Traitor by her court."

"And are you?"

"Not in a few centuries. Now"—she glanced down at Gwenvael—"help me tie him to the bed. And gag him."

It wasn't the first time he'd woken up to find himself tied to a bed. Nor was it the first time he'd woken up to find himself tied to the bed and gagged.

But usually when he woke up bound and gagged, he was always experiencing wonderful pleasure. Not pain. At least not this kind of pain. Pain so raw and brutal he tried to shift back to his true form several times but couldn't. He sensed it had something to do with the collar around his neck. It held great power and cut down on his.

Someone had tied him face down on the bed so they could rip something out of his body. Something vital? He had no idea. He only knew it hurt and he wanted the pain to stop. Needed it to. He couldn't think with all this pain. Couldn't understand where he was or how he'd gotten here. He couldn't see because of all the sweat pouring into his eyes, burning them. Yet he could hear a soft voice telling him it would be all right. *Nothing to worry about. Just a bit more.* But he knew she was lying. He knew this pain would last forever, and he didn't understand why she didn't just kill him. No one should suffer like this. Least of all him.

He felt the blade enter his flesh again and he screamed, the sound somewhat muffled behind his gag.

Gods, why wouldn't she just kill him?

Dagmar heard Gwenvael's muffled scream again and she pulled her legs up onto the boulder she sat on, wrapping her arms around them. She'd tried to stay inside but her constant threats to Esyld finally forced the dragoness to order her to leave.

She'd gone, Dagmar was ashamed to admit, willingly.

She didn't know hearing someone suffer could bother her so. She'd been through childbirths with her sisters-in-law, some of them terribly difficult, and she'd been the cold, responsible one in the room the midwife always relied upon. She'd also assisted healers when her kinsmen had been badly wounded. One of her cousins had gotten his leg crushed by his own horse. She'd been the only one who'd stayed to help the healer cut it off. He'd been awake during the whole procedure, begging them not to do it, but Dagmar knew the healer had no choice.

Although she'd been relieved when her cousin finally passed out, not once, during any of that, had she ever felt like this—as if she could feel every blade cut, every pull when Esyld tore the jagged pieces of metal from Gwenvael's exhausted body. Dagmar even felt like she could taste the vile concoction Esyld had poured down his throat before she'd begun cutting him open. She'd hoped it would be something for the pain, but it had only been to help Gwenvael's body flush out the poison through his skin.

Gwenvael screamed again, and Dagmar closed her eyes

tight, resting her forehead against her knees. She took deep breaths and willed herself to be calm.

Small noises from the woods surrounding her caught Dagmar's attention. She lifted her head and watched the immense wolf pad softly toward her. She smiled at the sight of him.

A canine, any canine, was a welcome sight to her. Without Canute she was quite willing to risk a good mauling for the comfort of a four-legged friend.

"Hello." He came up to her without hesitation and, keeping her fingers curled in, Dagmar brushed her knuckles across his head. "You need a bath," she teased.

"You're a brave one." A woman trekked out of the woods and over to Dagmar. "Those who see him are usually afraid of him."

"I do well with canines."

"You mind?" The woman motioned to the part of the boulder Dagmar wasn't sitting on.

"No."

"Thanks." She tugged the large pack she had on her back off and sat down hard, exhaling. "I'm bloody exhausted."

She was a warrior woman. A warrior woman who had seen better days . . . or years. She looked to be somewhere near her fortieth winter and was covered in scars. There were scars on her face, hands, and neck. Dagmar assumed she had more, but they were covered by her clothes. It seemed the warrior was too poor for proper armor and had only an undertunic and a padded top, linen pants, and extremely worn leather boots. Her brown hair was long and curly with several warrior braids weaved throughout. But what fascinated Dagmar the most was the color of her skin. She was one of the desert people. Rarely did someone born that far south find their way to the Northlands. And especially not a female alone.

"I'm Eir," the woman said, pulling off her boot and revealing extremely large feet that bled from several blistered spots. She wiggled her toes and groaned in pain.

"I'm Dagmar. No socks?"

"They were so frayed, didn't see the point."

Dagmar opened her satchel. "Here. You can have these."

Eir took the wool socks from her. "You sure?"

"Yes. A . . . My friend gave me a new pair. So you can have the extra one. You should wash them first, though."

The warrior shrugged and pulled them on, making Dagmar wince at the lack of hygiene.

"I can wash them later," she promised, and Dagmar decided not to question that.

Gwenvael screamed again, and Dagmar gritted her teeth. The wolf that settled at her feet pressed his extremely large head against her legs. She appreciated the comfort.

"That your friend?"

"Yes."

"Sounds like he's having a rough time of it."

"He is."

"I wouldn't worry. I hear the witch is a good healer." She pulled her old boots over her new socks and sighed. "Much better. Thank you."

"You're welcome." Dagmar, desperate to focus on anything but Gwenvael's pain and her panic, asked, "Why are you here?"

"Doing what I always do. Looking for a good battle to get into. A good fight. Nothing better than stumbling into a war that keeps you busy for a while."

A sword for hire. Some of the most unsteady work Dagmar knew of. "Do you enjoy that?"

"I enjoy wandering. Never staying in one place for too long. A really good battle keeps me busy for a bit, and then I move to the next place." She nudged Dagmar's shoulder with a hand missing its smallest finger. "Know of anything?"

"I wouldn't send you farther into the north. Your kind wouldn't do well there."

"My kind?"

"Yes. Female." Eir laughed, and Dagmar went on. "You'll find more work in the south and I hear there's a huge war in the west. You should go to Dark Plains. I've been told Queen Annwyl has quite a few females in her troops."

"I'll do that. Is that where you're heading?"

"I don't know. I don't know what I'm doing right now."

"I understand." She stood again, and her size roused Dagmar's suspicions. "You're not a dragon, are you?"

"Me?" She laughed. "Gods, no! I wish. I'd love having a tail."

For the first time in hours, Dagmar smiled. "Wouldn't we all. Uh . . ."

"Eir," she kindly reminded her.

"Eir. Yes. If you go that way about a half a league, you'll find a dead dragon."

Eir stared off in the direction Dagmar pointed. "Really?"

"There might be something you can scrounge off of him. He had a pouch. Might have something in there you could use." She held up her satchel. "It's as big as this. Although on him, it's just a pouch."

"All right."

Dagmar pointed off in front of her. "And out there somewhere, not sure how far, though, there are a couple of other dead dragons. You might be able to get something off them as well."

Eir grinned at her and Dagmar counted at least twelve scars on that face, one of them a huge gash that ran from her hairline to under her chin. "Thanks. I owe you one. For the socks," she added and laughed.

"You're very welcome." Dagmar rubbed the wolf's head and back as he got to his feet. "Take good care of this one. He has a wonderful temperament."

"Only when he's in the mood." She pulled her heavy pack on and headed off. "Good night to you, Dagmar."

"And to you, Eir." She smiled at the wolf. "Good-bye, new friend." The wolf nuzzled her nose and padded off after its handler.

She watched them disappear into the woods until the door of Esyld's house opened. The dragoness walked out, using a wet cloth to wipe blood from her hands. "It's done."

Chapter 16

Izzy stared at her mother. The early morning light poured through the bedroom window she stood in front of, making her look even more beautiful than Izzy already thought she was. All that curly, long black hair and that soft, womanly body. Not at all like Izzy with her giant feet, too-long arms, and absolutely no curves to speak of. There wasn't much about herself that she'd consider womanly . . . or soft.

She was just plain old Izzy whose life was completely unraveling at the moment.

"What do you mean I can't go?"

"Was I unclear in my wording? I'm not sending you off to war. You're barely seventeen winters."

"My eighteenth is a few months off."

"Then it won't be a painfully long wait."

How could her mother be so flippant about this? Everything Izzy had been training for, everything she wanted to do was moments from her grasp. They wanted her to go with one of the legions to fight a baron lord near the Southland coasts. He'd created his own army and was said to be preparing to march on Dark Plains. Annwyl, as always, wanted to attack first.

Izzy's entire training unit would be going, and it could be the perfect opportunity for Izzy to prove her worth to Annwyl. How could her mother just take that from her?

"This isn't fair." She hated that she sounded like a whining child, but it *wasn't* fair!

Talaith sighed and faced the window, looking out over the courtyard. "The world is not fair, Izzy. But you'll go nowhere until I give my leave. And don't bother trying to get your father to change my mind. We went round and round about it for the last two days, and my mind is made up."

Izzy knew if her father couldn't convince her mum, no one could.

Tears filling her eyes, Izzy stormed out of her mother's room and down the castle stairs. Her comrades, a few of her fellow trainees heading off to the coast in the next day or so, called to her as she quickly walked through the courtyard, but she ignored them, wanting to be away. She even heard her father call out to her, but she ignored him as well as she ran out the castle gates and toward the river. Once she reached it, she stopped at a random tree and punched it. Bark flew everywhere and the five-hundred-year-old tree jerked a bit. Then Izzy burst into tears.

None of this was fair. She was a good soldier. Very good. And she had every intention of being the best warrior. She wanted to be the Queen's Champion. Hell, she wanted to be the Queen's General one day. But all that took work and time. Every moment delayed seemed to take her dream farther and farther from her until it was nothing but the pipe dream of a silly girl.

"Why are you crying?"

Izzy turned toward the voice, her gaze rudely examining the girl standing in front of her. She had straight black hair that reached her shoulders and black eyes. She sported a large

wound on one side of her face that appeared nearly healed up
and she wore a chain-mail shirt and leggings but no surcoat.
Izzy would guess they were about the same age, but Izzy
damn well knew better.

"You're a dragon."

"I am. I'm Branwen the Black."

And based on that wound on her face and the other bruises
and scratches, Branwen the Black had been in battle.

Izzy hated her.

"I'm Iseabail, Daughter of Talaith." *The most difficult, uncaring, unfeeling mother in the world!*

The girl stepped closer, not realizing how jealous Izzy was
of her at this very moment. If Izzy had a temper like Annwyl's
she would have hit her by now. Oh, if only she had a temper
like Annwyl's!

"So why do you cry?" she asked.

Izzy swallowed back her tears and anger. "My mum." She
swallowed again, almost losing that battle to her tears. "She
won't let me go off to combat with the rest of my comrades."

"How old are you?"

Izzy glared. "How old are *you*?" she shot back.

"Eighty-three."

"Oh." *Damn.*

Then Branwen grinned. "But for dragons that makes me
about your age, I reckon. And me mum gives me such a hard
time. She acts like I'm still a hatchling. She won't let me go
into any battles by myself. I always have to be by her side. My
brother's not yet a hundred and he gets to go into battle by himself. It's not fair."

"It's not! But they never see that, do they?"

"No, they don't. Becomes a real pain in the arse, doesn't it?"

Izzy finally smiled. "It does."

Branwen looked Izzy up and down.

"So you done crying now, Iseabail, Daughter of Talaith?

Because I must tell you that from experience, tears never work with the mothers. Only the fathers. So why bother?"

Now Izzy grinned. She simply couldn't hate Branwen. "You're right. Why bother? And everyone calls me Izzy."

"All right then, Izzy."

"Oy!" a voice called from a distance behind them. "Branwen! Where are you, you dizzy cow?"

Branwen sighed. "That's me idiot brother and me cousins." She tugged Izzy's arm and together they began to walk. "So what does your father say about you going off to war?"

"He fought on my behalf. I know he did. But if he can't convince my mum . . . no one can." Feeling comfortable, she added, "My father is Briec the Mighty, by the way. Not my blood father, but . . . you understand. My mum's his mate."

"Briec?" Branwen stopped and looked at her, her dark eyes wide. "You're Briec's daughter?"

Her sudden eagerness surprised Izzy a bit. Although Briec's brothers and sisters had been welcoming, the other dragons— "the idiot royals," as her grandfather would always mutter—had been tolerant of her, but she could easily tell they didn't consider her anything but another human and a possible meal.

"Aye," she said with a bit of confidence. "I am."

Branwen slapped Izzy's arm and Izzy grunted in pain. "Well then, you sobbing cow, you're me cousin!"

Izzy blinked. "I am?"

"Aye! I'm a Cadwaladr. Briec's cousin. Me mum is your grandfather's sister. Which makes us second cousins . . . I think. Anyway, we're kin. Ya know? Family."

"All right then." Izzy couldn't ignore Branwen's eagerness. She seemed so happy to know her.

"This is brilliant! Changes everything."

"It does?"

Branwen threw her arm around Izzy's shoulders. "Tell me, cousin, have you ever played Run and Jump?"

"No."

"Well as your older cousin, it's my right to teach it to you. That's the beauty of blood relations."

"Will it upset my mother?"

"Beyond comprehension, I'd wager."

Izzy didn't even hesitate. "Then lead the way, cousin."

He could smell incense and herbs, fresh vegetables, and what smelled deliciously like stew.

Gwenvael slowly looked around him, confused about where he was and yet for some strange reason recognizing this place. It was a house. He'd dreamt about it long ago, yet he knew he'd never been here.

Maybe he wasn't awake after all. He couldn't really tell at the moment. He closed his eyes, but he caught those scents again. And, above them all, he scented her. His nostrils flared and his eyes opened again, his gaze searching her out. She was sitting at a small eating table beside the pit fire built into the wall. She had a metal cup in front of her and her head in her hands. Her head scarf and spectacles lay on the table, and her satchel was at her feet.

Seeing her there, alive and well, did more for him than anything else could.

Her head lifted from her hands and she turned in his direction. He smiled at her, but she didn't smile back. Instead she lowered her head and squinted at him.

"If you can't see me, you lazy sow, put your bloody spectacles on."

Her back straightened and she glared. "I see you perfectly, which is barely at all."

"You're keeping me waiting?"

"Until the end of time."

Gwenvael stuck his lower lip out, shuddered a bit. "But I'm in such pain."

"By all reason, have you no shame?"

"Not an ounce." He held his arm out, hand open for her to take. "Now come here."

Putting her spectacles back on, she rose from the chair and moved across the room. She placed her hand in his, and he tugged her close until she crouched beside him.

"Are you all right?" And he was no longer teasing, because he needed a straight answer to his question.

"I'm fine."

"Good." He kissed her knuckles. "Where are we?"

"The Outerplains between the Southland and Northland territories. By the Aatsa Mountains."

"How the hell did we get here?"

"You brought us here."

"I did? I don't remember."

"What do you remember?"

"Kissing you." He grinned. "In the library stacks."

"That, of course, you couldn't be kind enough to forget."

"Not ever. But do tell me, Lady Dagmar, why do I hurt? Did you try to skin me alive with your hidden passion?"

"My hidden . . . oh. Forget it. You've been through hell the last few hours is what happened. Kidnapped and tortured and a pitch battle with Horde dragons."

"Really?" He lowered his head and his voice. "Am I fiercer to you now that you've seen me in battle? Do you want me more than you ever thought possible? Are you ready to take me at this moment?"

"Perhaps when the scabs fall off."

Not knowing what she meant, Gwenvael looked down at his body. Horrified, he sat up. "What is this? What's happened to me?"

"Calm down. It'll heal quick enough, I'm sure."

"Heal? I'm hideous!"

"You're alive."

"Hideously alive!" He covered her face with his hands. "Don't look at me! Look away!"

"Stop it!" She pulled at his hands. "Have you lost your mind?"

Gwenvael dropped back to the bed, turned his face toward the wall. "You know what this means, don't you?"

"Gwenvael—"

"I'll have to live alone, at the top of a castle somewhere. I'll hide from the daylight and only come out at night."

"Please stop this."

"I'll be alone but not for long because you'll all want me more. You'll lust for the beautiful warrior I once was and pity the hideous creature I've become. Most importantly, you'll want to soothe my pain." He looked at her again. "Don't you want to soothe my pain? Right now? Without that dress on?"

"No. I do not."

Dagmar tried to stand, and Gwenvael caught her hand, pulling her back down. "You can't leave me. I'm tortured and brooding. You need to show me how much you adore me so I can learn to love myself again."

"You've never stopped loving yourself."

"Because I'm amazing."

She yanked her hand away, but Gwenvael simply caught it again and dragged her until she was on top of him.

"Let me go!"

"Not until you kiss away my torturous brooding."

"I'm not kissing anything away." Dagmar froze. "And move your hands, sir."

"But they are warm and comfortable where they are."

* * *

He was impossible! To think she was actually *worried* about him. Why? What was the point of worrying about someone who was insane?

"Get your hands off my rear."

"Not until you kiss me."

"I'm not kissing you."

"It's because I'm hideous!"

"You're not . . ." Why was she arguing with him? Didn't that make her *more* insane than he was? "Release me."

"Kiss me, and I will."

"Fine." She leaned down and planted a quick, closed-mouth kiss on his lips. "There."

"You can do better than that."

"No. I can't. So just—" Dagmar gasped when his hands squeezed her rear through all her layers of gown and undergarments. And with her mouth open, he swooped in, rising up and kissing her hard. In seconds his tongue had invaded her mouth and swirled insistently around hers.

That was all it took. She melted against him, her hands reaching up to frame his face. Her stomach tensed, and everything went wet and warm between her legs.

She wanted him. Beyond reason, she wanted him. No matter how strange, demanding, or annoying he seemed to be.

His grip on her rear tightened almost to the point of pain, but she didn't mind. Nor did she mind when he pulled her so close she could feel the hardness he had for her between his legs. Taking his time, he rocked her sex against his groin, the hands on her ass not only moving her but squeezing her cheeks each time.

She began to groan, the power of a climax beginning to grow inside her.

"What are you doing?" Strong hands grabbed Dagmar's arm and yanked her off Gwenvael.

Stunned, panting, and incredibly aroused, she could only stare at Esyld, unable to speak.

"He's still healing!" the dragoness chastised. "He doesn't have the energy for all that sort of thing."

"She was all over me," Gwenvael chimed in, causing Dagmar's mouth to drop open in shock. "I couldn't stop her."

"Honestly!" Esyld dragged her toward the door, shoved a bucket in her hand. "Go get some water from the well. Perhaps that'll help you cool off and get some control!"

The door slammed in her face and Dagmar could only stand there, staring at it, her mouth still open.

Gwenvael grinned at the dragoness peering at him.

"Do you enjoy torturing her?" she asked.

"Depends on the torture."

She snickered. "I assume you're hungry, Gwenvael."

"I am." He inclined his head. "You look awfully familiar. Have we . . . uh . . . met?"

She rested her hands on her knees and bent at the waist, leaning in close. "Look in my face and say that again. With the same inflection."

Gwenvael did look into her face and he knew what he saw smirking back at him.

His mother.

"I'm feeling really uncomfortable."

"Good. You should." She went to the pit fire and spooned stew into a bowl. "I'm your aunt Esyld."

Gwenvael only knew of one Aunt Esyld and to this day she was still hunted by his kin.

"Then I'm eternally grateful for your help." Gwenvael pushed himself up, his back resting against the metal rails of the bed frame. Air hissed between his teeth, the pain reminding him he had a ways to go before he was back to his old self.

Tell that to his cock, though. He would have taken Dagmar right then and there if his aunt hadn't returned. For his life, he didn't understand that woman's effect on him.

"Surprised I didn't kill you in your sleep?" She handed him the bowl and a spoon.

"There's no good answer for that. So I choose to eat instead."

Esyld pulled a chair close to the bed and sat, crossing one leg over the other. "She said you were smart."

"Do you mean the beautiful Dagmar?"

She frowned. "Beauti—forget it. I mean Keita."

"My sister?" Gwenvael dropped his spoon back into the bowl with a plop. "My sister's been here?"

"More than once. We've become very close." Gwenvael didn't like the sound of that one bit, but before he could say anything about it, "Calm yourself, Gwenvael the Gold. Your sister found me. And I can assure you I have no intention of corrupting her."

"You're still wanted by my mother's court."

"I'm well aware of that. But I have no intention of challenging your mother for her throne."

"Why did Keita come to you?"

"Why else? Because she knew it would drive your mother insane if she ever found out. They get along as well as Rhiannon got along with our mother. Hopefully it will not meet the same end."

Considering Rhiannon had to kill her own mother to secure her throne and protect the life of Bercelak and his family, Gwenvael didn't much appreciate the last part of that statement. "If it does, I'll blame you."

"I'm sure you will. But I want nothing more than what I have, Gwenvael. I don't want her throne or her power. I just want to be left alone."

"If that's all you really want, then let me talk to my mother."

"No."

"You should be in the south, among your own. Not here among the barbarians."

"That's very sweet. And perhaps your mother would seriously consider it. But your father wouldn't. Those kin of his still search for me. If they know I'm here, I won't live another day. So I'd prefer they both knew nothing of my presence."

He couldn't argue with her; she was absolutely right. There were few dragons who took their commitments as seriously as Bercelak the Great. And he had no greater commitment than Queen Rhiannon.

"As you wish. You saved my life; I owe you at least that."

She gestured toward his food. "It's getting cold. Eat."

The stew had cooled, but it was still warm enough and quite satisfying. While he ate, Dagmar returned. "That took you forever," he said around a mouthful.

She slammed the filled bucket on the table and marched across the room. She flicked one of his still-healing wounds.

"Ow!" he cried out, pulling his arm away.

"I had no idea where the well is, you clod. So I've been stumbling all over the place looking for that bloody thing! I could have fallen in for all you lot care!"

"Don't say that, Dagmar. Tonight, tomorrow . . . *eventually* we would have noticed you were gone. Ow!" he cried out when Dagmar flicked another one of his wounds. "Stop doing that!"

Vigholf the Vicious of the Olgeirsson Horde waited impatiently by the Spikenhammer Gardens. A quiet place of beauty and silence that Vigholf would avoid like the plague if he knew of any safer place to talk. But he didn't. His father's spies were everywhere, looking for his betraying son.

That was not Vigholf. As far as his father was concerned, Vigholf was still loyal to him. His brother had begged him to keep that illusion, although it grated on Vigholf's nerves to do so. He was normally such an honest dragon that his mother often hit him in the back of his head with her tail and yelled at him to, *"think before you speak!"*

But to his great disappointment, Olgeir the Wastrel no longer earned his son's devotion. The old dragon had broken the truce they had with the Southlanders and had betrayed one of the warlord dragons he had an alliance with. The Northland Code was all, to dragons like Vigholf. A clear set of rules and guidelines with loyalty being the most important. Yet his father was loyal to no one but himself, so how could he expect others to be loyal to him in return?

Vigholf heard the pounding hooves of his brother's war horse and turned to watch him ride up. It still amazed Vigholf how his brother did that. Most hoofed animals wisely stayed away from their kind because they knew how easy it was to become dinner. But his brother never had that problem. Animals were drawn to him, birds perching on his shoulders, wolves and deer resting at his feet, and horses taking him anywhere he needed to go though he could easily fly.

They'd never been very close growing up, Ragnar the Cunning a confusing mix of brilliant fighting skills with talk of philosophers and Magick. But Vigholf had learned to appreciate the skills his brother held and his true Northland spirit.

"Ho, brother!"

"Vigholf. You have news for me?"

"I do."

His brother dismounted and got his horse to wait simply by sliding the palm of his hand down his forehead.

"Well?"

"I found out why our kinsmen have been heading back to the Horde lair. Da's got himself a prize."

Ragnar's face twisted as if he expected to get punched. "Tell me it's not that bloody Gold again." Then he looked panicked. "Tell me Father doesn't have Dagmar."

His loyalty to that human female had always managed to stun Vigholf. She seemed quite plain and uninteresting to him, but for twenty years Ragnar kept his eye on her. Protecting her when he could, comforting her when he couldn't.

"Calm yourself, brother. It's neither. In fact, our father has gotten himself something much more valuable than one of the Dragon Queen's sons."

"Which is?"

"The Dragon Queen's daughter."

Ragnar stepped close, his excitement evident. "The Dragonwitch? Morfyd?"

"No. The other one."

His brother's face fell. "The slag?"

Vigholf shoved his brother's shoulder. "Don't be a bastard, Ragnar! Not all of us follow the dictates of monks."

"It doesn't make me a monk because I'm a bit choosy about my bed partners. How did he get his claws on her anyway?"

"She was on the wrong side of the Outerplains, it seems."

"Foolish dragoness, and *again* he's breaking the truce by snatching one of their females." Ragnar began to pace. What he always did when he was trying to work something out. "So they're all going back for The Honour."

"Of course. A fresh dragoness to fight for until the last dragon is standing? Who among our kinsmen would miss out on that?"

"When is it?"

"I don't know. Da hasn't given a date yet, which is strange for him. He usually likes to get them mated off and out of his hair as fast as possible. I'm not sure what he's waiting for."

"I know. He wants her to call on her kin. Get them to fly in here to help her, and then he can get his war."

"And every warlord will side with him if they think the queen made the first move. But I don't think the little Red called on anyone. The Gold, her brother—if he knew about his sister, he didn't show it."

"He didn't know. Neither did Dagmar, or she would have told me."

"Even after she found out you'd been lying to her all these years?"

"She has more to gain by giving me information than withholding it. And what I did is not something I'm proud of, brother, so do not speak of it again."

Vigholf had no idea why his brother would let it bother him so, but Ragnar was not an easy dragon to understand.

Ragnar stopped pacing. "The Southland dragons haven't arrived because she hasn't called to them. She's going to try and get out on her own."

"Why the hell would she try that?"

Ragnar faced him, his smile bright. "The beauty, my dear brother, of a mother-daughter relationship."

"What does that mean?"

"It means she'll move heaven, earth, and any number of hells to get out of there without her mother finding out."

Vigholf shook his head. "You're going to use this, aren't you?"

Ragnar threw his arm around his younger brother, giving him a rough hug. "What kind of scheming, plotting bastard would I be if I didn't?"

Gwenvael slept on and off for the rest of the day and well into the night. The scent of more food woke him up, and another meal and a delicious concoction of wine mixed with healing herbs had him up and wandering around his aunt's house. It seemed a large step down for a princess who'd hoped to inherit her mother's throne upon her death—and the death of any other siblings in her way—but Esyld seemed to be quite content.

They chatted for a while, Gwenvael busy bringing her up to date on his kin while leaving out any political talk completely. He left her tying dried herbs together and still laughing when he went out to find where Dagmar had wandered off to.

He found her behind Esyld's house, sitting on an overturned trunk and staring out over a small stream. With bottle of wine and fresh fruit in hand, he walked up to her.

"See?" he teased. "I noticed you were gone."

She jumped at the sound of his voice and kept her head down. "I didn't hear you coming."

"Most don't." He stepped in front of her and examined her closely. Her spectacles were on top of her head, and she was digging in the pocket of her gown for something. She was nervous and sniffling.

Knowing he wouldn't get a straight answer out of her, Gwenvael gripped her chin and tilted it up until she looked him in the eye.

Tears. Real ones.

She jerked away from him. "I'm fine. You can stop looking at me like that."

"Tell me."

"No."

He sat down next to her on the trunk. "I have wine."

She wiped her eyes and ignored him until he opened the bottle and held it out for her.

"It's good wine."

She took the bottle from him and swigged several gulps down. She handed it back to him and muttered, "It's a bit weak."

Gwenvael took a healthy gulp and almost choked it back up. "Weak," he squeaked out. "Definitely."

Locking the top on the bottle, Gwenvael placed it down in

front of them. "Now I want you to tell me everything. Tell me the price you had to pay to free me from the Horde."

She began to sob and when Gwenvael tried to put his arms around her shoulders, she shrugged him off. He felt cold fear grip him. "Gods, Dagmar, what did they do to you?"

Still sobbing, she reached into a hidden pocket of her skirt and pulled out a piece of parchment. She shoved it at him.

He glanced at the seal but didn't recognize it. Quickly tearing it open, he read it. It was written in the ancient language of all dragons; although a few of the letters were penned slightly different, a few of the words possessing different meanings, it was still readable to his eye, if not to a human's like Dagmar.

"It's to my mother. From a Ragnar of the Olgeirsson Horde."

He blinked, raised a brow. "Ragnar? That wouldn't be sweet, caring Brother Ragnar you told me about, would it?"

She nodded, continuing to sob.

Gwenvael winced. "I understand how that could upset you, Dagmar, but I can assure you it's a very common practice. My grandmother attended colleges all over the Southlands as human and no one ever knew."

She pointed at the letter and continued to sob.

"Dagmar, all it says is that he's responsible for me being alive and safe and wants to talk to my mother about an alliance to help him overthrow his father."

When she continued to cry, he went on, "This is standard political crap. I don't understand why you're so upset."

Swallowing back her tears, "We both know this"—she pointed at the parchment in his hand—"is, excuse my father's term, elk shit. We both know he doesn't simply want me to convince you to take me to the Southlands just to get this ridiculous letter into the Dragon Queen's hands."

"So?"

"Which means he really wants me there for another reason. Once I'm there, he'll want me to do something to benefit him."

"Probably true . . . so?"

"And normally, I would jump at the chance. To travel into the Southlands. To meet Queen Annwyl and bargain for a much better deal than I got with *you*."

"That was an excellent deal."

"Normally, I'd lie and connive and do whatever necessary to make you take me into the south."

"But . . ."

More tears began to flow. "But that thing . . ."

"Thing? What thing?"

"That thing . . . in one's head . . . that tells you when something would be wrong to do. It won't let me do it."

Feeling a sudden high level of annoyance, Gwenvael carefully asked, "Do you mean your . . . conscience?"

Her tears turned into hysterical sobs, and she went down on her side, her head dropping into his lap.

"Dagmar! Everyone has a conscience."

"I don't!"

"Of course you do."

"I'm a politician, Gwenvael! Of course, I don't have a conscience. At least I didn't. Now I'm cursed with one. And it's your fault!"

Somehow he knew that last bit would happen.

Why didn't he understand? Why couldn't he see? A conscience made her weak and vulnerable. Another poor female to be taken advantage of. Next thing she knew, she'd be planning parties, begging her father to arrange for suitors, and thinking about having children.

This was a nightmare!

"Stop it," he ordered, grabbing her shoulders and forcing her to sit up. "Stop it right now."

"Just say it. Say that I'm pathetic. That I allowed that bastard to trick me for twenty years and I never realized it and now I have a bloody conscience. Just say that I'm worthless and get it over with."

"I will do no such thing. You have a conscience. You've always had a conscience. You might as well face it."

She scowled at him through her tears. "Liar! I've never had a conscience before now."

"Dagmar, you attacked a dragon that breathes fire because he was going to eat your puppy."

"I had to protect him." And when he smirked, she quickly added, "He has a use."

"Looks a little small to be one of your battle dogs. So what use does he have?"

"Who else would eat up all the scraps off the floor?"

"Dagmar."

"All right, all right. Fine. I have a conscience. There. Happy?"

"Ecstatic." He crouched in front of her and wiped her face with the sleeve of his linen shirt. "Annwyl's going to like you. She doesn't like to think she has a conscience either."

"I'm not going with you, but I will give you the information you need and I have maps that should help."

"Good. You'll bring them with you when we leave for the Southlands in the morning."

He had to know this was dangerous. Ragnar wanted her in the south for a reason, but neither of them knew why. "Don't be foolish, Gwenvael."

"I'm not." He grabbed the wine and settled on the ground, his back against the trunk. He took her hand and tugged her to his side. The thought of sitting on the ground did nothing for her, but it seemed an evening for such things.

Taking a sip, he handed her the bottle. "Before we do

anything, though, I need answers to important questions. Honest, direct answers."

"All right."

"What's coming for Annwyl?"

"Minotaurs."

He sighed. "I asked for honest, direct answers."

"And that's what you got."

"Minotaurs? Standing cows are coming for Annwyl? You want me to believe that?"

"Standing cows that are trained from birth to kill in the name of whatever gods their elders worship."

"Did Ragnar tell you about the Minotaurs?"

"He did. But I heard it from others. I believe it's true."

"Fine. Then I'll believe it's true as well." Gwenvael took another drink of wine. "I have to say the day is getting stranger."

"And your second question?"

"How did you get the name Beast?"

Dagmar rubbed her forehead, the pain of her past returning violently. "And that's important to know why?"

"Tell me."

Dagmar held her hand out. "More wine."

"When I was thirteen," she began, suddenly looking much younger than her thirty winters, "one of my father's nephews came to visit. He was much older than I, but we'd never gotten along. Apparently I was a 'know-it-all bitch who should be tossed into a convent' while he 'should have been strangled at birth and thrown off a mountainside as our ancestors used to do.' Needless to say, when he came to visit this time, we kept our distance. Yet he was never a smart boy and rumors quickly spread that he'd been making fun of me to his men. Telling them I was 'growing into a right beast.' I ignored it, even though my father and brothers had also heard the same rumors. But I didn't say a word or complain. Just didn't see the point.

"One night, a day or so before he was supposed to return to his father's lands, I left the kennels and was about to enter the fortress. I heard one of the servant girls and went around the corner to make sure everything was all right. I didn't like what I saw and she seemed to be even unhappier, so I grabbed my cousin and pulled him away. Angry and drunk, he grabbed my throat and punched me in the face, breaking my spectacles."

"Bastard."

She chuckled, but kept with her story. "As usual, however, I was not alone. I had Canute's great-grandfather with me. As he'd been trained to do, he took my cousin to the ground by the throat and held him there, waiting for my next command." She stopped, took another gulp of wine. "My cousin was begging me to call him off, and by this point my father and three eldest brothers were standing behind me after they'd been fetched by the servants. I looked at my father and said, 'I shouldn't.' He replied, 'But as a Northlander, we all know you will.' I knew what was expected, so I did it." She swallowed. "I gave the command and my dog . . . finished him. The next day my father sent the remains back to my uncle with a note that read, 'A little gift from The Beast.'"

"And that uncle was Jökull?"

She nodded. "And that was Jökull's favorite son. Not long after was the siege that killed my brother's wife."

"You blame yourself."

"Sometimes. I can't help but wonder where we'd be if I'd only given a different command."

"Too late for those thoughts. They don't help. Besides, I don't worry about what I should have done. I only worry about what I'm going to do now."

"Yes. That sounds about right for you."

He got to his feet. "Come on. We need to get ready."

"You still plan to bring me to the Southlands?" She held out her hand and he grabbed it, easily hauling her to her feet. "Seems foolish to me."

"Maybe. We'll see." But he didn't think so. Nothing had ever felt more right before in Gwenvael's life than taking Dagmar Reinholdt to Dark Plains with him.

"I'll need to send my father another letter before we go." She wiped the dirt from the back of her skirt with both hands and gave that wicked little grin he'd learned to enjoy. "And I think I could use your help with wording."

Sigmar shoveled food into his mouth and completely ignored his daughter-in-law. Ever since Dagmar had gone off with the dragon, his oldest boy's wife had been more and more impossible.

It wasn't news that she hated his daughter, but she needed to face the fact that she didn't stand a chance against The Beast. Few did.

"All I'm suggesting is that a marriage between her and Lord Tryggvi would do you very well."

"Is that right?" Sigmar asked, putting down his spoon. "What do you know about him?"

"He's the ruler of Spikenhammer and is an excellent warrior."

"True enough. What else?"

"What else? Well, I know his mother is—"

"His mother? What do I care about his mother? I mean what about him? Which gods does he worship?"

"I don't know. Who cares?"

"You should. What if he worships them gods that demand sacrifices? Human sacrifices," he said before she could mention oxen or deer. "How does he handle crime in his city?

What kind of executions does he run? Does he believe in torture? If so, what kind?"

Her mouth opened and closed several times, but she had no answers.

"That's the difference between you two." He looked at his sons, each of them eating heartily before they headed off for training. "Isn't that right?"

They grunted agreements around their food.

"You don't know those answers, girl, but *she* would. She sure as fuck wouldn't come to me with some half-thought-out idea. She'd have already asked the questions and found the answers." He slammed his finger into his temple several times. "'Cause she *thinks* that one does. Which is more than I can say about you."

She looked at Sigmar's oldest. "You going to let him talk to me that way?"

"Only if he's right. And he's right."

"My lord." One of the servants rushed in. He was the one Dagmar worked closest with, and he now handled many of her duties now that she was gone. He was smarter than most but feared Sigmar enough not to push anything. "Another missive from Lady Dagmar. It seems to be nearly three days old."

"Read it," Sigmar ordered him.

Opening the sealed parchment quickly he began, "'Dearest Father. I hope this letter finds you well. I know I promised to be at Gestur's by now, but there's been another change of plan.'"

Sigmar sighed, leaning back in his seat. "Bloody 'ell."

"A-ha!" His daughter-in-law said, but when they all stared at her, she simmered down.

"Go on," Sigmar prompted.

"'I am heading into the Southlands to meet with Queen

Annwyl personally. I hope to get you at least one more legion. Perhaps two.'"

"Damn that girl."

"Should we go after her?" his oldest asked, motioning to one of the serving girls for more food.

"A few weeks ago I would have said yes. But that monk, Ragnar, stopped by here two days ago and told me Jökull's on the move. I'd feel better if I knew she was someplace else. Even with that"—he sneered—"weeper."

"As would I," his son agreed. "And hopefully she can work her way around the Mad Bitch of Garbhán Isle."

"So you're going to let her get away with disobeying you?" his daughter-in-law nearly screamed.

"Quiet!" He motioned to the servant holding the letter. "Finish it."

"'I know this is not what you wanted to hear from me, but I need you to trust that I'll do what is best for our people.'" That Sigmar already knew. Of *that* he had no doubt and never would. "'Please be safe and think before you act.'"

Sigmar and his sons laughed at that one as the servant continued to read.

"'And Kikka has been having it off with the stablemaster. The Weeper and I watched her get used like a whore for nearly two hours. I am sorry I had to tell you this way, but I thought it was best you know. Yours . . . Dagmar.'"

The entire room had fallen silent, and everyone, even the servants, now gawked at his daughter-in-law.

"She's lying!" she cried desperately.

But no one had any doubts to the truth of what Dagmar had written, and Sigmar knew both his daughter and daughter-in-law well enough to know that if he searched for proof, he'd find more than enough of it.

Such a foolish girl, Sigmar thought as he stood and picked up his favored battle ax. He'd leave his eldest to deal with that wife of his while he dealt with the stablemaster.

As he walked out into the courtyard, eleven of his sons behind him, he did have to chuckle and wonder, *did that stupid girl really think she could take on The Beast—and win?*

Chapter 17

"Dagmar!"

Dagmar instantly sat up, her eyes snapping open, and she yelled, *"I am not lying!"*

The big dragon beneath her sighed. "Wake up, ya dozy cow. We're almost home."

She yawned and stretched, rubbing her hands across her face before digging into her satchel for her spectacles. She'd stopped wearing them an hour into their return flight. Too many times the dragon had dipped or spun to the side in mid-flight, and Dagmar had realized that if she was holding onto the dragon's mane within an inch of her life, she couldn't be expected to make a wild grab for her spectacles as well.

Putting them on, making sure they fit properly behind her ears, she glanced around. "It's beautiful," she finally said. All lush greenery and thick-leafed trees.

"Yes. Nearly as beautiful as I am."

With her hands tangled in his mane, Dagmar leaned over a bit and looked toward one of the many lakes covering the land. "What's going on there?"

The dragon looked down. "By the gods, they actually talked the old bastard into it. Hold on!"

She managed only a yelp before they seemed to be diving

directly at the lake and the dragons surrounding it. Even more horrifying was the dark brown dragon heading right for them. They seemed to be on a collision course, and there was nothing Dagmar could do except grit her teeth and prepare to leap for safety into the lake. Of course, as high up as they were, she'd die on impact, but what choice did she have?

But the pair of dragons stopped with barely an inch between them.

"You idiot bastard! Did you think you could take me on?" the dark brown one demanded.

"Of course I can. But didn't want to have to explain to the queen how I had to kill one of my own blood."

Laughing, they reared up and hugged, which left Dagmar sliding off the dragon's back, the only thing keeping her from falling to her death the grip she had on his hair.

"Falling!" she screamed. "Falling! Falling! Falling!"

"What?" Gwenvael glanced back at her. "Oh!" He went back to a more lateral hover and Dagmar rested against his back, her breath panting out of her.

"Sorry. Forgot you were back there."

"Bastard," she muttered.

The other dragon flew around to look at her. "Well . . . hello." He gave her a smile that she assumed he thought was endearing but, considering the number of fangs in his mouth, was anything but. "I'm Fal of the Cadwaladr Clan. Mightiest dragons of the land."

She heard Gwenvael snort but ignored him. "Dagmar Reinholdt. Of the Northlands."

"A Northland woman? Ho, ho, cousin! You've outdone yourself."

"Shut up."

He held out a long black talon and Dagmar took hold. A sort of dragon-to-human handshake. "I am very glad to meet you, Lady Dagmar." He leaned in a bit, his snout extremely close. "Whatever this golden bastard has told you is a lie and *I'm* the pretty one."

"I already know that, and I'm sure you are." She winked at him, and Fal laughed.

"I like her, cousin."

"Mitts off, boy. She's under my protection."

"Is she?" Fal looked at her and back at Gwenvael. "Isn't that what humans call putting the wolf in charge of the barn?"

"You're still talking. I still hear you talking."

Worried these two might get into a friendly family battle that would leave her dead next to the lake, Dagmar cut in, "You know, I'd love to have the ground beneath my feet once more before I die."

"What?" Gwenvael asked. "Oh! Sorry. Sorry." He bumped his cousin. "Move, you big-headed bastard. I need to get my lady to safety."

"I'd stop here first before heading to the castle. Unless my lady is afraid of so many dragons in one place?"

Dagmar sniffed. "I've tolerated him for far longer than I thought I'd have to. I'm certain I can handle anything at this point."

"What's that mean?"

But Fal was laughing. "I like her. She'll do fine here. Come on!" The brown headed down and Gwenvael followed.

"I like your cousin," Dagmar said offhandedly and was shocked when Gwenvael abruptly stopped.

"And he's a whore, so keep away from him."

"But"—Dagmar tapped her chin—"Ragnar told me you're The Defiler."

"It's *Ruiner*. Stop getting it wrong. And I have boundaries. My cousin has none. So no matter what he tells you, he's simply trying to get under your skirt."

Having never been warned off a male before, Dagmar sat back and enjoyed herself. "But what if I don't mind him being under my skirt? What if I'd, in fact, like him to be under my skirt?"

"If you suddenly decide you simply must have someone under that skirt, you're to let me know."

Dagmar felt a sharp thrill. The dragon hadn't kissed her or anything else since that time on Eslyd's bed. For the three days they'd been traveling together he'd been polite, protective, and extremely chatty, but he'd never touched her. She'd assumed he'd simply lost interest as she knew males of every species would do no matter how beautiful or not a woman might be.

"I'm to let you know? And why is that again?"

"Because you're safe among my kin now, Beast, which allows me to focus on getting what I need." He glanced back at her. "What we both need, I'd wager."

"You really so sure?"

"As a matter of fact, Lady Dagmar"—Dagmar squeaked when she felt Gwenvael's tail slap her rear—"I'm quite sure."

Gwenvael wanted to shift to human as soon as he landed and get Dagmar back to the castle, but his family swarmed over him and before he knew it he was in the midst of hugs and slaps on the back that nearly broke his spine in two. Some of his kin he hadn't seen in quite a while, but it would be hard for anyone to tell, they'd so easily fallen back into their comfortable camaraderie.

While he greeted his kin, he kept a watchful eye on Dagmar. Although she appeared completely out of place, she didn't seem unnerved or frightened by the dragons surrounding her. She didn't try to hide or get herself to a safe place behind a tree. She simply stood there. His little self-contained volcano.

For nearly three nights he'd been alone with Dagmar. For nearly three nights he went out of his way not to make her feel uncomfortable or unsafe. And for three days his cock insisted on telling him what an idiot he was. Yet she was entrusting him with her life, even after finding out about the Lightning's betrayal.

He wouldn't take that trust for granted.

Glancing down, he watched as Dagmar wandered comfortably among his kin, her steady gaze focused on the ground. She'd stop, stare at something, and move on. Finally, when he pulled away from one of his many cousins and saw her doing it again, he had to ask, "What are you doing?"

"Comparing."

"Comparing what?"

She looked up at him, her brows drawn together in a slight frown. "Why is your tail different from the others?"

In a group that was never silent, the sound of small birds could suddenly be heard.

"They all have this sharp spike at the end," she said while pointing at one of his cousins' tail. "Except yours." He saw her fighting that wicked smile when she asked, "Were you *born* this horribly deformed? Or are all the royals missing basic defenses all other dragons are gifted with?"

Fal leaned forward before his cousin could and began, "What you need to do, my lady, is ask his brothers—"

Grabbing one of Fal's horns, Gwenvael twisted and yanked his cousin back, sending him skidding into the lake.

"Let's go." He motioned at Dagmar with his talon.

"Aren't you going to answer my very innocent question?"

"No, cheeky wench." He slapped her ass with his "horribly deformed" tail. "Now walk!"

"Gwenvael! Gwenvael!"

He turned, looking for the voice he knew so well, already getting an uncomfortable feeling in the pit of his stomach.

"Up here!"

Slowly Gwenvael raised his eyes to the sky—and cringed. "Iseabail! What in all the hells are you doing?"

She grinned. "Flying!"

Yes. She was. And her mother would have a fit. Izzy wasn't even on the back of one of the older dragons but had found her way to the youngsters . . . and Celyn, son of Gwenvael's battle-honored Aunt Ghleanna. He would be a fine and well-known warrior one day when he came into his own. Until then he was like every other male of the Cadwaladr Clan at that age: lusty.

"Get down from there!"

"What? Can't hear you!"

He rolled his eyes as Celyn winked and did an impressive dip that had Izzy squealing and laughing.

"Stop worrying, nephew. We won't let anything happen to Briec's girl."

He looked at his aunt Ghleanna. Her black hair with the silver streaks of age was cut short, ready for battle as always, battle scars littering the face and torso of her dragonform.

"Her mother doesn't want her flying. And I don't want her flying with Celyn."

"Celyn knows she's family. And she and Branwen have become fast friends. Besides, we'll watch out for her." She motioned him away with her front claws. "Go. Take your lady to the castle and see your sister. I know she's been worried for you."

He smiled and leaned in, kissing her cheek. Before pulling back, he whispered, "She's young, Ghleanna. Too young for Celyn."

"She's not as young as you'd like to believe," she whispered back. "But I think we both know her heart belongs to another."

Startled, Gwenvael leaned back and asked, "It does?"

She laughed and shoved his shoulder, nearly sending him flying. "Go on with ya, boy."

Gwenvael took one last look at his niece, wincing when she raised her arms in the air and cheered when she should be holding on to Celyn with both hands.

No. Best not to think about it. But he would need to let Briec know to keep an eye out. Izzy listened to him above all others.

"All right, Beast, let's go." He motioned Dagmar forward with his claw. "Time for you to meet the queen."

They had an array of human clothes lined up right outside the gates of Garbhán Isle, and yet none of the peasants or entering travelers went near them. They all seemed to know they were clothes for the dragons.

It must have been odd, Dagmar realized, for the Southland humans to suddenly realize they had dragons living among them so casually. As it was, Dagmar was still getting used to it. Believing a being existed was quite different from finding out you'd been tutored by at least one for the last twenty years.

Gwenvael changed into his human clothes, and they entered Garbhán Isle through the massive iron gates. It was then that Dagmar decided she might have actually chosen well with this ally. She didn't know firsthand what Garbhán Isle was like under the former warlord's rule, but now it was a thriving city, pulsating with power—and soldiers. Merchants sold everything from fruits, vegetables, and meats, to furs, and jewels, to more weapons than she could ever imagine. Weapons not only for humans but for dragons as well. In fact, there seemed to be just as many items for dragons as humans, ranging from whole skinned cows and deer for dinner to enormous lances made from the finest steel for battle.

"It's all amazing, isn't it?" Gwenvael asked her, his hand against her back as he led her through the large crowds of soldiers, travelers, merchants, and peasants.

"It is that."

"I hope my family wasn't too overwhelming back there by the lake," he murmured as he gently led her around two arguing merchants.

"I find it amusing you'd ask that after meeting my kinsmen."

He chuckled, his hand lingering on her waist as he pulled her to a stop. "Now before we go inside—"

"Gwenvael!" The trio of shrieks startled Dagmar, and she turned in time to see three young and rather attractive women throw themselves onto the Gold, their arms wrapping around his neck, shoulders, and chest. They squealed again, showering his face with kisses.

Dagmar glanced around and quickly surmised they were in a section of the market where sex was sold. She rolled her eyes, wondering why the idiot couldn't have found a less obvious place to have a chat.

Remembering each woman's name, Gwenvael greeted them kindly and kissed each on the cheek. He asked questions about their children and business, surprising Dagmar with his knowledge of their personal lives. Her brothers barely knew the camp girls' names, much less whether they had children or not.

Dagmar turned when she felt a tug on her sleeve, a human male standing next to her. "Yes?"

"Yeah, how much for the blonde?"

Dagmar blinked, glanced back at Gwenvael and the three girls before asking, "Pardon?"

"The blonde. How much for the blonde? The bigger one. Just for an hour or so?"

Of course. Dagmar would never be one of the whores . . . she must be *selling* the whores.

"Five coppers for an hour," she replied. "Any more than that and it'll cost you."

"An hour will do." He reached into his pocket and handed

her five copper pieces. She dropped them into her satchel, tapped Gwenvael on the shoulder, and said, "He's bought you for an hour of sex. Enjoy."

She walked off, heading toward another set of gates that would lead her to more stables, more soldiers' quarters, a main courtyard, and, eventually, the queen's castle. But she laughed when the man behind her yelled, "Wait one damn minute!"

Why was *she* the villain in this scenario? Why was she the one everyone was clucking their tongues at when all she wanted to do was protect her only daughter?

For the last three days she'd heard nothing but pleas on Izzy's behalf, as if Talaith had ordered her execution. It was unfair, and she was tired of it. She was especially tired of her mate. As much as she loved him, there were some days she knew she'd have no trouble kicking the living crap out of him.

Why could no one remember? Izzy was her only child and would remain her only child. The Nolwenn witches of Alsandair were only allowed one child by the gods. It was the price her ancestors had agreed to for their longevity and power.

"I don't want to talk about this anymore," she snapped at Briec, storming past him and out of their room.

"You can't keep walking away from this conversation," he said from behind her. "You will have to face this. And I'm thinking you'll have to face this soon."

"There is nothing to face. She can stay here, protect these borders. It was only seven months ago that we were under attack."

"That was a completely different situation and you know it. And staying here is not what Izzy wants."

Talaith cut through the Great Hall, pushing past some sad-faced, grey-cloaked traveler standing around looking confused and lost. Most times she'd question a stranger's presence, but she was too annoyed to really notice and went straight outside, Briec still on her heels.

"She's a child," she reminded her mate for, perhaps, the ten-millionth time.

"She's a warrior. Or she will be."

"She's a child." *Her* child, dammit, but everyone kept forgetting that. "I don't care how good she is with a sword or a spear or anything else she's trained with. A real battle is very different from taking on someone wearing protective padding."

"I know that. But she'll never learn how to survive in a real battle without being in one. And where the hell are you going?"

"For three days your family has been down by the lake, and no one has properly greeted them. I told Fearghus I'd handle it since none of you could be—" Briec caught her arm and spun her around so fast she didn't even finish her sentence.

"He did what?"

Before Talaith could tell her mate to get his damn hands off of her, Gwenvael walked up to them. "Ho, brother!"

"Shut up," Briec snarled, immediately turning his attention back to her.

"And I'm so glad to be back, too!" Gwenvael went on cheerfully. "And it means so much everyone cares that I suffered such pain and nearly died while trying to protect our secrets."

"We have no secrets, you idiot."

Talaith yanked her arm away from Briec's grip and went on her toes to kiss Gwenvael's misleadingly sweet face. "Hello, handsome."

"My sweet, sweet Talaith. Did you miss me?"

"Every day and night, my love."

Gwenvael had grown on her as no other oversexed male ever had before. There was a lot of heart hidden behind so much idiocy.

"Morfyd's waiting for you," Briec snapped. "Now piss off."

Talaith pinched Briec's arm.

"Ow!"

"Be nice! And stop snarling and snapping at everyone. What exactly is wrong with you?"

"Don't yell at me."

"I'm not yelling at you! *Trust me*," she yelled, *"you'll know when I'm yelling!"*

She stalked off, Briec right behind her, both of them ignoring Gwenvael's ominous warning: "I wouldn't go down to the lake if I were you."

"Talaith, slow down!"

"No. I'm done with this conversation, and you."

She went through the first gate, pushing against the flow of foot traffic in the market, until she made it out the second gate and into the surrounding forests. She headed toward the biggest lake that was closest to Garbhán Isle. Fearghus had told her that was where she could find his family.

"I can handle this," Briec demanded gruffly.

"No, Briec. You can't. Gwenvael's been gone near on two weeks in dangerous enemy territory, he's covered in all sorts of scars, and still you couldn't keep a civil tongue in that fat head of yours when speaking to him. So I will handle this, and you'll piss off!"

Talaith stomped past the line of trees and out onto the clearing by the lake. The Cadwaladr Clan had made themselves quite at home. She'd never seen so many dragons lounging around in both human and dragon form. They all seemed to be talking at once. Or was it arguing? She really couldn't tell since they seemed to be yelling everything. They reminded her of a tree filled with crows. Chatty, squawking crows.

"I'll deal with them," Briec said, trying to pass her.

"Oh, no." She grabbed his arm and stepped in front of him

to stop his progress, her back to the other dragons. "Fearghus specifically said you're *not* to deal with them."

His violet eyes narrowed. "When did you two become so damn chummy?"

"Stop barking at me!"

"I'll bark at you all I want! And another thing . . . I . . . I . . ." His gaze had traveled past her—and up.

"What's wrong?" She'd never seen such a blank expression on his face before. As if he didn't know what to make of whatever it was he saw.

"Please," he said calmly, too calmly, "for the love of all that's holy, don't turn around."

That didn't sound remotely good, so that's exactly what Talaith did.

Her eyes searching, she looked at the crowd of dragons and saw nothing, but then she heard it. That giggle she'd known only a short time but had learned to love more than anything else in her world. Terrified of what she'd see, but knowing she had to see, Talaith raised her gaze to the open skies. Her mouth opened and she stared in shock as she watched her daughter—again her *only* daughter—charge across the back of some dragon Talaith had never seen before. And then to add to the horror, Izzy didn't stop running. No, she simply kept going. Right over that dragon's back and neck until she reached his head . . . and that's when she dived right off.

And just when Talaith assumed her daughter was committing some sort of ritual suicide, she crashed onto another dragon that had come up under the first. Unfortunately, she lost her seat and slid right off. Grabbing hold of his mane, she held on while he zigged and zagged through the sky.

All of this on its own was nightmarish enough. Truly, it was. But the fact that Izzy was laughing and goading the dragon on did nothing but make it all that more terrifying. Well, terrifying at least for Talaith.

Because who, in their right minds, enjoyed this? As it was, Briec still had to find ways to trick Talaith onto his back for a simple ride to his den.

Another dragon flew under the one Izzy held on to, and that's when Izzy released her grip on the mane. Her body fell toward the next dragon, but one of them must have miscalculated because she slammed against his side and went flipping off. Her body spiraled and plummeted to earth until a black-haired dragon raced forward and caught hold of Izzy in her talons.

That's when Izzy screamed. Not in fear or panic—as Talaith would have truly appreciated at this moment to prove her daughter had an ounce of common sense—but in unabashed joy. Pure, unadulterated enjoyment of what she was doing.

"Talaith?" She felt Briec's hand on her back. "Talaith, love, you've stopped breathing. I need you to breathe."

"I—" She motioned to his kin. "You—"

"I'll deal with them."

She nodded, still unable to speak or form a coherent thought. Then she turned and stumbled back to the castle, trying the whole time not to throw up.

Dagmar wandered through the castle since she found herself in no mood to wait for Gwenvael's appearance. Especially since part of her worried that he *wouldn't* appear at all, and the thought of him with those women did nothing but annoy her.

She noticed right away that nothing about this place seemed royal. There were expensive tapestries here and there and marble flooring in certain hallways. But otherwise . . . It reminded Dagmar of her father's house. There were weapons at the ready in nearly every room, in nearly every corner. And a few weapons adorned the walls, but Dagmar had to smile when she saw that some still had dried blood on them. A slightly less frightening way to threaten one's enemies when the heads you have outside your walls had become nothing more than crumbling bone.

She also noticed that everyone seemed rather . . . casual. Dagmar had expected a lot more pomp and circumstance from the Queen of Dark Plains and her royal court. A lot more scurrying servants and whispered court drama. There didn't seem to be any of that.

In fact, the more she wandered, the more Dagmar wanted to meet the infamous Blood Queen. But first, she'd have to track down Gwenvael. She'd have to tidy up before she could be presented to a queen. She was covered in traveler dirt, and her poor cloak and dress needed a good scrubbing. Grinning, she wondered if her recently earned five coppers could get her an already-made gown. Nothing fancy, of course, but a less heavy material that would be presentable for her first court appearance.

Dagmar walked past a room and then stopped. She immediately walked back and glanced in. The library. A very nice one, too, although a bit small. She wandered in and began to study the books on the shelves. Lots of fictional work here. Not really to Dagmar's tastes, but she usually read everything she could get her hands on. She turned a corner and found books on history and philosophy. This was definitely more along the lines of what she enjoyed reading, especially when she found a rare copy of *The Battle Strategies of Dubnogartos*. He was one of the greatest warlords of the long-dead Western armies. And although some of his methods were outdated, to know how the man thought and strategized was a boon she simply couldn't pass up.

Grabbing the book, Dagmar began to carefully skim through the pages. Finding it old but beautifully maintained, she immediately began to look for a chair to sit in so she could read a few pages . . . or chapters. Just a few. She went deeper into the library, surprised to find that it wasn't very wide but awfully deep. Near the back, where daylight from the front windows no longer crept in, Dagmar followed the candlelight. As she came around the corner, she saw her. A woman sitting at a table, her elbows resting on the wood, her face, chest, and arms all that could be seen in the dim candlelight. She had a book open at midpoint in front of her and several lit candles on the table. But she wasn't reading . . . she was crying.

Not wanting to interrupt—or be forced to comfort anyone—Dagmar began a quiet retreat. But she hit a loose floorboard and the woman's head snapped up.

Dagmar winced. The poor woman had been crying for a while. "I'm sorry. I was just—"

"It's all right." The woman wiped her face with her hands. "Just having a moment." Rubbing the back of her hand against her dripping nose, she asked, "What are you reading?"

"Oh. Uh . . . *The Battle Strategies of Dubnogartos.*"

Her face lit up and Dagmar suddenly saw all the scars that the dim lighting had been hiding. "Great book," she enthused. "His battle against the Centaurs at Hicca . . . bloody amazing read."

She motioned to a chair. "You can sit down if you like. I'm done with my crying fit, I think."

Dagmar slowly walked over to the table. "Rough morning?"

"You could say that."

Dagmar pulled out the chair across from the woman and sat down, placing the book on the table.

She watched as the woman let out a sigh and stretched her neck. But it was when she again raised her hands to wipe her face that Dagmar saw them—from her wrist to her forearm, on both arms.

The woman raised a brow. "Something wrong?"

"Uh . . ." Dagmar couldn't stop staring and finally she blurted out, "You're Queen Annwyl. Aren't you?" If nothing else, the dragon brands burned into her arms gave it away. Only a monarch would be brave enough to wear those markings for the world to see.

"Some days. But you can call me Annwyl."

This softly sobbing woman was the Queen of Dark Plains?

And Dagmar began to wonder if her arranged alliance with this monarch had been a bit hasty. Her father needed a strong leader as his ally, not some whimpering mess hiding in a library. It was true enough, she knew, that being with child was hard on any woman, but even Dagmar's sisters-in-law hid their misery better than this.

"And you are . . . ?"

"Dagmar," she said quickly, realizing she had to hide any disappointment she may have at the moment. "Dagmar Reinholdt."

The queen frowned. "I don't recognize you, but that name sounds awfully familiar."

"Dagmar Reinholdt. Only Daughter of The Reinholdt."

"Dagmar? You're a woman."

She couldn't help but smile. "Yes. I'm also called The Beast, in some parts."

"I was unaware that The Reinholdt had any daughters." She leaned in a bit. "How did you get here?"

"Oh. Gwenvael brought me."

It was strange watching it. That soft, sweet, scar-covered face so quickly and brutally becoming hard and very, *very* angry.

The queen's fist slammed down against the thick wood table, and Dagmar felt it bend under the pressure, heard the sound of it splintering.

"That idiot!"

It took her a bit, to get that bulk up and out of its seat, but she managed without any help, her rage giving her a fluidity Dagmar guessed was denied the queen at most times. Then she lumbered off, words pouring out of her mouth that made

Dagmar's brothers seem more like holy priests than the salty warriors of the Reinholdt Clan.

She sat there a moment, letting out a breath. "So that's the Blood Queen." She knew now the rumors were true . . . The woman was completely insane.

"Oh!" Her hand covered her mouth as she realized what she'd done. "Gwenvael!"

Then she was up and running.

"Is there something wrong with you? Beyond that which we already know of?"

Gwenvael looked at his sister, the piece of fresh fruit he'd just taken off her plate still in his hand. "Huh?"

Morfyd sat down at the table where battle plans and decisions regarding Annwyl's kingdom were made on a daily basis.

"What possessed you to bring her here?"

"I had no choice."

"What do you mean you had no choice?"

"How was I going to find out why that Lightning wants her here if I didn't bring her with me? Of course"—he glanced around—"I seemed to have misplaced her. But I'm sure I'll find her again."

Morfyd rubbed her eyes and took another breath. "Gwenvael, she is the *Only* Daughter of The Reinholdt. And the Northland men are intensely, almost rabidly, protective of their daughters. And you just traipse off with one."

"I didn't traipse. There was no traipsing. And I don't know why you're so angry at—"

"Don't speak." She held her hand up, palm facing him. "Just don't speak. We have to figure out what we're going to tell Annwyl before she finds out"—the door slammed open behind them, Annwyl glowering at them both—"on her own."

"You idiot!"

"Annwyl! My heart!"

Annwyl stalked across the room, her belly leading the way. Actually, her rage led the way, her belly right behind it. "What the hell were you thinking?"

"Well—"

"Don't speak!" Morfyd cut in. "Just don't speak."

Dagmar charged into the room after Annwyl. She was out of breath and slightly sweaty. Did the woman exercise anything besides her manipulation skills? *Weak as a kitten.*

"If you could just give me a moment, Your Majesty," she panted out. "I can explain what brings me here."

Gwenvael snickered. "She called you 'Majesty.'"

Annwyl hit him on the forehead with the flat of her hand. "Ow!"

"How do you do that?" Annwyl demanded of Gwenvael. "How do you convince them to take the blame for you?"

"It's all in the hands," he countered.

"I assure you I'm not taking the blame for anything, Your Maj—"

"Call me that again, and I'll tear you open from bowels to nose. It's Annwyl, you sod."

Gwenvael saw Dagmar's eyes narrow, her nostrils flare, and he quickly jumped in before the little barbarian could say something that would forfeit her head. "Tell them how you blackmailed me."

Dagmar's back snapped straight, Annwyl's rudeness immediately forgotten. "What?"

"She's just using me," he explained to Annwyl. "Using me to get to you."

Adjusting her frames, Dagmar said, "It's time for you to stop talking."

"I don't want to."

"But you will stop talking."

"We're on my territory now, Beast. You can't strut around here and pretend you rule all—"

"Quiet."

"But—"

She raised her right forefinger.

"She—"

Dagmar raised that damn forefinger higher.

"It's just—"

Now she brandished both forefingers. "Stop."

He gave Dagmar his best pout, which she completely ignored, turning her back on him to again face Annwyl. "Think there might be some place *private* we can talk, my lady?"

Gwenvael's mouth dropped open. "Did you just dismiss—"

Dagmar held up that damn forefinger again but didn't even bother to look at him when she did.

Annwyl's grin was wide and bright. A smile Gwenvael hadn't seen from her in far too long. "Right this way, Lady Dagmar."

"Thank you." Dagmar brusquely snapped her fingers at Gwenvael. "And don't forget to bring my bags up once I get a room, Defiler."

Annwyl fairly glowed as she followed Dagmar from the room, her smile growing by the second. Gwenvael faced his sister. "It's Ruiner, which is a vast difference."

"Uh . . ."

"So get it right!" he yelled at the empty doorway. He shook his head, fighting his smile. "Rude cow."

His sister stared at him so long he began to worry. "What?" He brushed his hands over his face. "Is something marring my beauty? Besides these hideous scars that I received while protecting those I love?"

"You like her."

"I like everyone. I'm filled with joy and love and—"

"No. Nitwit. You *like* her."

"Don't be ridiculous. She's not even the kind of female I'd be attracted to."

"Because she can construct and verbally repeat full and complete sentences?"

"That's top of my list."

Morfyd leaned forward. "Good gods . . . you haven't fucked her. Have you?"

"What kind of language is that from my sister?" He wagged his finger at her. "It's that Brastias. A bad influence. I know something's going on there. I'll find out."

"Don't try to turn this on me. You like a girl."

"I do not."

"You do. You like her."

"Shut up."

Laughing, Morfyd pushed away from the table and stood. "This is a great day in Dark Plains! I must trumpet it from the rooftops!"

"You'll do no such thing. And does no one care that I had a near-death experience with Lightnings?"

"No!" his sister crowed, still laughing as she left the room.

"Your betrayal will not be forgotten!" he cried dramatically.

The statement would have meant more, however, if someone was there to witness it.

Chapter 18

Dagmar couldn't believe the room the servants led her to, with the queen and Lady Morfyd following behind—laughing hysterically. She had no clear idea what they found so amusing, but she was used to the ways of bitchy women. She'd lived with a group of them for years. Yet for her people and her father, she'd suck it up and pretend that she was no better than they were.

The room she was to use as her own for the next few days was enormous, with a huge bed, a table that could be used as a desk or for eating, a pit fire built right into the wall, several plush chairs of different styles, several straight-back chairs, a big standing chest filled with drawers that could hold anything she may have, a large claw-footed tub she couldn't wait to make use of, and a standing washbasin.

"This is wonderful," she said, pivoting in a circle. When she'd spun completely around, she found Lady Morfyd whispering to the queen and the queen leaning against the wall so she could be held upright while *Her Majesty* howled in laughter.

This was almost as bad as her first meeting with Gwenvael.

"We're done, Lady Annwyl," one of the servants said.

"Good. Have food sent up and—" She took a long look at Dagmar before adding, "Fannie."

"Right away."

The servant left and Morfyd helped Annwyl to one of the chairs. Once the queen sat down, she said, "I have to say, Lady Dagmar, and I mean this very deeply . . . I love you."

Now Dagmar was beginning to panic. "Uh . . . my lady—"

"The bit with the forefingers. I thought he was going to break a blood vessel."

The laughter started all over again, so badly that Morfyd had to sit on the floor and Annwyl kept trying to stop.

"We've got to stop, I'm about to have an accident."

"But the look on his face!"

"That was the best part!" Then Annwyl started laughing all over again.

That's when Dagmar understood. They weren't laughing at her. Not at all.

There was a knock on the door, and a woman at least a

decade older than Dagmar stepped in. "My lady? You asked for me?"

"Aye, Fannie." Annwyl wiped tears from her face and took a breath. At least now she was no longer crying from sadness. "This is Lady Dagmar Reinholdt. While she's here, I want you to help her with what she needs."

"Of course."

Annwyl relaxed back in her chair. "Tell her what you need."

Dagmar had no idea what to ask for. Ask for too much or the wrong thing and she could alienate Annwyl. And considering the monarch nearly snapped Dagmar's neck for using her proper title, this was a far bigger risk than she'd imagined.

Dagmar stared at the kind-faced servant, and Fannie leaned back a bit so she could examine Dagmar closely.

"Water for a bath, fresh clothes, and I believe food is already being sent up," Fannie suggested.

Dagmar nodded in agreement. "That's fine."

"Wait." Annwyl pointed at her. "I thought you told Gwenvael you had bags. Should I send someone to—"

Wincing, Dagmar shook her head. "Uh . . . I was . . . I was just being rude. I don't have any bags."

The four women glanced back and forth among them, and then, the laughter started all over again. Only this time Dagmar happily joined in.

Gwenvael walked into the queen's bedchamber. Fearghus sat at a desk, writing. Éibhear on the floor with a book in his lap.

"Does no one care that I'm not dead?"

Éibhear looked up and smiled. "I care."

"You don't count."

Fearghus spoke to Gwenvael without pausing in his self-important scribbles. "Why are the servants telling me you brought back a trophy from the north?"

"She's not a trophy." He sat down on the bed. "She's more a toy for my amusement."

Éibhear snickered until Fearghus glared at him.

The eldest of the siblings placed down his quill and turned in his chair to focus on Gwenvael. "I know I'm going to regret asking, but what the hell is going on?"

"You're right. You're going to regret asking."

The door opened and Briec walked in. He saw Gwenvael and slammed the door behind him. "Thanks for the warning about Izzy, you idiot."

"I did warn you, but you were too busy doing the Briec-Talaith form of oral sex to hear me."

"Well, if you thought she was mad before . . ." he announced to the room.

Fearghus rested his elbows against his knees. "What happened with Izzy?"

Briec went face down on the bed, mumbling something into the fur covering it.

"What?"

He lifted his head. "I said, 'she was playing Run and Jump.'"

Fearghus cringed. "And Talaith saw her? Gods."

"You forgot the best part," Gwenvael added. "She was playing Run and Jump with Celyn."

Briec buried his head back into the bedding while Fearghus sat up straight, scowling. "That dirty little bastard."

"My thoughts exactly, brother. I say we go out there and kick the shit out of him."

Éibhear let out a bored sigh. "Who cares?"

Gwenvael looked at Fearghus, Fearghus looked at Briec, and Briec's head popped back up off the bed.

Leaning over the foot of the bed, Gwenvael asked, "What was that?"

"I said 'who cares?'"

"You don't?"

"No. I don't."

"He's such a liar," Gwenvael mouthed to Fearghus.

"I know!" Fearghus mouthed back.

Éibhear slammed his book closed. "And whatever you two bastards are doing, stop it."

Dagmar soaked in the tub, her hair and body scrubbed clean. And while she relaxed in the steaming water, Annwyl and Lady Morfyd ate from large platters of food placed on the table in front of them.

Morfyd, it turned out, was another bloody dragon in disguise, and Gwenvael's older sister. She was beautiful with long white hair and a long, lean body, easily seen once she pulled off the voluminous witches' robes she wore and relaxed at the table in a thin pale pink gown. She was nothing like Gwenvael, however; that was clear enough. Sweet, borderline shy, and soft-spoken, she didn't seem to have anything in common with her sibling.

"Here." Morfyd handed her a small plate piled with food easily eaten without utensils. "A little something while you relax."

"Thank you." Dagmar popped a round ball of fried dough into her mouth and sighed.

Oh, yes, she could definitely get used to this.

"Minotaurs?" Annwyl asked again. "I didn't think they existed."

"You said the same thing about Centaurs," Morfyd reminded the monarch, "until you got that hoof to the back of the head."

"She snuck up on me," Annwyl snarled between clenched teeth. And, just as quickly, her anger faded and she held up a bottle. "Wine, Dagmar?"

"Yes, please."

The queen poured a chalice of wine, and Dagmar asked what had been perplexing her for some time. "Why do they want you dead? It's the question I haven't been able to get answered."

"That's easy—" Annwyl began, but Morfyd quickly cut her off.

"It's vey complicated. There's much that leads us to this point. So I will start from the beginning—"

"Fearghus knocked me up," Annwyl blurted out.

"Gods dammit, Annwyl!" Morfyd exploded.

"That's the main part of the story."

"I'm not sure why it matters." Dagmar picked up another piece of baked something or other and nearly melted away in her bath it tasted so delicious.

"Gwenvael didn't tell you who Fearghus is, did he?"

"He's Annwyl's consort."

"And our brother."

Dagmar swallowed her food. "So he's a . . ."

"Yes."

"But Annwyl is . . ."

"Yes."

"How is that possible?"

"Again," Morfyd said patiently. "It gets very complex. If we look back at history and the beginning of—"

"The god Rhydderch Hael has been playing with my insides."

"Gods dammit, Annwyl!"

"You're taking too bloody long!"

"Before this gets ugly," Dagmar easily coasted in, "perhaps we should discuss the tunnels I told you about?"

Morfyd studied her closely and asked, "Does it not bother you?"

She knew she didn't mean the tunnels. "Bothered by what?"

"The soon-to-happen unholy birth of Annwyl's spawn?"

"Oy!" Annwyl objected.

"Pardon?" Dagmar asked before popping another delicious something in her mouth.

"No offense, Dagmar, but so far every human who's been told about Annwyl's pregnancy without the necessary backstory has been quick to label Annwyl a whore and her babes demons. Yet you don't seem to care."

"Am *I* carrying her children?" Dagmar inquired while licking her fingers.

Morfyd raised a white brow. "Not that I'm aware."

"Then to quote my father, 'I really don't give a battle-fuck.'"

Annwyl coughed up whatever she'd just put in her mouth, hitting Morfyd in the face.

"I do, however, have concerns over those tunnels, so we'll focus on that."

Gwenvael stretched his legs out and wiggled his toes. "I'm so exhausted. All that bloody flying."

"Don't sleep yet," Briec said, comfortably sitting next to him. "You have to come to the dinner tonight, or you'll never hear the end of if it from the aunts."

"Do I have to?"

"Don't whine," Fearghus snapped, sitting next to Briec. "And yes, you have to. At the very least you need to entertain your Northland guest. And I still haven't heard why you brought her here."

"Because that Lightning wants her here, and until I find out why he wants her here—here she stays."

"You just want to fuck her."

"Yes," he hissed at Briec's question. "But that's not all. She's extremely smart and has a delightful sense of evil that I truly appreciate."

"And you want to fuck her."

He sighed. "Is it too much to ask that my brothers take their minds from the gutter and into the fresh air?"

"Watch your back, Gwenvael," Fearghus warned. "She has been chumming around for twenty years with Olgeir's son."

"She didn't know."

"So she says. But at the end of the day, you have to remember, she is and always will be a Northlander. They live by a different set of rules than we do."

"I know. They have a Code. How come we don't have a code?"

"We can't get you to adhere to the general rules of decency . . . how do we enforce a code?"

"Good point." Gwenvael looked between his brothers. "One more time?"

They nodded in agreement.

"All right. On three. One, two . . . *three*!"

All three of them stood and as quickly dropped back down, slamming once more into Éibhear's back. He let out a yelp of pain and tried again to struggle out from under them.

"You're all bastards!"

"Don't whine!" Gwenvael chastised. "Just admit that you're crazy about Iz—"

"Shut up!"

Dagmar pulled on the much-too-large, but lusciously soft robe, belting it in the middle. She took another glass of wine from Morfyd and dropped into the chair Annwyl had vacated. "Thank you."

"You're very welcome." Morfyd again studied the maps Dagmar had given her. "I'll give these to Brastias. Perhaps he can figure out where all these lines go. Or my brother, Éibhear. He's very good with maps."

"I'll help as much as I can," she promised.

Morfyd looked up from her notes. "Tell me, Dagmar, do you talk to Gwenvael?"

"Yes."

"*Full* conversations?"

"Yes."

"And he holds your interest?"

Annwyl laughed at that, but Dagmar didn't. "As a matter of fact, Lady Morfyd, I find your brother quite intelligent, with excellent ideas and thoughts on a range of topics. Perhaps *you* should find the time to have a full conversation with him before you judge what you don't know."

Morfyd stared at her with wide eyes and Dagmar felt a little guilty. But before she could apologize the bedroom door flew open and another woman marched in. She was a few inches taller than Dagmar and stunningly beautiful with brown skin just like the soldier-for-hire Dagmar had met. Now she'd seen two women of the desert lands in less than a week, when she'd seen none for the thirty years before that.

"I've been looking everywhere for you two," the woman snarled, slamming the door closed behind her. "And anyone like to explain what the hell Run and Jump is?"

Annwyl slowly rolled onto her side, *away* from the woman glaring at everyone in the room.

"Waiting for an answer!" she bellowed, looking quite comfortable yet gorgeous in the plain black leggings she wore with black boots, a loose off-white linen shirt, and a thin leather tie that pulled back her long mass of black curly hair. Nothing else adorned her body except a silver chain necklace that disappeared under her shirt and a small sheathed dagger she had tied to her upper thigh.

It probably took her all of five minutes to dress every day, but Dagmar knew her brothers' wives spent hours attempting to look as effortlessly beautiful as this woman.

"Well . . ." Morfyd gave a small shrug. "If you're talking

about dragons, it's a little game hatchlings play with their parents. You know, before their wings can actually carry them, when the family's out flying. The hatchlings will run and jump from one parent to the next. I did it with mine. It was fun, but it also helps the hatchlings learn how to fly because very often you'll catch the wind and you learn to coast."

"Right," the woman said, her smile not fooling Dagmar at all, "fun and a learning experience." That's when she leaned down and screamed into poor Morfyd's face, *"And that's why my daughter is doing it with your family!"*

Morfyd's eyes grew wide. "Oh."

"Yeah! 'Oh'!" She turned toward Annwyl. "And I blame your fat ass for this, you pregnant sow!"

"Me?" Rolling back to her other side, Annwyl faced them. "How is this *my* bloody fault?"

"She's out of control and it is your fault." The woman threw herself into a chair and said in a mocking, childlike voice, "'They say I can go to war. They say I'm really good. I want to be the Queen's Champion one day.' *Your* fault!" she finished in her own healthy yell.

"I haven't watched training in three months, how is this my fault?"

"Brastias speaks for you now, does he not?"

Annwyl pursed her lips before slowly stating, "He is in complete charge of my armies until I can mount my war horse without him whinnying in terror, yes."

"Then it's your fault! Because he says she's ready to go to war and so she wants to go."

Morfyd leaned forward a bit, her hands clasped in front of her. "Perhaps—"

"Shut up, scaly!"

Morfyd leaned back in her chair. "All right then."

Finally, the woman caught sight of Dagmar, her dark eyes raking over her before she said, "Talaith."

Dagmar had no idea what that meant until Morfyd cut in, "Sorry. Talaith, Daughter of Haldane. This is Dagmar Reinholdt. Of the Northland Reinholdts."

Ahh. Talaith was her name.

Talaith focused her lethal gaze back on Morfyd. "Are there Reinholdts in the south?"

Morfyd's eyes narrowed dangerously. "Not that I'm aware of."

"Then don't embellish!" she screamed.

"I'm not!" Morfyd screamed back.

Suddenly Annwyl sat up, one hand on her belly, a cry exploding from her lips. Immediately the women stopped bickering.

"Gods, Annwyl. What's wrong?" Morfyd demanded.

Green eyes turned to them and Annwyl sneered, "Nothing. I just wanted the two of you to shut up. You're going to make us look bad in front of the barbarian!"

The silence that followed was awkward, to say the least. And lasted a good thirty seconds. Until Morfyd spit out that first laugh, and then all of them followed suit. They couldn't seem to stop either. Even when Gwenvael walked in, stared at them all for a bit, and then walked back out, slamming the door behind him, they kept right on going.

Chapter 19

Gwenvael returned to Dagmar's room several hours later when he was sure his sister and brothers' mates were gone. She was stretched out facedown on a bed she was way too small for, her long hair, now clean and smelling delightfully of flowers, hanging over the side and nearly touching the floor. Her freshly washed body was covered only in a robe, and one small hand was balled into a fist, resting by her mouth. The other hand rested by her hip, palm up, and her spectacles were on the side table across the room.

She also snored, but only a little.

He walked around the bed and crouched down by her head. Reaching out, he gently brushed her hair off her face, smiling at how innocent she looked. Not at all like the manipulative little barbarian he'd been traveling with for days.

"Dagmar." He said her name softly, gently, his fingers petting her cheek. He liked how her skin felt under his fingertips. "Dagmar," he said softly again.

And, when she didn't answer, *"Dagmar!"*

She snapped awake, head and chest off the bed, her eyes immediately open and alert. *"It is not a lie!"*

"Sorry, love," he said softly again. "Did I wake you?"

Rolling her eyes, Dagmar dropped back to the bed. "Go away."

"No. You were mean to me, and I want reparations."

"You want—what are you doing?"

"Getting comfortable," he explained while crawling onto the bed and over her until he'd draped himself across her back. Once in position, he sort of dropped on top of her, and he enjoyed the sound of air abruptly shoved out of her lungs.

"Get off me!"

"Not until you apologize and make me feel better. *Much* better."

She tried to drag herself out from under him, but he wouldn't budge, making sure all his weight stayed on her back.

"Apologize for what?"

"For being mean to me in front of my much-loved kin."

"I don't know what you're talking about."

Gwenvael bounced his lower body up and down, causing his groin to slam against her ass.

"Stop! Stop!"

"Take it back."

There was a long pause, and then what suspiciously sounded like a giggle. "No."

She squealed when he started slamming into her again.

When Gwenvael finally lifted himself up, Dagmar scrambled off the bed and stumbled across the floor.

Turning around, she gripped her loosening robe closed. "Stay away from me, you mad bastard."

Gwenvael went up on all fours and began to crawl across the bed. "Apologize."

"Never."

"Beast."

"Defiler."

With his knees resting on the edge of the bed, Gwenvael reached out to grab Dagmar. She squealed again and made another run for it. Charging off the bed, Gwenvael reached for her again. He lost her . . . but he got the robe.

He held it up. "Look what I have here."

Dagmar stopped in mid-run and spun around to face him. She had her right arm over her chest and her left hand over her sex. "Give that back!"

"I don't think so."

"Gwenvael, give it back."

He tossed it over his arm and planted his feet firmly. "No, my lady, what I think I'm going to do is . . ."

"Gwenvael," she pushed when he stopped talking. "What's wrong with you?"

He let out a hard breath, his gaze locked onto her body. Her hands and arms blocked much of it, but still . . .

"Gods, woman, what have you been hiding?"

Dagmar looked around and down at herself. "Nothing, I don't think. I mean, I told what I knew to Morfyd and Annwyl—"

Gwenvael shook his head. "Not that. This." He walked

toward her and she quickly stepped back. "We really must find you clothes that do you justice."

"I don't know what you mean."

"Don't move," he snapped, and Dagmar immediately stopped moving away from him.

Gwenvael walked slowly around her, his gaze feasting on her.

"What, in the name of reason, are you doing?"

Behind her, Gwenvael slowly went to his knees. "Enjoying myself."

When Dagmar felt something brush against her ass, her entire body jolted. "Did you just—" She cleared her throat. "Did you just kiss my . . . uh . . . backside?"

Gwenvael didn't respond, but when she felt a warm tongue lazily wind its way up to her hip, she jumped away.

"What are you doing?" she asked again, quickly facing him.

"If you turn back around"—he purred—"you'll eventually find out."

"I can't . . . We can't . . . I know we've danced around it, but . . . uh . . ."

She took a step back when Gwenvael stood. "It's all right."

Dagmar realized she was panting, as if she were running down that main road toward Spikenhammer again.

"I didn't mean to panic. I just . . . I'm not used to . . ."

"Sssh." He walked toward her and she took another step back.

"Stop moving," he ordered.

And she did.

Gwenvael put her robe over her shoulders, took one arm and put it through the sleeve and did the same with the other. He closed the robe tightly and belted it.

"Feel better?"

She let out a shaky breath. "Yes."

"Do I make you uncomfortable?"

"No."

"Do you want me to leave?"

She swallowed. "No."

Gripping her hand, he walked her over to the bed and knelt on top of it, tugging at her until she joined him.

Kneeling across from each other, he said, "You know, Dagmar, not everything has to be so serious. Every moment involving a life or death issue that needs to be analyzed and sussed out."

She winced. "I try not to be stuffy."

"And you're not, thankfully. But the games played that involve whole kingdoms don't need to be played here. Here it's just us—and we can do whatever we want."

It dawned on Dagmar that he was right. She wasn't at her father's fortress, one of her brothers liable to walk in unannounced at any time. Nor did she have to worry about her sisters-in-law listening at the door or bribing the servants for information. She was thousands of miles from her kinsmen and in a place that knew nothing of her.

Dagmar felt a delicious, wicked thrill lash through her and carefully stated, "I don't have your freedom, my lord. I have my . . . *honor* to think of. To protect."

"Your honor?" Confused, Gwenvael stared at her for a long moment, and then his expression cleared and slowly, carefully, he began to play the game with her. "Ahh, yes. Your precious honor. There will be no protecting that tonight. Not with me."

Gwenvael lowered his head, his mouth heading toward hers. Dagmar turned her face away, her hands firmly pressed against his chest, trying to push him back even while her hands begged to explore.

But he wouldn't let her turn away, grabbing a handful of

her hair and forcing her head back until she had to look at him, his mouth again lowering toward hers.

His tongue slid inside, taking full ownership as it stroked and teased her and Dagmar whimpered desperately, her fingers digging into his shirt-covered chest. There was no rush to this kiss, no desperate invasion. He simply took what he wanted in his own time—and she let him.

So lost in his kiss, she didn't know he'd opened her robe again until he palmed her breast. Startled by the contact, Dagmar instinctively tried to pull back, but his grip on her hair kept her firmly in place. Unable to escape.

In this moment, on this bed, the dragon had complete control of her. And the violence of the shudder that went through her told its own tale. She needed this moment, this break from responsibilities. A longed-for break that had nothing to do with getting what she wanted or protecting those she cared for, and everything to do with her pleasure.

His lips nibbled their way down her chin to her neck and kept going. His warm mouth closed over her nipple and began to suck as a finger slid inside her.

Dagmar's hips jerked, attempting to move away from the finger so easily sliding in and out of her. But the fingers still gripping her hair tugged hard, and he gave a low warning growl.

Without a word, he made it clear he wouldn't let her go until he was done, and she rewarded him with fresh wetness between her legs that allowed him to add a second finger to the first.

She winced a bit, sucking air between her teeth, remembering that her few relations had been extremely short, years apart, and mostly unpleasant.

Her whimper this time had nothing to do with unpleasantness, however. She couldn't explain the difference, but it was there. His gentleness, his control without ever being vicious. It had her melting into him, giving herself over as she'd never done before. His mouth moved to her other breast, sucking until the nipple was hard and begging.

He had her bent back now, over his forearm, her body completely open to him and whatever he wanted to do. Her hands moved across his shoulders, holding onto him as her hips began to rock back and forth, riding the fingers inside her. She tried to stop herself, but her body had long left her behind. It had a mind of its own, and it seemed to know exactly what it wanted.

The pace of the fingers inside her increased, taking her roughly, the tips curling and rubbing against some nameless spot that had her legs shaking. She could no longer hold herself up, but the dragon took care of that. He took care of everything as his mouth returned to hers, his tongue forcing its way back in while he held her tightly with his arm. And when he had full control of her mouth and her whimpers had turned to short, desperate cries, Gwenvael placed his thumb against her clitoris and began to swirl it in circles, pressing down hard.

It was the last thing she needed, and she was grateful for the mouth covering hers as she screamed out the first release she'd had without use of her own hand.

She held on to Gwenvael as her body shuddered and shook, and when she felt the wave ebb and thought she was done, he turned his fingers a bit and readjusted where he'd placed his thumb. Then the wave was back again, twisting and turning her body, wringing it out like a rag. She tried to beg him to stop, to release her, but his mouth on hers seemed a permanent thing as he readjusted yet again, and again her body was dragged up and over.

When she could no longer breathe and sobs clogged her throat, he finally pulled back. His thumb slowed its pace before finally stopping, his fingers slid out of her with a gentleness she found startling, and the brutal assault on her mouth turned to tender kisses along her jaw.

He held her until her panting turned to slow, deep breaths and her fingers unclenched from his shoulder.

He'd just begun to lower her to the bed when she heard a brisk knock against the door.

"My lady?" Fannie's voice said from the other side.

Gwenvael pulled her back up and whispered harshly against her ear, "Answer her. Answer her now."

"Yes?" Dagmar stated clearly.

"Evening meal will be in another hour. I have a gown for you. Do you need help dressing?"

Still unable to organize her always organized thoughts, Dagmar was grateful when Gwenvael prompted, "Tell her yes, but you need another ten minutes to yourself."

Dagmar swallowed and said, "Yes, but I'm still napping. Another ten minutes, please."

"Of course, my lady."

"Thank you."

She never heard the woman leave, but the shadow under the door vanished.

The dragon finally released her, and Dagmar immediately pulled her robe over her body as he climbed off the bed and headed toward the door. She remained where he'd left her, unable to move.

"I'll be back later tonight," he told her as he walked away.

"Who says I'll be here?"

He stopped before opening the door and faced her. "You'll leave the window open for me and you'll be naked. When I come back, I'll take what I want from you, as many times as I want to." He grinned; it was pure and raw and astonishingly beautiful. "Understand me, Lady Dagmar?"

She shook her head. "No. You'll have to explain it to me."

"I will. Even if I have to tie you to the bed and explain it to you again and again and again." He looked her over one more time. "And don't play with yourself after I'm gone. Don't want you wearing my pussy out before I've had a chance to use it." With his hand on the door handle, Gwenvael rewarded her with the warmest smile she'd seen from anyone. "Besides, you look so beautiful when you come, I don't want to miss a second of it."

Then he was gone, the door shutting quietly behind him. A few minutes later when Fannie returned with the gown, she found Dagmar in the same position Gwenvael had left her in— kneeling on the bed, clutching her robe closed . . . and panting.

"She should have warned me, Jack."

"Aye, my Lord Gwenvael. She should have."

"She should have told me the truth about herself."

"Very true, my lord."

"Spinster? Spinster, my perfect ass! That woman is a volcano, Jack. Self-contained, waiting-to-go-off-and-melt-my-scales volcano. And, if I might add, a wee bit of a tease."

"Sounds that way, my lord. Now . . . are you sure about this?"

"If I hope to get through dinner . . . I have little choice. Just do it."

"As you wish."

Jack stepped back and motioned to several of the male servants under his direction. One after another, they poured the ice water pulled from a deep well discovered not long after Annwyl took over Garbhán Isle.

As soon as the water hit Gwenvael's human form, it sizzled and popped, the large chunks of ice melting completely on contact, steam rising after only a few seconds. Thankfully, however, it did its job.

Resting back in the tub, Gwenvael sighed, "Thank you, Jack."

"You're more than welcome, my lord. Will there be anything else?"

"A return of my sanity would be nice."

"You're on your own with that, my lord. I'm afraid there's only so much a servant can do."

Chapter 20

Gwenvael closed his bedroom door and headed down the hallway toward the stairs. He felt calmer now. More in control. He wasn't used to a woman who could rattle his tail. Even worse, he didn't know he'd like it.

Nearing the stairs to take him to the Great Hall, Gwenvael almost missed it. He stopped walking, his nostrils flaring, instantly recognizing all the scents coming from one room. He took several steps back and gave one knock on the door before pushing it open.

His young cousin Branwen lay stretched out on the bed, stomach down, her gaze focused on a book. She still wore her chain-mail shirt and leggings while her worn boots stood at attention by the bed, ready to be pulled on at a moment's notice. Like her mother, Branwen seemed more comfortable in her battle clothes than in the gowns her sisters often wore when not in the middle of combat. It reminded him of why he'd always liked Branwen.

Across the room were Izzy and Celyn. Together they held one of the battle lances developed by Gwenvael's ancestors, the Cadwaladr Twins. The weapon could be lengthened or shortened, should a dragon decide to shift from dragon form to human or back again. The twins, like his grandfather, had spent as much time human as dragon during their warrior years and found the use of the weapon important, and to this day they were still considered two of the deadliest beings who'd ever lived.

Yet Izzy's form would never change, so there was no real point in teaching her to use the weapon other than it allowed Celyn a chance to stand behind her with his arms around her and his hands on hers, slowly moving from battle stance to battle stance together.

In Gwenvael's extremely educated opinion, Celyn's pelvis snuggled just a little too close to his niece's rear.

As he stepped into the room, Izzy's head came up. The intense expression—or scowl, depending on who you spoke to—she always possessed when learning anything to do with war or combat, quickly changed into that welcoming smile Gwenvael simply adored. For a niece, he couldn't have asked for better than Izzy.

"Gwenvael! You're back!"

"Hello, my heart. Dinner will be soon. You sure you want your mum to see you looking like that?"

Izzy glanced down at her dirt-covered clothes. Spending a day playing with young dragons was hard and messy work, and clearly his Izzy had enjoyed every second of it.

"You've got a point. Mum's going to be pissed as it is, eh?"

"After watching you play Run and Jump? What do you think?"

She gave him her biggest grin, which caused her adorable pug nose to crinkle, making him laugh.

Glancing down at his young female cousin, he asked, "And how are you, Branwen?"

"Starving. When do we eat?"

"Soon. You two had best get dressed, so you won't hear complaints from your mothers." He looked at Celyn. "Mind if I talk to you for a bit, Celyn?"

Celyn didn't even bother trying to hide his smug grin as he

pulled away from Izzy. No doubt this was not the first time a male relative of some female Celyn had set his sights on had asked to speak to him, nor would it be the last time. "Of course. See you at dinner, Cousin Izzy." He winked at her, his smug grin in place.

Gwenvael followed the young dragon out, closing the door behind him, quite pleased to hear the hysterical feminine laughter that followed their exit. As long as Izzy didn't take Celyn seriously, Gwenvael would have less to worry about.

Still, it wouldn't hurt to have a talk with the young hatchling. To calmly remind him that although Izzy was not blood, she was still the niece of Gwenvael and Fearghus and the very much loved and cherished daughter of Briec.

Celyn turned to face him. "Is this the bit where you remind me little Izzy there's kin and I should keep my distance?"

And then Gwenvael remembered. Celyn was a Cadwaladr. Explanations and calm warnings would be a waste of Gwenvael's precious breath.

Keeping that in mind, Gwenvael grabbed his young cousin by the back of the neck and slammed him face first into the stone wall. When he pulled him back, a lovely splash of blood was left behind where Celyn's nose had been shattered.

The hatchling almost dropped to his knees, but Gwenvael held onto the back of his neck and walked—or dragged—him toward the steps.

"I'll make it simple for you, Celyn. You keep your hands off my niece, or you'll be able to serve the virgin witches of the east as a eunuch. Understood?"

Celyn nodded, his hands covering his shattered nose.

"Good. Now run away." And the hatchling did, tearing off down the hallway and disappearing from Gwenvael's sight.

"It should be a good night," he said with a smile.

* * *

Dagmar stopped midway down the stairs leading to the Great Hall. The room was packed, every table filled with laughing, talking, and arguing people. Platters of food were passed down from person to person, each taking what they wanted before sending it on its way. Servants bustled back and forth between bringing fresh food out and taking empty platters back. Several of the serving women poured wine and laughed right along with those at the table.

Thankfully, there was no uncomfortable grabbing, nor warnings to "mind your hands."

"My Lady Dagmar."

Gwenvael's cousin Fal charged up the stairs and took her hand. "If I may escort you, my lady."

"Thank you."

"Don't let this lot frighten you. They're loud but harmless."

"Harmless unless I'm the enemy."

"Exactly." They reached the last step. "You can sit near me. I'd love to find out more about the Northlands."

She'd rather eat bark, but she didn't have a moment to come up with an excuse before Gwenvael came up behind them and grabbed Fal by the hair. With one good yank, the youngster went flying and Gwenvael took her hand. "Beast."

"Defiler."

He grinned and placed her hand in the crook of his arm. "Come along. There's much to observe and mock."

She laughed. "Sounds delightful."

Gwenvael led her to the queen's table, but they stopped when a large wall stepped in front of them.

"Lady Dagmar, this is my baby brother, Éibhear."

Dagmar looked up into a handsome but fierce face . . . until he smiled. That adorable smile took up his entire face and Dagmar was helpless to do anything but smile back.

"Hello," he said.

"Hello." By all reason . . . His hair was blue. Not so black it appeared blue, but blue! She briefly wondered if Gwenvael would mind if she ran her hands through it.

"Is it true you went to the Great Library of Spikenhammer?"

"Very true."

"I've always wanted to go. I've heard their collection of books is phenomenal."

"It is. And your brother was thrown out for lewd behavior."

Éibhear's enchanting smile faded, replaced by a rather frightening frown. "Can't take you anywhere," he accused his brother.

"It wasn't me," Gwenvael lied. "She molested me in the stacks. She treats me like a whore."

"He's right," she agreed, surprising the brothers. "Sold him for five copper pieces in the market, too. Thinking about buying myself a new dress with my earnings."

"I'll have you know," Gwenvael said over his brother's laugh, "I'm worth more than five copper pieces. If you're going to sell my ass on the street, at least get my true worth!"

Izzy and Branwen quickly stepped apart as Branwen's older brother Fal crashed past them, then stepped back together as they continued down the stairs.

"Who's that?" Branwen asked, watching as Gwenvael led a woman toward the queen's table with all of Gwenvael's siblings—and Izzy's mum. Who Izzy still wasn't talking to!

"Must be the Northlander."

"Cousin Gwenvael seems quite taken with her."

"She must be smart then. He only truly likes the smart ones."

Once off the stairs, Izzy glanced toward the main table. She knew they had a seat for her—right next to her mother.

Branwen grabbed her arm. "Come, cousin. You'll sit with us." The young dragoness pulled Izzy to a table. There were several seats open, but Bran still took hold of the hair of one of her sisters, and yanked her from the chair.

"*Ack!* You crazed cow!"

Yelling ensued, and Izzy tried to avoid the swinging arms.

"Sit, Izzy." Ghleanna waved her into a seat. "Sit. Ignore them two. Never know how to act right." She sucked the marrow from a chicken bone and tossed it over her shoulder, hitting a servant in the head. "It's embarrassing."

Izzy had just dumped several delicious-smelling ribs onto her plate from a passing platter, when Celyn walked up and shoved his sisters aside. He'd barely sat down in the seat beside Izzy when Branwen started yelling at him while her sister was still yelling at her. A solid blast of flame from their mother put a halt to it all.

"Branwen. Here. Dera. Here. Now both of you shut up!"

Wiping soot from their faces, the sisters sat down, and Izzy turned to Celyn.

"By the gods!" she gasped when she saw him. "What happened to your face? Are you all right? I'll see if Morfyd has something for you."

She went to stand, but his hand on her arm kept her right where she was.

"I don't need anything, Iz. And this"—he pointed at his swollen nose and black eyes—"was just a warning off from Gwenvael."

"A warning off? For what?"

He grinned. Even with his face swollen, Celyn was extremely handsome—and he knew it. But Izzy still liked him. He made her laugh and showed her all the interesting weapons the dragons used. "He tried to warn me off you."

"Me?" She couldn't help but giggle. "Really?"

"Really. Your uncles and father are very protective of you. Briec threw me into a tree. One of those really old ones that never move. Your uncle Fearghus bit me."

Izzy placed her hand on Celyn's. "He . . . *bit* you?"

"Aye. He was on the floor and—"

"Why was he on the floor?"

"I don't know."

"Did you think to ask?"

"No." He pointed at his leg. "Bastard nearly tore out me calf muscle."

Using the tips of her fingers, she toyed with one of the ribs on her plate. "And Éibhear?"

"What about him?"

"He's an uncle. Has he violently attacked you for no good reason?"

"No. A cousin I was quite close to hasn't said a word to me in three days." Celyn took one of the ribs off her plate. "Not since he saw me flying you around."

Celyn leaned in closer, his shoulder pressing into hers. "And if I may be so bold—if you want to call Éibhear your uncle that's on you, but that would make him a very dirty, naughty uncle, because I've seen how he looks at you."

Under the table, Izzy wiped her suddenly sweaty palms on the skirt of her gown. "How does he look at me?"

"The same way I do."

Startled, Izzy quickly looked away. "I thought my father and uncles warned you off."

"I said they tried." He took another rib from her plate, laughing when she grabbed the other end and began to tug. "I never said they succeeded."

When he saw Brastias lean over and whisper something to his sister, Gwenvael thought about setting the big bastard on fire.

"Stop it," Dagmar murmured.

"Stop what?"

Dagmar laughed. "Don't give *me* that innocent look. I invented it. And I don't see what's wrong with him."

"He's not good enough for her. She deserves—"

"Better than a human?"

"Did I say that?"

"You don't have to." A chalice of wine in her hand, Dagmar relaxed back in her chair while Gwenvael did the same. After the first fifteen minutes, Dagmar had held that pose most of the night. They leaned in close and chatted, her asking questions, him answering; then he would do the asking and she the answering. He loved how sly she looked as she watched everyone and listened to everything. He knew she didn't realize it, but she'd let her guard down. The ongoing threats in Annwyl's court among the House of Gwalchmai fab Gwyar royals and the Cadwaladr Clan were slight in comparison to life among the humans. His family dealt with things straight on. A fist here, a blast of flame there. It kept the general peace and didn't kill an evening—or someone's favorite cousin. The humans, however, were much more dangerous.

She'd probably never admit it, but she was enjoying herself. He could tell. She tugged on his shirt and he leaned back again.

"Why does sweet Éibhear look so angry? He hasn't smiled once since we sat down."

"He's pretending he's not jealous about my niece Izzy."

"That pretty girl you pointed out to me? Talaith's daughter?" She snorted. "Foolish, foolish boy."

Gwenvael chuckled. "I know."

She studied others at the table before she asked, "And do those two ever stop arguing?" He didn't need to look to see who she spoke of, but he did anyway to find out what the argument of the evening was.

Talaith held up an apple in front of Briec, dangerously

close to his nose. "This doesn't look ripe enough. Why isn't this ripe?"

"As ruler of all fruits and vegetables, I'll make sure to get right on that."

"You can't expect me to eat fruit that's not perfectly ripe, and I'm extremely disappointed you didn't consider my needs."

"I don't expect you to have a sound thought in that head of yours, either, but I do like to keep hope alive. And your needs, woman, will be met later tonight."

Gwenvael bit into his own piece of fruit before shrugging. "It's not an argument. It's their bizarre idea of foreplay."

"Really? And what's your idea of foreplay?"

The fruit he'd only moments ago swallowed became lodged in his throat. He coughed, twice, until it moved a bit, able to freely go down his gullet.

"You all right?"

"I'll be better when I get you back in your room."

"That won't happen for hours." She held her chalice up so a servant could pour more wine into it.

"I never knew you were such a little tease, Beast."

"Do you want me to stop?"

"Not on your life."

The pair reared back a little when they realized the dining table was no longer in front of them.

"Were we done eating?" Dagmar asked, glancing suspiciously into her wineglass.

"You haven't had too much to drink—the table's really gone. And it seems it's time for dancing."

He held out his hand and opened his mouth to speak, but Dagmar cut him off.

"No."

"You don't even want to try?"

"No. Trust me. There are other things I'd rather do."

"Such as?"

"Set myself on fire. Drown myself. Or hang myself from the roof. These are all preferable to dancing."

Gwenvael laughed until his niece grabbed his hand. "Come on, Gwenvael! We're dancing!" Izzy pulled him out of his seat with that healthy strength of hers.

"You'll be all right?" he asked Dagmar, letting his niece grip his hand and put all her weight into trying to drag him forward.

"I'll be fine." She motioned him away with her chalice. "Go. Dance. Find me later—if you can."

Evil little tease! "I will."

He let Izzy's hand go abruptly, and his niece squealed and crashed to the floor. "Iseabail! What are you doing on the floor? Get up, girl! Have some pride!"

Dagmar was in love. Madly, adoringly in love.

She never dreamed she'd find a love as deep as this. But who knew? Who knew a sweet-faced, soft-spoken dragoness would have so much gossip and, even more importantly, be so willing to share it all with Dagmar!

Yes, it was love. Deep, never-ending love!

"And see the short red-haired male standing near Briec? The royal?"

Dagmar wanted to squint through her spectacles—those at a distance were fuzzier than usual due to her excesses of wine this evening—but she didn't want to be obvious. Luckily, however, Morfyd's brother Briec was quite easy to spot. Arrogance like that filled a room. "Yes."

"I've been told," she whispered, leaning close, "that he enjoys wearing his wife's gowns. And when he does, his wife accidentally catches him in said gowns."

"Is there scolding?"

"Aye!" Morfyd lowered her voice again. "Apparently she enjoys scolding him very, very, *very* firmly. In fact, she scolds him until they're both quite exhausted and happy."

Dagmar put her hand to her chest. "That is *fabulous*."

"Isn't it?" Morfyd patted her leg. "I have to say, Dagmar, I am so glad you've visited. There are very few who have a true appreciation of delicious gossip. Except, of course, Gwenvael."

"I expected that," she admitted. "But no one else?"

"Fearghus doesn't like to be bothered with anybody or anything. Everything irritates my eldest brother. Everything. Except Annwyl, of course, but even she can get on his nerves. Briec could care less about anybody or anything except himself and whether he can find something to argue with Talaith about."

Wanting more on that, Dagmar began to ask, but Morfyd held up a halting hand. "Don't ask. The whole thing is between the two of them and is idiotic. Éibhear is of no use to me because he refuses to believe the worst of anyone so he constantly interrupts me to say, 'That can't be true. That can't be true.' Which takes the piss right out of it."

"Annwyl?"

"All she does is read. The woman lives in that library and she absolutely hates when you distract her from her precious books. If she isn't killing, she's reading. If she isn't reading, she's killing. There's no middle ground with her."

"And Talaith?"

"My one saving grace, but I can't go on too long with her or she starts getting paranoid."

"Paranoid?"

She rolled her eyes. "'What are they saying about me? And what are you saying about me?' Again, takes the piss right out."

Dagmar laughed. "Well, you'll be glad to know, I keep my

paranoia for the important things." Her gaze swept the room. "All I care about is what everyone else is up to."

Morfyd grabbed hold of Dagmar's hand, holding it close to her chest. "Don't take this the wrong way, but . . . I love you."

Dagmar laid her free hand on top of Morfyd's. "And I you."

They began laughing again—something she'd done more in this one night than she'd done in her entire life.

Talaith swooped in, crash-landing on the chair on the other side of Dagmar. "I'm having a wonderful time!"

Morfyd whispered against Dagmar's ear. "She's drunk off her ass."

"I am not drunk," Talaith protested. "You witch. Bitch." She giggled. "You bitchy witch."

Talaith waved her hands. "All right. I may have had more wine than I should. But I still know the important question of the day."

"And what is that?"

"Has little Dagmar here fucked our Gwenvael?"

Dagmar rubbed her leg where Talaith had slapped her to emphasize her rude question, and Morfyd turned a lovely shade of red, gasping out, "That's none of our business!"

"Come on. I want to hear it from someone who isn't completely captivated by those big, dumb dragon eyes of his. I want the truth! Is he as good as he claims to be?"

"Quiet!" Morfyd hissed.

"I don't know the truth." When the women stared at her, Dagmar shrugged. "I don't."

"Then don't do it," Talaith said earnestly. "Trust me on this."

"Why not?"

Putting one arm around Dagmar, she motioned to Morfyd with the other. "Close your ears, woman, you don't want to hear this."

"Gods help me."

Talaith leaned in close. "As I said, Magdar—"

"It's Dagmar."

"Whatever. You don't want to do this because if he's anything like his brother, you'll be trapped. Caught for eternity."

"And why will that happen?"

"Because he'll fuck you until your eyes roll into the back of your head and that'll be it! There will be no getting free from that, my dear. You'll be trapped here. In this hell."

Dagmar calmly glanced around. "This hell?" she asked flatly. "This castle-hell with pleasant servants to do your bidding, beautiful rolling hills and forests filled with fresh game, a benevolent queen, fierce dragons bent on protecting you and your daughter, and a gorgeous silver-haired warrior who's madly in love with you? That hell?"

"Yes! You understand!"

"Perfectly. And I will keep this in mind if and when I get around to . . . uh . . . fucking Gwenvael."

"Just make sure it's what you want. Because once you're in, you're not getting out. And don't let him brand you. You'll be trapped with him forever!"

"Talaith!" Morfyd exclaimed.

"Branding? With actual irons?"

"No! It's not like that," Morfyd argued. "It's called a Claiming. The brand is placed on you by the dragon you love *without* implements. It's quite mystical and . . . romantic."

"It's hardly romantic," Talaith muttered before she perked up and nearly shouted, "But it will make you come!"

Morfyd dropped her head into her hands. "Gods, please stop drinking and talking." She glared at the human witch. "Just pass out already!"

Dagmar simply had to ask. "Talaith, are you unhappy with Briec?"

"Absolutely not!" She sighed deeply and looked moments from emotional tears. "I love him so much."

"All right then."

Morfyd shook her head when Dagmar glanced at her. "I won't discuss it. I just accept they're my kin and go on about my day."

Patting Morfyd's leg, Dagmar offered what comfort she could, "That's probably for the best."

Éibhear handed his brother a pint of ale when Gwenvael stumbled to a stop beside him. He grinned. "Duchess Bantor again?"

"It may appear that she only has two hands, but clearly she has six."

"She's been trying to get you into her bed for over a year."

"Although never acknowledged by the lot of you, I do have standards."

"She's very pretty—huge breasts—and from what I understand willing to do anything."

"Her hands grip me like claws. It makes me uncomfortable. *She* makes me uncomfortable."

"And you have your sights set on someone else tonight."

Now Gwenvael grinned. "I do."

Éibhear pursed his lips and glanced away.

"What?" Gwenvael sighed. "What was that look for?"

"Nothing."

"Just spit it out, little brother."

Éibhear peered at his brother, wondering how to broach the topic tactfully. "It's just . . ."

"It's just what?"

"Don't you think Lady Dagmar's just a little . . . well . . . that she's . . ."

"That she's what?"

Éibhear decided to be cautiously direct. "A little bit beyond you?"

"Sorry?"

"She reads an awful lot. I talked to her for quite a bit, and she's so knowledgeable. *Extremely* knowledgeable."

Gwenvael put his hands on his hips. "You think she's too smart for me?"

"Perhaps 'more savvy' is a better phrase."

"You oversized cub!"

"Don't get mad. I'm only suggesting you should aim . . . a little . . . lower."

"What kind of brother are you?"

"An honest one. Would you prefer I lie to you?"

"Yes!" Gwenvael yelled, slamming the ale back into Éibhear's hand. "As a matter of fact, I *would* prefer that!"

Dagmar was sneaking out the back of the castle when she saw her leaning against some fencing, her head on her folded arms. She approached slowly, cautiously.

"Annwyl?"

The queen's head snapped up. "Oh. Dagmar."

"Are you all right?"

"I'm fine. Just needed some fresh air."

She needed bed. There was a light sheen of sweat on her and her hands trembled.

Dagmar heard the soft mutterings all evening from the few human royals who were at the court. Annwyl was not the Annwyl they remembered. Her hair had thinned; her face had lost its luster, becoming drawn and lined. Her arms and legs were much too thin for someone so weighed down with child. Since Dagmar knew nothing of the queen before she'd met her—except for the rumors, of course—she couldn't tell one way or the other. But Dagmar did know when a birth was at risk. She knew the signs well.

"Why don't I get Fearghus to—"

"Please don't." She forced a smile. "It's been so long since he's had some time to himself and he's enjoying his kin—for once."

Dagmar chuckled. "I understand that. I can help you up, though. To your room."

"You don't have to." Yet her eyes were begging for that bit of help.

"You're giving me a reason to get out of there." She went over to Annwyl and slipped one arm around what remained of her waist. Dagmar forced herself not to physically flinch when her fingers felt actual ribs beneath the queen's gown. She took Annwyl's arm with her free hand. "Come on. I think two mere humans can manage this, don't you?"

Annwyl laughed. "I would hope so."

Together they made their plodding way to the back stairs and up them. It wasn't easy and Dagmar wasn't exactly known for her momentous strength, but she handled it better than she could have hoped. Keeping the conversation light with stories of her vapid sisters-in-law, Dagmar helped the queen to get out of her gown and washed up. Then she helped her into bed, smiling when she realized the queen was already asleep before Dagmar was able to cover her with the fur bedding.

She silently slipped out of the room, closing the door, when she heard a woman's voice. "Oh, Gwenvael! I simply adore you!"

Dagmar looked down the hallway and watched as Gwenvael led some big-breasted royal toward his room.

Shaking her head at her own idiocy—*Did you really think you had a bolt's chance in hell with that?*—Dagmar turned and headed back to the stairs and the fresh night air.

Chapter 21

Gwenvael didn't think he'd ever pry Duchess Bantor off his neck. She clung to him like a vine, the wine she'd been guzzling all evening making her much bolder and harder to get rid of than usual. He finally dumped her off at her room into the arms of a giggling servant girl who liked the way he crossed his eyes when her ladyship drunkenly told him to "take me, Gwenvael. Take me now!"

Chuckling, Gwenvael went down the four flights of stairs to the second floor, walked past his own room, and rounded a corner, walking right into Briec.

"Ho there, Briec! What a delightful ass you're carrying."

"A delightful *drunken* ass."

"I'm not drunk."

Gwenvael grinned. "The ass speaks."

"Put me down!" the ass demanded. "I can walk on my own."

"As you wish." Briec dropped his package, and Talaith grabbed hold of her mate's arm to prevent her rear from hitting the floor.

"See?" she said, when she'd finally found her balance. "I'm as dry as the desert sands."

And to prove it, Briec pulled his arm away. With nothing to hold on to, Talaith went down like a stone statue Gwenvael once stole.

Talaith glared up at Briec. "Bastard."

"I told you, my beautiful Talaith, that *I* was the dragon for you," Gwenvael reminded her. "But no. You had to go with the arrogant one. Whereas I am always loving and charming and simply wonderful to be around. There isn't an arrogant bone in my beautiful, perfect body."

Briec's eye twitched seconds before he jerked toward his brother, but Gwenvael held up his hands. "Not the face! Not the face! I have plans for this evening and my perfection must remain unmarred."

"You're an idiot."

"Prove it."

Looking down at his brother's mate, "Speaking of which, last I saw you, you were with the cunning"—Gwenvael flashed his teeth at his brother, making Briec laugh—"Lady Dagmar."

"Last I saw her," Talaith said while trying to get herself to her feet, "she was heading outside."

Gwenvael threw up his hands. "I order a woman to be in her room, naked, waiting for me, and she traipses off."

Shaking his head, Briec reached down and grabbed hold of his mate's shoulders, lifting her to her feet. "Next time use the chains. That way they can't get away."

"Good idea. Perhaps I can borrow your set."

Now that she was on her feet, Talaith slammed her hands against Gwenvael's chest. When he didn't fall back, she frowned and hit him again.

"We do not have a set. Borrow Annwyl and Fearghus's like everyone else. And another thing, slag, keep your dirty, dirty, whorish hands off Lady Dagmar. She's nice."

Gwenvael stared down at his hands. "They're not whorish."

"A bit slutty, though," Briec joked.

"And what makes you think I plan to take advantage of Lady Dagmar?"

"She has a pussy, doesn't she?" Talaith sneered.

Gwenvael's laugh rang out through the hallway. "We should keep her drunk *every* day!"

Briec sighed. "Once a year is quite enough, thank you. But I will say this one is different from the others you've rutted with. She's well read. Well spoken, too. And her thoughts progress in a nice logical order. She actually kept my interest in our conversation for five . . . maybe even six minutes before my mind wandered away to something much more interesting."

"Talaith's ass?"

"Rude," Talaith hissed. "Tell him he's rude!"

Briec shook his finger at Gwenvael. "You're rude! Don't speak to her that way!" He pulled Talaith into his body, holding her tight against him before he added a wink and mouthed at Gwenvael, "Definitely her ass."

Dagmar marched up the hill and awkwardly climbed on top of a boulder. It was a good choice. Gave her a lovely view of the entire valley that separated Garbhán Isle from Dark Plains as a whole.

"So many lakes," she said out loud. "So much potential defense." The queen had asked for her help and Dagmar happily accepted, determined to prove her worth, at least to the Southlanders.

About to step down, Dagmar noticed the tall male standing beside the boulder. It wasn't Gwenvael, but definitely another sneaky dragon. She could tell easily now, which made her wonder how she'd ever missed it before. Of course, Ragnar had been different. He had an entire backstory and even play-acted as if he were old and wounded. All very brilliant, and it still pissed her off.

"Good evening to you," she said.

The male looked up at her and then around as if he expected her to be speaking to someone else.

"Um . . . good evening?"

"I don't remember seeing you at the dinner." She held her hand out for him to grasp it, and, after a pause, he did just that, helping her to settle comfortably on the boulder.

"I didn't attend. I'm searching for my wandering mate. Some days I don't think she loves me at all."

"Traveling has an allure of its own. I know that now. And perhaps the time away strengthens her love for you."

"She may have said that one or two times. But I miss her."

He smiled and Dagmar had to hold back a little sigh. He was astoundingly beautiful with his long dark hair and violet-colored eyes. She'd love to meet the female, dragon or human, who'd willingly wander away from him.

"Are you meeting someone out here tonight?" he asked.

"Doubtful." The image of Gwenvael taking that royal back to his room had not left her head. "I just needed a bit of fresh air."

"And some time to yourself. Noisy lot," he added, motioning toward the castle.

"Very noisy. But not what I expected."

"Everyone expects the worst of dragons. They can't help themselves." His head cocked to the side. "I think it's time for me to go."

Dagmar nodded. "As you wish."

"It was nice"—he looked at her strangely—"talking to you."

She didn't know why he seemed so surprised she'd talked to him, but she didn't care enough to ask.

"And you."

He gave her a very courtly bow before walking off into the surrounding woods. She watched him go, impressed with the rear view as much as the front one.

"Reason preserve me," she muttered, appalled with herself.

She turned back around, her entire body jolting when she heard, "I thought I told you to wait in your room and be naked?"

With one hand against her chest, she raised the other. She was appalled at herself even more now that she'd allowed the Gold to startle her.

"Well?" he pushed.

"Don't snarl at me. And I didn't see the point of being in my room waiting for you when you seemed to be off with someone else."

"I was?"

"Do you not remember the royal draped around your neck like a noose?"

"The duchess you mean?"

"Yes. Her."

"Why would I waste my time with her when I *thought* I had you waiting in your room for me?"

"To quote my father, 'Bigger tits?'"

"You think so little of me."

"No, actually. I don't."

He casually walked around the boulder until he faced her. "My brother Éibhear says you're too smart for me."

"Your brother Éibhear spends too much time in his books and staring at Izzy."

"Annwyl said you defended me to Morfyd."

"I was simply clarifying the situation to her."

"I appreciate your clarification then. It means much to me."

He grabbed her hands and held her arms away from her body. "I do like this dress on you. Fannie has a good eye."

"She knew not to bring me something garish. I appreciate that. And thank you for the compliment."

"You're very welcome. Now come down here."

Gwenvael stepped back and she carefully slid to the ground. "Take off your dress."

Startled, Dagmar glanced around. No kiss? No romance? Just orders? And even more annoying was how her nipples hardened at the thought.

"Out here? Now?"

"Yes. Here. Now."

"Lord Gwenvael, there's quite a difference between enjoying the observation of others and enjoying *being* observed."

"I know that. Take off the dress." He stepped closer. "Unless, you'd prefer I hold you down and tear it off."

"These perverted fantasies of yours—"

"Make you wet?"

She held her thumb and forefinger up, a bit apart. "A little," she whispered.

Before Dagmar knew it, they were both laughing. Should there be laughing? Listening to her sisters-in-law, she thought there should be something desperate and uncontrollable and wild. And although she felt all those things, she also felt . . . happy.

Gwenvael pressed his forehead against hers and kept his voice low, "It's just you and me here, Beast. We're not involving anyone else except maybe the crows sleeping in the trees. Whatever we do between the two of us, with only the two of us, is our business. That, my lady, is the beauty of fantasy."

"As always, your words are smooth as glass, Defiler."

"That doesn't mean they're not truthful." He carefully removed her spectacles, taking the time to slip them into the hidden pocket of her gown. "Take off your dress. I'd hate for you to have to explain to Fannie what happened to the gown she got for you."

Trying to focus her vision, Dagmar reached for the ties of her bodice. "You don't think the mauling bear story would work with her?" she asked with a giggle.

* * *

Gwenvael silently watched while Dagmar untied the ribbon holding her bodice together. To keep some females calm, Gwenvael would talk. About their beauty, their wit, anything that would keep their focus on him and him alone. But he knew he had Dagmar's attention and mere words were something the pair of them played with. They tortured others with their words, used their words to get what they wanted or needed.

He didn't want any of that between them right now. He only wanted Dagmar, the woman boldly leering at him as she pulled the slightly too large bodice apart. His gaze remained on her face, watching the flush that flowed across her cheeks as she became more excited. Her scent teased his senses, making it hard for him not to throw her to the ground and take what he wanted.

Dagmar pulled the dress off her shoulders and off her body. It dropped to the ground, quickly followed by her shift. Hands on her hips, she stood there with her brow raised in silent challenge.

With a quick swirl of his forefinger, he motioned for her to remove the bit of material covering her sex.

Letting out an annoyed little grunt, she muttered, "Lazy," under her breath before tugging at the ribbons on each hip until they split apart and she could add the cloth to the growing pile at her feet.

Although she stood before him completely naked while he was clothed, her stance was defiant, brave, and demanding. It aroused him more than he could have imagined.

Uncrossing his arms, Gwenvael gently removed the scarf covering her head and pulled her braid around to the front. Untying the ribbon at the end, he took his time unbraiding the silky mass. When done, Gwenvael combed his fingers through her hair until it hung loose and free to her hips.

Now that he had her as he wanted her, he cupped her breasts, his thumbs toying with her nipples. Her eyes closed, body trembling, while Gwenvael amused himself.

His cock pushed hard and heavy inside his leggings, and with every passing second it became harder and harder not to simply mount her and fuck them both into oblivion. But he needed her more ready than this.

Using gentle pressure, he pushed her back until her rear was pressed up against the boulder. He took her hands and kissed them. "I want to see what these small fingers of yours can do."

She automatically reached for him, but he took firm hold of her hands and pushed them back against her body. "No. Show me on yourself."

"You're being lazy," she teased.

"Desperate," he replied. "Not sure I can get you ready before I take what's mine." Gripping her hips, he lifted her until she was spread out on the boulder.

"Lie back and show me," he calmly ordered.

She didn't move right away, her head leaning back a bit as her squinty gaze searched the darkness.

"Here," he said softly, lifting her dominant hand with his own, "let me help you." He sucked her middle finger into his mouth, his tongue slowly swirling around the tip. She moaned, sounding in pain as her mind fought what her body wanted so badly. When she began to squirm, he released her finger and placed it against what was quickly becoming a very wet pussy.

"Show me," he whispered, and waited.

This was insanity. Out here in the open, naked except for her boots, with a dragon everyone knew to be an unrepentant slag. Not simply naked, though, but splayed open across a boulder with her hands between her legs.

Yet this had been the substance of her fantasies for years.

Fantasies, where everything was safe and hers without the involvement of anyone else. She used those fantasies to help her fall asleep at night after pleasuring herself once, maybe twice. And she'd had no intention of telling anyone about those fantasies. No husband or female friend because there had been no one she'd trust enough with that information. How could she? When she'd been forced more than once to use that kind of information to protect herself against someone else?

But what she kept coming back to, again and again, was that she hadn't told the dragon anything. She hadn't let him in on her secrets. True enough, he'd discovered her enjoyment of watching others, but there were few she knew of who wouldn't stop and watch when stumbling across a coupling.

Yet Gwenvael the Handsome kept getting to the heart of her desires with little to no help from her. Was that where his reputation stemmed from? Was that why so many women came back to him again and again? Would she?

His fingers brushed across hers. Gentle, but insistent. Whisper soft, but demanding.

He understood so well the rudiments of taking control. Ropes and chains were merely one element. And although fun to talk about, it was not an element necessary at all times.

Unwilling to stop herself any longer, Dagmar began to stroke her sex with the tips of her fingers. Playing with herself as she'd want a man to. She took her time, allowing her body to heat up as her fingers slid deeper and deeper inside, writhing as she'd occasionally touch her clitoris. She didn't rush anything but, instead, took her own sweet time making her body ache.

It seemed to work well as a strong grip took hold of her fingers and pushed the middle and forefinger inside her body.

"Fuck yourself," he growled. She did, her hips rocking against her own hand, her own moans getting louder with each thrust.

She felt the dragon's human hands press against the inside

of her thighs, pushing her legs apart. And then his mouth was on her, his tongue taking up the teasing of her clitoris. She began to squirm harder, the intensity of it almost too much to bear. But his hands pinned her down against the boulder, holding her in place as he took his turn making her body ache.

Dagmar's back arched as he did things with the tip of his tongue that had her crying out, her voice echoing in the dark clearing. She had no time to worry whether she may be alerting anyone to their presence as he sucked the small bundle of nerves between his lips and proceeded to roll it back and forth gently until her body jerked out its climax, her free hand pinning his head against her body, unwilling to release him until the last shudder had passed.

This was no quick release, however, made to simply unleash the tension in her body. As she began to settle down, his mouth readjusted, the flat of his tongue pushing and grinding against her clitoris again. Her back arched in response, her head thrown back as the air left her lungs in one surprised gasp. Almost immediately it started again—not the slow buildup, but right back into another climax. A stronger, more powerful one that, if he hadn't been holding her down, would have rolled her right off the boulder onto the hard ground.

She didn't know how long he had her pinned to that rock, laying one climax on top of another, on top of another. Each one new and different, crashing up against the one that had been fading until she begged him—weakly, her strength nearly gone—to stop.

"Once more," he murmured, and she shook her head, her voice catching.

"I can't."

"You will. Once more." Then he was inside her, his cock pushing past still-pulsating tissue, her body still shuddering from the last few climaxes.

She had no idea when he took his clothes off, but nothing

had ever felt more wicked or delicious than his naked body pressing into hers. His weight held her down as he roughly rocked into her, taking her, his arms braced on either side of her shoulders. His long hair fell around them, draping them like the finest silk while his groans worked into her system, taking her up again. And what she'd thought impossible happened once more. Her climax so brutally intense and harsh, her hands slapped against his sides, her fingers yanking down against the flesh. She felt skin tear under her nails, and his cry of pain led right into his gasp and moans of pleasure.

He came hard inside her, his body jerking against her during each release, her pussy tightening around him over and over again, until she pulled the last bit of come from his balls.

Gwenvael dropped on top of her, his mind unable to care if she could breathe or not. At the moment, he simply couldn't think straight . . . or at all. He had no idea how long he lay on top of her, but when he finally lifted himself off, she was asleep beneath him. Snoring.

Grinning, he shook her shoulder. "Oy!"

Her eyes snapped open. *That was not what I said!*

He laughed and said, "Stay awake, you lazy sow."

She blinked, grey eyes able to focus on him since he was only mere inches from her face. "I'm tired," she haughtily complained.

"Yes," he said softly, a fingertip tracing along her cheek and jaw. "I guess you are."

"But you're not."

"Not even a little." He leaned down and kissed her, his tongue slowly tasting hers.

She moaned, her body automatically responding to him and his touch. But she pulled her mouth away, her head shaking.

"No. I can't do that again. It was too much."

"There's no such thing." He grabbed the hands pushing against his chest, feebly trying to shove him away. "And you will do it again," he told her, pinning her hands against the boulder beneath them. "As many times as I want you to."

He was still inside her and felt her pussy pulse to life with the action of pinning her hands. It became warm again at his words.

Gods, she was delicious—the cunning, clever Lady Dagmar.

"And if I say no?" she asked softly, playing the shy virgin beautifully. "To protect my honor?"

He leaned into her, kissing her neck and then biting it until he heard her gasp, the walls of her pussy clenching him so tightly he feared she'd snap his already-hard-again cock in two.

"When I'm done, you'll have no honor. I'll take what I want, Lady Dagmar," he whispered against her ear, his grip tightening on her wrists. "And no matter how much you struggle or fight, I'll keep taking what I want. Again. And again. And again."

It was small. A human male would miss it completely. A dragon not as in tune with her body would miss it as well.

But he didn't.

At his words, Dagmar came again—and he almost came with her.

Chapter 22

Dagmar knew she was back in her bed and not alone when that horrifying sound jolted her awake.

Her eyes snapped open and she blinked, squinting, trying to figure out where she was and how she got there. Then the sound moved closer, and Dagmar couldn't help but turn her nose up in disgust.

He snored. The great Gwenvael the Handsome snored. Good thing he'd brought her such pleasure or she'd have him removed from her room—perhaps from the castle!

But he had, truly had, brought her pleasure. From that boulder to this bed, he'd taken her again and again until she'd begged for sleep. Yet it hadn't been simply that, had it? There were many in the world who knew how to give pleasure. No, it was something else when it came to Gwenvael. She argued to herself that many of his conquests probably had the same feelings about him when all was said and done, but she wasn't foolish like the others. She'd had no grand illusions of a perfect love that would have Gwenvael dropping to his knees and begging for her hand in marriage. From the beginning, she'd been quite determined to keep a clear perspective on all of this.

She knew she'd be returning to her father's fortress. She knew her future was meant to be spent behind the massive gates of that fortress. She also knew that with luck and skill, she'd be able to get her small house somewhere on her father's lands, similar to Esyld's, in another decade or so. These were the absolutes of her life and she refused to let a few nights bedding Gwenvael change any of that, because she couldn't afford to hope for more.

Yet even with all that cold, calculated thinking, she couldn't stop that small dart of hope that had struck her heart.

Dagmar leaned in close and focused on the face beside her. He looked so innocent while he slept. Very misleading. She also marveled at how much heat he gave off. She kicked off the furs covering her and stared up at the ceiling.

It was late and she should go back to sleep, but that snoring made it near-impossible.

Rolling onto her side, she rested her arm around his waist and snuggled in close. She kissed a line across his shoulders to his neck, smiling when he groaned in his sleep. Dagmar teased his ear with the tip of her tongue and draped her legs around his thighs. Still he slept on. So she slid her body directly over his, her knees resting on either side of his hips. Sitting up straight, she rested her rear against his groin and smiled down at him.

He certainly is handsome, she thought, moments before slamming the pillow down over his face.

Instantly his arms reached up wildly and Dagmar leaned in, putting her weight into the attack.

She snickered madly, even as he grabbed her arms and flipped her to her back.

"You barbarian! What did you think you were doing?" he demanded.

"I couldn't stand the snoring anymore!"

Gwenvael gasped in outrage. "I do *not* snore!"

"You sound like a hoofed animal in rutting season."

Dagmar wasn't exactly surprised when he became merciless, tickling the sensitive flesh on her sides while she tried to fight him off. His weight kept her pinned down as she'd been unable to do to him, and her slaps against his arms and chest did nothing but make him laugh.

Her squeals, however, did get them a sound banging against the wall from one of their neighbors.

They froze, both looking horribly guilty, she was sure.

"This is your fault," he whispered.

"*My fault?* I can't believe no one's complained before about that horrid noise. You could destroy whole armies with that noise alone!"

His hands gripped her sides again and she resumed her kicking and squealing, but his mouth silenced hers, his body pinning her in place. Her fists, which had been hitting his chest and shoulders while he tickled her, unfurled and her fingers dived into his hair, her arms tugging him closer.

He slid inside her, the length and width of him stretching her, demanding more.

Dagmar's body arched up and her hands loosened from his

hair, her arms flailing back, trying to find purchase. Her fingers touched the wall and she braced her hands against it as Gwenvael's strong, hard strokes pounded into her. Short of breath, she pulled out of their kiss and turned her face away, panting and moaning, feeling that climax building within her.

When it came, it ripped through her, leaving her gasping and sweating, her body shaking from the release. Gwenvael pulled back, but only to flip her over. Lifting her hips up, he entered her from behind. Dagmar moaned decadently at the ruthlessness of it while her body raced toward another climax.

His hand slipped between her thighs, his fingers toying with her clitoris until Dagmar had to bury her face into the bedding so she could scream without the worry of terrifying their neighbors.

Now both of Gwenvael's hands viciously gripped her hips again, holding her up and steady as he pounded into her. When he came, he shouted, cutting off the sound by clenching his teeth. He released inside her again and again, keeping her tight against him, her rear pressing into his abdomen.

As the last shudder passed through her, Dagmar dropped listlessly to the bed. Gwenvael managed to pull out of her, his hands releasing their grip. She felt him move away from her, but he didn't get far before he fell forward, his head against her ass, his snoring filling the room.

But now Dagmar was simply too tired to care.

Gwenvael felt the cold hand of death slap against his shoulder and he sat up in bed, screaming, *"I only touched her once!"*

The smirk that greeted him wasn't unkind, but it didn't seem convinced of his statement either.

He blinked, trying to wake up. "Fannie?"

The servant gave a small bow. "My Lord Gwenvael."

Fannie was one of those servants a body could rely on in

almost any situation. Always calm, dignified, and smart, she seemed to know exactly when to appear and when to leave. He liked that about her.

"Good morn, Fannie." He frowned. "But why are you in my room?"

"Her ladyship has asked that you leave *her room* as soon as possible while the rest of the royal house is downstairs having first meal."

He rubbed his eyes. "She's throwing me out? What did I say to Annwyl this time?"

"Not Lady Annwyl, who gets very angry should we call her 'ladyship,' but Lady Dagmar, who I am currently tending until she returns to the north. She seems to have no concerns with the correct usage of proper titles." While her hands stayed primly laced together, her eyes swept the room. "And this is not your room, but Lady Dagmar's."

As Fannie had done, he looked around the room. "It certainly is." He focused back on the servant. "And why is she throwing me out?"

"She'd prefer that the turn in your relationship be kept quiet, and since the bulk of your family is all downstairs for breakfast, she feels it is the best time for you to return to your own room."

That was a first. Most females begged for him to stay, but Dagmar Reinholdt was tossing him out. Even worse, she was having her servant do it. He should be insulted, but he realized he was more disappointed.

"So she used me and she's tossing me aside?" He gave Fannie his best pout.

"Apparently. Although I must say I admire her for it."

He placed his hand over his heart. "Fannie . . . my love. You wound me. Do you not care for me at all? After all we've been through?"

"My Lord Gwenvael, I care for you as I care for one of my

sons. But I also send off my sons at eighteen and bid them not to return until they have a wife, a babe, and coin in their pocket."

"I have the coin . . ."

Her smirk turned into a smile. Fannie always had a warm spot for him, even while she openly teased him. Of course, she'd made it clear from his first night at Garbhán Isle that he was to keep a respectful distance from her and any of the servant girls who were under her command.

"I believe you're taking too long, my lord, to remove that shiftless rear from my lady's bed."

"Fine. I'll go." He stood, one of the furs around his hips to protect dear Fannie's modesty. "But you tell her I'll be back and she is to follow my orders this time."

"Somehow I doubt Lady Dagmar follows any orders but her own, my lord."

"Very good point. But," he added, pinching Fannie's hip and enjoying the way she jumped and slapped his hand, "that is the challenge."

It had been hard leaving that overly warm bed this morning, but Fannie had eased her awake with a cup of hot tea and they both knew she wasn't in the mood for sly looks and brotherly nudges. The servant arranged for her to bathe in another room and presented her with another grey gown. This one simple and comfortable, easy to move around in.

If Dagmar thought she could lure Fannie away from Annwyl, she'd do it in a second.

Holding on to a mug of hot tea, Dagmar slowly walked around the Great Hall, her eyes taking in everything. The large number of tables from the previous eve were gone, replaced by one long table that went down the middle of the room. Talaith sat on one side, her feet up and a book in her lap that had her complete attention. She'd dismissed the porridge without even looking at it and absently munched on dry toast while fresh water was her morning drink. Talaith's young daughter had already shoveled food down the way Dagmar's father always did and then ran off to meet up with her cousins. Her mother screamed, "And no flying!" after her, but Dagmar seriously doubted the young girl would follow that edict.

Annwyl had come downstairs, but she'd kept right on going out the door. Walking was no easy feat for her, but she'd made it out eventually. She never said a word to anyone and she looked even worse than she did the previous eve. Still, even in her state, everyone seemed to give her a healthy distance.

The bulk of Gwenvael's low-born family camped at the lake where Dagmar had first seen them and apparently enjoyed their morning meals there. The servants set out early with fresh bread and porridge for them.

Gwenvael's brothers and Morfyd had the hall mostly to themselves and they focused on the business of defenses. They had open maps and discussed all the ways the cult could gain entrance to Garbhán Isle. They paid her no mind, so she wandered closer and closer until she stood behind them. She wasn't surprised they ignored her. She was always ignored until she openly involved herself in something that garnered everyone's attention. She wasn't ready for that yet. She was still figuring out all the players for this game, trying to understand the dynamics. The previous evening had helped with that, but there was still so much for her to learn.

Until she learned the risks and rewards involved in this world, she'd simply keep her distance and her own council until she decided that it was the right time to—

"Are you going to keep standing back there, hovering, or are you actually going to help us?"

It took Dagmar a good ten seconds before she realized that Briec had directed that question at her. Raising her gaze, she saw Gwenvael's siblings all staring at her over their shoulders.

"Pardon?"

Briec, who seemed to be in a constant state of boredom, rolled his eyes. "Gwenvael said you were knowledgeable in this. Is that true or was he blowing flame up my ass?"

The visual that particular phrase gave her was *not* attractive, but she ignored it and asked, "You mean knowledge about the Minotaurs?"

"Well, that would help." And his tone was so rife with sarcasm one would think Dagmar had known him for decades and had been annoying him all that time. "But he said you helped your father with his defenses. True or not?" he demanded.

"Briec . . . tone," Talaith said from her spot across the hall, her gaze firmly on the book in front of her.

"Is it true you helped your father with the defenses of the Reinholdt lands?"

His tone hadn't changed, but he seemed to think reworking the sentence covered that.

"Yes. I did. We worked quite closely together." Of course, she really had to pry her way into all that and, in the end, she worked with her father at night, giving him her ideas and suggestions, often trying to make him think he came up with it all on his own. In the morning, he would give instructions to his men to build the defenses she'd designed and she doubted anyone among her father's troops had any idea of her involvement.

"Then help or go away. I can't stand hovering."

"I'm still hearing tone," Talaith said dryly, the book continuing to hold her interest.

The silver dragon's violet-colored eyes narrowed on his mate, and he asked, "You must be hungry, my love. Shouldn't you have a big, steaming bowl of porridge? All big, thick, and gloppy yellow, coating your tongue and throat as it slides down—"

Talaith dropped her book, put one hand over her mouth, and held the other up to silence Briec. She choked, and Dagmar remembered how Talaith had taken quite a liking to the wine the previous eve.

"You are a bastard," Talaith finally snapped before she stood and ran out of the room, her hand firmly back over her mouth.

"That was rude, Briec," Morfyd chastised, although Briec's grin clearly stated he didn't care what his sister thought. Morfyd tapped the table and said to Dagmar, "We could use any and all help at this time. Between your maps and ours, we have to admit we're a little lost."

Dagmar simply wasn't used to this straightforward approach. She was used to having to ease or extort her way into most important situations that were the domain of men. Walking in and taking over wasn't in her nature because she'd been unable to get anything done with that approach.

Yet the dragons were leaving her little choice.

She stepped toward the table and Fearghus moved his chair over a bit, giving her space. She leaned down and focused on the maps.

Well, if they wanted help . . .

"These maps are useless," she stated plainly. "Minotaurs travel underground. I need a map that shows any tunnels you may have built or underground entrances. Also possible accesses from caves, and any places you think it would be easy for them to dig through."

"I think we have something," Éibhear offered as he jumped up and quickly left the room, surprising her with how fast he moved considering his overwhelming size.

"Could they already be here?" Briec asked.

"Doubtful. Minotaurs attack as soon as they gain entrance. They do not give warnings; you will not see them coming. They will not bargain. Ever. If they have a task, they will complete it."

"So if we capture one . . ."

She shook her head at Fearghus's question. "You'll get nothing from a Minotaur. Like most bovines, they are unbelievably stubborn and highly dangerous. Even though their kind hasn't been seen in the Northlands in decades, most of the Northland warlords have defenses aimed solely at protecting themselves from the Minotaurs. I know of no warlord who has a dungeon, just for that reason. It makes it too easy for them to get in."

The dragons all passed glances before Fearghus admitted, "We have six."

Dagmar tilted her head to the side, studying them. "You have six dungeons here? Why?"

"They were all built by Annwyl's father. We no longer use them."

"Ever?"

"Annwyl's a cut-off-your-head, ask-question-later kind of leader."

"I see. And does that philosophy include someone who's merely, say, a petty thief?"

Fearghus and Briec stared at each other, perhaps trying to figure out the correct answer to that question.

Morfyd sighed. "You're all idiots." She looked at Dagmar. "No. There's a town jail for that. Annwyl chose a magistrate to handle simple crimes. Although anyone who feels they've been wrongly treated can, of course, request an audience with her. Although in my opinion she chose well with the current magistrate. But for anything political or involving more than one dead body, she gets involved, and those who are found guilty, don't leave Garbhán Isle."

Harsh, but surprisingly fair.

Éibhear returned with several rolled maps under his arm. He placed them on the table and unrolled them. "Did you mean something more like this?"

Placing her now-cold tea down on the table, Dagmar rested her hands on the worn wood and stared at the maps. "Yes. This will do very nicely. I think I'll be able to match these to the tunnel maps I brought with me. Thank you, Éibhear."

He grinned, quite pleased with himself. "You're welcome."

"Suck up," Briec muttered.

She studied the maps closely. How the queen had lasted this long without an attack, Dagmar would never know. There were so many weak spots, so many easy points of entry, Dagmar was shocked no one had tried before now.

"We have much work to be done here."

Briec nodded solemnly. "And I bet you work much better on your own, don't you?"

Morfyd slammed her hand down on the table. "Gods dammit, Briec!"

"What? I'm merely trying to be helpful."

"No," Dagmar replied. "You're trying to pass the hard work off on me."

He shrugged. "Perhaps."

"And although I find your lack of work ethic appalling"— Dagmar let out a sigh while ignoring Fearghus's accompanying snort—"he does have a point." She glanced at Morfyd before focusing back on the maps. "I actually do much better on my own. So if you can just give me a few hours to—"

The scraping sound of chairs hastily pushed back against a stone floor cut off her words and Dagmar swiveled on her heel, her gaze sweeping the room. In seconds, they'd all run off. She could still hear a door slamming somewhere off in the distance as they scurried away.

"Dragons," she hissed. "No better than rats from a sinking—"

"Good morn, my family! I—" Gwenvael stopped at the bottom of the stairs, his overly cheery greeting cut off when he realized only Dagmar and the servants remained. "Where is everyone?"

"They've deserted me." Dagmar grabbed the seat Fearghus had so hastily vacated and yanked it closer. "I'm not even from here. For all they know I could be a brilliant spy, bent on destroying Annwyl's kingdom—and yet *I'm* the one working on their defenses."

Gwenvael stood next to her now, staring down at the maps. "Are those the most recent maps?"

She dropped into the chair and pulled it closer to the table. "Éibhear seems to think they are."

"He'd know. He loves maps."

Strong fingers brushed the back of her neck and Dagmar forced her body to not writhe in the chair.

"You left me this morning," he murmured.

"I believe 'leaving' you would be me heading back to the Northlands. All I did this morning was travel down the stairs to enjoy first meal while it was still hot."

"You should have woken me."

"And why would I do that?"

In answer, he leaned down and kissed her. His mouth was gentle, the kiss playful, and his tongue stroking hers felt absolutely divine. Her body relaxed, the hand on the back of her neck keeping her head from slapping against the hard wood of the chair back.

When she was nothing more than one of her dogs' limp rag dolls lying in a corner, he pulled slightly away. "Next time, you check with me before you leave my bed. I often have plans first thing in the morning."

"It's my bed, Lord Gwenvael. And who said there'd be a next time?" Her eyes locked with his. "Who said I'd ever let you back into my bed again?"

"It entertains me that you think you have a choice. Now come back upstairs. I have needs that you're required to fulfill."

Dagmar took a breath, appalled at how shaky it sounded going in and coming out. "I have work to do, Defiler."

"Give me an hour upstairs and the day is yours, Beast."

That sounded like an incredibly fair trade-off, especially

when his lips kept rubbing against hers. "All right. But only one—"

"So," a voice said from in front of them, "do you even know this one's name? Or is all that part of the mystery?"

Dagmar only had a second to see a flash of fang and true, bright anger in Gwenvael's gold eyes before he hid all that and turned to face the man who clearly wasn't a man. If she hadn't have been able to tell by his size, the fact that he was an older version of Fearghus would have told her the same dragon's tale.

"Father," Gwenvael said, the smile on his face looking intensely unpleasant. "Don't you look virile this morning? Is Mother chained to the wall again?"

"Don't test me, boy." The dragon placed big hands on narrow hips, black hair streaked with silver and grey brushed off his face. He glanced down at Dagmar. "So can this one actually read, or does she just pretend to have a brain in that head like so many of the others?"

Gwenvael's smile didn't falter, but Dagmar knew it took much out of him. "Is there a reason you're here? Or were you simply in the mood to torture your offspring for old time's sake?"

"I'm here to see Fearghus's nightmare. Where is she?"

"I thought you'd left her chained to the wall. And shouldn't we just call her Mum?"

That cold, black gaze latched onto Gwenvael, and Dagmar quickly stood, resting her hand on Gwenvael's arm. "If you speak of Queen Annwyl, I'm sure I can help you find her."

Now that cold, black gaze was on her. "Who the hell are you?"

"I am Dagmar." She kept it simple, unwilling to give the older dragon more than that.

"I see." He sighed in boredom. "Well, Dagmar, I'm sure your services last night were greatly appreciated, but you can return to whatever brothel he dragged you out of. There's important work to be done, and I don't need one of the local whores interfering."

Gwenvael let out a startled laugh, but he recognized it as the kind one lets out when he's realized he's accidentally cut off his finger or set his house on fire. That startled laugh before the real horror sets in.

Dagmar stepped away from Gwenvael and he grabbed hold of her arm, but she shook him off. She walked sedately over to his father, her hands folded primly in front of her, her head scarf perfectly in place over that simple braid. She looked as he'd first seen her, back in her grey, wool dress that had been scrubbed clean the day before.

The boring, quiet, demure spinster daughter of a warlord.

But that volcano inside her simmered beneath and that's what Bercelak the Great was not expecting. He was used to humans like Annwyl, Talaith. Fighters. Assassins. Those who went in for the direct kill.

Little did his father know, Dagmar was more lethal.

"Perhaps I should make myself clear, Lord—" She gestured with a slight dip of her head.

"Bercelak. Bercelak the Great."

"Oh." She stopped, sized him up carefully. "*You're* Bercelak the Great? My tutors didn't describe you well at all."

"Tutors?" He glanced at Gwenvael, but if he thought he'd be getting any help from him . . .

"Yes. I realize I didn't make myself clear. I am Dagmar Reinholdt. Thirteenth offspring of The Reinholdt and Only Daughter."

His scowl deepened. "You're the daughter of The Reinholdt?"

"Yes. I am."

"What are you doing here?"

"I've come to see Queen Annwyl."

"Right. Except I find you playing with my boy."

"I don't think Fearghus would appreciate me *playing* with Annwyl."

Gwenvael snorted another laugh, which earned him another glare from his father.

"I have to admit," Dagmar went on as she leisurely walked around Bercelak. "You're not what I expected."

"Is that right?"

"You seem much braver than I heard you were."

Confused, Bercelak looked down at Dagmar, his gaze following her as she circled him. "What?"

"You know. How you ran away from the Battle of Ødven."

This little barbarian truly was evil. It had been Gwenvael who had told Dagmar those stories about Bercelak on their long flight to Dark Plains. And he'd told them to her as he'd been told, showing Bercelak for the killer he was, as a warning to her to keep her distance from Bercelak the Great should she meet him.

But she'd turned all that to gain her own vengeful ends— and Gwenvael adored her for it.

"I did no such thing," Bercelak huffed, shocked.

"Or when you were found crying and whimpering near the Mountains of Urpa."

"That's a damn lie!"

"Doubtful. These are common stories among my people. And tell me," she went on, "is it true that you only survived your battle with Finnbjörn the Callous after you begged him for mercy?"

Black smoke eased from Bercelak's human nostrils. "The only thing that protected Finnbjörn from *me* was when he returned my sister!"

She blinked up at him, her face beautifully blank. "No need to yell."

"You vicious little—"

"Father," Gwenvael warned.

"And you brought her here!"

Gwenvael shrugged. "I begged her to marry me in the Northlands, but she wanted to get to know me first. You know how girls are," he finished in a conspiratorial whisper.

"What the hell are you talking about?"

Dagmar easily—and rather bravely, in Gwenvael's estimation—stepped between the two.

"Gwenvael, why don't you get Fearghus?"

"I'm not leaving you alone when he's snorting smoke, woman."

"I'll be fine. Go get Fearghus."

"I can call him here. I don't have to leave."

"No. Go get him." She peered at Gwenvael over her shoulder. "Or would you prefer your father found Annwyl on his own?"

No. That wouldn't be good either. But he didn't understand why she wanted to be alone with Bercelak. The old bastard still had no problems eating humans when the mood struck him, often bringing them home as treats to Gwenvael's mother.

"Dagmar—"

"I'll be fine here. Go."

He was reluctant, that was obvious; but he eventually did as she asked.

"I'll be two minutes." He glared at his father. "No flame."

Dagmar watched Gwenvael disappear down a hallway before she turned back to face his father.

In all her years, she'd never seen a scowl quite like that. As if the dragon were filled with nothing but hate and rage. She'd thought Fearghus's scowl was bad, but nothing, absolutely nothing, like this.

Taunting him had been pleasurable since she hadn't

appreciated the way he'd spoken to his son. And although Gwenvael had described the older dragon to her as some kind of murdering lizard, her instincts told her something else— she just wasn't sure what that was yet. Who was Bercelak the Great, and why oh why did she desire to taunt him the way she did her own father?

"Why are you really here, Northlander?" he demanded.

She smiled because she could tell it annoyed him. He wanted her frightened and scurrying away. Not likely.

"Why I'm here is my business and the business of Queen Annwyl. Perhaps you should tend to your own, Consort."

He stepped closer to her. "Do you really want to challenge me, *human*?"

"I don't know. Do I?"

"Do you think I'm like my son? That the fact that you're female sways me in any way as it does him?" He leaned down a bit, his face a tad closer than she would have liked. "There is no kindness in me. No softness. No caring. And I'll stop at nothing to protect my kind."

"Then you and I, Lord Bercelak, have much in common."

"Tell me why you're here, little girl. Tell me, or I'll tear you apart."

She debated whether to believe him. Was he evil? Pure and simple? Was there no reasoning with someone so filled with hate and rage, who had no softness about him at all?

Following her instincts as she'd always had, she challenged, "Do your worst. I *dare* you."

His nostrils flared, the black smoke curling out from them increasing, and she saw fangs. *That's new.*

"Granddaddy!"

Both Dagmar and Bercelak jumped as Izzy charged into the Great Hall from the courtyard, running across the table, only to throw herself directly onto the dragon's body.

"They told me I'd just missed you at the lake," she squealed, delighted.

Her arms wrapped tight around his neck, her legs around his waist, she kissed his cheek. "I haven't seen you in ages! Where have you been?"

"Uh . . . Izzy . . ." He folded his arms across his chest, trying desperately to keep that scowl on his face. "Get down from there," he snapped.

Without seeming to notice his tone, Izzy did just that.

"Morning, Lady Dagmar," she said cheerfully.

"Good morn to you, Izzy."

The young warrior stood in front of Bercelak, her light brown eyes glowing. "So what did you bring me?" she asked, though it sounded a bit more like a demand.

"What?" He shook his head. "Nothing."

Her entire body shimmied like one of Dagmar's dogs when she held up a favored toy. "You always bring me something! What did you bring me?"

"Can we not talk about this later?" he snarled viciously, even making Dagmar think of running.

But Izzy only stomped her foot and snarled back, "Give me!"

Through gritted teeth, "Back."

Now she frowned. "What?"

"Back," he said again and added a quick motion of his head.

Izzy walked behind the dragon and squealed again, making Dagmar wince. The young girl ran back around, a gold and jeweled dagger in her hand.

"This is beautiful!" She danced from foot to foot in front of the dragon and said in one long rush of words, "I've never had anything so beautiful before in my entire life and I love you and I can't wait to show Branwen—she's going to be so jealous— and you are so amazing!" Then she added, "I love you, love you, love you!" She leaped up into his arms and kissed his face until the dragon couldn't hold the smile back anymore.

"Would you stop that!" But he didn't seem to really mind.

"You are the best grandfather a girl could ever have!" She kissed his forehead and jumped back down. "I can't wait to show Branwen!" she cheered again, running toward the exit of the Great Hall. "And Celyn!"

He'd been trying for that angry gaze again, glaring at Dagmar, when Izzy's last words caused him to look nothing but panicked. "You stay away from Celyn!"

She only laughed. "You sound like Dad!" Then she was gone.

Turning back to face Dagmar, he seemed not to appreciate the smirk she couldn't stop.

"You can get that look off your face, little miss. Izzy's different. And she's the only one. Except for her, my soul is empty. No room for anyone human."

"That's it!" Talaith said as she marched down the stairs. "No more wine for me." As she landed on the bottom step, she stopped and smiled. "Bercelak! I didn't know you were here."

Much steadier now and recently bathed, she walked over to them and reached up to hug the dragon. "I'm so glad to see you. How are you doing?"

"Fine. Fine," he said gruffly.

She stepped away from him, his hand held by hers. "And what brings you here?"

"He's here to see Annwyl," Dagmar filled in. "I was just going to take him to find her myself." She grinned, making sure to flutter her eyes a bit as Gwenvael did. It annoyed her; why wouldn't it annoy his father? "I simply can't wait to get to know him better." She placed her hand over her heart. "He reminds me of my own dear father."

"Try the stables," Talaith suggested, completely missing the glower Bercelak seared Dagmar with. "She's been hiding in there lately. I think she misses that war ox of hers she has the nerve to call a horse." She beamed up at Bercelak. "I do hope you're staying. We haven't talked in ages."

"Um . . . yeah, well . . ."

She released his hand and stepped away.

"Oh . . . uh . . ." Bercelak glanced at Dagmar, then muttered, "The queen wanted me to give you this." He yanked a pouch hanging from his belt and handed it to her.

Talaith tugged the pouch open. "The Fianait root!" And just as quickly her face fell.

"It's not the right one?" he asked, obviously concerned.

"It's not that." She let out a breath. "I'm just so frustrated. I work on these spells, and I see what I want. But dammit, Bercelak, I just cannot make it come together. The power is there. The energy. But I simply can't control it. I'm getting frustrated."

"It'll take time to hone the power within you, Talaith," he patiently explained. "You're being too hard on yourself. Too impatient."

She rolled her eyes and smirked. "I know. I don't need you to tell me; I hear it enough from your son."

"But apparently you're not listening. The queen has already offered to help you; you should take her up on it."

"She must be busy, though."

"She'll make the time for you. Besides, she needs the break. The Elders are making her insane, and her worries over Annwyl . . ." His gaze strayed to Dagmar and he finished with a mutter, "Just have Briec bring you. Or I can take you."

"That is so sweet!" Then Bercelak was being hugged again. He glared at Dagmar over Talaith's back, and Dagmar grinned, making sure to show him *all* her teeth.

"I simply don't understand it," Talaith said, pulling away from Bercelak. "How can *you* possibly be the father of Briec the Arrogant? You are so nice and he's so not. It amazes me."

Talaith winked. "Try to stay for dinner tonight," she said before walking away.

Dagmar absolutely adored the silence that followed

Talaith's exit, knowing the growling, snarling dragon was feeling completely uncomfortable.

"This changes nothing," he finally barked.

"Oh, I know. Big, scary . . . *you*." She mockingly slashed at him with her hand and added a little roar sound.

"Now you're just irritating me."

"I know." She took his arm. "So why don't we find Annwyl? I'm positive she detests you and I'm sure nothing will change that."

"I guess that's something," he grumbled.

Chapter 23

Morfyd held her hands up, her body blocking the doorway. "No one is going back to the hall until you all calm down. There will not be a family free-for-all."

"I say free-for-all for everyone!" Gwenvael cheered.

"Would you shut up?"

Really, she didn't understand her kin. They all knew their father could be a bit of a prat; why her brothers insisted on fighting with him, she'd never know. There was no point. Although Gwenvael was in high spirits. Not surprising since he'd apparently consummated his alliance with the sharp-witted Lady Dagmar.

It had taken mere seconds for rumors of his being in her room to make the castle rounds this morning.

"I think we should all calmly go and talk to Father and see what he wants."

"Fine. We'll do that. Now move." Briec grabbed her arm

and yanked her away from the door while Fearghus snatched it open and stormed out, the other two right behind him.

"Dammit!" She went after them but found them standing around the Great Hall, looking confused.

"Where did he go?" Fearghus asked. Morfyd knew how her brother hated when he was ready for a fight and there was no one there to fight him.

Gwenvael, however, appeared the most panicked. "Where's Dagmar?"

Briec stared at his brother. "Finding out what dragon stomach acid is like?"

As Talaith had suggested, the Blood Queen was in the stables. Not the main Garbhán Isle stables where the army commanders kept their war horses. No, she was in a separate stable specifically for the queen's war stallion, Violence. *Lovely name. And what a lucky horse, too.* So he wouldn't be lonely, he had his own stable dog—a delightful 50-pound mixed breed who ran up to Dagmar and licked her boots—and a bevy of worthy mares. The one in the stall closest to him kept nuzzling his side, while Annwyl petted his muzzle.

It all appeared very serene and a bit sad, but something was off. Dagmar could feel it. She held her hand up, silently ordering Bercelak the Great to hold his position at the door. And, one of the greatest warriors of the Southland dragons did as she bade.

She approached cautiously, not wanting to startle the queen, but as she neared, the feeling that something was wrong grew until it nearly strangled her.

"My queen?"

"What?"

The first sign Dagmar was right: She'd only been here for less than two days, but she'd never known the woman not to correct anyone stupid enough to title her with anything but "Annwyl." Or, at the very least, a simple "my lady."

Dagmar moved closer, her eyes examining everything. "I'm sorry to bother you, my lady, but you have a visitor."

The queen wouldn't look at her, her gaze focused on the horse she petted with one hand. The other hand was not resting on her belly as it had been since Dagmar had met her, but instead gripping the stable gate penning in her horse. Readjusting her spectacles a bit, Dagmar watched as the long, strong fingers of the queen dug into the wood until it began to splinter.

Now Dagmar understood.

"How long have you been having the contractions, Annwyl?"

She'd thought Annwyl merely had quickened breathing due to the load she currently carried; now Dagmar saw that she'd been panting. Not dramatically, but as a way to control her pain. Something a warrior learned early in training, just as Dagmar's kinsmen had.

Annwyl swallowed but still wouldn't look at her. "Days."

Days? She'd been having contractions for days and she'd said nothing?

Dagmar let out a breath. Yelling at the nitwit wouldn't help; she needed the queen calm and pliable at this moment.

"But it's gotten worse in the last few hours?" she asked, keeping her voice even and unaffected.

Annwyl nodded. "But it's too soon, Dagmar. They can't come out yet."

"I believe it's no longer your choice, my lady."

"Yes, but I—" The pain was so brutal and swift, the queen's words were cut off and she had to use both hands on the gate to prevent herself from dropping to the floor.

"Annwyl—"

"It's too soon," she repeated, once she could speak.

"Perhaps not," Bercelak said softly, now standing behind Dagmar.

"You?" the queen fairly snarled. "What are you doing here?"

He ignored her question and said instead, "Mostly all my offspring were hatched after six months. Why should my grandchildren be any different?"

Seemingly stunned by his statement, Annwyl stared at Bercelak for a long moment. Then she asked, "Mostly?"

"Gwenvael lasted eight months. But I think that's because he is and always will be a lazy prat. He lounged in that egg for months until, I'm convinced, he fell asleep and accidentally broke the shell while turning over. As I said, lazy prat."

The queen smiled, her laugh a little breathy. "Then you don't think this is . . . uh . . ."

"Ill timed?" Bercelak shook his head. "No. Not at all. But we need to get you back inside, Annwyl. To a bed, so the grandchildren of someone as great as I can be born in luxury and comfort."

Her smile quickly turned into an intense expression of distrust. "Why are you being so nice to me?"

"Because I am in the mood to do so. *Do not question me!*" he bellowed.

"Don't yell at me!" she bellowed back.

Dagmar held her hands up. "Perhaps we could have this delightful yelling another time." She leaned over and whispered to Annwyl, "And how many times do you think you can get him to carry you?"

"You may have a point," she said moments before another contraction tore through her. Her fingers ripped into the wooden slats of the gate, a piece breaking apart in her hands. This was no ordinary pain, Dagmar knew that now. She also knew they were quickly running out of time.

She passed a hard glance at Bercelak, and he nodded.

When the contraction passed, he stepped forward. "Let's

get you inside. Unless you'd prefer to have your children out here among the horses and hay like a homeless peasant?"

"Was there really no nicer way for you to ask me that question?" she asked once he had her in his arms, the two hated enemies staring each other in the eye.

"I'm sure there was, but I chose not to use it."

"Of course."

He headed out, Dagmar beside them, but halfway to the Great Hall, Annwyl made Bercelak stop.

"Before we go inside," she said, panting heavily, sweat now covering her entire body. "I need you both to promise me something . . ."

Gwenvael stood in the middle of the Great Hall and tried hard not to panic.

"I doubt he'd actually kill her," he said.

Morfyd slugged his shoulder.

"Ow."

"You're an idiot. Of course he's not going to kill her."

"All I know is that I left them here together and now they're gone. Remember what happened the first time we left him alone with Annwyl?"

"That was the only time we left him alone with Annwyl." Fearghus sat on the table closest to his brothers and sister. "So," Fearghus asked casually, "how was last night?"

Gwenvael, not in the mood to tell his kin anything at the moment, shrugged. "Last night was fine; why?"

Fearghus's eyes narrowed a bit, and then he snarled in disgust, "Gods dammit!"

He snatched a small leather pouch off his belt and tossed it to Briec.

Grinning, their silver-haired brother said, "Told you he'd fuck her."

"I knew he'd try, but I thought she was smarter than that."

Gwenvael folded his arms across his chest. "What the hell does that mean?"

His brothers glanced at him and then turned back toward each other.

"A woman has needs," Briec explained to Fearghus. "Even a Northland woman."

"I still thought she'd think better of herself."

Now he was really getting pissed. *"And what the hell does that mean?"*

Before anyone could answer, Izzy charged into the hall and up the stairs.

"Look, brother, you have to face it," Briec said. "You're not exactly in her class."

Gwenvael's mouth dropped open in astonishment and he glared at Éibhear, who'd walked in a few moments after the rest of them.

"I didn't say anything!" the pup cried out desperately.

"*I* am not in her class?" Gwenvael snarled. "I'm a Dragon Prince of royal blood and *I'm* not in her class?"

"She's smart," Fearghus said simply.

"And I'm not?"

Morfyd patted his shoulder. "You have your own special talents."

"Yeah," Briec said simply. "Fucking."

"Briec," Morfyd chastised. Sort of. She didn't put any real venom into it.

"You're all bloody bastards, you know that?"

Izzy charged back down the stairs, stopping briefly in front of them while she danced back and forth on her toes. Then she sighed in disgust and ran off down the closest hallway. "Mum! Come quick!"

Gwenvael began to pace. "As much as I do for this family and you have the gall—"

His tirade was cut off when they all started laughing at him. Briec and Fearghus were lying back on the table, laughing. Morfyd was doubled over. Only Éibhear wasn't laughing, but he did look guilty.

Gwenvael guessed that was something.

Unreasonably hurt, he watched as Izzy and now Talaith ran through the hall and out the big doorway.

"You know what?" he said, turning toward his kin. "You can all burn in the deepest, fiery pits of hell. Because none of you bloody bastards—" His eyes strayed to the front of the hall and his words choked in his throat. "Fearghus."

His brother sat up, wiping tears of laughter from his eyes, until he saw what Gwenvael saw.

Talaith tapped her daughter's shoulder. "Go upstairs to the room we've set up and turn the furs down." Izzy charged off. "And then go find Brastias!"

There were things in the world Gwenvael never thought he'd see. A dragon with two heads—although humans did love to write about them as if they existed—his oldest sister performing a human sacrifice since she did seem to adore the humans so, and his father, Bercelak the Great, carrying Annwyl the Bloody as if she were spun of the finest glass.

Talaith had her hand on Annwyl's shoulder as her gaze locked with Morfyd's. "It's time, sister."

Morfyd nodded and snapped her fingers at Éibhear, yanking him out of the panic attack he was about to have, if the expression on his face was any indication. "Éibhear, go to the servants and tell them it's time. They already know what to do. Then go down to the lake and tell the family. Everyone, and I mean *everyone*, is to be battle ready, just in case."

Éibhear nodded and ran off.

Bercelak walked over to Fearghus. "You'd best take her. I think her desire to slit my throat is growing."

"I'd have already tried," Annwyl whispered, "but I feared you'd drop me."

Grinning, Bercelak placed Annwyl in Fearghus's arms.

"Take her up, Fearghus," Morfyd ordered, Talaith already running up the stairs as Izzy charged back down and out the door to fetch Brastias.

Fearghus pulled his mate tight against his chest and nodded at his father. "Thank you."

Bercelak grunted and watched until his son had disappeared up the stairs and down the hall. Once he was gone, he silently turned and headed back toward the doors.

"Where are you going?" Morfyd asked.

"To get your mother." He stopped long enough to look at them over his shoulder. "I think we all know she needs to be here."

Morfyd swallowed, her eyes intent on their father's face. "Aye. We do."

Without another word, their father left, and Morfyd headed toward the stairs.

Briec stood. "Morfyd?"

She stopped on the first step, her hand gripping the railing. "You'll both need to be ready."

"Ready?" Briec asked.

The breath she took was shaky, and Gwenvael knew his sister was fighting for strength. "You'll need to watch out for Éibhear." She looked at both of them, her blue eyes clear as was her meaning. "You know how close he is to her."

With that, she lifted her witches' robes so she wouldn't trip and jogged up the steps.

Briec and Gwenvael stared at each other for a long time until Briec said, "I'll go work with Brastias to make sure everything is locked down."

Dagmar laid her hand on Briec's arm. "I can handle the defenses while the rest of you handle this. I'll need someone from

Annwyl's army to work with and a few laborers. I'll take care of everything else. You won't need to worry."

Briec nodded. "I'll arrange it." Then he was gone.

Gwenvael sat down hard on the table, his eyes focused on the floor. He didn't see the worn stone where everyone stomped day after day. He saw nothing. Felt nothing. Except lost. For the first time in his life, he felt hopelessly lost.

He didn't realize Dagmar sat beside him until he felt her take his hand, interlacing their fingers.

"You wouldn't lie to me—even if I begged you to, would you?" he asked.

Dagmar shook her head. "No, Gwenvael. Not about something like this."

"I understand."

"But I will be here. As long as you need me. If that helps."

"It helps."

She nodded and squeezed his hand.

And when the screaming started, she squeezed his hand tighter.

Chapter 24

Standing in the middle of the courtyard, the afternoon suns beginning their descent to nighttime, Dagmar gave the guard captain further instructions on what she wanted and sent him off. She pulled out her plans and studied them. Her overwhelming feeling of dread had made her choices confusing. Usually she knew what to do and when to do it almost immediately. Quick decision-making something she'd always prided herself on. But the gut instinct she often relied on was too clouded by the dread that had settled over Garbhán Isle. A dread that had magnified in the past hour. Because in the past hour, the screaming had stopped.

Dagmar had assisted on many births over the years. Not by choice but because it was expected of her. And in all those years the one thing she'd always known was that it was never a quiet affair. There was always screaming, crying, some laughing, and, in the case of many of her brothers' wives, lots of cursing and promises of brutal retribution.

One look at Annwyl and Dagmar knew she was a curser. And yet now the queen lay quiet behind her closed door. Only Morfyd, Talaith, and several healers allowed inside. And outside that bedroom were Gwenvael's kin—waiting.

Suddenly Dagmar heard screaming, but it was not Annwyl. It was the humans around her in the courtyard. They screamed and ran off. She only had a few seconds to wonder why when the wind stirred and lifted around her. She looked up and watched in fascination as a great white dragon touched her claws to the ground, her wings scraping against the nearby buildings. A black dragon landed behind her, and almost immediately they shifted to human.

Dagmar had to fight her urge to stare. The female was beautiful. Astonishingly beautiful with white hair that reached down to her toes and a long, strong body. But it was the markings that had Dagmar wanting to move closer to take a long look. The dragoness had been branded with the image of a dragon from the tip of one toe, across her foot, around her leg, swirling around her torso, back, chest, until it reached her neck. It was not a nasty brand she might have received while being held prisoner either. It was a beautiful brand of a dragon. Almost elegant in its execution with the darkest black markings against white skin. It should have marred her beauty, but it didn't. And she clearly wore it with pride.

The Claiming that Morfyd and Talaith had told Dagmar about. Romantic? Really? Looked more painful than romantic.

Cold blue eyes immediately locked on Dagmar. "You. Servant girl. Where is your queen?"

Bercelak placed his hand on the female's shoulder and turned so he could speak to her in hushed tones. That was when Dagmar realized Bercelak had his own brand. This one covered his back all the way down until his ass met his thighs.

"This is Dagmar Reinholdt, my love. Of the north." He gave something of a smile to Dagmar while motioning to the female. "Dagmar, this is the Dragon Queen of Dark Plains."

Sizing the monarch up almost instantly, Dagmar dropped to one knee and bowed her head. "My liege. It is a great and overwhelming honor to meet you."

"Hhhhm," the Dragon Queen said. "One who knows the proper ways of things."

Long legs, one of them branded, now stood in front of Dagmar. "Rise, Northlander."

Dagmar did. "What is thy bidding, my liege?"

"Yes," she said. "This one has been taught well." She motioned toward the castle. "Take me to Annwyl."

Dagmar headed back to the castle, the two dragons behind her.

"We need to put clothes on," her consort told the Dragon Queen.

"I don't have time for that."

Dagmar stopped right inside the doorway leading to the Great Hall. "Your daughter left you clothes for your convenience, my liege."

"Honestly! Humans and their weakness."

"I couldn't agree more, my lady."

The queen sniffed and held her hand out. "Just give me the damn things."

Once the queen had slipped the simple sheath gown over

her head and Bercelak had pulled on black leggings and boots, Dagmar led them up the stairs and to the back of the hallway. The room had been set up specifically for when Annwyl was ready to give birth. Supplies had been stocked and at the ready and the bed had been much smaller than her own so that the healers and Morfyd could move around it easily.

As soon as they stepped into the hallway, the Dragon Queen's offspring pulled themselves up from the floor.

The queen's blue eyes swept across the group before she stepped next to Briec. "Where is Keita?" she demanded softly.

The silver-haired dragon shrugged and rolled his eyes. "I have no idea."

The queen let out a sigh. "Foolish brat. I should have known . . . Never mind. I'll deal with her later." She leaned over and kissed her son's cheek. "Briec."

"Mother."

She moved down the hallway, greeting each of her children.

Smiling at Éibhear, she brushed his blue hair off his worried face. "My baby boy."

"Hello, Mum." She went up on her toes and he came down a bit so she could kiss his forehead. She greeted Gwenvael next, kissing his cheek. "And my brat."

"Mother."

She stopped in front of Izzy, placing her hand on the girl's cheek, wiping a tear with her thumb. "Hello, my little Izzy."

Izzy choked on a sob. "Grandmum."

The queen leaned down and kissed her cheek, then whispered something in the girl's ear. Izzy let out a breath and nodded.

Several more steps took the queen to the front of the door Annwyl lay behind—and her eldest son.

"My son."

"Mother."

She petted his cheek, and Dagmar saw more affection in that single gesture than she'd ever seen before. The queen turned away from her son and grabbed the handle on the door. She snapped her fingers. "Northlander. With me."

Gwenvael's eyes widened and he reached for Dagmar. She shook her head. "It's all right," she whispered as she passed him and followed the queen.

The door closed behind them, and Dagmar saw the relief on Morfyd's face at the sight of her mother. She stepped away from the bed and motioned her mother closer. The two began to speak in soft whispers while Talaith held Annwyl's hand and wiped her brow. Three other healers worked with herbs and roots, creating different concoctions they hoped would help.

Dagmar looked down at Annwyl and she felt suddenly cold all over. The strong—albeit crying—female she'd met just yesterday in the library was gone. All that remained was a pale, sweat-covered body lying in soaked furs. The only sign of life was when her body would stiffen as another bout of pain shot through her. It would last twenty or so seconds, and then she'd be still again.

For the first time in years, Dagmar thought of her own mother. Had she looked like this before Dagmar came screaming into the world? Did she seem so weak and near death to Sigmar? And would these children spend their lives blaming themselves for their mother's death as Dagmar secretly did?

Would they be right?

The Dragon Queen stepped away from her daughter and over to Talaith's side. She took Annwyl's hand from Briec's mate and closed her eyes. Dagmar had no concept of how long the queen stood like that. A few seconds, minutes, days? She didn't know. They all crowded around the bed, waiting for her to say something. Anything.

But she didn't have to say a word. Not once she opened those eyes. Those blue eyes that had been so cold only minutes before when she'd looked at Dagmar, now appeared . . . devastated. She was devastated. Devastated because there was absolutely nothing she could do.

Dagmar knew this even before Talaith turned away and walked to the window. Even before Morfyd shook her head and said, "No, Mother. You have to do something. There must be something."

The queen gently laid Annwyl's arm back down, placing it carefully. "You already know there's nothing I can do. That you can do. Nothing except one thing."

"No." Tears flowed freely down Morfyd's cheeks as she stepped away from the bed and her mother. "No. I won't do it."

"Tell her what she told you, Northlander."

Dagmar's head snapped up and both Talaith and Morfyd turn to stare at her. "My liege, I—"

"This is no time for games, little girl. In fact, we are running out of time quite quickly, so you tell them. Tell them what she said to you and Bercelak when you brought her back here from the stables. Tell them what she made you promise her."

Dagmar had never planned to say anything about what Annwyl had said, hoping it was merely the words of a scared, first-time mother. And when Bercelak had only grunted at Annwyl's words, Dagmar had assumed he'd say nothing either. And perhaps he hadn't. Perhaps his mate knew him so well he'd not had to say a word for her to know the truth of things.

Dagmar cleared her throat, wishing for the first time in days she was back at home with her idiot sisters-in-law and her dangerously stupid brothers.

"She . . . um . . . She told us that no matter what, you were to save the babes. Even if it meant her life, you were to save them."

Morfyd's head bowed at Dagmar's words while Talaith's gaze moved to the ceiling.

"She knows the price," the Dragon Queen explained. "She knows and she's made her choice. We can not ignore that."

"But Fearghus . . ."

"Has to know before we start." The queen nodded. "I will tell him."

"No." Morfyd wiped her face with the palms of her hands. "I'll tell him." She headed toward the door, but stopped long enough to tell the healers, "Prepare everything we need."

Gwenvael looked up from his place on the floor as the door slowly creaked open and Morfyd stepped out. She kept her eyes down and immediately reached for Fearghus. She took his hand and walked him down the hall a bit, pulling him into the doorway of an unused room at the very end of the hall.

The rest of them got to their feet, pulling themselves up off the floor and watching as Morfyd placed her hand on their brother's shoulder and stepped in close. She kept her voice low, but whatever she said, whatever she told him, had Fearghus sitting hard on the floor, the door slamming against the wall as his back fell into it. Morfyd dropped in front of him, both hands now on his shoulders as she spoke to him. He shook his head and pressed the palms of his hands against his eyes.

Gwenvael immediately looked at Briec and he saw the same shock and pain in his brother's face that he felt. Éibhear simply kept shaking his head, as if refusing to believe what he knew was truth.

But it was Izzy, Izzy who loved Annwyl as more than a favorite aunt, who burst into hysterical tears. She pushed herself away from the wall and tried to run. But Bercelak grabbed hold of her and swept her up in his arms.

"It's all right, Izzy. It's all right," he whispered as he stroked her back and let her sob uncontrollably into his neck, her arms wrapped around his shoulders, her legs around his waist.

Gwenvael looked back at Fearghus and Morfyd. His brother finally nodded to something his sister said. She kissed his forehead and stood, walking back toward them. She reached out and grasped the door handle. Before pushing it open, she said to them all, "We'll let you know when we're done."

Then she slipped inside, the door closing behind her.

Fearghus sat on the castle roof, staring out over Dark Plains. He'd stayed human, knowing he'd have to go back inside at any moment. But he'd discovered this particular spot long ago that he could easily reach while human or dragon.

He sat and stared, his boot-shod feet pressed against the slats all that kept him in place.

He'd always known that any time Annwyl went off to battle, she may not return to him except on the shields of her men. They both knew it was a risk they took because they were monarchs who did not hide behind fortress walls waiting for wars to end. They fought alongside their kind. And with that choice, they risked death.

Yet this had not been their choice. They'd never sat down and discussed having children and when. Instead the gods had chosen for them, taking away any choice they had.

And because of the gods, Fearghus was going to lose his mate. The only female he would ever truly love. Even when they were thousands of leagues apart from each other, Fearghus always knew Annwyl was part of his world, part of his life.

Now he'd no longer have that comfort, that certainty.

He heard two strong cries ring out through the castle and he shut his eyes, trying so very hard not to feel resentment toward innocents who had even less choice in all of this than he and Annwyl had.

He knew he should go down to be with his twins, but he simply didn't have the heart. The pain tore at him like knives.

As he sat, relieved when the crying eventually stopped, he felt his mother sit down next to him. He wasn't surprised she'd tracked him down. The only other who could have was Annwyl.

"A boy and a girl," she said. "Beautiful. Healthy." She shrugged. "Seem human."

"And Annwyl's dead."

"No. Not yet."

Fearghus looked at his mother. "But you're the only thing keeping her alive."

"For as long as I can."

"And how long is that?"

She took a breath. "Three days. Perhaps four."

"Three days." Three days out of what should have been another four- or five-hundred years at least. "Is she awake?"

He knew each answer she had to give caused his mother more pain, but he had to know. "No."

"And she won't be again, will she?"

"No."

He gave a snort that couldn't possibly pass for a laugh. "Then why bother keeping her alive?"

"Because you'll need to say good-bye. You all will." She cleared her throat. "Now, I'll stay until—" She cleared her throat again. "I'll stay for as long as you need me. And I'll do what I can."

Which, at the moment was nothing, but instead of saying that, he simply said, "Thank you."

Briec stared into the large crib holding his niece and nephew while around him healers and midwives bustled about.

They were both extremely—he frowned—well-developed babes. They didn't look like newborns at all. They seemed older. In fact, they seemed to be more like dragon hatchlings in many ways. Both had full heads of hair—the boy with his mother's brown hair with light brown streaks and the girl with her father's pitch-black hair—and their eyes were open, able to focus. Already they reached for things they wanted and could grab with their small hands.

Truly, if Briec didn't know better, he'd swear they were nearly three months old, rather than born no more than an hour ago.

Annwyl is dying. That's what his sister had told him a few minutes before. They'd cut the human queen open to get to her babes and then sewn her back up again. It wasn't the procedure that was killing her. It was rare but had been done before by well-trained healers and witches, including Morfyd who helped most women in the nearby village through easy and hard births.

No, it wasn't the procedure. It had been the babes. They'd literally sucked the life from their mother, growing too fast and becoming too powerful for her human body to contain them. Now Annwyl was almost skeletal on her bed, the skin that was always taut around powerful muscle sagging on her.

Unintentionally, the babes had drained her of her life's energy, and now the only thing keeping her heart beating and her lungs breathing was the Dragon Queen. The most powerful Dragonwitch that Briec knew of.

He finally tore his gaze away from the sleeping babes and looked at one of the midwives. "Talaith?"

"She went to fetch the nursemaid who will feed the twins, my lord."

He nodded, but Briec had already seen the nursemaid outside the room, talking to another healer.

With one last look at his niece and nephew, he slipped from the room, glad to see the guards placed outside the door. He checked his room and the kitchens, the Great Hall, and the library. He went outside and eventually caught her scent. He followed it through the woods to a small lake that few thought about because it was hidden by the trees and several large boulders. Many a night they'd come here and Briec had spent hours making Talaith sob his name.

Now his Talaith sobbed for a different reason.

She kneeled by the lake, her torso bent over her legs, her arms around her waist—and she wailed. She wailed as he'd never heard her before. This woman, who'd been through absolute hell and back, wailed for a friend she'd come to love as a sister and for the heartbreak of a family she now saw as her own.

Briec kneeled down behind her, his knees spread so he could pull her into his body. He held her tight in his arms, leaning over her so she could feel him surrounding her. So she could know that she didn't have to go through this alone.

Her hands gripped his arms, the small fingers digging into the chain-mail shirt covering him.

And he let her wail. He let her wail not only for herself but for all of them. Because Talaith no longer had to be anything but what she was. She was no monarch. She had no kingdom to rule. No politics to concern herself with.

She was simply a woman whose heart was breaking. And Briec was grateful that at least one of them could show it.

Dagmar had learned very early in life that animals felt and understood more than humans ever gave them credit for. Knowing this, she went to the stables where they kept Annwyl's horse. As soon as she saw the powerful stallion, she knew he knew. He was pushed up against the back wall, the mare in the stall beside him, pressing her majestic head against his neck.

Cautiously, Dagmar opened the gate to his stall and stepped inside, making sure to close the gate behind her. This would definitely be one of those times her father would yank her by the hair and tell her not to be stupid, but when it came to animals, Dagmar always followed her instincts—and they'd never failed her.

She approached the enormous beast, wondering how Annwyl ever sat, much less fought, on top of such an animal. She moved carefully, doing her best not to startle him. The mare watched her closely, wanting to see what she might be up to.

Once she stood next to him, Dagmar reached out and brushed her hand against his side. The stallion moved restlessly but didn't strike out.

She held up the fur blanket she had in her arms, showing it to the mare. Soft brown eyes blinked at Dagmar but the mare didn't do much of anything else.

Dagmar really wished this was a dog. Dogs she understood so easily. But horses were different and she knew that. She also knew that the horse would be forgotten for the next few days, even though he loved Annwyl as much as anyone else. The bond between a horse and rider was the same as between dog and handler. It went beyond being a mere pet. It was a partnership where one trusted the other and vice versa. Of all the bonds she knew, it was the most indestructible and the most unappreciated.

Taking a deep breath, Dagmar lifted the fur blanket she'd nicked from Annwyl's room and slowly placed it over the stallion's back. She adjusted it so it rested high on his shoulders and he could catch her scent.

The stallion's head lifted up and over his mate's, his black eyes looking down at her. After a moment, he lowered his head, his muzzle near her. She reached up and stroked him there.

"I am so very sorry," she said softly, and his eyes closed.

She walked away, making sure to lock the gate behind her. Once outside, Dagmar looked around. It was late and she hadn't eaten, but she wasn't very hungry, truth be told. Nor was she tired.

With a sigh, she started back to the castle, but stopped

when she heard sniffles. Following the sound, she came around the stables and what she'd always considered a painfully hard heart melted right inside her chest.

She crouched down beside him, but didn't know why. He was so large, she wasn't that much bigger than him when she stood up.

Dagmar placed her hand on his knee, smiling into the teary silver eyes that peered up at her beneath long dark blue lashes.

"I'm so sorry," she said again, knowing words would do nothing at the moment.

"I'll miss her," Éibhear said while trying to wipe the tears away. "I'll miss her so bloody much."

"I know. I've barely known her and I know I'm going to miss her."

He shrugged sheepishly. "Guess your kin don't blubber, though."

"My father cried once. He doesn't know that I know, but my old nursemaid told me before she died."

"Why did he cry?"

"Because my mother died while having me. She made the choice to save me. Just as Annwyl did to save her own babes."

He nodded. "I know it was her choice and that she'd make no other. Not Annwyl. She'll risk everything for the ones she loves."

The great blue dragon in human form relaxed his head back against the wall behind him. "But Fearghus . . . He'll never recover from this. Not really."

"And all you can do is be there for him. To let him know that he's not in this alone."

"I will." He tried to wipe his face and Dagmar took a clean cloth from the pocket of her dress and wiped his tears for him.

"You won't tell, will you?" he asked. "That you found me crying."

Dagmar rested back on her calves and said, "Your secret will always be safe with me, Éibhear the Blue."

Gwenvael leaned over and stared down into the crib. The girl frowned like her father—no, that wasn't right. She frowned like *his* father. And that did nothing but make Gwenvael rather nervous. Especially with those bright green eyes watching him so intently as if she were debating whether to cut his throat or not. Her brother, however, had quickly grown bored of staring and gone back to sleep.

Thankfully, his niece and nephew *looked* human. More human than he'd hoped to expect. They had no scales, no wings—no tail, which would have been awkward in the best of situations. They looked like every other human baby he'd ever seen.

Except that they appeared to be three or four months old physically and yet they already moved as if older than that. He'd give them a few days before they could roll over and crawl just like most hatchlings.

Gods, what else did their future hold? As it was, he could feel the Magick surrounding them. No, that was wrong. It didn't surround them. It poured from them. Out of every pore. They were still weak and terribly vulnerable, but one day . . . One day their power would be phenomenal.

"How are they?"

Gwenvael glanced over his shoulder. Fearghus lurked in the doorway, unwilling to enter.

"They're doing well. They're healthy. Seem to have all the important parts and nothing in addition we have to worry about." *At least not yet.* "You should take a look."

"No. I need to go back to Annwyl."

"I understand." Gwenvael reached down and scooped up the girl. He'd done that earlier and immediately put her back down. She clearly wanted to be left alone, but he needed the same reaction he got the first time. And he got it. Her face turned red and she began screaming.

"What are you doing?" Fearghus demanded. "You're upsetting . . . her or him."

"Her. And she'll stop eventually."

But he knew she wouldn't. Gwenvael's arms weren't the ones she wanted holding her at the moment.

Aye, very similar to how newly hatched dragons behaved.

The boy's eyes snapped open. Like his father's and grandfather's, they were a coal black and at the moment, quite angry. He started screaming too, because his sister was and he was not happy about it.

"What the hell are you doing?"

Fearghus reached over and took his daughter from Gwenvael's arms.

"Clearly she wants to be left alone!"

"I was just trying to help."

"That was not helpful, you idiot. That was stupid."

"She's not crying now."

Fearghus blinked and immediately gazed down at his daughter.

"She has Annwyl's eyes."

"True." He sat his brother down in the chair beside the cribs. "But the boy has yours."

He readjusted the girl into the crook of her father's left arm and then placed her brother in the opposite arm.

"See? Your eyes."

"But Annwyl's hair."

"Aye. And I can tell by the look in his eye—he already knows he's trouble."

"I'm sure you'll help him with that."

"Me? Of course not. I don't need any competition."

Gwenvael busied himself around the room until he knew

Fearghus was comfortable with the children he held in his arms; then he crouched in front of his brother. "You know, Fearghus, I bet they'd like to meet their mum."

Fearghus winced, his eyes blinking rapidly. "What?" he asked, torn between being confused and angry.

"Just for a few minutes."

He calmed down, understanding what Gwenvael meant, and nodded. "Right. You're right."

Gwenvael helped his brother stand and followed him to Annwyl's room. It was unbearably quiet except for the sounds of Annwyl's labored breathing. Together, they placed the babes next to their mother on the bed. Immediately, the little ones clung to her, their tiny fists already able to grab what they wanted.

Fearghus knelt by the side of the bed, picking Annwyl's limp hand up and holding it between his much bigger ones.

Gwenvael briefly squeezed his brother's shoulder and started toward the door. It was only a flash, but he saw the hem of white robes pass by. He rushed out, closing the door behind him.

"Morfyd. Wait."

She waved him off. "Leave me be, Gwenvael. Please."

He watched her run away, for once unsure of what he should do next. A few minutes later, Brastias stalked around the corner, stopping abruptly when he saw Gwenvael standing there.

"Well?"

Gwenvael started to say something, but really he had nothing to say. He shook his head instead.

"Is she—"

"Not yet. Soon."

Brastias rested back against the wall, his eyes staring off. He and Annwyl had always been close. A kind of brother and sister who had been through hell together. The general glanced around the hallway, suddenly standing up straight. "Where's Morfyd?"

Gwenvael watched the human male for a long moment before he motioned with his hand down the hallway. "In her room, I suspect."

Brastias headed off, and Gwenvael felt his heart break for all the things he couldn't do to help his kin.

Morfyd ran into her room and slammed the door shut. She pressed her forehead against it and finally let the tears explode out of her.

She'd failed. She'd failed everyone. Her brother. Her friend. And now her niece and nephew.

And it had been she who'd held the dagger that cut Annwyl open. Something her mother had never done before, but Morfyd had. Only two of the ten she'd helped this way had not survived, their pregnancies troublesome from the beginning. Yet Annwyl had been too weak. Her body simply drained. They'd had no choice but to cut the twins out or risk losing both mother and children.

She knew Annwyl had made her choice. She believed what Dagmar had told them. But none of that made Morfyd's failure any easier.

Then she'd come in as Fearghus and Gwenvael placed the babes on their mother. Like any hatchlings would, they wanted their mother's attention and were annoyed they weren't getting it, but were not yet at the age they could reason why. But Fearghus knew why, and the pain of that showed on his face.

Of all her kin, she was closest to Fearghus and the thought that she'd let him down, that she'd failed him in something so important, tore her in ways she never thought possible.

"Morfyd?"

Startled at the voice from the other side of the door, she stumbled back.

"Morfyd, open the door."

"I . . . I need some time. . . ."

"Open the door."

Not bothering to wipe her face, Morfyd pulled open the door and quickly stepped away from it, turning her back.

She'd let Brastias down too. She knew how he felt about his queen and his comrade. They'd faced death together many times, Annwyl and Brastias. This was hurting him too.

"I'm so sorry, Brastias," she sobbed. "I'm so—"

He was there, in front of her, pulling her close, his arms tight around her.

"You'll not say that again," he told her gruffly. "You've done all you could. Now I want you to let it go, love."

She did. For hours. Sobbing into the poor man's surcoat until she practically passed out in his arms from exhaustion.

Izzy dashed up one of the highest hills within three leagues of Dark Plains and screamed into the night, *"What have you done?"*

When there was no immediate answer, she bellowed, "Don't you dare . . . *Don't you dare ignore me!"*

The flame-imbued lightning flashed out and Izzy barely moved in time as it struck at her feet.

"Ordering me?" a voice she knew as well as her mother's boomed. *"Me?"*

"You should have protected her! I told her to trust you!"

Rhydderch Hael, the father god of all dragons, appeared. He did not come out of the darkness as much as he was a vast part of it. His dragon body stretched for what looked like miles and his hair glowed in the moonlight. She'd seen him three times now like this. Before her mum had sacrificed herself to save Izzy seven months ago, she'd only met Rhydderch Hael in her dreams. If it was urgent, she'd hear him in her head.

Lately, however, things had changed. He'd appeared the first time while she'd been off practicing with her spear by one of the lakes. She'd tried to hug him, but she couldn't even hope to reach her arms around him, so she sort of ended up squeezing his enormous dragon neck. They'd talked for hours, and Izzy had promised never to tell that he'd come to her in physical form. But his voice could still pop in her head unbidden. Like it had that morning when he told her it was time for Annwyl's babes to be born.

She'd given her childhood heart to Rhydderch Hael a long time ago. And then she'd given her soul in order to save her mother.

"We all make sacrifices, little Izzy."

"You're a bastard," she snapped. "A right bastard."

His dark violet eyes flashed and his twelve-horned head lowered a bit. "And I'm still the god you've committed your life to. Your loyalty is to me."

"My loyalty is to my kin. And they're my kin. You're not."

"You say dangerous words, little Izzy."

"I don't care. I don't care because my queen is dying. And it's all your fault." She wiped her face and realized at that moment that she was crying. "I know you're a god, and we mean nothing to you. But just remember, those babes are your creation. No one will protect them like their own mother. Like Annwyl. No one."

Rhydderch Hael yawned and motioned her away with his claw. "Go home, little Izzy."

His black dragon body shimmered, and then he was gone. And she felt the betrayal all the way to her bones.

* * *

Dagmar stood outside Gwenvael's door. She'd almost knocked three times. This wasn't like her. Not knowing how to handle something. She handled *everything*. But she didn't know whether stopping by would be . . . inappropriate? That seemed the best word.

Their one night together did not mean anything more than what it was.

But she was worried about him. Everyone seemed to be taking all of this so hard. Even the servants and the soldiers. On her way in, she'd passed poor Izzy running out. She didn't bother trying to stop her, knowing the girl needed her own time to deal with this.

She knew Gwenvael loved Annwyl, and she felt the almost overwhelming need to care for him, which seemed absolutely ridiculous.

Besides, would Gwenvael even want that kind of comfort? At least from her?

She hated feeling like this. Insecure and confused. It wasn't like her, but she guessed everyone had these moments.

The door was snatched open and she looked up into Gwenvael's face.

"How long were you going to stand out here?"

"I didn't want to bother you. I just—"

He grabbed her hand and dragged her into the room, slamming the door shut. He pulled her over to the bed and pushed her onto it.

"Roll onto your side," he ordered. "Facing the window."

"All right." She did as he bade, the bed behind her dipping a bit as Gwenvael, fully dressed, crawled in behind her. His arm wrapped around her waist and he moved in close behind her. He rested his chin against the top of her head, and they both lay there staring out the window.

Neither spoke, nor moved, and they remained where they were until the two suns rose the next morning.

Chapter 25

Keita the Virtuous, a name recently given to her that would cause her brother Gwenvael to roll around the floor and laugh like a hatchling should he hear it, stared out over the cold, hard lands of the Northlands. She was in Horde territory, standing on the flat mountaintop of the Olgeirsson Horde lair, and all she could see for miles and miles in either direction were more snow-covered mountaintops.

But for nearing two weeks now, she'd been trapped in this place . . . with *these* dragons.

She had yet to meet a Lightning who wasn't a barbarian. Appalling manners, distasteful habits, and brains the size of cooked peas. Every day had been a new experience in dealing with idiots.

Yet, as with most idiots, they were crafty enough.

Her talons brushed the steel collar locked around her neck. A long chain went from it to the spike buried in the floor and surrounded by several-feet-deep marble.

Aye. Crafty cretins, one and all. They weren't smarter than her, but she'd realized quickly that aggression would only put her in deeper. They were used to Southland females like Keita's mother, Queen Rhiannon. No matter the situation, Rhiannon only reacted with aggression and violence. Morfyd had always been weaker, but she wasn't above using her Magicks to fight off her enemies. Unfortunately for Keita, her Magick skills were basic. She was a dragon, so automatically a Magickal being by nature, but she had no spells that could move mountains or turn a dragon's blood to metal spikes. When she shot flame, it came out straight and true. Her mother's flame could snake around corners and into crevices. She used it like a whip.

Her brother Briec also had skills far superior to many dragons, Fearghus a little less. But Keita, Gwenvael, and Éibhear only had the dragon basics, which meant she had to find other ways out of this hell.

What helped her, though, was the fact that there seemed to be nothing but males around her. Big, lonely males who were ready to settle down with a mate and have hatchlings of their own. Because females were so scarce, they'd have to fight for her in a tournament called The Honour. Brother against brother, kin against kin—all to be the one to Claim Keita. To put their brand on her, as if she were some farmer's cattle.

That may have been her mother's way, but it wasn't what Keita wanted. It never would be. She liked her life just as it was. With human males hard and ready at the asking, beautiful gowns, and the freedom to go anywhere she pleased at any time. She answered to no one, and that included her mother or some male who thought he might own her.

For two weeks, she'd been amusing herself with the idiot kin of Olgeir the Wastrel, blocking her whereabouts from her parents and siblings. She knew her brothers well enough to know they'd come for her. They'd die for her, and she'd die for them. But after one night among the Olgeirsson Horde, she knew the risk they would most surely take would be unnecessary.

Even more importantly, it would also be unnecessary to let her mother know Keita had gotten herself into this mess. And, oh, how Rhiannon would love to know about all this. There were few things in this world Keita dreaded, but her mother's mocking laughter was definitely top of her list. From her hatching, the great Dragon Queen had made it perfectly clear

Keita was not remotely what she'd wanted for an offspring. No great Magick like her older sister and no battle-honed skills like her brothers. "She's good enough for a fist fight, I suppose," Rhiannon would often say, "but I'd never put a battle lance in her claws."

In the end, letting her mother know she'd been captured by the Horde was unacceptable, but more importantly it was unnecessary. Although it would take time, she knew she'd get out of here without even having to crack a talon.

And, steadily, every day, she'd been nearing that goal. Until last night. Until she felt pain like she'd never felt before. Not physical as she'd briefly felt from Gwenvael almost a week ago. Something else. Something from her Fearghus that tore into her like a spear.

She'd felt his loss. Felt it as if it were her own. She knew then she had to get home. She'd played with these fools long enough and she'd run out of time. As had Annwyl, apparently.

"Lady Keita?"

She gave herself one more moment to stare off into the distance before she turned to face the Lightning behind her. He threw down a half-eaten carcass at her feet.

"For you," he said gruffly.

It took everything not to let out a sigh and roll her eyes, but she plastered on her sweetest smile, making sure her fangs twinkled in the torch light. "That is so kind of you," she said sweetly. "I was just thinking I was a little hungry."

He stepped closer. "The Honour is to take place in three days, my lady. I will make you mine then."

She lowered her eyes and sauntered toward him.

"Your words," she said against his ear as she passed him, her tail easing up his chest, "arouse me, my lord."

She heard his panting, knew he wanted her. It did not surprise her when he suddenly turned and grabbed her, pulling her until their scales touched. He was much bigger than her; she had to bend her head back to get a good look at him.

"I will make you mine," he growled.

."Lady Keita, I—"

The younger Lightning stopped as Keita jerked out of the other's arms. She made sure to look alarmed, confused—weak.

The younger Lightning slammed down his gift on top of the older one's. Keita blinked. *Good Gods. Is that a tree? Who gifts a tree?*

She absolutely dreamed of the day she could tell Gwenvael this story.

"You cheatin' bastard."

"Back off, little snake. Wouldn't want you to lose your head over somethin' you'll never get."

The younger one—who had yet to learn to control his passions, whether love or hate—went for his brother.

Keita moved back as much as she could with the chain still holding her in place. But as she knew it would, the sound of their scuffle lured the others.

"What's going on?" one of the older ones demanded.

"He was going to fuck her! I caught him!"

She almost laughed outright. Cocky bunch of dumbasses, weren't they?

But with more of Olgeir's brood joining in, the fight was getting ugly and the guards were called. She moved toward the door as two dragon guards ran in.

"Stop them please!" she begged. She'd convinced them all she only wanted the best for Olgeir and his kin—as if she cared. They rushed forward, first one and then the other. It was the other's neck that Keita's tail whipped around, yanking him back at such an angle that it snapped his neck clean. A lovely trick her father had taught her. "You may be smaller than the males," he'd always told her, "but you can use their weight and stupidity against them. Never forget that." She hadn't.

She snatched the key ring hanging from his breastplate and unlocked the collar at her throat.

Backing into the shadows, she waited as more kinsmen tore into the room and joined the fray. Then she inched her way to the edge of the flat mountaintop. She gave herself another second, enjoying the spray of blood beginning to cover the floor, and then she dropped backward off the landing.

She stayed silent as she fell toward the ground, her eyes focused on the area she'd just escaped from. The fight continued, but calls of her disappearance didn't come.

Grinning, Keita flipped forward and unfurled her wings. The power of the wind at her back took her and she headed south.

Nothing stopped her and she stayed near the tops of the trees. Eventually they'd realize she'd gone and would send out scouts to track her down. She'd have to be wily and fast to stay out of their grasp. But her brothers needed her, and she wouldn't let anything stop her.

It was when she passed over the Torment River that she knew she had two males on her tail. She did her best flying, using trees and rocks and even birds to keep them off her back.

They were persistent, though. Determined. Finally throwing a net over her. She sneered, her talons slashing against the soft material. But when nothing happened, she looked down. Yet it was not her claw she saw . . . but her hand.

"What in all the hells—"

The net closed fully around her human body, and Keita fell like a stone. She screamed as land rushed up to meet her, the sound cutting off abruptly when strong dragon arms caught her and carefully brought her to the ground.

"Here we are, Princess Keita." Lightning strikes dotted around her for a moment as the Lightning shifted from dragon to human before he carefully placed her on the ground. "Nice and safe."

She waited while the net was slowly removed, biding her time. She stayed curled on her side, panting.

"Is she hurt?" another voice asked.

"No. But she wants us to believe she is. Don't you, my lady?"

Realizing she had no more time to spare, Keita came up. She had her hands curled into fists and punched twice, knocking her abductor back several steps. She ran, needing to get her feet off that cursed netting. But she didn't get far as her abductor's arm swung out and, without him even touching her, sent Keita flying back. Her squeal of surprise and outrage at the brutal use of Magick was cut short as her human form rammed into the base of the nearby mountain.

Now she wasn't pretending anything. She couldn't move or speak, too exhausted to fight as the Lightning crouched beside her and clipped the small, human-sized collar around her throat. The power of that Magickal item plowed through her, leaving her a shuddering pile of human flesh at his feet.

Big fingers brushed her hair from her face.

"Red," another voice said about her hair.

"Pretty," said another.

"Tricky," said the one looking down at her. He smiled when she glared up into his face. "Hello, Princess Keita. I'm Ragnar. I am sorry I had to end your trip back to your brother and his dying pet, but I have need of you. And until I tell you differently, princess . . . you're mine."

Dagmar closed the doors to Violence's stables. She'd brought him and his mares a basket of apples and stayed with them until Violence finally ate. The stable dog whined on the other side of the door, more than ready to follow her back to her room. He was a very sweet dog, but he had other responsibilities.

"Quiet now," she said through the thick wood. "Go lie down."

The mutt sniffed a bit under the crack, but eventually went back to his warm bed and cold food.

Dagmar turned to head back to the castle but stopped short when she saw Queen Rhiannon standing behind her—staring.

"You have a way with animals, I see."

"Yes, my lady. I raise dogs for my father's troops."

"You do?" She frowned in disapproval. "Is that an appropriate task for the Only Daughter of a Northland warlord?"

"No. But my father could not deny my talents."

The dragoness moved toward her. She seemed to glide, in a way. "My son tells me you have other talents."

Dagmar couldn't help it. Her eyes widened in shock and she felt as if she'd wandered into the Great Hall completely naked.

The queen frowned again and then gasped. "Oh, gods! No, no. Not like that."

The pair began to laugh and immediately stopped, realizing how out of place it sounded and felt. But they had both been startled.

"I forget sometimes that Gwenvael is not like his brothers. What I meant to say is he told me you have a skill with words and negotiations."

This time Dagmar was surprised but flattered. She'd had no idea Gwenvael had praised her so to his mother. "I . . . have helped my father when—"

The queen raised her hand and swiped it through the air. "Please, Lady Dagmar. I am in no mood for false modesty."

Dagmar folded her arms across her chest. "Is this about Ragnar?"

She snorted. "I can handle that Horde hatchling myself. He's a mage, you know? Not a bad one either. I can feel his power among the lines of Magick. But I guess all that means nothing to you as a follower of Aoibhell."

"I'm not a follower. I agree with her teachings."

Rhiannon gave a small snicker. "Even suggesting you may

worship Aoibhell herself is an insult to those who believe in her word."

"To turn her into a god would go against everything she believed." Dagmar briefly glanced at the ground. "What is it you want from me, my lady?"

"I'll be blunt since I'm not good with subtlety. I'm having an issue. It involves Annwyl's twins. I need the help of a devious mind combined with a . . ."

"Barbarian will?"

The Dragon Queen leered. "Exactly."

"I can help you." As she'd promised to help Annwyl. And as long as the human queen breathed, she'd keep that promise.

Dagmar motioned away from the stables with a wave of her hand. "Tell me everything, Majesty, and we'll figure it out from there."

Olgeir stared out over the edge where he'd guessed Lady Keita had made her escape. At his feet, one of his favorite guards lay dead from an expertly broken neck, and behind him were the idiots he called sons.

"We'll go after her," his oldest said. "We'll find her."

"It's too late!" He turned and his sons backed up. He may be old, but for dragons that only made them harder to kill. "Can't you smell him? On the air? He already has her."

"Who? Who has her?"

"The boy. That treacherous, bastard boy."

One of his younger sons raised a brow. "Ragnar would never be fool enough to come back here."

But Olgeir knew he had. Knew his son was fool enough to risk everything to become warlord of the Olgeirsson Horde.

"We'll find him, Da," his oldest said, the others roaring behind him. "We'll find him and kill him. Bring his head back to you."

"No." Olgeir sneered. "Stay here. I'll handle the boy. Like I always have."

He stormed off, motioning to three of his best guards to follow.

Olgeir would bring Ragnar's head back himself and mount it over his treasure.

His idiot offspring's mother would complain, but she'd have to get over it.

Chapter 26

For three days the Blood Queen of Dark Plains held on. For three days the entire kingdom had been in mourning.

Yet the pain felt by the dragons who considered her family was a palpable thing, rippling through them all. Every day she'd see servants rush from the castle so they could sob among their own without upsetting the dragons any more than they already were. Even those cousins and aunts and uncles who hadn't had a chance to get to know Annwyl before the birth mourned for the loss their kin suffered.

To be blunt, Dagmar simply wasn't used to it. The Northlanders didn't show their pain. They didn't mourn. They simply set their dead to flame, either on pyres or at sea, and once the remains were nothing but ashes, three to five days of drinking ensued. Neighbor enemies didn't attack at these times, probably one of the only lines not even Jökull crossed when at war. Drunken tears and sobbing were allowed only because they could be written off. "It was the drink," she'd heard her kinsmen say more than once. "More than six kegs of ale and I'm a blubbering mess."

Yet there had been no drinking in Dark Plains. Only the grim readying for battle and defense, and the painful expressions of those who were feeling the loss of Queen Annwyl.

To combat all of it, Dagmar had kept busy doing what she did best: planning, plotting, and executing.

A good portion of the defenses were up and ready. Some of them were buried deep in the ground beneath them, ensuring it would at least be hard for the Minotaurs to break through into the Garbhán Isle dungeons. Others were topside and at the ready. And a few were tests she'd insisted upon. She'd argued over the tests with Brastias, who seemed grateful to have something else to focus on. He thought they were simply too limited and specific, which may have been correct, but Dagmar still liked to test out her ideas when she could.

While the defenses were being built, the merchants and prostitutes had been moved from inside the main gates to a town about a league away from the edge of Garbhán Isle. This way the servants didn't have to travel too far to get daily supplies, but strong defenses could now be erected that would protect the main gate.

Dagmar had happily helped with all that as well, glad to be of some assistance during this time. Yet there was still much work to be done, and she had every intention of making sure as much as possible was finished before she returned home.

As Dagmar walked across the enormous courtyard studying her list carefully, wind whipped around her, lifting the hem of her dress and her hair. It reminded her she had yet again forgotten to braid her hair and wear her scarf over it. She raised her gaze to the sky, her eyes momentarily blinded by the two suns blaring overhead. She saw the dragons at the last minute, dashing to the side as five of them landed.

She didn't recognize them as any of Gwenvael's kin, but she could tell they were old. No matter the color of their scales, their manes were nearly white and grey with age. They landed and looked around. The old Gold in front looked down at her and she knew immediately this male was a problem.

They weren't here to give their condolences, or to offer assistance. In fact, she knew exactly what they were here for.

Knowing this would turn ugly very fast, Dagmar went to put her plan in motion.

Gwenvael cut in front of his father, pressing his hands against the old dragon's shoulders and stopping him midway down the Great Hall steps.

"Father, no."

"You dare come here?" Bercelak snarled at the dragons in the courtyard with such lethal anger that Gwenvael feared the veins pulsing across his father's temples would burst.

The Elders had shifted to human and wore the boring brown robes they brought with them. Four of them stepped hastily back at Bercelak's angry words, but only Elder Eanruig had the balls to look bored.

"There is no disrespect intended, Lord Bercelak," Eanruig sighed. "But I made it clear to Her Majesty that we would come for the babes after they were born."

Gwenvael and his father locked gazes before Gwenvael swung around and demanded, "What now?"

"We've come for the babes, young Prince. They will leave with us and be raised where we choose is best for them."

"You're not taking those children."

"The Elders have decided, Lord Gwenvael, and there's nothing you can do about it."

"I don't care. You'll not take those children. Fearghus will decide where they live and how they are raised. Not you. And not some bloody council."

Briec came down the steps from the Great Hall, stopping beside Gwenvael. "What's going on?"

Their father couldn't even answer. He simply shook his head, his hands resting on his hips as he paced back and forth on the long step.

Gwenvael looked at his brother, the anger fairly choking him. "They've come for the babes."

Briec focused on Eanruig. "Under whose authority? Clearly not our mother's."

The Elder smirked, and Gwenvael winced when Briec began to yell in his head, *We're killing him! We're killing him right now!*

Gwenvael placed his hand on Briec's shoulder. *We can't. Let's just be calm.*

Fuck calm!

"The Council has made its decision, Bercelak the Black—"

"*You've* made the decision," Becelak cut in. "This is about you!"

"—I would strongly suggest you don't stop us from doing what we've come to do."

Dagmar came around the corner of the castle. She gave Gwenvael a small wink and motioned to Addolgar and Ghleanna who stalked in behind her.

"Lord Gwenvael," she said, smiling softly, "who do we have here?"

He passed a quick glance to Briec.

What the hell is she doing? Briec demanded.

Trust her, brother. For Gwenvael certainly did.

Going down the stairs, Gwenvael grasped Dagmar's outstretched hand and said, "Lady Dagmar this is Elder Eanruig of our Council. Elder Eanruig, this is Dagmar Reinholdt of the Northlands. Only Daughter of The Reinholdt."

Eanruig puffed up a bit when he realized Dagmar was as close to Northland royalty as one could find among the warlords. "Lady Dagmar. It's an honor."

She gave a small bow of her head. "I've read so much

about the mighty Dragon Elders of the Southlands. And I am most honored to meet you." She gave the most innocent of smiles. "So what brings you here today?"

Eanruig sighed sadly, making Gwenvael want to pull the bastard's lungs out through his nose. "We heard about poor Queen Annwyl and we've decided that for the safety of her children, we should take them under our protection."

"Ahhh." Dagmar nodded. "I see."

"What's this?" Ghleanna asked, stomping forward. "I don't understand. What are they saying, Dagmar?"

"It's very simple," Dagmar explained cheerfully. "For the safety of the twins, the Council has decided to rip them—in a sense only, of course—from Fearghus even as we are preparing the funeral pyre for Annwyl's eventual death."

Eanruig gave a smug chortle. "It's not that simple, my lady."

"No, it is," Dagmar countered, still cheerfully. "You see, Ghleanna, if Elder Eanruig has the twins, he has control over the queen, because she'd never do anything to risk her own grandchildren."

Now Eanruig frowned. "That's not true."

"Don't be shy," she praised, latching on to the Elder's arm, a bright smile on her face. "It's brilliant politically. Think of it. He who controls the twins, controls the queen. Yet if she denies Elder Eanruig the babes, he can rally those who've never been large fans of Queen Rhiannon anyway to his side and start a delightful civil war."

Ghleanna crossed her arms in front of her chest. "And we're letting him get away with this?"

Eanruig snatched his arm away from Dagmar. "There is nothing to get away with, Low Born," he sneered. "What the Council decides to do is none of the business of the Cadwaladr Clan."

"He's right, Ghleanna," Dagmar cut in. "This has to do with the royal bloodline and those connected directly to it like Bercelak. Unfortunately"—she seemed to mock

Ghleanna by winking at Eanruig—"that has little to do with you or Addolgar."

"Bercelak is our brother."

Dagmar patted Ghleanna's forearm. "This is about bloodline, dearest. Am I correct, Elder Eanruig?"

"You are," he snidely agreed.

"And coming from a low-born bloodine, you have no real connection to the Dragon Queen or any say in these decisions. Now, why don't I get the babes?" She smiled at Eanruig.

"Thank you kindly, Lady Dagmar."

As Dagmar walked up the stairs, Ghleanna scowled up at Bercelak. "You're going to let him get away with this, brother?"

Sighing dramatically, Dagmar took hold of Bercelak's arm. "What choice does he have?"

"He can strike the bastard down."

"No. He can't. Nor can Briec or Gwenvael. Because of their connection to Queen Rhiannon, they could never strike an unarmed Elder down. Even if openly challenged . . . as some might consider this situation to be."

Ghleanna blinked, her scowl lessening. "'Cause they're directly connected to Rhiannon?"

"Right."

"But we're not?"

"Unfortunately, you're just meaningless low borns who could easily interpret this as a threat to the twins and act accordingly."

Eanruig frowned. "Wait . . . what?"

"Well, they are low borns, my lord," Dagmar stated flatly as they all watched him back away. "What exactly did you expect?"

Even if Eanruig was hundreds of years younger, he'd never have been able to move fast enough. He was a politician, like Dagmar, not a trained warrior. He had no speed, no skills, and no hope of outrunning a battle-trained dragoness who was quite pissed off.

Ghleanna sliced through Eanruig's human body with her sword, cutting him from right shoulder to left hip. As she pulled her blade from his torso, his screams making the observing humans run for their lives and the other Elders scramble away in fear, Addolgar's blade was slicing through the air overhead, slamming into the middle of Eanruig's skull. The weapon didn't stop its descent until it came sliding through the Elder's groin.

And with that, the screaming stopped.

Flames briefly burst and Eanruig's human remains returned to their natural form. Dagmar felt nothing as she stared down at what remained of Elder Eanruig. Perhaps it should have been other babes he'd set his sights on, but he'd come after Annwyl's. That had made it almost a pleasure to work with the Dragon Queen to make sure the laws of her kind would protect Ghleanna and Addolgar, who'd been told nothing and yet reacted as Rhiannon guessed they would.

Ghleanna raised her blood-covered weapon and pointed it at the remaining Elders falling over each other. "Now listen up, you lot. As of this moment, Fearghus the Destroyer's twins are under the protection of the Cadwaladr Clan. You come near them again without express permission from one of us or the queen herself, and the Cadwaladrs will come down on you like wolves on a wounded deer. We will tear the walls of Devenallt down around you and show you what the true meaning of civil war is." She stepped closer. "Don't fuck with my kin, or I'll kill every last one of you and leave your rotting bones in front of the dens of your offspring." She flicked her sword up, Eanruig's blood splattering across the Elders, before she shoved it into the sheath tied to her back.

"Get out of our sight. And never come back here again

without an invitation." When the Elders only stared at her in mute horror . . . *"Move!"*

The old dragons shifted and slammed into each other as they fought to get away.

Brushing one hand against the other, Ghleanna headed back toward the training grounds Dagmar had dragged her and her brother from.

With a wink and a smile, Addolgar followed after his sister.

Dagmar realized she had the attention of Gwenvael, Briec, and Bercelak. "Yes?"

"She's good," Briec muttered.

"That she is." Gwenvael slid his arm around her shoulders, his lips grazing against her temple. "With an impeccable sense of timing and knowledge of our bloodlines."

"Don't be nosey."

"Tricky, tricky, tricky."

"My Lady Dagmar!" A young soldier called out as he ran toward her. "Lady Dagmar!" He slid to a stop at the bottom of the stairs.

"Take your breath first, lad, and then tell me what you think I need to know."

Hands on his knees, his breath coming in gasps as he bent over at the waist, he finally spit out, "You told me to tell you if I heard anything—"

"Yes, yes. What is it?"

"About three hundred leagues from here, my lady. Hoof prints."

"You'll have to tell me something a little more interesting than that, I'm afraid."

"Pairs. What I mean to say is pairs of two hooves, marching, side by side. And then they just disappear. We can't find where, although it looks as if they disappeared into rock."

Not disappeared into rock, she'd wager, but *under* it. The

way of the Ice Land Minotaur. Not only could they find their way underground with ease, but they could also cover their tracks quite well. They didn't fool her. She'd bet they'd gone underground several leagues from where those tracks were found, most likely aware Annwyl's army had been warned of their coming.

Dagmar motioned the young soldier away. "Good work. Tell General Brastias if he doesn't already know."

"Aye, m'lady," the young soldier promised before running off again.

She nodded at the dragons who watched her expectantly.

"They're here."

Chapter 27

Gwenvael found his brother where he'd been for the last three days. He hated to bother him now, but he'd received his orders from Fearghus himself three days before.

"Brother."

Fearghus raised his head. "Aye?"

"Dagmar has received word that the Minotaurs are near. We're all meeting now with Father, Ghleanna, and Addolgar in the war room to discuss next steps."

"Fine," Fearghus said, his voice sounding very weary. "I'll be right there."

"You don't have to. We can take care of—"

"These are my children's lives we're talking about," he cut in. "I'll be right there."

Fearghus didn't raise his voice. He didn't get snappy as he

was known to do in simpler times. Instead he no longer showed any emotion at all.

"We'll wait for you," Gwenvael said, and left.

Dagmar heard another shout and then more slamming from behind closed doors, but it was Talaith who jumped at the noise yet again.

"I can't concentrate when they get like this!" She looked at Dagmar. "How do you ignore it?"

"You so clearly have not met any of my family."

Talaith let out a breath and returned to the book in front of her.

Dagmar glanced over at the woman. She hadn't been sleeping, the circles under her eyes a clear indication of that. Instead she spent nearly every moment trying to help Annwyl in a last ditch effort to save her life. Or, on occasion, helping Dagmar. "Talaith, perhaps you should get some rest?"

"I can rest when she's dead," she answered gruffly. Then, horrified at her own words, she shoved the book away from her and covered her mouth with her hand. "Good gods."

Dagmar rested her hand on Talaith's shoulder. "There's only so much you can do."

"I know. But I can't stop hoping that Morfyd or I will find something, anything, that can bring her back. Even Rhiannon's power won't hold for much longer."

Dagmar sat back in her chair, her maps and notes spread out in front of her. "Tomorrow?"

Talaith shook her head, immediately understanding what Dagmar's real question was.

"More like tonight."

"Does Fearghus know?"

"Has anyone told him? No. Does he *know*? I strongly think yes."

Letting out a breath, Dagmar sat up and began to lean over the maps again when she saw him. He strode through the doors and absolutely no one paid him any mind. Considering the way the security had been ridiculously amplified—at Gwenvael's firm direction—the fact that no one would even look his way irked her. She'd specifically added that even dragons in human form were to be questioned or Gwenvael's kin alerted.

"Who is that?" She motioned to him with her chin and Talaith looked directly at the dragon.

"Who? Samuel the washing boy?"

Dagmar frowned and looked again, quickly realizing Talaith spoke of the boy currently on his knees scrubbing the floor.

"Not him." She searched for him again and saw him casually walking up the stairs. "Him."

Talaith stared blankly at the stairs. "Who?"

"You see nothing?"

"Am I supposed to see something?" She made it sound as if Dagmar had lost her mind. Dagmar knew witches like Talaith and Morfyd could see what others could not, but as long as Dagmar wore her spectacles, she wasn't blind. She knew what she saw . . . so why hadn't Talaith seen as well?

Pushing her chair back, she stood. "I'll be back in a moment."

Lifting the skirt of her gown, Dagmar went up the stairs after him. As she stepped into the hall, she realized he'd disappeared. Perhaps he was someone's lover, stopping in for a visit. Yet she heard no doors opening or closing. Saw no midmorning light momentarily streaking into the hallway as someone entered a room.

She headed down one hall, turned, and went down another. She walked toward the room Annwyl lay in but stopped short when she saw the man reappear from the twins' nursery. This time he held Annwyl's twins in his arms. He stood in the hallway, bold as brass, in front of the guards who were supposed to be protecting the babes and their nursemaids. But the guards didn't move. They didn't even acknowledge his presence.

Then she understood. They didn't see him, Talaith didn't see him—no one saw him. No one but Dagmar.

It was something Aoibhell herself used to complain about in the letters Ragnar had given Dagmar. She wrote faithfully to a friend, mostly reiterating her beliefs—or lack thereof. But a few times, something she said hadn't made much sense to Dagmar. Until now.

"At first they were always so surprised when I could see them, Anne. Now they stop by for chats. Tea. It's like I can't get rid of them. It seems to only happen to those who truly do not worship. Not the ones trying to annoy their family or who feel betrayed when someone close to them dies. But the ones who truly understand that the gods are no better than anyone else."

Dagmar studied the male holding Annwyl's babes. His mouth twisted a bit as he debated something and, with a small shrug, moved forward, heading toward Annwyl's room.

Dagmar followed right behind him, the guards noticing her immediately. She waited a moment, took a breath, and entered the queen's dying chamber.

He stood beside the bed, staring down at Annwyl.

"Wanted to give them a chance to say good-bye?" she asked coldly.

Looking up in surprise, he smiled. "Amazing. That you can see me, I mean." When she didn't comment on that, he seemed to lose interest.

"It seemed only fair to bring them to their mother. Don't you think?" He placed the babes on their mother's chest and stomach. His smile was indulgent, like a father's over a puppy his children had grown fond of but could no longer have. "Now say bye-bye," he told them, his voice teasing. "Can you say bye-bye?"

Dagmar's eyes narrowed, her top lip curled, and her hands turned into tight fists.

God or not, she wouldn't be letting this bastard off that easily.

Briec, thoroughly disgusted with his kin, rolled his eyes. The mate of his brother lay dying in the rooms above and all these idiots could do was argue about the best way to track down and decimate Minotaurs.

A waste of energy in his opinion. But typical of the way the Cadwaladr Clan handled something like this.

They couldn't help Annwyl, and his father's kin did like to "help." So they would do what they did best: kill and destroy. But they couldn't do that if what the tiny barbarian female had told them was true—that the Minotaur tracks may be in one location, but that only meant the Minotaurs themselves were surely in another. So they stood over maps and argued and debated and disagreed. All while Fearghus sat in a chair, staring at the table with the maps. Briec knew his brother saw nothing that was in front of him. Felt nothing except the loss of his mate.

Late every night Briec had to track an exhausted Talaith down and pull her away from her books so she could get at least a few hours of sleep. She didn't sleep, though. She mostly cried. It was heartless and cruel, he knew, but it would be better for all if their mother—who sat silent across the room staring at Fearghus—would simply let Annwyl go. Let her go so they could release her ashes to the wind, and then move on to the business of raising her offspring the way she would have wanted.

It wasn't that Briec wanted her to die. He'd never disliked her *that* much. But keeping her around for no reason other than to give Fearghus a still-breathing corpse to stare at every day and night didn't seem like a much better idea.

Of course, whenever he thought of himself going through

any of this—losing his Talaith this way—he felt the pain as a physical thing. Never before had he wanted so badly to do something, anything, that would help his brother. Fearghus had never been a happy-go-lucky dragon like Gwenvael, but Fearghus had never been like this.

Broken.

His brother was broken. And although Fearghus's devastation would have been great if Annwyl had fallen in battle, his enemy would have been clear. His task clearer—to kill and destroy all those who'd had a hand in Annwyl's death.

But how did one kill a god?

If Briec knew, he would have done it himself long ago.

As Bercelak's bad temper lashed out at his own brother and Addolgar—whose temper could be much worse—lashed back, Briec glanced around the room.

Something . . . he felt *something*.

He immediately glanced at his sister. Her expression didn't change, her annoyance didn't dwindle.

If Morfyd felt nothing then perhaps there was nothing to feel.

He dismissed it all and focused on his father, wondering which one of them would throw the first punch.

Ahh. Bercelak, of course. Not surprising.

The god in human form stood tall and looked at her. His hair was wildly long, a good portion of it dragging along the floor, and it seemed to have an array of colors streaking through all that black. When she'd first seen him, it had been too dark to tell all the nuances, but now she saw it all clearly. Even his eyes were a strange color. Violet perhaps? Very much the color of Briec's eyes, although more vibrant—and surprisingly warmer than Briec's. More friendly. Just like his handsome face.

Everything about him said handsome, charming, and

sweet—and Dagmar didn't believe any of that for even a second.

"So you don't worship the gods."

Dagmar moved farther into the room.

"Reason and logic are all I need."

"But so cold and unfeeling are dear reason and logic."

"They've done well enough for me. I've seen my people worship at the altars of gods like you and I have yet to see the benefit. Men cut down in their prime during battle, leaving wife and babes to their own. So the wife prays to her god. 'Please god, help me now that my husband is gone.'" Dagmar shrugged. "Within a month or two, when she's worked her way through the paltry sum given to her by the army, I'll see her in the market, selling herself on the street to the highest bidder. Hoping to earn enough to put food on the table for babes who'll grow up as thieves and murderers. Or maybe as soldiers, because their father was, and then it can start all over again. No, I'm sorry. That I cannot worship."

"But to save your friend, won't you lie to me? Tell me what I want to hear? Won't you play those same games you play with others?"

"I've read enough about the dragon gods to know that will be of no use to me. I can flatter you with compliments, but what will it buy me?"

"So then why are you here, my good Lady Dagmar?"

"I want to understand why."

"Why what?"

"Why you'd do this to them. There was no one protecting my mother or me, so her death was unavoidable. But these babes"—she pointed at the twins, who tugged on their mother trying to get her attention—"they're your creation. Why would you do this to them?"

"I've done nothing to them."

"Taking their mother from them? Do you think they'll forgive you?"

"They'll have to understand. She's too weak to protect them."

"Now, yes, she is. But not before she was pregnant. And you're a god. You could give that back to her."

"If I deemed her worthy. I don't. But fear not, sweet Dagmar, I'm taking them away from here. I'll protect them and make sure they're raised properly. I did a very good job with Izzy."

"You don't think their father will do a good job?"

"He's very angry. He doesn't want to blame them, but he does."

"He wouldn't have to if you gave him his mate back. Only she can protect these children."

"That's what I thought." He glanced down at her, an insulting pout on his lips. Insulting because he wasn't nearly as sad as he pretended.

"They will *never* forgive you," she promised.

"They won't have to know."

"Ahhh, I see. Take them from their kin and they'll never hear the stories about how you killed their mother."

"I didn't kill her."

"Yes, you did. This is down to you, my lord. You and only you."

"Well, it's too late now." He dismissed her with a wave, becoming frustrated. "By tonight, she'll be greeting her ancestors. Now if you'll excuse me——"

Her mind moving fast, Dagmar tried to find a way out of this. A way to help the babes first and perhaps, if she were lucky, Annwyl second. But for some reason, she could only think about wool socks. What in all of reason did wool socks have to do with anything?

She no longer even had that pair she brought with her. She'd given it to . . .

Dagmar rested her hand on the baseboard of the bed,

steadying herself. She had only one chance here; she'd better make it good.

"And what of your mate, Rhydderch Hael?"

He stared at her. "What of her?"

"Ragnar told me the stories about the dragon gods."

He laughed. "You mean when you thought he was a monk?" When she didn't laugh along, he let out a bored sigh. "So what about my mate? And can we make this speedy?"

"I have a theory."

"That does not sound speedy."

"Everything I've read by humans or been told by Ragnar and those who traveled with him is that Eirianwen, your mate and the most feared goddess of war, is a dragoness."

"I grow so bored," he suddenly said.

"I'm sure you do. But just hear me out. I found this very old text written by a monk believed to be completely insane—"

"That's always a good source."

"—and he wrote about a tale of two goddesses. One, Arzhela. A goddess of beauty, light, and fertility. Loved by all the human gods. Worshipped as one of the most loved deities. Then there was her younger *sister*. Eirianwen. A dark goddess. Opposite in purpose and even looks. She favored the desert gods. Brown of skin and hair and eyes. And"—now she made a sad, pouting face—"so unfairly feared. Even by her own sisters and brothers. Because she looked nothing like them and she had a blood thirst rivaled by few. It makes sense she'd become a god of war. Aaah." She wagged her finger. "But few human warriors would worship her. Those who followed Arzhela had nothing but horrible things to say about poor Eirianwen and gave her nothing but a horrible reputation throughout the land. Saddened, Eirianwen wandered away, becoming the traveling war god. Until she eventually wandered into the midst of the dragon gods. Unfortunately, she was human and they did not like human gods."

Feeling her confidence return, Dagmar moved closer toward

him. "And just as Eirianwen was about to give up and wander away yet again, tragically dismissed by everyone, she met the father of all dragons. Oh, and he took quite a shine to her, and so he and she could . . . well . . . you know, he turned himself to human. A skill he only had because he was a god. None of his own creations could turn to human, which had never been a problem until the humans began to fight back on being dinner.

"Then Arzhela found out about you and Eirianwen, didn't she? And she was not happy, mostly because she still had no mate of her own. How could her scary, over-muscled, blood-drenched, murderous baby sister have a mate and not she? Even worse, he wasn't one of the human gods but one of those scaly reptiles."

When that received a raised eyebrow, she held her hands up. "Merely repeating the text I read, my lord."

"Of course."

"So there was war because that's how things are handled between gods. A surprise attack was planned, with the retrieval of Eirianwen added in for good measure. Because it wouldn't be right if they didn't bring her back to her own kind who had been treating her so wonderfully up to this point." He smirked at her dry tone. "But Arzhela, always a little too confident, forgot that her sister was a god of war. Battle, blood, and strategy are her friends, just as reason and logic are mine. She knew this would be coming and planned a counterattack, rallying all the other dragon gods to your side. And by doing so, she risked everything for you." Dagmar moved in until the hem of her dress mingled with his long hair. "Because when the battle was done and the air cleared, there was no more crossing over from one god domain to the next. She was now part of the dragon pantheon."

"So what?"

"Dragons' ability to shift to human is not a gift from you at all, is it? It's a gift from *her*. Because of her love for you and desire to protect your kind as best she could." Dagmar tapped his chest with her forefinger. "That explains why, when the dragons of the Southlands fly into battle, it is her colors they wear under their armor. It is *her* powers that their battle mages call upon. Not yours."

The Dragon God said nothing, merely stared.

"That was Morfyd and Talaith's mistake all along, wasn't it? It should have been Eirianwen they called upon. Eirianwen to protect Annwyl. Because of the two of you, she seems to be the one with the heart. The one who cares."

She stepped back from him. "I know! Perhaps I will call on her. I've never called on a god before, but as a follower of Aoibhell, I'm sure my call will be heard by all the gods. Dragon, human or otherwise. Perhaps she will be able to do," she sneered, "what you are not powerful enough to do!"

Then his hand was wrapped tightly around her throat, stopping any more words or air from escaping her mouth. He lifted Dagmar from the floor, ignoring the way she clawed at his fingers.

"So very smart, Dagmar Reinholdt. So very, very smart. Let's see just how smart you are."

He released her, tossing her back in the process. Coughing and trying to get her breath back, Dagmar didn't have a moment to ask what he meant before he slipped his hand under Annwyl's neck and tilted her head back. He kissed her then, and Dagmar watched as he pulled the last breath from her lungs, the Magicks that had kept her breathing, harshly ripped from her.

The dragon god stepped back and Annwyl's arm fell to the side, her eyes staring blankly at the ceiling.

He'd killed her.

Dagmar felt panic sweep through her, her body trembling as she stared at the dead queen.

"Now her death is on your head, human." He placed

Annwyl's twins in Dagmar's arms. "The question is . . . Will the twins' deaths be on your head as well? I think so."

"Wait—"

He turned from her, snapped his fingers, and when Dagmar blinked again she was no longer safe in the Garbhán Isle castle. She was underground in a tunnel somewhere, the babes in her arms crying because they'd felt the last gasp of their mother.

And at her feet was Annwyl's naked corpse, the wound from where they'd opened her up to get to the babes no longer bleeding since there was nothing left inside her to bleed out.

Slowly Dagmar raised her gaze and kept raising it until she could look into the face of the nine-foot beast standing before her. The light from the torches they used to allow them to clearly see their work as they dug out one of the recently closed tunnels glinted off the creature's horns.

"It seems today," the Minotaur said softly, grinning down at her and the babes, "the gods have decided to treat their most loyal servants with gifts."

Chapter 28

It was something none of them had ever heard before. At least not in the context of true pain.

Their mother cried out.

Gwenvael spun around to look at her, along with everyone else in the room, as Rhiannon sat forward, her hand over her chest.

"Oh, gods. She's dead, Fearghus." She looked at her eldest

son. "He took her from me. He ripped the life right from her body."

They were all moving for the door when she said, "No." She shook her head, still trying to get her breath back. "She's gone."

"What do you mean she's gone?" Fearghus snapped.

"I mean she's gone. The babes are gone. They're gone. He took them."

"No." Morfyd stepped forward, her eyes unfocused as she saw what her mother saw. "He didn't take them. He sent the babes away."

"Where?" Gwenvael asked. "Where did he take them?"

Rhiannon closed her eyes, going inside herself for more information.

Bercelak pushed past his children and siblings and crouched in front of his mate. "What is it, Rhiannon?"

"He wanted me to see. To see what he did because seeing through her pain makes it harder—" She gripped Bercelak's hand, her face contorting as she tried to see past a god's tricks to the truth.

Rhiannon snatched her hand away from Bercelak and abruptly stood, her face red with rage as she snarled, *"That bastard."*

Fearghus moved toward his mother. "What is it? What has he done?"

"He sent them to the Minotaurs."

The room fell silent, everyone standing for a moment, brutally stunned. Then Fearghus was stalking across the room and tearing the door open. Without even realizing it, he ripped it off its hinges, Briec and Gwenvael forced to step aside as it flew by.

They all stormed into the Great Hall, Talaith and Izzy waiting for them all.

The Nolwenn witch had felt it, too. She knew what had happened to her friend and the twins.

"They're not alone," Rhiannon called after them, and as one they all turned to face her.

"Who's with her?" Fearghus demanded.

When his mother's eyes rested on him, Gwenvael felt the breath stop in his lungs. "Dagmar?"

His brother asked him something, but he couldn't hear him. He couldn't hear anything above the roar in his ears as Gwenvael realized what had happened to Dagmar—and what *would* happen to Dagmar if they didn't get to her and the babes in time.

Fearghus slammed his shoulder, snapping his attention back in the room.

"What?" Gwenvael snarled.

"Will Dagmar buy us time?" Fearghus demanded.

"Yes," Gwenvael nodded, already running toward the Great Hall doors. "She'll buy us time."

Dagmar stared up at the Minotaur standing over her. His eyes were brown, his hair shaggy and unclean, his face bovine with a flat, moist snout covered in some kind of unpleasant-looking mucus. He wore nothing more than a cloth made of some animal skin around his hips and a necklace made of what she would guess was pure gold. The chain was thick and broad and the medallion that hung at the end of it, the size of a small plate. She recognized the symbol of the goddess Arzhela immediately.

Dropping to one knee in front of the head Minotaur, Dagmar said, "I'm so happy to have found you, my lords. I'd taken the children when the chance presented itself, but it was not easy."

"You took the spawn?"

She nodded, but did not raise her gaze. "I knew you waited here, and at the death of their mother it seemed the most opportune time."

He shoved the body at Dagmar's feet with his hoof. She

was glad her head was lowered and he couldn't see the wince his actions caused.

"This one. *This* is the great Blood Queen of the South?"

"Yes. Giving birth is what killed her, my lord. As you can see, the . . . uh . . . spawn drained her of her very life."

"Good. The whore deserved it."

Another Minotaur stepped closer, crouching beside the body. He pressed big, meaty fingers against her throat, then nodded. "She's dead."

The head Minotaur stepped around Annwyl's body and kicked it, sending it flying.

Dagmar bit the inside of her cheek when she heard it slam into a far wall, bones crushed from the pressure. The great human queen landed limply on the rocky ground, her remains unnaturally twisted.

It took all of Dagmar's self-training to not cry out. To not order them as Only Daughter of the Reinholdt to treat the remains of the Great Blood Queen with reverence . . .

The Only Daughter of the Reinholdt . . .

"And as for you—"

She saw fur-covered hands reaching for her. "I am the Only Daughter of the Reinholdt," she snapped. "You will not put your hands on me! And know that my father sent me here as an ambassador to the south so that I may assist you in your holy quest in retrieving the spawn of the demon queen."

"Why"—another of them demanded—"would he send his daughter on such a mission?"

She got to her feet, the babes still tight in her arms. "He knew the demon queen would only trust a woman. And because I am The Beast."

"You? You're The Beast?"

"My father knew sending me here was dangerous, but no one else would be able to get close enough."

"Or had the strength of will of The Beast to be around the whore."

"Very true, my lord." She looked at Annwyl's broken body and her expression of disgust was real enough—but most likely not for the reasons they thought. "I've seen many things in that place that will keep me up at nights. Many horrors. But my father will be proud, for I have retrieved the spawn as he has commanded."

"You've done well." The head Minotaur praised, reaching for them. "Now we can cut their throats and head home this very night."

"No." Dagmar turned her body away from him to keep his hands off them. "We cannot kill them here. We must return with them to the north and give my father the prize of cutting off their useless little heads."

"We cannot do that. They need to die before those dragons can find us."

"We'll have more to bargain with if they live."

"Going home was never our intent, my lady. Killing them is. If any of us survive that and make it home alive, then it will be an extra gift from the gods. But our main goal—our only goal—is to see these atrocities dead before we do anything else."

Would they understand the hypocrisy of referring to the twins as atrocities when they were standing cows? *Talking* standing cows?

No. Probably not.

"I cannot allow that," she said with as much royal rudeness as she could muster. "Their deaths are not for . . . *you*."

"But the gods—"

"Your only purpose here, bovine, is to ensure my safe passage home. They will come for us and you will fight to protect me and most likely die. That is your only task."

The males stood in confusion, glancing between each

other. She knew she had them. Men were always so easy for her to twist when she needed to.

Tragically, Dagmar hadn't counted on the female.

"She lies," the female hissed, moving out from the shadows. Her dress was also made of animal skin but covered her from shoulders to hooves. She had no horns as the males did, but was slightly shorter than the tallest among them. The brown cape over her dress was wool. She had the hood pulled up to cover her hair and Dagmar could see the runes sewn into the fabric.

A priestess of Arzhela. Of some power, too.

"She protects those things she carries, with her very life." She slammed her fist into the shoulder of whatever male stood closest to her, eliciting a grunt. "And you fools believe her."

Dagmar could barely understand the female's words because of the damage that had been done to her throat, which bore the old scar of a sword cut that went right across it. She could have gotten it in battle, but most likely it was the sacrifice she made to Arzhela. A true servant of the goddess that once was.

The priestess came closer, her hooves stomping loudly on the rocky ground. She stared hard at Dagmar as she approached.

"You're wrong," Dagmar tried again, attempting to sound bored and unimpressed. "My task is as simple as yours. Retrieve the spawn, return to my father. The Reinholdt."

"She lies," she hissed again.

"Are you doubting my word as a Northlander? Are you doubting I'm a Reinholdt?"

"You are a Reinholdt, Lady Dagmar. I have seen you before when I've passed through the Reinholdt lands. You *are* Dagmar Reinholdt. But you lie." She leaned in close, her wet nose sniffing around her. "She has the smell of Rhydderch Hael all over her."

"She is his disciple!" one of the males accused.

"No." The priestess gave a small smile. "No. She worships

no one. No god protects her. Cares for her. Even Rhydderch Hael. He is the one who sent her here. For us."

"And the spawn?"

"They have failed him. He wants nothing to do with them."

She reached to touch one and Dagmar immediately turned her body away.

Her voice low and controlled, she growled, "Keep your grubby, cow hands off them."

The priestess leered. "The spawn are mine." Her gaze moved to the males. "The woman . . . is all yours."

Dagmar didn't even manage the thought that she should run before a hand gripped her hair and yanked her back, the priestess quickly ripping Annwyl's babes from her arms.

"No!" She reached out for the babes, desperate to get them back. Desperate to protect them with her life.

The head Minotaur stepped in front of her, his hand wrapping around her throat. "How could you not worship the gods? Even now they reward our sacrifice"—he shoved her back into the other Minotaurs—"with you."

Soldiers, guards, and servants—the humans—all quickly moved out of their way as Gwenvael and his kin poured from the castle into the courtyard. They immediately shifted, Addolgar and Ghleanna heading off in opposite directions to scour the countryside, calling on their sons and daughters to join them. Rhiannon and Morfyd headed toward the lake to call upon gods to help them. Leaving the four brothers and their father.

Gwenvael, Briec, Éibhear, Bercelak, and Fearghus would start where the hoof prints were first located and move out from there, hoping that they were no more than a few leagues off.

But as Gwenvael took to the air, he heard a voice calling to him. He looked down and saw that it was Izzy. She waved her hands wildly and screamed his name.

He dropped lower. "What is it, Izzy?"

"Annwyl's horse! Can you not hear him?"

Briec was by him now and they hovered for a moment, trying to hear around and through the other noises of humans.

"I hear him," Briec said. They both could. The horse was banging against his stall. He could have merely gone mad, sensing his mistress was dead. But Gwenvael didn't think so. And neither did Izzy, it seemed. She took off running, cutting through and around humans with ease while her uncle and father flew low until they reached the queen's personal stable.

Izzy ran inside even as her mother ran up behind her telling her to wait.

Éibhear moved past them all, grabbing hold of the stable roof and yanking it off with one great pull.

None of them had ever seen Violence act this way. He'd always been the calm center of the storm that was Annwyl, which was why Fearghus had chosen the stallion for his mate in the first place.

"Mourning?" Briec asked.

"I don't think so." Fearghus dropped a bit lower. "Izzy. Let him out."

Izzy gripped the metal bolt holding the stall gate closed and locked, and yanked it back. The gate slammed open as the horse hit it again with his front hooves and without a moment's hesitation, he charged out, running toward the great gates.

The horse no longer seemed mad with grief. Instead, he had a purpose and a destination.

"Open the gates! Now!" Fearghus yelled to the guards before taking off after the beast, his brothers and father right by his side.

They grabbed her now-empty arms—and reason help her but she felt that emptiness to her soul—and dragged her back across the tunnel floor to where they'd stopped digging. They threw her to the ground and she scrambled back up.

Her mind desperately searched for a way out of this, but the power of the priestess over these males was absolute. In the north, a priestess of power was the one woman no man would dare argue with. Unfortunately the Minotaurs were no different from her kinsmen.

"You'll have to forgive our roughness, my lady," the head Minotaur said with absolute disdain. "It's been months that we've been on this road and our priestess is rarely accommodating. But truly you won't live long enough to mind that much."

"You will pay for your betrayal of the Northland Code."

"We are from the mighty Ice Lands. We are the true Northlanders. So any code you southerners use means nothing to us."

And it was as the males were moving closer to her that Dagmar saw her, standing in the midst of them—unseen. Except by Dagmar. She seemed taller this time and no longer the poor sword-for-hire. How could Dagmar not have seen it before? How could she not have known?

"Are you just going to stand there?" Dagmar snapped, angry. "Are you going to do nothing?"

The Minotaurs stopped, glancing at each other while a few muttered, wondering who she was talking to.

"You hurt his feelings," she chastised. "That's why you're here, Dagmar Reinholdt. You really have no one to blame but yourself."

"You're blaming *me* for this?"

"We weren't blaming you for anything," one of the Minotaurs contested.

"Shut up," she snapped and focused again on Eir. "You have to do something."

"Like what? Kill them all?"

"Excellent start."

"I can't. They haven't actually done anything to me. And

you don't worship me . . . or anyone. The twins aren't mine to protect. I really shouldn't interfere with other gods."

"Are you kidding me?"

"This isn't going to work," the head Minotaur said. "Pretending to be crazy won't help you."

"Gods have rules," Eir went on, ignoring the Minotaur as Dagmar was. "A code, if you will, like you have in the north."

"So that's it? You're going to walk away?"

"You talked yourself down here . . . Seems to me, you're on your own."

The goddess began to turn away, but Dagmar pulled her arm away from one of her captors and pointed it at her. "You said you owe me one!"

Eir faced her again, blinking in surprise. "For your wool socks."

"It was an open-ended 'I owe you one.'"

"What?"

"If you'd specifically stated, 'I owe you one set of wool socks,' that would be one thing. But you just said you owe me for the wool socks. Thereby leaving it completely open to interpretation and final payment."

One of the Minotaurs leaned close to his commander. "She's centaur-shit crazy."

"The fear must have scrambled her mind," the commander suggested.

Eir stared at her for a moment before nodding her head. "You *are* good. But it was only one favor. So you choose who I save. The twins or—"

"The twins," she said, and all the Minotaurs looked over at their priestess, busy pulling out daggers and herbs for a proper sacrifice.

"The twins," Dagmar repeated.

"All right. Think you can keep them busy for a bit?"

"I have to ask you again, are you kidding?"

"Come on. You're very good. You'll come up with something."

Frustrated, confused, and quite terrified, Dagmar threw up her hands and said, "Hear me, Minotaurs!" And all those bovine faces looked at her. "The dragon gods will not stand for this! And it will not be you they come after. It will be your people. Your females. Your calves. They will wipe your people from the earth for this betrayal!"

That made the males pause. They were on a suicide mission, but that didn't mean their families were.

Eir raised her thumb up and smiled. "Nice!"

"Ignore her," the priestess said while carefully arranging the now screaming twins to her liking on a quickly made altar. "Use her as you will—no one will care."

"But"—one said carefully through his teeth—"we think this one's crazy."

The priestess gaped at him. "That's never stopped you before."

While the Minotaurs debated the rape and murder of the insane, Dagmar watched Eir. She'd promised to help the twins and yet she wasn't walking toward them, but away, eventually stopping at Annwyl's prone body. She knelt down beside the dead queen and turned the body over. She placed her hand on Annwyl's head and dragged it down the length of her body, down her face, across her chest and stomach, down her legs to her feet. Annwyl herself didn't move, her eyes still staring unseeing at the ceiling, but her corpse twitched as bones locked back into place.

With a hand under Annwyl's neck, her head gently tilted back, the goddess, like Rhydderch Hael had done a short while ago, pressed her lips against Annwyl's . . .

The Minotaurs, obviously overcoming their moral dilemma, grabbed Dagmar and pulled her to the floor, onto her back. She fought back at the hands grabbing for her, but her focus was on the babes and the priestess who had them. The callous cow hummed as she prepared her ritual, ignoring everything else that was going on around her.

"Look at me, human."

Dagmar did, staring up at the Minotaur now over her while the others held her pinned to the ground.

"Your pain," he said softly, "will be my pleasure."

"And your death," said Annwyl behind him, "will be mine."

The Blood Queen then grabbed his head, her fingers digging into his eyes, pressing in until she had them deep into the sockets.

The Minotaur screeched and stood, Annwyl attached to his back, holding on as he desperately tried to get her off.

The others released Dagmar as they went to their commander's aid. But he was shrieking and turning in circles, unintentionally keeping Annwyl from their grasp while at the same time using her body as a weapon.

Dagmar quickly got to her feet as Annwyl pulled one hand from the Minotaur's face and reached down yanking the eating dagger he kept on his loin cloth. She raised the blade above him and brought it down into his skull. He squealed, and Annwyl laughed, hysterically, dragging the blade out and slamming it home, again and again.

Finally one of the Minotaurs grabbed hold of her and yanked her off their commander, tossing her across the room. Annwyl hit the wall, the floor, and then jumped right back to her feet.

Now Annwyl screamed, the likes of which Dagmar had never heard before and prayed to never hear again. Annwyl screamed and, covered in blood, charged full into the Minotaurs. They were so stunned it took them a moment to react. One of them went for his blade, but Annwyl snatched it from him, using it to cut his stomach open before turning and boldly swinging the weapon as she did.

Dagmar forced herself to look away and to the priestess.

The priestess was angry, but she didn't lose her head. Instead she grabbed the dagger and raised it above the girl. Dagmar ran at her, stepped on the weak altar for leverage, and launched herself at the priestess. Well aware she was no fighter, Dagmar wrapped her arms around the heifer's head and held on.

"Get off me!" the priestess bellowed in outrage and shoved, sending Dagmar flying back. Dagmar hit the ground but kept her head up so it wouldn't smash into the floor. When she stopped sliding, she grabbed one of the torches and forced her aching body back up. She felt the pain immediately, having never been trained in controlling it, and quickly limped back to the female Minotaur. She slapped the torch into her face, startling and angering her yet again.

"Bitch!"

Dagmar kicked at the bowl filled with oil, aiming for the priestess. It hit her on the side and Dagmar quickly slammed the torch at her. The flame caught and the priestess cried out, yanking off her cloak. Using the time, Dagmar grabbed hold of the twins and quickly retreated. She saw the exit from where she stood, but a slashing, killing Annwyl and still quite a few Minotaurs stood between her and freedom.

The priestess, cloak and flame free, stepped over the altar. She stared at them all, and then she opened her mouth and yelled, *"Stop!"*

They all did, too. Even Annwyl.

The priestess glanced at Dagmar but seemed confident in her current situation of being unable to escape. Right now, they both knew that Annwyl was her bigger concern.

She raised her arm and stepped a little closer to the queen. "I call upon the darkest powers to come to me," she chanted, her finger pointing at Annwyl. "I call upon them to possess me and give me the power to destroy this abomination."

Dagmar stepped forward. "Annwyl, kill her!" she shouted. *"Kill her before she can finish!"*

She'd never know if Annwyl had heard her words, had

understood her words, or simply responded to the sound of yelling. Whatever prompted the queen, the Mad Bitch of Garbhán Isle, it was quite enough.

Pulling back her arm—the skin no longer pale and flaccid but strong, powerful, and filled with well-trained muscles—she threw the sword she had in her hand. A Minotaur's blade, much longer and wider than any human sword, and Annwyl handled it like it was a small eating dagger.

The weapon flew across the tunnel and slammed into the Minotaur female, forcing her back several steps.

The priestess stared down at it, but she didn't die.

She raised her arms and shouted, *"Kill—"*

But Annwyl's hysterical scream drowned her out, and then the Blood Queen was charging the Minotaur female, slamming into her, knocking her into the ground. She yanked the blade from the female's chest and raised it. Still screaming, she slammed it into her. The priestess's howl of pain filled the tunnel, but it still couldn't block out Annwyl's scream. It went beyond a battle cry. It went beyond anything.

And while she screamed, over and over again, Annwyl yanked the weapon out, and slammed it back in.

Unable to turn away, they all watched her, even Dagmar. The Minotaur males didn't move. Their commander was dead and their priestess was being murdered right before them.

And it was murder. A brutal, vicious murder. Blood and gore flew everywhere, even striking Dagmar and the babes, but Annwyl kept going until the tip of the blade slammed into the ground beneath them. That's when she released it and tore at the priestess's chest using only her bare hands. She tore the ribs apart and began to slam her fist inside the open chest cavity again and again.

By now the female Minotaur had long died, but apparently Annwyl's rage was still going strong.

Dagmar lost count of how many times Annwyl struck at

the open chest in front of her. How many times she yanked organs out and tossed them over her shoulder. For the first time in her life, Dagmar was mesmerized, unable to think or reason or do much of anything but stare.

It took them long minutes before the Minotaurs finally snapped out of their own state of shock, and one of them, a giant with an absolutely enormous head, moved toward her. He slowly raised his sword and Dagmar went to warn Annwyl, but a blade held against her throat cut off the sound.

The Minotaur now stood behind Annwyl, the sword held in both hands over her naked back. Without a sound, he brought it down. But as the tip of the blade neared her spine, Annwyl moved. She simply lifted her right arm and reared to her left side. The blade slammed into the Minotaur female's empty chest. The male stared dumbly at what he'd done, and then his gaze turned to Annwyl. Her smile was mad, one corner of her mouth lifting, her green eyes rising up to look at him through the wild tumble of hair in her face.

"Missed," she hissed, and the Minotaur stumbled back. He was terrified. He couldn't hide it, not from his comrades, not from himself. For the first time in his life, Dagmar was sure, an Ice Lander was terrified and everyone knew it—because they were all terrified as well.

Terrified as they watched Annwyl grab the hilt of the Minotaur's blade still sticking up from the female's chest. Terrified as the much smaller human and naked female got to her feet. Annwyl panted, not from exertion . . . but from lust. From desire. The desire for the kill. Dagmar had never seen it like this before. Not like this. Not as if the warrior would climax at any moment merely from the threat she presented.

The queen's crazed gaze shifted to Dagmar and the Minotaur behind her lowered his blade and moved away. He held his hands up, the palms coated with a lighter, paler fur than the brown and white on top.

As one, the Minotaurs all moved back, watching her closely, so closely.

Annwyl wet her lips, her panting getting heavier, her body more aroused by the second. Then she screamed; she screamed and the Minotaurs ran. Down the tunnel they'd built and out into the sunlight they rarely saw.

And Annwyl? She was right behind them.

Fearghus stopped short and Gwenvael almost ran into the back of him. His brother turned, his eyes wild as he searched the area. Annwyl's horse reared up and held its ground.

"What? What is it?"

"Listen!"

Gwenvael heard it then. Something he thought never to hear again. The battle cry of the Blood Queen.

"There! She's there!"

And Annwyl was there, tearing out of a hole dug into the base of a small hill. She wasn't running away, though; she was running after. Running after the Minotaurs she'd chased off. At least nine feet tall and outweighing her by more than twenty stone, the Minotaurs ran. But she caught up with them. As he, Fearghus, Briec, and Bercelak all landed nearly a hundred feet away, Annwyl caught up with the first one. She slashed the back of his ankles and he tumbled forward. As he rolled onto his back, she cut his throat and kept moving, slashing at another. The Minotaurs had hoped to outrun her, but now there were dragons in their way, cutting them off.

Briec took in a breath, ready to douse them all in flame, but Fearghus shook his head. "No. Leave it."

"But Annwyl will be safe." A gift from their mother protected Annwyl from a dragon's flame. It had helped her more than once during a messy battle.

"Leave it," Fearghus said again.

They did, and the Minotaurs, realizing they couldn't escape, spun around to face Annwyl. They attacked as one fighting unit, nearly twelve of them remaining from what Dagmar had assured Fearghus would be a force of at least fifty. But the blade Annwyl carried—a short sword for a Minotaur, but nearly double the length of Annwyl's own broad sword—flashed in the sun as she went to work.

It was a brutal battle, the Blood Queen once again proving her name as she hacked away at arms, legs, and heads. The heads were hard to take, so she crippled most of them first and then went from one to the other to the other, finishing them off. As the brothers and their father watched, Morfyd and Rhiannon landed, followed by Talaith and Izzy arriving on horseback. Then the Cadwaladr Clan arrived, dropping from the sky and watching as Annwyl did what she'd always done best.

She went to the last one, who no longer had legs but was still struggling to get away. She planted her foot into his back and held him in place. Then she raised the sword in her hands and brought it down against his neck. The first strike did not take his head, so she hacked and hacked until it fell off.

Then Annwyl stood there, panting, her naked body covered in blood. But she was alive. Very much alive.

And completely insane.

Gwenvael heard a small cry and looked up to see Dagmar walk out of the tunnel. She was dirty, her clothes torn, and she had some blood on her, but she was alive and so were the twins. They were the ones crying, annoyed, it seemed, more than anything. But all four were fine—four because he now included Dagmar's spectacles in all estimates.

She looked at him, her relieved smile warming him in a way he'd never felt before. He stepped forward, determined to get to her, but her eyes widened and she quickly shook her head. Good thing, too, because Annwyl turned on him so fast,

Gwenvael took a hasty step back. She held the blade in both hands, raised high on her side. A move for a running attack.

Fearghus scowled, more confused than angry. "Annwyl?"

Her green eyes shifted toward Fearghus, but Gwenvael saw no recognition of her mate. No undying love and loyalty. As far as Annwyl the Bloody was concerned, all of them were enemies.

"Get on the horse," Annwyl ordered Dagmar.

Gwenvael shook his head. "Wait—" But his mother caught his arm, pulled him back. She stepped in front of him, prepared to protect her son, and kept her eyes on Annwyl.

"Move!" Annwyl commanded again.

Dagmar did, going to Annwyl's stallion. The horse lowered himself to the ground and Dagmar climbed onto his back, the babes in her arms making it an awkward ordeal. Annwyl moved toward the horse, her gaze constantly scanning from one dragon to the other. She reached Violence and slid on behind Dagmar. She still held the sword and appeared ready to use it at any second.

"Take his mane," she ordered Dagmar as the horse stood tall. "Now hold on. He knows where to go."

Annwyl pointed her sword at Celyn and Branwen. *"Move!"* The two youngsters fell over each other trying to get out of the way, until their mother grabbed them by their hair and yanked them back.

"Go," Annwyl told her horse.

Violence reared up then shot off, tearing through the empty space the young siblings left.

As the horse disappeared over a hill, Gwenvael's Dragon Kin stood silent, unsure what to do next.

Then Addolgar earnestly asked, "I'm confused. Is she dead or not?"

Chapter 29

After all that, Dagmar had really hoped they were heading back to Garbhán Isle, but no. A nice inn somewhere in one of the villages? No. A pub for a pint . . . or twelve pints, one after the other until she could no longer see straight with or without her spectacles? No.

Instead of any of those lovely ideas, the Queen of Dark Plains took her to a cave. A dark, dank cave. She couldn't even see her hand in front of her face or the babes in her arms, but of course this place must be safer than the tunnel they'd just escaped from.

She hoped so, anyway.

Thankfully the horse seemed to know where he was going, happily trotting along through the winding black tunnels. Eventually he stopped and Annwyl jumped off. Dagmar could hear the queen moving around and some cursing when she walked into things. But then flint struck rock and a torch was lit. Annwyl walked around the cavern, lighting more torches attached to the walls, and as she did, Dagmar could now see she was not in some random cave Annwyl had stumbled upon. They were in a furnished cave. A dragon's cave. She let out a sigh of relief and the horse lowered himself to the ground, allowing Dagmar to slip off. Not easy when she was desperately trying not to drop the sobbing babes in her arms.

"Why are they crying?"

The naked queen stood before her, blood covering most of

her, and there seemed to be a fresh wound or two, but this . . . this was the queen Dagmar had always heard of. Tall, powerfully built. Muscles any male warrior would envy and generous breasts any woman would love to have been gifted with. The only sign that showed Annwyl had once been with child was the horizontal scar across her lower abdomen. But it looked as if it had been there for years.

It seemed Annwyl had a new patron goddess who took much better care of her subjects than Rhydderch Hael, bringing Annwyl back to the way she was before the babes were born—at least physically.

Emotionally, the woman was a mess.

"They're crying because they're frightened," Dagmar explained, hoping the queen took her babes soon. Her arms were growing tired, their abnormally large size turning them into quite the burdens.

Annwyl looked at the Minotaur sword in her hands, then set it down. After that she walked around the large cavern, rubbing her hands together. Dagmar noticed a table and chairs, so she sat down.

The queen turned and faced her again. "I put the sword down, why are they still crying?"

"They're probably hungry."

"Then feed them."

Uh-oh.

"They're not mine to feed."

"Who do they belong to?"

This is just bloody wonderful!

Dagmar cleared her throat, and spoke carefully. "They're yours."

"I don't have children."

Dagmar was so tired, the patience she prided herself on quickly deserting her. "What do you remember?"

The queen thought for a moment, pointed at the horse. "I remember him."

"Do you remember his name?"

Annwyl frowned. "Black . . . ie?"

Dagmar exhaled. "Do you remember your name?"

She chewed the inside of her mouth, stared up at the ceiling. After several *minutes*, the queen asked, "Do I need to?"

"Reason preserve me," Dagmar sighed. The babes cried louder and she looked down at them. "You need to settle down."

And when they did, she found herself more disturbed than she'd been by their crazed mother.

"See?" Annwyl said, smiling with relief. "They are yours."

"No, my lady, they are most definitely—"

"They couldn't be mine," she cut in quickly. "I'd make a horrible mother. Five minutes with me and they're already covered in blood."

"Yes, but—"

"I'll be back." Abruptly, the queen walked away down a dark tunnel Dagmar had no intention of following her into.

Gwenvael turned to his mother. "So she's gone 'round the bend then?"

"Well, she's clearly not sane."

"I'm going after her," Fearghus said.

Rhiannon grabbed her eldest son by the hair.

"Mother!"

"For once, don't be a prat, Fearghus. She doesn't even recognize you. Go near her now and she'll kill you."

"If that's true, then it's a good thing she's alone with the children," Briec stated dryly.

"And she has Dagmar." When they all looked at him, Gwenvael added, "She matters, too."

"They'll be fine," Izzy said, positive as always. "Annwyl just needs a little time to get back to her old self."

Éibhear snorted. "And aren't you the one who said we should trust Rhydderch Hael and he'd never hurt her?"

Izzy's mouth dropped open and her eyes widened. "You blue haired—"

"That's it!" Talaith stood between the enormous blue dragon and her daughter. "Separate. Separate! You're both irritating me!" Talaith took a deep breath. "Fearghus, go to her, but approach her carefully. Think of it as battle fatigue. Go slowly, don't startle her, don't rush her. Take it slow and easy. Understand?"

"I understand. Now I just have to figure out where she's gone."

"We'll fly until we find her."

Talaith shook her head at Gwenvael's suggestion. "She's going to go where she feels safe."

"Even if she doesn't remember?"

"She knew to protect the babes. She knew her horse. Fearghus, she'd go where she feels safest. Where she's always felt safest."

Fearghus's smile was small, but there. "Dark Glen." He nodded, knowing he was right. "She'd go to Dark Glen. She'd go home."

Dagmar was asleep on the large bed she'd found in one of the caverns. She placed the babes down first on the fur, surrounding them with protective pillows in case she rolled over while she slept. Once done, she stretched out lengthwise on the bed and that was the last thing she remembered until she sensed someone near her.

Before opening her eyes, she went for the small dagger tucked into her girdle and sat up. But as she tried to focus on the man in front of her, the dagger slipped from her fingers and spun away.

Thankfully the human male was quick of hand and caught the blade before it slammed into his forehead. Squinting, she leaned in and winced. "Sorry, Fearghus."

First she gets his mate killed, then his twins almost get killed, and now she was throwing knives at his head.

"I am teaching you how to use that damn thing," a voice said behind her. "You're bloody hopeless with it."

Dagmar could barely make out that gorgeous body in brown leggings and long gold hair, but she knew her Gwenvael. Jumping off the bed and into his open arms, she gasped out, "I'm so glad you found us!"

Gwenvael hugged her tight against his body so her feet didn't touch the floor. "*I'm* glad we found you." He kissed her cheeks, forehead, and chin. "Are you all right? Are you hurt? Tell me you're all right."

"I'm fine." Although she had the irrational desire to cry. "I'm not hurt. And the babes are fine."

"And where is Lady Madness?"

Without moving her head from the wonderful spot on his shoulder, Dagmar pointed in the direction she remembered Annwyl going. "She and that stallion from the underworld went that way. She said she'd be back. I decided not to take it as a threat."

Fearghus sat on the bed, stroking his hand across each babe's head. "The lake is in that direction."

"Considering she's positively saturated in Minotaur blood, that would make sense."

Gwenvael put her back on her feet, but before stepping away from her, he placed the sweetest kiss on her forehead. "Before my brother goes off after his crazed mate, think you can tell us what happened? The more we know, the better he'll be able to deal with Annwyl."

Dagmar nodded. "Yes. Of course." She sat down on the bed. "First off, Fearghus, I must apologize." And that's when the first tear fell.

"Dagmar?"

"It's all my fault, Gwenvael. All of it. I only wanted to help, but instead I nearly wipe out your entire family!"

Gwenvael crouched in front of her, taking her hands in his. The simple feel of his flesh against hers, his thumbs rubbing across her knuckles, calmed her down almost immediately.

"I want you to listen to me well, Dagmar Reinholdt," he said. "No one's blaming you for anything."

"Yet."

Dagmar and Gwenvael looked at Fearghus.

"Did I say that out loud?" Then he winked, and Dagmar almost started to cry again, even while he got her to smile.

"Ignore him, Beast." Gwenvael grabbed a straight-back chair and sat down in front of her. He took hold of her hands again. "Now tell us everything."

She kept it clean and direct, no emotions tossed in. No mentions of her own mother and the desire to prevent the twins from going through what she went through herself.

Instead, she told them as she would have told her own father. In plain words, with "none of that fancy analyzing you do" and that her father hated.

Fearghus stayed on the bed, near his babes, his eyes constantly straying over to them. Neither spoke while she did. Neither asked questions. Instead they waited until she finished.

"I know the babes are hungry," she said when she was done. "But they've been surprisingly good natured about the whole thing and went right to sleep when I put them down. But at some point they are going to need to eat, and either Annwyl has to pull those udders out or we need to get a nursemaid in here because I'll be of no use. Other than that"—she shrugged—"that's pretty much the whole story."

The following silence nearly choked her and she was moments from a good bout of panic when Fearghus leaned forward and rested his elbows on his knees.

Clasping his hands together, he said, "I'm sorry. Can we go back for a moment—you bargained your way out of that with socks?"

That hadn't been what she'd expected the future Dragon King of Dark Plains to ask, but . . . all right.

"Yes, but it was because she was vague that—"

"Now aren't you glad I bought you the socks?"

Dagmar scrutinized Gwenvael. "Pardon?"

"If I hadn't gotten you that new pair, you wouldn't have given up your socks to a traveling goddess."

"He has a point," Fearghus tossed in.

"Yes, but—"

"Which means you owe me your life." Gwenvael glanced at his brother. "Like Talaith and Briec—I can keep her."

"No, you cannot!" Dagmar snapped, completely confused.

"But I bought you the socks," Gwenvael insisted.

"Only because I made you take back the puppy."

Regarding his brother, Fearghus asked, "Puppy?"

"I was trying to make her feel better. She was all upset because I wouldn't bring that bloody dog of hers."

"Was he a nice one?"

"Large. Lots of meat. With the right seasoning . . ." Gwenvael sighed, his eyes staring far off. "Gods, I'm hungry."

Dagmar dragged both her hands through her hair. "Shouldn't both of you be a little more . . . livid with me?"

"But I have my Annwyl back," Fearghus said. "Sort of. She doesn't know who she is."

"Or that she's a mother."

"Let's not be negative," Fearghus insisted lightly. "All that matters is that my Annwyl wiped out an entire murderous unit of Minotaurs."

"Fearghus," Gwenvael asked, appearing sincere, "can Annwyl fight naked all the time?"

"Don't make me kill you. I'm in a good mood, and it'll just upset Mother." He stood and bundled the fur around his children, carefully lifting them. "I'm off to find Annwyl."

Gwenvael tapped his leg. "Remember what Talaith said, Fearghus. Take it slow with her. Give her time to remember who she is."

"I will."

Fearghus took several steps away, but stopped. He faced her. "Dagmar?"

"Yes?"

He gazed down at his twins and then at her. "Thank you." He smiled and it was something so beautiful and sincere she didn't know what to say. "For everything. I'm eternally grateful."

Unable to speak, she nodded, and Fearghus disappeared down one of the dark tunnels.

"You keep staring at my brother like that and I'm sending Annwyl after you."

Startled, Dagmar's spine snapped straight and she gave Gwenvael her haughtiest look. "I don't know what you mean. I'm not wearing my spectacles, so I can't see anyway."

"Ohhh. That's what that was. It wasn't you staring longingly at the spot where that deep, low voice told you 'Thank you, Daughter of The Reinholdt . . . for everything.'"

"I hate you," she managed before she started laughing.

Gwenvael rested his hands on the bed, braced on either side of her legs. As he moved forward he teased in a high-pitched voice, "Oh, Fearghus! I'll happily help you because you're so big and strong!"

He kept moving forward, forcing her back, even as she pushed at his shoulders. "Stop it! I did not say that, nor do I sound like that."

"I'll save you *any* day, little Dagmar."

"You're just jealous," she shot back.

"I am." He caught her off guard with the quick reply. "I don't want you looking at anyone like that but me."

He stretched out on top of her, bracing his weight on his right forearm while his left hand brushed against her cheek. His teasing expression turned serious and he studied her face so intently, she became uneasy.

"What?"

"I've never been so scared for anyone before in my life, Dagmar. Not like that. But I knew, I had no doubt, that you'd give us time to get to you. I knew you'd never go down without a fight."

She didn't doubt his words for a moment. She knew they were as truthful and unadorned as what she'd recounted for him and his brother.

"I . . ." she swallowed, unable to fight the emotions surging through her at that moment. "I think I need to have a slight breakdown right now."

"Feel free." He kissed her forehead and pulled her close to his body, rolling to his back so she could lie on top of him. "You've had a very long day, Lady Dagmar."

She rested her chin on his chest. "I truly have, Lord Gwenvael. I truly have."

Chapter 30

He found her by the lake, as he knew he would. They'd fallen in love here, made love here, argued here, and even trained for battle together here. Whenever Annwyl needed time away from her day-to-day responsibilities as the Queen of Dark Plains, Fearghus brought her here. It was here she felt safe and sane and loved.

The fact that she'd returned here now gave him hope he hadn't lost her completely.

Still naked and covered in blood, she stood at the edge of the lake, peering into the water. She didn't move as he approached, although he sensed she knew he was there.

"Annwyl?"

She glanced at him, saw the babes, and turned away. "Why did you bring them here? They need their mother."

He kept his voice even, controlled. "Because they're hungry."

"I can't help them."

"Then who can?"

"I have no idea, but it's not my problem."

Fearghus began to speak but realized the next words out of his mouth were probably the wrong ones. Slow and easy, he needed to remember that.

Deciding to settle the babes first, he walked over to a pile of furs he kept by the lake and spread the softest one out. Crouching down, he placed the twins on their stomachs, across the fur. It amazed him how healthy and well developed they already were. How beautiful.

He covered them with a much smaller fur and smiled when the boy rolled to his back as his sister did and grabbed hold of the fur, pulling it up until it covered his sister's face. She slapped the fur aside, then slapped her brother. The crack of her small hand against her brother's face made Fearghus wince and the boy cry.

"If you cry every time one of your kin hits you," Fearghus murmured, "you're doomed before you've even begun."

"What's wrong?" Annwyl demanded from behind him. "Why is he crying?"

"His sister hit him, but he needs to toughen up."

Annwyl's fist slammed into his shoulder and he was grateful he wasn't really human. Shattered shoulders were almost impossible to repair, even for a healer as good as his sister.

"What kind of response is that? What kind of man are you?" Annwyl snarled at him.

Still crouching, he looked at her over his shoulder. He took a breath, trying desperately to maintain his temper. "I'm not a man, Annwyl. I never have been. And you know this."

"I don't know what you're talking about." She motioned to their still-crying son. "Pick him up. He wants you to pick him up."

"No. He wants *you* to pick him up. He wants his mother."

"I'm not—"

Fearghus stood and the words tumbled out of his mouth before he could stop them, "Stop pissing about and pick him up."

Those green eyes turned dark and her glare dangerously nasty. "Go to hell."

Fearghus stepped into her body, scowling down into her face. "I said . . . pick him up." He waited one beat . . . then two, before he yelled, *"Now!"*

Her fist flew out, slamming into the side of his jaw, the power of it sending him stumbling back while colors burst behind his eyes. And since he'd taught Annwyl to punch like that, he had no one to blame but himself.

She swung her fist at him again, but he caught her hands this time, yanking her close by her arms.

"Pick him up," he snarled in her face, unclear as to why he wanted to force this down her throat.

"No!" Then she brought her head forward, slamming it into his chin.

"Dammit!" Fearghus shoved Annwyl away and she hit the ground, rolled, and was on her feet in seconds.

They stared at each other, both panting.

Fearghus pointed at the boy. "Pick him up."

Annwyl dragged her tongue across her top lip and said, "No." Then she was moving, stalking across the cave floor to the weapons they kept piled in several corners. Fearghus went to the pile closest to him, snatching up a spear with a steel staff and turning just as two blades swung down on him. Grasping the spear in both hands, he blocked the weapons and shoved Annwyl away. She took quick steps back and spun on her heel, swinging the weapons up and behind her. Fearghus again blocked both weapons, turned the spear, and twisted until Annwyl fell on her ass.

He leered down at her. "Just where I've always liked you, Annwyl the Bloody. On the ground, at my feet."

Her cry of rage ricocheted off the walls and Fearghus barely moved before the swords cut through the air where his legs had been.

Fearghus brought the spear over his head and down, using enough force to spear a man clean through. But Annwyl was already on her feet, the swords slamming into the side of the spear. The power of the move spun Fearghus around. When he faced her again, he smashed his weapon against her ass.

The momentum sent Annwyl into the cave wall, the impact dazing her for a moment. Fearghus threw the spear to the ground and stalked over to his mate. He grabbed the swords from her hands and tossed them back on the pile; then he grabbed her around the waist.

"Let me go!"

"Talaith said I need to take this slow." He lifted her struggling body off the ground. "To give you time. Unfortunately for you, Lady Annwyl, I don't have that kind of patience. As you well know, I never have."

"Put me down!"

"What it all comes down to is what I want. And I want my mate back. And gods be damned, Annwyl the Bloody, *I will have her*!"

* * *

One second she was fighting with some handsome bastard who looked remotely familiar, and the next thing she knew she was airborne, flying face first into the clean, cool water.

As she went under, her arms swinging wildly to try to right herself, images inundated her. Images and thoughts and . . . and . . . memories.

Clawing her way back to the top, Annwyl burst through the surface. She wiped hair and water from her eyes, trying to find—

"There you are, you whiny sow." He leered at her, looking smug and self-righteous. "You going to feed these brats of yours, or am I going to throw you in a few more times?"

Annwyl scowled at the dragon she was cursed to love for eternity. "You. Big. *Bastard!*"

He grinned, his body crouched by the lake's edge as he watched her swim closer. "Now is that any way for you to talk to your mate? The dragon you love above all others?"

"Love you? I'd be better off loving one of those Minotaurs!"

Annwyl reached the edge of the lake, but before she could take hold of the edge, Fearghus slammed his hand against her forehead. "You're not nearly clean enough. You still have Minotaur all over you."

Then he shoved her under the water.

Now past all reason, Annwyl reached up and grabbed hold of Fearghus's arm. Using both hands, she yanked the big bastard into the water with her. She swam back to the surface and took deep breaths, making sure to keep her eyes on Fearghus.

He came up laughing. "What did you do that for?"

"I hate you!"

"Liar!" He swam to her side and shoved her under the water a few more times, his hands scrubbing her hair and body until he'd gotten most of the blood and Minotaur gore off.

"There!" he said, when she'd finally gotten away from him. "Much better."

"What is *wrong* with you?"

"What's wrong with me?" His hand slipped behind the back of her neck and tugged her closer. "I almost lost you, Annwyl. I almost lost the only female I'll ever love. That's what's wrong with me."

"That's all very sweet, but shouldn't you be a bit nicer to me then? A few flowers, maybe a candlelight dinner?" Her teeth clenched and she spit out, "Is it beyond your capabilities to be a little bit romantic?"

"Yes, it is."

"I give up." She swam back to the lake's edge, Fearghus right behind her. "I don't know why I put up with you."

He grabbed hold of her and turned her to face him. "You put up with me because you love me. And I love you, Annwyl."

Then he was kissing her, his hands digging into her wet hair, holding her steady as he plundered her mouth with his own. This she knew. This she'd craved.

She'd been there. On the other side. But not where anyone expected her to go. It hadn't been her ancestors who'd met her when she arrived. It had been Fearghus's. She'd had her ass pinched by Ailean the Wicked and a discussion on books with Baudwin the Wise, Fearghus's great-grandfather. And as wonderful as it had all been, sitting on that soft grass, that one sun shining over their heads, surrounded by trees and many lakes, she'd still missed her Fearghus.

When Shalin, Ailean's mate and Fearghus's grandmother, saw Annwyl gazing off, she put her arm around her waist and said, "Don't worry. It's not over for you. She's coming for you." Annwyl had no idea who the pretty dragoness meant, but then she was being pulled, yanked from one world into another. Into blood and pain and misery.

Until Annwyl had that sword in her hand—then all had been right.

But with Fearghus at her side . . . now all was perfect.

He pulled his mouth away, but kept his forehead pressed against hers, his hands holding her steady. They gazed long and hard at each other. There were words they could say, but none were needed. Not for them.

Then, together, they both turned their heads toward the cave floor. When Annwyl looked at the baby boy it was Fearghus's eyes that glared at her under all that brown hair with gold streaks.

The boy focused on both of them while his sister crawled toward the closest weapons.

And until Annwyl left this world—for the second time, anyway—she'd never know what disturbed her more at the moment. The fact that her three-day-old children could already crawl, that her daughter went right for the battle ax, or that her son planted his hands down on the lake's edge, leaned into her, and screamed.

Fearghus floated beside her, his body rubbing against hers. "He *really* wants you to pick him up."

Annwyl nodded. "I'm sensing that."

Chapter 31

Dagmar sat on the tree stump by the small stream. It was getting late, the two suns just beginning to set. But this was Dark Glen, according to Gwenvael, and aptly named because the surrounding trees were so dense it felt late at night rather than early in the evening.

It didn't matter, though. Not at the moment. Not when she was clean, her hair gently scrubbed of all blood and gore by Gwenvael. He'd seemed to enjoy washing her from head to toe. He'd seemed to be relieved simply to have her by his side.

Whether he was or not, Dagmar knew she was relieved to have him. As soon as she'd heard his voice, felt his presence, she'd known she was safe. He made her feel safe without making her feel trapped; she adored that.

Not surprisingly, Annwyl and Fearghus had not returned to them. Dagmar had been a little worried when she heard the distinct sounds of battle—swords clanging, battle cries, a lot of yelling—but Gwenvael didn't even seem to notice, busy tending to the few wounds she had. Nothing serious. Mostly scratches here and there, but he'd treated each one like a sword wound.

She glanced down at the cotton shirt she wore. Her dress was hopelessly soiled and she had no real desire to ever put it back on. She had found one of Annwyl's rare gowns, but it kept falling off her shoulders and baring her breasts. Although Gwenvael seemed to appreciate that, Dagmar had been in no mood to give Fearghus any additional entertainment when he returned. So she'd settled on Gwenvael's shirt. It was simple and cotton, reaching down to her knees. Never before had she worn so little and been out in full view of anyone who could wander into this glen.

She smiled softly, glad her spectacles hadn't been broken so that she could see everything around her. The old and beautiful trees, the small stream, the lovely flowers, the running deer . . . being chased by Gwenvael.

He flew low, tearing after the large buck. He got in close and bumped the animal with his snout. The deer flipped forward and into a tree, stunning itself. Gwenvael picked it up between his fangs and crushed it. Then he spit it out on the ground and followed that with a ball of fire, engulfing the deer's body.

Gwenvael landed, sitting back on his haunches, his tail swinging out behind him.

"Hungry?" he asked.

Dagmar pulled off her spectacles, carefully folding them and putting them into a small protective box Gwenvael found for her in the cave. "I think I'll stick with the fruit and cheese."

"All right then."

Letting out a satisfied sigh, Dagmar looked up at the trees, now nothing more than fuzzy outlines, and gleefully ignored the sounds of flesh being torn from bone.

Because she had no doubts that at this moment . . . Life could have been so much worse.

Gwenvael watched as she crawled into the big guest bed Annwyl and Fearghus had in their cave. He'd used it himself more than once, but because he always liked his head right on his shoulders, he'd always used it alone. "Don't bring any of your whores here," Annwyl had commanded on more than one occasion. And he'd grudgingly obeyed.

But now he had Dagmar in that bed and he knew he couldn't get in with her. How could he? She'd been through too much in one day. Gods and Minotaurs and Annwyl. Yet all he wanted, all he could think about, was getting into that bed with her and Claiming her as his own.

It was those damn wool socks. He didn't realize he loved her until she told him about out-negotiating a god of war— the most haggle-loving of the gods—with socks! He knew now, though. He knew he loved her and knew that he'd never let her go back to her life in the cold Northlands. Not when he had a warm place for her in his bed and his heart.

Yet knowing all that, he still couldn't take her. Not now. If he got in bed with her at this moment, he'd brand her as his and forever wonder if it was what she truly wanted or if she'd still been overwhelmed at witnessing an Annwyl-slaughter of fifty Minotaurs.

He had to wait.

Yet she didn't make it easy on him, looking so vulnerable and enticing. Her hair had dried into loose waves down her back, and without her spectacles on all he could see were those lovely grey eyes blinking up at him. His shirt was much too big on her and made her appear innocent, like a virgin on the altar of his cock.

No, he had to wait.

Gwenvael handed her two books he'd grabbed off Annwyl's bookcase. The couple had not returned and Gwenvael wasn't exactly shocked. Nor did he blame them. They needed the time alone. He'd offered to take Dagmar back to Garbhán Isle, but she'd softly said, "No. That's all right. I'd rather stay here for a bit, if we could."

He knew his brother wouldn't mind so they stayed. But now it was late and she looked exhausted. Exhausted and vulnerable. And delicious.

Gwenvael shook his head. "I have to go out for a bit."

"Oh. All right." She didn't argue about it, or complain. Simply pulled open one of the books and started reading.

"You'll be safe here. My kin are all over, so there's nothing to be afraid of."

She nodded but kept reading.

Without another word, Gwenvael headed out of the cave and to the closest, coldest lake.

Dagmar growled and sat up. She'd tried to sleep. For at least an hour she'd tried. She knew she was exhausted. Knew she needed the rest.

But he'd left her!

Was he already that bored with her? Already that ready to move on and find some bar whore to warm his bed?

Dagmar knew there were ways to entice males into a woman's bed, but she'd never been good at that sort of thing. In fact, she'd never even tried to be. Instead she'd taken off her spectacles and forced herself not to squint. She'd hoped that would have done the trick. It didn't. He ran out of the cavern like one of her dogs was chasing after him.

Throwing off the furs, Dagmar slipped out of bed. She grabbed her spectacles from off the side table and rebelliously put them on before walking into the main alcove. The thought of returning to that empty bed was not enticing, nor was sitting at the table reading. There were only a few torches still lit, but she decided to follow the light and see where it took her. Anything was better than lying in bed, staring up at the cave ceiling, worrying about whether bats hid up there until the suns rose.

The interior of the dragon's cave could almost be called plain. He had few adornments on his walls. A tapestry here and there, and several weapons tacked up as decorations. But, she noted on closer inspection, they could easily be pulled down and used as necessary.

There were many alcoves, several filled with riches. But what surprised her were all the books. At least three alcoves had books from floor to her shoulder. She cut through one of these alcoves, a few torches against the wall lighting her way, until she slipped through a large crevice in the wall. Yet she didn't expect the crevice to suddenly bow inward, making her feel trapped and wonder if she'd ever get out. But she wiggled a bit and pulled herself through. She let out a breath, suddenly grateful for her small breasts, and kept going, determined to find another way back around.

As she stepped out on the other end, she realized she was on a large, naturally made ledge that curled up at the end. It was sturdy and allowed her to walk across and place her hands on the raised part so she could lean over and look down onto an amazing indoor lake. The lake itself was breathtaking, the water crystal clear and beautiful, a small underground stream constantly refilling and churning it so it didn't become stagnant.

For a very brief moment, she wondered why Gwenvael had not brought her here to bathe, but then she caught sight of Annwyl and Fearghus by the lake's edge. The babes were in a large crib, big enough for the both of them. And they slept while their parents clung to each other. Dagmar could hear low moans from him and soft sighs from her. Could see the queen's body arch, her head thrown back as her mate entered her. He kissed her neck, his hands stroking her body with a reverence Dagmar had only seen from monks when touching their most holy of artifacts. From where she stood, unseen, she could hear words of undying love and promises of a grand future.

She lowered her head. This wasn't the usual sort of coupling she'd secretly watched over the years. Sordid liaisons to be grabbed and hurriedly done with before husbands or wives came to investigate. Dirty secrets to be kept and fantasized over while at first meal the following morning. To be forgotten months, if not days, later.

No. This was love. In its purest form.

And Dagmar felt nothing but regret knowing she'd never have this herself. She couldn't even blame the men who found her not to their tastes because she understood that to have this kind of love was simply not in her nature. To open herself this way to anyone was not possible for her. Who could she ever trust like this?

Feeling a sadness from deep within, Dagmar stepped back, determined to tackle the tight fit of the crevice again so she could leave Annwyl and Fearghus to their privacy. But her back moved into something hard but not nearly as hard as a cave wall.

A hand slipped around her mouth, silencing her surprised gasp, and soft lips pressed against her ear.

"I leave you alone for a few minutes"—that low voice whispered—"and I always find you up to something very naughty, my Lady Dagmar."

She shook her head in denial, absurdly delighted when she felt his other arm slip around her waist and hold her tight against his body.

"You can deny it, but we both know. Know how much you enjoy watching others."

Perhaps. But she didn't enjoy it nearly as much as she enjoyed the feeling of Gwenvael's hand sliding down her leg and grasping hold of the shirt she'd worn to bed. He pulled it up until it rested above her hips.

"Aaaah," he sighed as two of his fingers slipped deep inside her. "I knew it, my lady. Knew you'd be soaking wet from watching."

She'd known it too, but it had little to do with what Annwyl and Fearghus were up to.

"Can't leave you like this, now can we? Wet and needy, with no relief." He thrust hard with his fingers, and Dagmar immediately gripped the fingers covering her mouth with both her hands. She didn't try to pry them off, but pinned them there, hoping they would help her control her desire to cry out.

"Watch them," he said against her ear, while his tongue explored. "Watch how my brother takes his mate. With such skill, he brings her to climax. And I will do the same for you."

As her hips began to match Gwenvael's fingers, thrust for thrust, she had no doubt he'd do as he promised, but again, it had nothing to do with what went on near the lake's edge. She couldn't see the other couple anyway, her eyes closing as she focused on the feel of Gwenvael's fingers inside her, the way his breath caressed the sensitive place behind her ear, and the way his naked body felt pressed against her back.

"Gods, Dagmar. You're so tight." He bit her shoulder, nipped her neck before returning to her ear, his whispers feverish. "I tried to give you time alone, but I can't. Not now. This night you'll spend with me." His thumb pressed against her clit, moving in slow circles. "You'll spend it with my cock deep inside you, making you come again and again."

Her body jerked in his arms, the climax wrenching through her. He turned them so she was now facing the wall, trying to use his big body to block out the cries. It was unnecessary, though, as the queen's own choked cries of pleasure overrode Dagmar's.

Her body shook in his arms, her knees weakening from the power of her climax. Yet Dagmar had no fear of falling, because Gwenvael held her. He held her until her last shudder passed and she slumped, boneless, against his body.

Gwenvael placed her on the bed, tossing the shirt he'd removed from her across the room. Her eyes fluttered open and, smiling, he carefully removed her spectacles, placing them on the side table. He leaned over and waved his hands in her face. "Can you still see me?" he teased loudly.

She lightly slapped at his hands. "Stop doing that."

"What would you like me to do instead?"

Soft hands reached for him, grabbing hold of his shoulders, pulling him down on top of her. "I want you inside me."

Nothing had sounded more perfect before.

He pushed inside her, his way eased by her recent climax. She gasped as his cock stretched her open, her neck arching as she gripped his biceps.

When her lips parted, Gwenvael kissed her, spearing his tongue inside her moist mouth as his cock speared inside her warm pussy. Her fingers dug into his skin, her thighs opening wide beneath him.

For more than an hour he'd sat in that freezing cold lake as human. Even with chattering teeth and shaking body, he was still hard. And hard only for her.

It never even occurred to him to find another. To track down a bar wench or two and do what he normally did when in this part of Dark Plains for a night. It never occurred to him that anyone but Dagmar would be in his bed ever again.

Eventually he had headed back inside with the intent of trying to get some sleep in one of the alcoves. He was a dragon; sleeping on jewels and treasure was par for the course. But as soon as he'd entered the cavern, he'd immediately known Dagmar was gone. Locking on her scent, he was relieved to discover she'd only gone deeper into the cave rather than out of it. He followed her scent until it disappeared into a crevice no one among his kin would ever be able to creep through. But he had an idea of where it led and he took another path he knew.

When he saw her standing there, watching his brother and Annwyl, he'd been shocked at the warmth he'd felt for her. The tenderness. As well as the blinding lust. He'd been torn between the desire to simply hold her close or bend her stomach down over that ledge.

She drew her knees up, allowing him to go deeper inside her, and he braced his arms on either side of her and slowly began to thrust. She cried out, the sound muffled because of his mouth covering hers. He drank the sound down and used his body to make her cry out more. She clung to him, shaking beneath him as another climax raced through her. He felt it as her muscles clenched around his cock, squeezing his own climax from him. Now he cried out; now his body shook as he drained into her.

He pulled out of their kiss and looked down at her. Those grey eyes, always so cold and aloof or so plotting and curious, now only seemed soft and caring. She smiled, the grip on his arms loosening.

"I'm staying the night," he said. It wasn't a request.

"I know you are." It seemed leaving wasn't an option.

And that was quite all right. Because tonight he'd take her body, as often as they both needed it. But tomorrow . . . Tomorrow he'd make her his own.

Dagmar rose up a bit, her lips pressing against his neck, under his jaw. Her legs wrapped around his waist, holding him inside her. As was the way of his kind when human, his cock began to harden again, and, as was the way of Dagmar Reinholdt, her body responded almost immediately, quite ready for what he could give her.

It had been a long time since Rhiannon had been summoned through the lines of Magick crisscrossing throughout the universe. Mostly because there were few who could break through the defenses she'd erected over the centuries. Those defenses had been built because she'd tired of the constant requests from lesser witches and mages for assistance or, even more dangerous, those who'd hoped to quietly steal her power for their own uses.

Yet the handsome Lightning standing before her had surprised her. First he'd sent that useless note through Dagmar, the human having handed it to Rhiannon as they'd plotted the handling of Elder Eanruig. But then he'd contacted her directly by bypassing all the defenses she'd built. Only the most powerful and experienced could manage that.

He was much younger than she'd assumed and nothing like the Lightnings she'd always known. Not only was he beautiful—a rarity among the Northland males—but he was quite . . . dare she say . . . elegant? An outsider from birth, she'd guess.

A confused, elegant outsider at the moment. Rhiannon did love confused males, although it wasn't as hard to do as they'd like to believe.

"You *knew* my father had your daughter?"

She couldn't help but smile. "I've always known." Although she'd thought Keita would have gotten herself out of there long before now.

"Yet you left her there."

"It wasn't so much she crossed through the Outerplains into the Northlands that bothered me. It was that she did it to see that treacherous bitch sister of mine. She only does these things to irritate me. And she could have called on her siblings to help her, but apparently she was too embarrassed for that—as well she should have been."

"I see."

"Now, now. Don't look so crestfallen, my little lightning strike." She patted his arm. "I am still quite interested in an alliance between us. Dagmar gave me your letter. Although I doubt you sent her here simply to get that message to me. So why did you?"

"Her uncle Jökull is on the move. Heading toward her father's lands as we speak. He's doubled his army and I knew no matter what I told her, she'd head right back there. Risking everything to—"

"You were protecting her," she cut in, surprised.

The Lightning glanced away. She couldn't tell if that was embarrassment or regret on his handsome face. "I know she doesn't believe it, but she means much to me."

Definitely regret.

Unfortunately it was too late for any of that. Rhiannon had seen her son's face when Dagmar walked out of that tunnel alive and well. It wasn't just relief he'd felt for the human. It was love. If it had been any of the whores she'd seen Gwenvael with over the years—dragon or human—Rhiannon would not be pleased. But Dagmar was not some mindless little slag begging for love.

That barbarian could destroy the world with her will alone—Rhiannon admired that.

"Where do we go from here, my lady?"

She headed off back to the humans' castle. "Find me at Garbhán Isle tomorrow. We will discuss an alliance."

"And your daughter?"

"Keep her. Let her go. Makes me no never mind. But"— she spun on her heel to look at him as she continued to walk away—"watch your back, boy. I know Olgeir quite well. He won't happily let that prize go."

Rhiannon left the Lightning to do as he wished and made her way back to the castle. She neared the gates when she heard her mate's voice.

"Where the hell did you go?"

Smiling, Rhiannon faced Bercelak. He was annoyed she'd left without telling him where she was going. He was annoyed she went off into the forest alone, without him or her guards. He was annoyed to wake up and find her gone. And she'd be paying for those little transgressions for the next few hours.

She couldn't wait.

Taking his hand, she tugged him toward the gates. "Don't snarl so, my love. I was getting us a war."

"You were getting us a what?"

"You heard me. I was getting us a nice, bloody war. Doesn't that sound fun?"

Chapter 32

Dagmar awoke when she heard soft laughter from one of the other caverns. It didn't amaze her that she heard that soft laughter in between bouts of the horrendous snoring going on next to her ear, but that she'd slept in spite of the horrendous snoring. But now that she was awake, going back to sleep with that level of noise was simply impossible. The trick was unwrapping the dragon who held on to her so tightly. Gwenvael's arms were around her waist, his head buried against her chest, his left leg wrapped around her right, his right buried between her thighs.

She knew she should feel horribly uncomfortable buried under so much male, but she didn't—until she couldn't get him to move. She pushed on his shoulders, shoved at his neck, tried to tug her legs out from under his weight. Nothing seemed to work and he didn't seem to be in any danger of snapping awake this early. Becoming desperate, Dagmar reached around his back and grabbed hold of his hair from the base of his skull. She pulled and Gwenvael angrily muttered in his sleep. She pulled again, going straight back, and, scowling but still asleep and snoring, the dragon rolled away from her.

Dagmar let out a breath and got out of bed before Gwenvael could roll back again. She found Gwenvael's shirt tossed on the floor and slipped it on. She needed a bath, but that would have to wait a bit. Hunger was winning the race this morning.

She found Annwyl and the twins in one of the small alcoves. Dagmar couldn't help but smile at the sight of the Blood Queen. She wore a sleeveless chain-mail shirt that brazenly revealed the brands Fearghus had given her upon Claiming, a black pair of leggings, and black leather boots. Two sheathed swords rested against the table leg closest to her.

So this is the true Blood Queen, eh?

Even with a child cradled in one arm and the other in his or her crib, rocked by Annwyl's rather large foot, Dagmar knew this was the warrior sane men had come to fear. And with good reason.

"Good morning, Annwyl."

Annwyl looked up and her smile was warm and welcoming.

"Dagmar. Good morn to you. Please"—she motioned to a chair—"sit."

Dagmar did, sitting catty-corner from the queen.

Annwyl gazed down at her son, pride and joy warring on that scarred but pretty face.

"Handsome, isn't he?" she sighed.

"He is."

"And Fearghus tells me I owe you much, Dagmar the Clever, she of the most lethal of tongues."

Dagmar laughed. "I like my new Southland name."

"As well you should." Annwyl motioned to the crib. "Mind picking her up? She'll let me feed her, but otherwise she has no use for me."

"You seem to have many"—Dagmar gave a quick glance around—"baby things around here."

"That was Morfyd. She insisted that here and Garbhán Isle have everything the babes may need. But I guess in retrospect . . ."

They smiled at each other. "She was right."

Dagmar went to the crib and looked down at the scowling little girl inside it. "She reminds me of Bercelak."

"I know. But when I mentioned that to Fearghus I thought he was going to skin me alive."

Lifting the babe, Dagmar cuddled her close. Tiny, strong fingers gripped her nose and twisted. "Have you named them yet?" she asked, the sudden nasal sound of her voice getting the queen to raise her head.

Chuckling, Annwyl uselessly remarked, "She's got a grip that one. And we can't agree on the names. Fearghus is partial to My Perfect Princess Daughter and The Right Little Bastard."

Dagmar laughed and pried the babe's fingers off her nose, wincing when the vicious little beast gripped her forefinger instead.

"I, however, prefer Adoring Perfect Son and Right Little

Bitch, which Fearghus will not even hear of." Annwyl kissed the small fingers carefully gripping her large one. Now Dagmar knew she should have asked to hold the son. The daughter was too much like her mother. "Any suggestions of your own, barbarian?"

Never in her life had Dagmar thought she'd find being called "barbarian" a compliment and sign of respect rather than an insult. But with Annwyl it sounded that way.

Dagmar looked down at the babe in her arms. Everything about the child spoke of power and beauty and strength. The proud, high forehead. The strong arms and legs. The fear-inducing scowl.

"Talwyn." She glanced at the boy. "And Talan."

Annwyl gazed up at her. "What?"

"Talwyn and Talan. They're good names. Very old, but have strength behind them." She nodded. "Yes. Talwyn and Talan."

Resting her head against the chair back, Annwyl said out loud, "Talwyn the Terrible. Talwyn the Terrorizing. Talan the Tenacious. Talan the Terrifying."

Annwyl nodded, her smile wide and bright. "I *like* it!"

Dagmar sat down at the table, the babe in the curve of her arm, as she reached for the pitcher of water and a cup. "I thought you might."

"Now, Lady Dagmar, tell me of your uncle Jökull."

She grimaced. "Why must we ruin a beautiful morning by speaking of him?"

"Because I need to know why Gwenvael's been insisting I send three legions to help your father."

Dagmar lowered the cup of water to the table, untouched. "How long has he been asking for three legions?"

"Since the beginning. That's what he told Briec when he was still in the Northlands and then what he told me upon his return." She rubbed noses with her son, making him giggle. "He's a little too young to giggle, isn't he?"

"Do you really want me to answer that?"

"No. Let's stay on topic. Your uncle."

For more than an hour Dagmar told Annwyl about Uncle Jökull and why her father needed the help. It was an amiable chat, but Dagmar couldn't tell if the Blood Queen would be giving her what she needed. The queen wasn't so easy to read when she wasn't psychotically trying to massacre someone.

Yet the most entertaining moment for Dagmar had to be when she watched the queen's reaction to her babe's diaper change. Eventually Dagmar had to take over, and the queen decided then, her face filled with disgust, "We need to get back to Garbhán Isle and let the nursemaids handle this sort of thing. Because I think I'm going to be sick."

Minotaur blood, gore, and brains she had no problems with. Her own children's dirty diapers—hell on earth.

As the children slept peacefully in their crib and the two women continued to chat, Dagmar noticed that Annwyl had slowly pulled one of her swords from her scabbard. Yet not once did she ever stop the flow of conversation.

Dagmar continued to talk until she, too, felt a presence in one of the tunnels closest to her.

It took another five minutes before Ghleanna cautiously stepped into the alcove. As she did, Annwyl was up, her blade raised and at the ready. Ghleanna automatically went for her own sword, and Dagmar stood.

"Stop it! Both of you. What do you think you're doing?"

There were others behind Ghleanna, but they seemed more than happy to let her take the first hit.

Ghleanna motioned to Annwyl. "She still mad? Do I need to protect the babes?"

"Of course not."

But for some unknown reason Annwyl suddenly jerked her entire body, forcing Ghleanna and the others to pull their weapons.

Dagmar gave Annwyl a scathing glare—which made the mad queen grin—and looked back at Ghleanna. "Everything is fine. Perhaps you should just tell me—"

Annwyl jerked again, making the Cadwaladr Clan extremely nervous. More swords were raised, more dragons in human form entered the getting-smaller-by-the-moment alcove with their weapons drawn, and things could turn ugly at any moment. That's when Dagmar lost patience and slammed her hands down on the wood table, yelling, "Whatever you're doing stop it right *now*!"

Her sudden outburst was followed by a loud thump from the alcove she'd slept in and a screamed, *"I never touched her!"*

Thoroughly embarrassed, Dagmar took off her spectacles and rubbed her eyes, while around her the room filled with hysterical laughter.

Gwenvael woke up naked on the floor and he wasn't sure how he got there. He distantly remembered laughter and the bellowed, *"Must you embarrass me?"* but that could have happened moments ago or twenty years ago. Gods knew it wouldn't have been the first time that question had been tossed at him. In his opinion, everyone was too easily embarrassed. If one feared embarrassment, they feared living.

He washed up in the basin, pulled on his brown leggings and boots, and walked out to the main cavern. But he stopped as soon as he stepped inside the alcove with the dining table and stared at his kin. They'd made themselves quite comfortable in Fearghus's den, which his brother would not appreciate one bit.

Ghleanna played with one babe, the girl, holding her high over her head and making unattractive silly faces, while Addolgar held the boy, bragging that, "he already snarls just like his grandfather."

And Dagmar was nowhere to be seen.

As Gwenvael stood there, dazed, Fearghus came out of another tunnel and walked up to him.

"Why are they all here?" Fearghus asked.

"I don't know."

"How do I get them to go away?"

"I don't know."

"What if I 'shoo' them?"

"They're like crows. They'll just come back."

"Dammit." Fearghus's gaze searched the room. "And where's Annwyl?"

As if summoned, she appeared from another corridor. "Found it." She held the still blood-covered Minotaur blade up. Gwenvael had no doubt it would one day be mounted on a wall either here or at Garbhán Isle. "Nice, huh?" she said to Fal, who stood at the other end of the alcove.

He held his hands out. "Let me see."

And that's when Annwyl threw it. Across the room, past their aunt holding one twin and their uncle, holding the other. Fearghus made a strangled noise of panic and Gwenvael went to dive for the weapon, especially when he saw his newborn niece reach for the bloody thing.

But before either brother could do anything, Fal snatched the blade from the air. He weighed it with his hands. "It's a nice one, all right."

"Told you. I think I'm going to mount it over my throne."

Panting, Fearghus looked at Gwenvael and he could only shrug.

"It's going to be a long eighteen years, isn't it, brother?"

Gwenvael patted Fearghus's shoulder. "Aye, brother. It is."

Lightnings! In the Southlands! Izzy had never been so excited. She nearly couldn't eat her morning meal. *But*, she thought as she reached for another loaf of bread and the servants gave her another helping of porridge, *no use in passing out from hunger at the Lightning's feet.*

That would definitely be embarrassing.

According to her grandmother, the Lightning would be coming this morning, and Izzy was putting off going flying with Branwen and Celyn just so she could meet him.

Purple! His hair would be purple!

She looked across the table at Éibhear. His hair was blue. A deep, dark, gorgeous blue. No, she doubted this Lightning would have hair as pretty as Éibhear's, but she still had to see purple hair.

What a perfect morning this was turning out to be! Her queen was alive and well, the queen's twins the same, and most of her family around her. "Most" because Annwyl and Fearghus were still at Fearghus's den. So were most of the Cadwaladr Clan who wanted to see for themselves the twins were all right. Clearly they weren't used to the darker side of Annwyl. But Izzy knew her queen would *never* harm her babes. Ever.

Also missing were Gwenvael and his Dagmar. She wondered if her uncle knew he was madly in love with that politician, as Briec called her. She doubted it. Males could be so stupid about that.

Again, she looked across the table at Éibhear. He seemed to be completely absorbed in the discussion between his parents and siblings, until he suddenly looked at her and crossed his eyes.

Trying not to laugh out loud, she put her head down only to have it snap back up again when her mother stormed into the Great Hall.

When Talaith left an hour earlier to "get some shopping done," she was in high spirits with the knowledge that all she loved were safe. But Izzy knew her mother well now and could easily tell that something had upset her. The question was what?

Briec watched his mate storm in, his usually bored expression turning concerned. "Talaith?"

Talaith ignored him and kept coming—right over to Izzy. Latching on to Izzy's arm, Talaith yanked her right out of her chair. "Mum!"

Without saying a word, Talaith grabbed hold of the left sleeve of Izzy's shirt and yanked it off her shoulder. Her mother snarled at the bandage she saw there. A bandage Izzy had worn every day for the last few months.

Knowing what her mother was about to do, Izzy begged, "Mum . . . please."

Her mother tore off the bandage, exposing the marked skin underneath.

"You stupid—"

"Mum!"

"—stupid girl!"

Now all her kin stood around her. All except Éibhear. He'd already known what Izzy had been hiding from everyone else. Had known from nearly the beginning, but she knew he hadn't told her mother. She knew he'd never betray her that way. Not when he'd promised.

But someone had told Talaith.

"What the bloody hell is that?" her father demanded.

"Gods, Izzy. What have you done?" Morfyd asked, her voice more concerned than angry.

They all could see it. All knew what it was. The mark of Rhydderch Hael. Izzy was to be his champion one day. His warrior.

"I did what I had to do," she said, trying to sound braver than she really felt. She didn't even realize she'd begun to cry until she felt the tears slide down her neck.

"For him?" Her mother still had hold of Izzy's arm and she shook her hard. "You did this for *him*?"

"I did this for you!" she yelled back, feeling hurt and angry and so very stupid. "He wouldn't bring you back unless I became his champion. So I agreed. *And I'd do it again!*"

The sound of her mother's palm colliding with her face echoed around the Great Hall.

Briec stepped between them, grabbing Talaith's arms and pushing her back.

Izzy rested her hand against her cheek, but the pain she felt was nothing compared to the pain she knew she'd caused her mother.

Talaith yanked her arms away from Briec and stared at Izzy.

"You idiot child." Her voice was so cold. "You don't just hand your life over to someone to save another."

"You did for me."

"I'm your mother. I can do any damn thing I want."

"But I—"

"I don't want to hear it." Talaith walked away from her, stopping as she neared one of the back hallways. "I've been fighting all this time to protect you and all this time he's had you anyway."

"Mum, *please*!"

"Tell Brastias he can have her. He can send her wherever he wants, train her to be whatever he or her precious god wants. I no longer care."

Without looking at Izzy again, Talaith stalked out.

Tears poured now, her sobs hurting her chest. She felt her father's arms go around her, but she didn't want that. She didn't want anything but to be left alone. She pulled away from him and ran, her Dragon Kin calling for her. She ignored them all and charged past the open gates.

* * *

Briec stood in the massive doorway of the Great Hall and debated.

Go after the hysterical daughter who'd given up her life to protect her mother or go after the devastated mother who'd given up her life to protect her daughter?

Dammit! His existence was much easier when he only had to worry about what to kill for dinner.

"Leave them be," Rhiannon said behind him. "They'll work it out."

"Like you and Keita?"

"She's breathing, isn't she? Besides Morfyd said she's gone back to her den, so she's fine. And your Talaith and Izzy will be fine. They just need to work this out."

"But when they're unhappy, I'm unhappy." He looked over his shoulder at his parents and siblings. "And that's unacceptable to me."

Éibhear let out a disgusted groan. "What is *wrong* with you?"

"Nothing."

"My Lord Briec."

Frowning at the title usage, Briec faced Brastias. "General. You've brought a friend."

Brastias glanced at the cloaked male behind him. "This is Lord Ragnar. He said your mother told him he could come to meet with her. Apparently he's from the Northlands."

"Aye, I can smell the difference."

The Lightning pulled the hood of his cloak back and grinned at Briec, not appearing remotely offended. "Good morning to you, Fire Breather."

"Lightning." Briec glanced at his kin. "Mother, our mortal enemy is here for tea and biscuits."

* * *

Dagmar escaped talks of weapons and Minotaurs in Fearghus's den by simply walking away and leaving the cave.

It was a beautiful day with the two suns shining brightly overhead. Yet a cooling breeze coming in from the east kept her from sweating, which she appreciated.

She strolled aimlessly among the thick foliage of Dark Glen, enjoying the quiet and the freedom.

"That dress looks very nice on you."

Dagmar stopped and examined the dress Annwyl had found for her among Fearghus's treasure. It was a simple frock with long sleeves and a neckline just below her collarbone, so she didn't feel choked but she didn't feel like a whore either. It was also grey, which pleased her the most. She had no desire to wear bright colors and was glad the queen hadn't asked her to.

"Thank you." Lifting her head she looked up at the top of a big boulder. The goddess sat on it casually, one arm resting on her raised knee. She wore no cape today and her padded shirt this time was sleeveless. The brown skin of her arms was covered in dragon brands, rune tattoos, and scars. She looked decidedly larger this time. Taller and wider.

"Hello, Eir," she said. "It's good to see you again."

"And you, my friend."

Eir's wolf companion pressed against Dagmar's side until she stroked his rough fur. "And you must be . . ." she thought back to her knowledge of the different pantheons. "Nannulf, Battle Guardian of war dogs!"

"That's very good," Eir commended. "We have been friends a very long time, he and I." Eirianwen, one of the most feared and violent goddesses in the known world, slid down the boulder and dropped to the ground beside Dagmar. "He's always liked you. Likes the way you train your dogs. You miss them, don't you?"

"Very much."

"And they you. Of course, you can breed and raise dogs

anywhere. Annwyl, she has no battle dogs. Not any real ones. Just blokes bringing their own pets with them into battle."

"That's my understanding. And I can always send Annwyl a breeding pair."

"That's one option."

Dagmar scratched a spot on Nannulf that had the whole wolf-god's body happily wiggling.

"Do I have other options?"

Eir placed a disturbingly large hand on Dagmar's shoulder. "Knowledge always allows for other options."

"Weren't you missing that finger?" Dagmar asked, staring at Eir's hand.

She raised her arm, wiggled her fingers. "They grow back . . . for me anyway."

"It must be nice to be a god."

"It has its moments. And stop trying to get me off the subject. You know what I'm trying to tell you."

"You can't seriously expect me to stay with Gwenvael."

Eir clapped her hands together, her grin wide. "But he likes you so much!"

"I find it horrifying that the most feared and deadly god of war is a romantic at heart."

"Don't you think the two of you are so adorable together?"

Dagmar eagerly clapped her hands together and said, "No!" before she let her face return to its natural state of disdain.

"It's not easy finding someone who not only accepts you for who you are but tolerates you as well."

"What does that mean?"

"It means that you're the type of woman only bloodthirsty battle dogs could love."

"Thank you," Dagmar replied flatly.

"Before you get insulted . . . I am too! And yet Rhy loves me anyway."

"Rhy?"

"Don't start." She gazed off, sighing. "Rhy loves me in spite of the—"

"Occasionally missing body parts?"

"Well—"

"The bits of blood and gore still caught in your hair?"

"That's—"

"The corpses piled high in your name?"

"Yes!" She let out a frustrated growl. "In spite of all that he loves me."

"And yet you brought Annwyl back. Against his wishes."

"She was already dead. His"—she shrugged—"proprietary rights, shall we say, over her were no longer in effect. Her corpse was mine to do with as I wish. The twins were a little more complicated. I couldn't simply take them since he'd sent them there. And I couldn't rescue you."

"Why not?"

She huffed indignantly. "I can't reward bad behavior."

"What bad behavior?"

"You don't worship me. Or any of us."

"How is that bad—"

"So I had to find another way and that's when I decided to bring Annwyl back." She pursed her lips. "It was a risk, though. She'd already been to the other side; she'd been swimming, laying out in the sun, had a little something to eat. Dragging her back here can sometimes cause problems, especially with humans. There was every chance she would have killed you and those babes as she did those Minotaurs."

"What an excellent plan then."

"It worked, didn't it, Lady Sarcasm? And so we understand each other, all I do is set the plan in motion. The rest is up to you."

"Yes, but I don't understand all these rules you have in place. Who you can help, who you can't, when, how . . . it's endless. They're all so complicated."

"But they have their reasons. I and the other gods of war built these rules for gods and the creatures we gods create for one simple reason."

"So that when the rules are broken, there's war?"

The goddess stilled for a moment and then giggled. Giggled like a child. "Yes." She bent over at the waist, her arms around her middle, the laughter becoming louder. "That is why! And it works every bloody time!"

For the life of her, Dagmar didn't understand what she liked about this goddess, but she did. She did like her. "I'm glad you're so amused by all this."

Wiping away tears, the goddess stood tall. She was a little smaller now. Dagmar wondered how big she could actually get. Or how small. Could she change into a hat?

"One gets her joy where she can," Eir added. "And that's all I want for you."

"Are we back at Gwenvael again?"

"He's perfect for you. And you love him. Don't you?"

Dagmar petted the large wolf-god standing beside her. She didn't have to crouch to reach his back. On all fours he neared her shoulder. "If I were to love anyone, it would be him. But I don't love anyone."

"Of course you—"

"I do care. For many things, many people. But I just don't think it's in me to love anyone."

"That very well could be true. But I think if gods can love, then I can hold out hope for you."

She patted Dagmar's shoulder. "Good-bye, my friend." Eir headed deeper into the glen. "It was good seeing you again."

"And you." Dagmar smiled at Nannulf. "And you as well."

After a moment of hesitation she whispered in the wolf-god's ear, "And watch out for Canute and the others. I don't think they worship the gods either, but . . . I think they deserve the protection just the same."

Dagmar stroked her hand down his head and across his fur. He leaned in, nuzzling her cheek, and, without warning, dragged his tongue across her collarbone.

Dagmar shuddered, unable to hide her disgust.

"Don't be too hard on him," Eir called back. "He likes you."

The wolf stepped back and stared at her expectantly, his tongue hanging out. For her dogs, she'd make the sacrifice. But only for her dogs.

Fighting her urge to wipe the slobber off her neck in front of him, Dagmar said, "Thank you, Nannulf."

The wolf barked. But he was a god, and the sound of it shook the glen, causing the trees to sway and the ground to vibrate.

Dagmar almost fell to her knees, so she quickly pressed her body against the boulder and held on.

"Don't do that, you big idiot!" Eir snapped. "Now come on."

Nannulf ran off after his traveling companion, and Dagmar finally wiped at the slobber on her neck. She felt slightly ill when she realized it had already dried on her skin and her flesh began to itch in response.

Determined to wash it off immediately, she turned and came face to chest with Gwenvael.

"Who are you talking to?"

"Powerful gods."

"Of course you are."

"You asked."

"I did." He brushed his hand across her collarbone. "Rash?"

She looked down at the red irritated area that was becoming redder and more irritated by the second. "Dog slobber."

"Lovely." He took her hand and led her through the trees. "Anyway, I heard from Morfyd this morning."

"Is everything all right?"

"Well, Izzy apparently has sold her soul to Rhydderch Hael. Talaith found out and it looks as if she's disowned her.

And our mother has invited Lightning dragons over for tea. Specifically Ragnar the Cunning."

Dagmar pouted. "We miss everything."

"Exactly. We need to get back to Garbhán Isle before everything implodes and we're not there to witness it—while enjoying wine and cheese."

"Good plan." Dagmar stopped walking and frowned.

"What is it?"

"Lord Ragnar's here? In Dark Plains?"

"That's what she said. Showed up last night. Why?"

Dagmar examined the ground at her feet. "I wonder if we got all those tunnels—or if Ragnar left a few open for himself."

Now Gwenvael stared down at the ground. "Shit."

It would be a much quicker trip with a horse, but she didn't care. She needed the run. She needed the freedom. She needed her lungs to ache and her muscles to burn. Izzy needed all of that to work through the pain she felt at her mother's anger.

What she didn't need, however, was to trip over her own two feet.

Izzy went down face first in the soft grass. Her hands braced her fall and she caught herself before smashing her nose into the ground and breaking it. The tumble itself did no harm and normally she'd be back up on her feet in seconds, but the dread of discovery she'd been living with for so many months had come full circle and all she could do was cry. She thought she'd cried herself out ages ago when Annwyl was dying. But it seemed she still had some tears left.

Izzy feared this crying jag would go on for hours, but she was easily distracted when the ground underneath her feet and legs moved a bit. What if there were snakes under there? She'd walked over a nest once and it had taken her father hours to calm her down.

Nervous, her hate of snakes a strong one, Izzy raised her chest up using her arms and looked down toward her feet. She didn't see any snakes, but they were tricky, weren't they? Plotting world domination, as far as she was concerned. She thought about running, but she had her sword sheathed at her side and her shield strapped to her back, so she felt somewhat ready. Her mother often asked her, "Do you sleep with those damn things on?" She didn't . . . not often anyway. But better safe than sorry, Izzy always felt.

And she knew her logic to be sound when the ground at her feet slowly rose up. She pulled her legs away and turned over, her palms flat on the ground as she crawled backward.

The ground broke apart and something thin and long poked out from the middle. A snake! Just like she thought. Tricky, evil snakes! But as the snake raised farther up, Izzy realized she knew no snakes that looked like that. Sharpened metal over scales. Purple scales.

Her grandmother had said a Lightning was coming to Garbhán Isle. But she knew something wasn't right. She could feel it . . . sense it.

Moving fast, Izzy flipped on to her stomach, her hands shoving hard at the ground as her feet pushed her off. But she'd barely run a foot when that tail wrapped around her neck, lifting her off the ground. The Lightning dragon attached to it pulled himself from the ground, three others doing the same from different spots.

"Find that son of mine," the dragon holding her ordered. "And bring him to me."

He shook dirt from his hair and face and lifted his head to look around. He squinted up at the sun, scowling. "Too bloody hot here."

Since he seemed distracted, Izzy slowly reached for her sword, but the sharpened tip of the tail pressed against her cheek until her head tilted all the way to the side.

"Don't do anything stupid, girl." The dragon brought her around so he could look directly at her. Izzy immediately pulled her hands away from her weapon and instead struggled with the bit of tail choking her.

The dragon was extremely old. Older than her grandparents. Unlike her grandparents, though, he was mean. Not unfriendly or grouchy or cranky . . . just mean. Mean because he could be and because he enjoyed it.

He brought her even closer until his breath hit her in the face—an unpleasant experience to be sure. His eyes examined her closely before he roared, *"Where's me son?"*

Chapter 33

Gwenvael took Dagmar's hand. He'd hoped to take his time walking back to Garbhán Isle. He had much to discuss with her and didn't want his family's dramas to distract either one of them from the fact that they were in love. . . . At least they'd better be, because he bloody well loved her.

Unfortunately their talk about the future would have to wait until he had Dagmar safely inside Garbhán Isle and the rest of his family dealing with any of the holes in their defenses.

"We need to talk to Ragnar," she said breathlessly as he dragged her through the trees to a clearing. "Find out how he got here and then—"

"I know. I know. It'll be—"

That tail blindsided him, Dagmar's screamed warning giving him only enough time to release her hand before he was sent flying into the forest. He shifted in mid-flight and when his body hit a tree, he plowed right through it and many others. He slid to a stop on his back and looked up into the old face of Olgeir the Wastrel.

"You."

Gwenvael grinned, slowly getting to his feet. "Hello, Olgeir. How are those granddaughters of yours doing? Such sweet, affectionate, saucy little slags."

"Where's me son, Ruiner?"

"Planning to become warlord. I hear he's quite pretty. My mother will enjoy helping him."

"I'm sure she will. And tell me, Fire Breather"—he brought his tail around—"is this one of your pets?"

The old bastard had little Izzy dangling from his tail.

"Ahhh. I see she is. Then maybe she'll be my pet now."

"You can't be that big a—" The blast of lightning to his right side sent Gwenvael slamming through more trees.

At the sight of his niece, he'd completely forgotten to notice that Olgeir wasn't alone.

Dagmar stood up, quickly removing her spectacles so she could wipe dirt from them. She did a poor job of it, but it still took off enough soil to allow her to see the hole Gwenvael's body made through the forest.

"She's not from here."

Dagmar looked behind her. Two Lightnings eyed her closely. They were big and purple and definitely true Northlanders.

"You become the pet of one of *them*?" There were times in her life when she could talk herself out of almost anything. And there were times when she should run.

She ran.

Talaith stood by one of the many lakes of Dark Plains. She stood and she stared out over the calm water.

"Now you know the truth. Don't you feel better for it?"

Her entire body taut with rage, Talaith glared up at the god who stood beside her. "How do I make you go away?"

Rhydderch Hael laughed. "You don't. The doorway is open now. I can come and go from this plane of existence or any other as I please."

"Lovely."

"Don't you prefer knowing the truth?"

"I'd prefer that you fuck off."

She felt his hand on her shoulder. "Talaith, I only told you the truth because I felt you should know exactly how much your only daughter loves you. How much she was willing to sacrifice for—"

The back of Talaith's fist met his throat, crushing part of it with the force of her move.

The god bent over, coughing and laughing. She could hear the bones and cartilage that she'd crushed immediately repairing themselves. As she stormed away, he was once again able to speak.

"Don't go away angry, Talaith," he said, still laughing at her. "I was only trying to help."

Talaith walked quickly back into Garbhán Isle, pushing past soldiers and servants. She needed to find Izzy. She needed to apologize, to beg her to forgive her foolish mother for letting another god manipulate her.

The crowd moving entirely too slowly for her at the moment, Talaith cut behind the stables and around toward the front gates where she knew Izzy had run. *She'll head to Dark Glen. She'll head to Annwyl.* And Annwyl would hold her there until Talaith found them. Feeling more and more desperate about her daughter, Talaith began to run. She'd nearly cleared the last stable when something barreled into her. Talaith's feet went out from under her and her body pitched forward, but strong hands grabbed her around the waist and pulled her back.

"Sorry about that," a woman said kindly. Talaith saw worn boots covered in mud and an even more worn brown cape scraping the ground. The hood of the cape covered the woman's face, but Talaith barely spared one of Annwyl's warriors another glance.

"You all right?" the woman asked. If Talaith had a moment, she would have heard the concern in that voice, but her daughter was all that mattered.

"I'm fine." She removed the hands still on her waist and took off running, a sudden, horrible fear for her daughter nearly choking her.

Gwenvael had no weapons, no armor, and no spiked tail—and if he survived, he'd make sure to yell at his brothers about it, too—but the Lightning trying to kill him had all those things.

He sent out a call to Addolgar, knowing he was closest to Fearghus's den, but he still had Izzy to worry about. He didn't have the time to wait for the others to get to them, so he'd simply have to risk his pretty face.

The sword flashed and Gwenvael jumped back, gripping the tree next to him. As the blade missed him by inches, he lifted the tree and tore it from the ground. He swung it and it slammed into the blade as it was making a return trip. The sword cut through the trunk with ease, and Gwenvael knew his head would be next. So he threw the remains of the tree into the face of the Lightning. It shoved the big bastard back, and Gwenvael rammed into him, dropping both of them to the ground.

Desperate, he grabbed hold of the Lightning's sword arm and held it down. That's when the bastard caught hold of his hair and snatched his head back, his spiked tail cutting at his snout.

Immeasurably pissed off—more about his hair than his face—Gwenvael brought his own tail down, feeling around the bastard's armor. He remembered from his combat days against the Lightnings that their armor didn't connect underneath as Southland dragon armor did. It was, in fact, wide open.

With that firmly in mind, Gwenvael slid his tail underneath the Lightning's armor and right between his legs.

Panicked, the Lightning tried to move out from under him, but Gwenvael held tight and, wrapping his tail around the bastard's cock—he yanked.

"You mother—"

He wouldn't release her. Merely carried her around in his tail like a treat or his favorite pet.

The Lightning sniffed the air and his lip curled. "All I smell are damn Fire Breathers. It's like they're everywhere." His head turned and he moved his tail, which he now had wrapped around her waist, closer. "Now where's me son, pet?"

"I don't know what you mean. I—"

The tail slammed Izzy into the ground twice before lifting her back up. "Don't lie to me, female! Where is he? *Tell me now!*"

Dazed, Izzy shook her head.

"You won't tell me?"

Tell him what? Who was talking? Where was she again? *Oh, look . . . pretty colors!*

"Let me guess. That Gold bedded you a few times and now you think he loves you? That he'll protect you?" His tail retracted, and Izzy fell several feet, her body landing hard. The colors multiplied and she could see nothing past them. "You humans are such pathetic fools." He grabbed hold of her sword with his tail and tore it off, tossing it into the trees.

"Do you really think some little whore like you would be important to any dragon?"

"She's not some little whore," her mother said, stalking from the base of the hill she'd just come over as Izzy's senses came back to her with stunning clarity. "She's Iseabail, Daughter of Talaith and Briec."

The Lightning leered down at Talaith. "Are you another pet?"

"I'm her mum." Talaith raised her right fist. "The most dangerous bitch you'll ever meet." She opened her hand and white flame shot from her palm, striking the dragon in the face.

He screamed, his claws covering his head, and Izzy quickly got to her feet.

"Izzy!" her mother yelled. "Run!"

"Oh, no!" The dragon's tail slammed down in front of Izzy. "You're not going anywhere, little whore!"

He spun to face her, his scales singed by her mother's flames and his tail lashing out at Talaith.

She watched as his maw opened up and Izzy immediately grabbed hold of the shield still strapped to her back, swinging it down in front of her body. Lightning strikes blasted from his mouth and rammed into the molded metal.

Izzy squealed, the power of the lightning lifting her off her feet and flipping her back into the forest even as the bolts ricocheted back to their owner.

Dagmar ran, her memory of the Dark Plains maps she'd created for herself leading her. She knew she'd never get back to Garbhán Isle and she wouldn't risk leading the Horde dragons to Fearghus's den and the twins. She'd nearly caused their death once; she wouldn't do it again. So she headed toward a very small lake that Gwenvael's kin never used for fear it was slightly tainted.

The Lightning dragons laughed and crashed after her, tearing the forest apart as they did.

"Come here, little human," one of them said, and she felt his claw swipe down to grab her. She ducked and changed course toward a large tree and one of her "test" defenses that Brastias had been so against.

Dagmar slipped around the tree and quickly untied the rope from the metal spike stuck into the wood. The dragons came into range as she released the rope on one of her favorite defenses and the huge trunk swung free.

The Lightnings were quick, their heads turning at the same time, and they both stepped back, the trunk swinging past them.

Unimpressed, they watched it swing back and forth until it stopped.

One of them snorted. "Ya can't be serious, lass. Do ya really think—"

The ground fell out from underneath them and both dragons let out startled cries as they fell into the deep pit.

Dagmar bent down and grubbed around in the soft soil by the tree. It took longer than she'd have liked, but she found the small box she'd planted there and held it close to her chest. Letting out a breath, she walked over to the edge of the pit and stared down.

"You crazed bitch!" one of them yelled up at her.

They couldn't climb out; there was nothing to cling to. And flying had become impossible because of the oil they'd fallen into. A special mix that Talaith devised one afternoon under Dagmar's direction that saturated them so their wings could do no more than hang limply from their backs.

Dagmar crouched beside the pit. "Do you know what my favorite word of the day is, my lords? It's 'seams.'"

She opened the small box and pulled out one of the simple, small sticks Morfyd had given her. "I don't mean as in 'He seems to be a prat.' More like 'The seams of my dress,' or 'The seams between a dragon's scales.'"

Dagmar held up the slim stick. "I got this from a witch. They know all sorts of things. It really is amazing what you learn when you become a . . . what was it you called me?"

She struck the slightly larger head of the stick against a rock and a small flame flared to life. "Ahh, yes. 'Pet.'"

Dagmar held the burning stick over the pit.

"Don't," one of them begged.

"But as a fellow Northlander . . . you already know I will." She opened her hand and the small stick fell. It grazed against the side of the pit—it, too, saturated with oil—and the tiny flame led to an eruption that tore down the wall and right into the pit.

The dragons screamed as the flames followed the oil under their scales to their flammable flesh beneath.

It was hard to hear over their screams, but the crackling told her to move and move now.

Dagmar did, standing and tripping backward on the hem of her gown.

Flames shot up into the sky and she turned to run, but scaled forearms grabbed her around the waist, pulling her close.

"Head down, love," Addolgar ordered, and then his wings surrounded them as he turned and everything in the pit exploded in a shower of flame and lightning.

Talaith wasn't surprised when Izzy got back to her feet so quickly. She'd, thankfully, taken after her birth father's side of the family—all of them quite hearty. But the sight of Izzy springing back from her dance with lightning, did nothing but piss off the old dragon who'd barely avoided his own strikes coming back at him as they were reflected by the shield.

Wanting them both dead now, he attacked Izzy with his tail and unleashed more lightning strikes at Talaith. She raised her hand, the shielding spell coming to her immediately. It wasn't as powerful as she would have liked and only absorbed the lightning strikes rather than turning them back on its sender. She didn't have time to worry about that, though, as she grabbed her dagger from the sheath tied to her thigh. Oh, how she wished she could tell her daughter to run and hide, but they simply didn't have that luxury.

The dragon swiped at Talaith with his claw and she dodged under and around it. He went for her again and Talaith neatly sidestepped the grasping appendage.

She was at his side now and she could see Izzy slam her foot on top of the dragon's tail. With the heavy shield braced in her hands, Izzy looked at her mother.

Talaith nodded once and yelled up at the dragon, "That all you can do, you old bastard? That all you have in you?"

The dragon swung a fist at Talaith as Izzy held the Lightning's tail in place long enough to bring the sharp edge of her shield down, severing the three-foot-long sharpened metal tip from the scale-covered muscled portion.

The dragon roared, his fist missing Talaith completely. Outraged, he slammed his bleeding tail down again and again, trying to crush a running and dodging Izzy.

Talaith thought he'd give his full attention to Izzy, but he was no fool. He reached down again, trying to grab Talaith. Debating her next move, she saw Izzy pick up the tip of the dragon's tail, readying to use the spiked piece as her weapon.

Impressed beyond reason, she bellowed, "Izzy!" Talaith quickly leaned back as swiping talons came entirely too close, the tip of one grazing along her chin. "Run and jump!"

Gwenvael snatched the sword from the Lightning's claw and stood, his tail still wrapped around the bastard's cock. He used it to throw him across the glen. Charging after him, Gwenvael went up in the air and came down with the sword in both claws. The blade tore through the Lightning's hard skull and out the back.

Twisting it, he yanked it free and ran back toward Izzy and Talaith, intent on saving them.

But as he slid to a stumbling stop beside Addolgar and his cousins, his mouth fell open. He'd be the first to admit this wasn't what he expected to see. Nor did his kin, based on the way they watched but didn't intervene.

He felt a small tap on his leg and looked down at Dagmar. Her clothes were covered in soot, which seemed strange, even for her, and his tail automatically wrapped around her legs as she took hold of one of his talons. Together they all stood and watched.

Talaith grabbed hold of Olgeir's talon as it tried to rip her open, that damn blade of hers caught between her teeth as the Lightning's claw rose. When he realized he had something attached, he lifted it to get a closer look and Talaith dropped from his talon to his snout. She landed on her knees and brought the blade down hard where two of his scales met tightly. Only a human as well trained as Talaith could hit that mark, the Lightning screaming in pain and rearing back on his haunches. Talaith stayed on his snout merely by holding onto the blade she'd impaled him with.

That's when Gwenvael's niece ran up the Lightning's back, sliding down when he went on his haunches, but charging forward again when he slammed back down to the ground. She ran, and she kept running.

Up the Lightning's back she charged until she'd reached the top of his head. That's when she used her right foot to lift off, her body forced away from the Lightning. Then, in midair, she turned with her arm going back at the same time, then forward as she faced the bastard. *Is that a . . . ?* Yes. It was the tip of a dragon's tail. *That* dragon's tail. And she used it to tear into Olgeir's eye, his roaring screams causing every dragon in an eighty league radius to flinch in empathy.

But Izzy always had strength and power and she used it to

drive that tip straight past his eye and the bluntly hard dragon's skull, right into Olgeir's brain.

The screams abruptly ended and the Lightning appeared dazed. He stumbled forward, stumbled back, and then his big body was falling. With both Izzy and Talaith still on the highest point.

Gwenvael went to catch them, but Addolgar held him back. He was glad, too. Otherwise, he would have missed the beautiful way mother and daughter took their leave of Olgeir. Talaith waited until the dragon neared the ground before jumping off and away, her body rolling effortlessly from him until she was right back to her feet. Even more impressive was that she still held her dagger, having pulled it out at the last second.

Izzy was a bit more flamboyant, releasing her hold on the dragon's tip and letting her body fall. When her feet touched Olgeir's forearm, she pushed off and backflipped away from the dragon. His knee tapped her on the way down so she flipped again, her head almost slamming into the ground. But she was a fast girl and her hands hit the ground first, pushing her off yet again. Three more backflips and she was standing by Gwenvael.

Panting, she smiled up at him. And, of course, she waved. "Hello, Gwenvael!"

He beamed back at her, loving his little niece more than he thought possible. "Izzy. Having a good day?"

She peeked at her mother and when Talaith blew her a kiss, her grin grew much wider. "It's getting better."

Chapter 34

Ragnar stepped past the doorway, the afternoon suns blazing down on his head. The Southland Dragon Queen stood next to him. They'd made their deal, and now the hard part would begin.

"Back to the Northlands, then?" she asked.

"Yes. I have many arrangements to make."

"And your father?"

"Will be a problem, but not my only one. There are others who hope to rule as well. They'll need to be dealt with." He exhaled. "But first . . . my father."

And that's when the land shook as Olgeir the Wastrel crash-landed in the middle of the courtyard.

"Sorry," someone yelled from above. "Lost me grip!"

That Gold dragon he'd sent Dagmar off with dropped to the ground beside the corpse. "It's all right," he called back up. "You didn't hit anyone."

The Gold lowered himself to the ground and three females slipped off his back, one of them Dagmar. Ragnar was so relieved to see her, he didn't have words.

The Dragon Queen's children rushed from the Great Hall to the courtyard stairs. "What the hell is this?" the arrogant, silver-haired one demanded.

A young girl pointed excitedly at Olgeir's body. "Daddy! Look what Mum and I did!" She held up Olgeir's horns. "And Addolgar gave me these! He said I could wear them on my helmet as a sign of honor!"

Bercelak the Great leaned against the doorway, his arms folded over his chest. "This is awkward," he said with a definite smirk.

The girl stared up at Ragnar, suddenly asking, "Do you know him?"

Rhiannon leaned forward and whispered quite loudly, "It's his father, dear."

Horrified, she said, "Gods. I'm so sorry."

The other human female, browner than the first but smaller, pushed the girl toward the stairs. "Let it go, Izzy."

"I didn't know." The girl held up his father's horns when she reached the step Ragnar stood on. "Do you want these back? Or his tail?"

"Izzy!" The woman pushed her into the Great Hall. "Stop talking."

"And what have you been up to?" the Silver snapped at the females. "First you don't want her fighting at all, and now you're throwing her into battles with this idiot's father!"

"Don't yell at me! It's not like we had a choice!" She nodded at Ragnar. "Sorry about your father." She marched into the Great Hall. "And just shut up about it, Briec!"

"I will not!"

The Gold shifted to human and brazenly walked naked up the stairs past Rhiannon. "Mother of my heart!" He stopped by Ragnar. "Liar monk."

"Ruiner."

He glanced back at Dagmar who was making her patient, cautious way up the stairs. "Go near her," the Gold said low, "and I'll let Talaith and Izzy do to you what they did to your father."

Ragnar raised a brow as the Gold slung his arm over Bercelak's shoulders.

"Father! I need to fill you in on a new fighting technique I've discovered. Come. Let me tell you all about it."

Ragnar smiled down at Dagmar. Her simple grey gown was torn, dirty, and covered in soot. Her spectacles were frighteningly dirty and one side of her face had scrapes. She'd never looked happier.

"Spot of trouble?" he teased as she climbed the stairs to him.

"A bit. Sorry I missed the meeting. But I'll do what I can as things progress though"—she reached up and tapped his chin as she came to a stop before him—"betray me again at your own peril, Horde dragon." Panting, exhausted, she still managed a smile. "I know Brastias thought my little trap was a waste of time. Now I can tell him it's not. I just have to make sure to account next time for the fire-lightning dynamics."

"What have I always told you, Lady Dagmar?"

She rolled her eyes. "Every action has a positive reaction—blah, blah, blah." Dagmar winked at the Dragon Queen. "Don't worry, though, Majesty. The Cadwaladrs are putting out the forest fire as we speak."

"Forest fire?" Rhiannon immediately went on her toes and tried to look over the buildings.

Deciding it was best to be on his way, Ragnar headed down the steps, the voice of the queen's consort bellowing behind him, "You grabbed his *what*?"

Yes. It was definitely time to get back to his people. The Northlanders had the usual problems—hate, violence, betrayal. But give him that over this oddness any day.

Walking past his father's body, Ragnar kept his gaze forward and didn't bother to look at the old dragon once more. It wasn't easy, but he was a Northlander in southern territory—he'd never show them how much it hurt to see a once-great dragon warrior like this. And felled by human females, no less. Yet the pain Ragnar felt wouldn't change anything. His father was gone and Ragnar's work was far from over. He still had those loyal to his father and those who would now want control of the Horde to contend with. Yet, knowing he wasn't the one who'd had to take his father's life did ease him in many ways.

Going on foot as human, Ragnar took his time walking his sorrow out so that as he neared the cave where his brother and cousins waited for him he felt much better. Then he caught movement from the corner of his eye and turned, instantly shifting to his dragon form and lifting his claws, a powerful spell on his tongue. But those brown eyes caught him off guard, momentarily stunning him as they'd done to him again and again since he'd caught her in his net. And because he was so trapped by those damn eyes, he didn't see that tail until it rammed full strength into his chest, barely missing his heart and several major arteries.

She stepped into him, the tail forced in deeper, pushing him back until he hit a tree.

Ragnar gritted his teeth, refusing to let her know exactly how much pain she was causing.

A lock of dark red hair fell across her forehead as her tail pushed in one last time before ripping out of him.

A single, strangled sound of pain escaped past his clenched fangs and he bent forward. Blood poured to the ground, but she hadn't wounded him enough to kill him. And, even bleeding as much as he was, he could still destroy her. For he was a battle mage of great power. Trained in the arts of claw-to-claw combat, weaponry, survival tactics, and warfare spell-casting, Ragnar was unfazed by most that life had to offer.

Until her. Until Keita the Viper.

To say they hadn't gotten along on their trip to the Southlands would be an understatement, and when he'd released her before the two suns rose, he truly never thought he'd see her again. For once, apparently, he'd been wrong.

And, more importantly, she was much braver than he'd given her credit for.

"Was it something I said?" he called after her as she stalked off into the trees, gone from his life forever . . .

He could only hope.

"You're still talking," Talaith complained. The warm cloth pressed over her face, although soothing, couldn't manage to block out the voice of her mate.

"Damn right, I'm still talking," he shot back. "It's bad enough you decided to play Lady Danger with a Lightning, but then you involved my daughter. Unacceptable!"

Talaith snatched the cloth off her face and glared across the too-small tub. She once had a bigger one, but she'd switched it out for the smaller one in the hopes of getting to do this sort of thing alone. And yet somehow Briec always managed to force his big dragon ass in with her. Nor did it help that he insisted on doing very distracting things with his toes. How could she stay angry or order him to leave when he kept touching her in a completely inappropriate and yet enjoyable way?

"We had little choice. I didn't see you running in to protect us, Lord Arrogant!"

"And what? You thought Izzy could take care of herself?"

"Of course I thought—" Talaith cut herself off, her eyes narrowing to slits on the smug bastard massaging her feet while he tricked her. "Bastard."

He rubbed a particularly sensitive spot on her instep. "You have to let her go."

"Don't you think I know that?" And she truly did know that. Talaith also knew she couldn't make up for sixteen lost years in seven months. She'd missed her child growing up and nothing would change that. Holding her back now would only put a wedge between them. She wouldn't allow for that.

"Then let her go to the west." She opened her mouth to instinctually protest, but he kept going right over her. "The

Forty-Fifth Legion is swapping out with the Eighteenth. Izzy
can go with the Eighteenth and have my kin to protect her.
And unlike the Forty-Fifth, the Eighteenth was trained by
Annwyl herself. They're good fighters and very loyal to each
other. Izzy will do well there."

"You've worked this out quite well, I see."

"I've learned that in order to hold my own with you in a
fight, I must see every potential argument you could come
up with, expect the most irrational decisions based on that,
and . . . uh . . . have all my . . . uh"—he looked up at the ceiling, trying to remember—"oh! All my dogs in a row."

"Dogs?" *That tricky viper!* Working behind Talaith's back,
was she?

Talaith yanked her foot from Briec and stood.

"Where are you going?"

"To kick some Northlander ass!"

"Oh, no you don't." He grabbed her forearm and easily
held her in place. "My brother is about to become well and
truly trapped by the most devious of females—I'll not have
that ruined by you."

"The love you have for your kin never ceases to amaze
me." She slapped at his hand. "Now let go. Let go!"

He didn't; instead, he studied her hip. "Where did you get
that bruise? From your fight with Olgeir?"

Talaith looked down at her naked body, holding her wet
hair off her face. "Some soldier slammed into me earlier
today. It's nothing. Now if you'll excuse me, I need to show
someone her teeth after I punch them out of her mouth!"

His grip only tightened as Briec got to his knees in front
of her.

"What are you doing?"

"Getting a closer look."

Talaith smirked. "That is *not* where the bruise is, Briec."

"Close enough."

* * *

Bercelak walked into the alcove of his eldest son's lair. The babes were alone in their crib, the boy asleep and the girl wide awake and scowling. Keeping his dragon form, he moved in closer, staring down at the babes. He hadn't spent any time with them after their birth, too busy handling defenses with his siblings.

Although that wasn't the full truth. In all honesty, he hadn't really known what to do with them. He'd always felt following the mandatory rule of his kind to never eat children was rather big of him and more than enough. And though he was glad the babes were in excellent health, he wasn't sure what to think or do with two human children.

Scowling himself, he leaned in closer to get a better look. He'd been told by his sons that the babes were much larger than most human children so recently born, and were quite advanced. But Rhiannon had been quick to assure them all that the twins wouldn't suddenly spring to forty winters. Advanced, they may be, but still mostly human.

Mostly human. What would he do with "mostly human" offspring?

Again Bercelak leaned in, until this time his snout was almost in the crib with the twins.

That's when the girl reached up and with absolutely no fear pressed her tiny hand flat against his snout.

Bercelak felt it immediately—a hard jolt through his system. A hard jolt of recognition.

This was his granddaughter. His blood. He knew it on so elemental a level, it nearly dropped him to his knees. She felt it, too, he knew, when her scowl eased away and she smiled at him.

"How's my darlin' girl?" he whispered, thrilled when she giggled and waved her tiny feet at him.

Bercelak let her tug on his hair with one hand and yank on his nostril with the other while he waved his claw at her and tried to coax her into saying his name.

Mutual scowls returned to grandfather and granddaughter at the exact same moment, however, when they both sensed the presence of another and looked over to see Annwyl the Bloody standing there—smirking. It was also the moment the boy decided to wake up, take one look at Bercelak, and scream his tiny human head off.

The girl, not appreciating that, punched her brother, who punched her back. They were in a healthy brawl in their crib when Annwyl walked over and yelled, "Pack it in!"

They separated, but not happily.

"Fearghus went out to find them separate cribs. One minute it looks like they're plotting to overthrow the world together, the next they're mauling each other."

"Get used to it. Most twin dragons usually fight their way out of their eggs."

Bercelak stepped back from Annwyl, feeling uncomfortable. He'd always disliked her; he'd tried to kill her once and he'd go to his afterlife remembering what it felt like to have the point of her sword pressed against his underbelly.

And yet, he had to admit at least to himself, his feelings for her had changed somewhat. The problem was he didn't know what to do with that.

"Why are you here?" she asked. At least this time she didn't sound confrontational, merely curious.

"Wanted to make sure you didn't burn to death in the forest fire."

"I thought I smelled something burning."

"And it didn't occur to you to—" He shook his head, pulling back his anger. "Forget it."

"I'm sure I would have found a way out for us somehow."

"Good to know. There's also a feast tonight at Garbhán Isle."

"All right."

"Well . . . now you know. I'm leaving."

Bercelak backed out of the alcove and turned to leave when Annwyl's voice stopped him.

"Wait. I . . ."

He forced himself to stop and look at her.

"I wanted to say . . . uh . . . what you did that day . . ."

Good gods, was she going to get emotional on him? Would there be tears and admissions of love and adoration? Would he be forced to comfort her?

Gods help me, where the hell is Fearghus?

She stared at him for a long bit, saying nothing and appearing as uncomfortable as he was, her gaze quickly moving around the alcove and cavern. Then she suddenly jerked— almost terrifying him—and quickly said, "I wanted to give you something!"

Disappearing into the alcove, she returned a moment later with one of the Minotaur blades. Considering the amount of blood on it, he assumed it was the one used by Annwyl to wipe out the Minotaurs' entire unit. "Here."

"What's this for?" he asked, not taking the weapon right away since he wouldn't put it past her to suddenly change her mind and take his head.

"Uh . . . well, I . . . I can't keep it here, now can I?"

"Why not?"

"Why not?"

Annwyl walked back into the alcove and held the blade over the babes' crib. The boy turned over and began to snore. But his sister . . . she reached for it with both hands, her dark eyes wide and excited. True, she might have that reaction to anything shiny and over her crib—but Bercelak doubted it.

"Does that answer your question?"

The human queen pulled the blade away and held it out for Bercelak—and he took it.

For a warrior like him or Annwyl, this was something to keep, to treasure as proof of superior fighting skills. She could easily mount it on her wall like other weapons she'd used before, thereby keeping it out of the reach of her daughter. But, instead, she'd given it to him.

"I'll keep it . . . uh . . . until it's safe enough to have it around her."

"That's fine. Thank you, Bercelak," she said, quickly adding, ". . . for taking it."

"You're more than welcome, Annwyl."

Then with a short nod and a smile at his grandchildren, Bercelak returned to Rhiannon, the prized Minotaur sword held tightly in his hand.

Gwenvael opened the door to his room and just as quickly closed it. His hand on the handle, he looked down at Dagmar. "Why don't we go to your room? It is so much nicer."

He didn't know why he bothered trying to lie to her. She simply studied his face for one second before she dug her short nails into his hand. "Ow!" Gwenvael released the handle and Dagmar pushed the door open.

The gorgeous blond—she had a name, but he'd be damned if he could remember what it was—sitting naked on the bed perked up when she saw Gwenvael again, but then her lip jutted out in a pout when she caught sight of Dagmar. "Oh."

"I know this looks bad," he began, but Dagmar walked into the room and over to the blonde. She leaned down and began whispering in her ear. He tried to hear her, but his damn human ears could be so useless sometimes!

The blonde went from being disturbed that a strange woman was so close to her and right into horrified. The problem was she was staring at Gwenvael in horror. Then she gasped, disgusted, and got off the bed. She picked up her clothes and ran out the door, easing past Gwenvael, as if afraid to touch him. He watched her tear off down the hall before walking into his room and closing the door.

"You going to tell me what you said?"

"No," Dagmar replied, diving back on the bed. "I'm not." Then she laughed, which he didn't like the sound of one bit since it was much more like a cackle.

"You know, I don't need you damaging my reputation."

"Yes, because there's such pride in being Gwenvael the Defiler."

"It's Ruiner! And that's only in the north. And those slappers had their own reputations long before I arrived. But here in the Dark Plains, I am Gwenvael the Handsome. Gwenvael the Loved. Gwenvael the Adored."

"Gwenvael the Whore."

"In some parts of Dark Plains, yes. Just remember, you're representing me now."

That made her cackle harder. "Oh, am I?"

"Yes. You are." He stepped farther into the room. "Which is why I brought you up here. We need to talk."

"I don't want to talk." She reached down and pulled the skirt of her gown up, raised her knees, and let her legs fall open. "All right, you. Get that mouth to work and it'd better not be for talking."

"Although I do find that strangely arousing, that's not why we're here."

She dropped her dress and sighed. "All right, what is it?"

He stared down at her and announced, "I've decided to give you the gift of making you my own by Claiming you as my mate. Isn't that wonderful?"

Dagmar pushed herself up, her palms flat on the bed. "Is that the best way you could come up with to ask me?"

"I didn't ask you."

"Yes. That's the problem."

"Why?"

"Is it too much to expect to be asked that sort of thing?"

"I'm a dragon. We don't ask; we take."

"You mean to tell me that Fearghus didn't ask Annwyl?"

"The rumor is he tied her to the bed."

"Talaith?"

"She woke up and boom, she'd been Claimed. And that's not a rumor; that's what she told me."

Dagmar narrowed her gaze then snapped her fingers. "Queen Rhiannon."

"Chains."

"No! Really?"

"Really. See? I'm the nice one. I'm trying to do it the polite way. Announcing it *before* tying you down." When she only stared at him, he snapped, "And why wouldn't you want to be my mate? We're perfect together."

"And we just found some naked woman on your bed, waiting for you."

"That was not my fault. Probably a gift from Fal."

"Why didn't I think of that?" She got off the bed, her hand scratching at her chest.

"That rash is getting worse."

"I know it's getting worse. I don't need you to tell me it's getting worse."

"Why are you snapping at me? I didn't give you a rash."

Still scratching, she began to pace. "I know you don't understand, but there are several reasons we should end this now."

He didn't like the sound of that. Why was she fighting this? Fighting what was so obvious to anyone with eyes? Did he need to get the woman new spectacles?

"Which are?" he tried not to snarl.

"One"—she held up her forefinger—"my father is expecting me home."

"You're right. And you were having such a good time there, too."

"It had its moments. Two," she didn't bother to raise another finger. "I have a good sixty or seventy years left, barring disease or an unpleasant fall down a flight of stairs. And I'd prefer my husband age with me."

"I'll talk to my mother about it."

"Your mother? What can she do?"

"Do we really need to argue about this now?"

"Fine. Three"—and still only that one finger—"I don't share."

"I never asked you to."

"You don't have to." She motioned to the bed with a wave of her hand. "They're laid out for you. Like treats."

"And that's my fault?"

"Yes. It is. Two hundred years of being a whore does not go away magically. And my life is simply too short to sit around being depressed over you. Or any man."

"Dragon."

"What?"

"I'm a dragon. I'm not a man."

"It doesn't matter. Once that cock grows between your legs, it doesn't matter what you are; it's all over. And if you think I'll be like my pathetic sisters-in-law, living and dying by a man's cock, you're sadly mistaken!"

She had no idea when she'd gotten so angry, but she was now. Livid, in fact. She hadn't been livid when she'd found that pathetic woman sitting on Gwenvael's bed, waiting for a male to show up and use her as a receptacle for his seed. Yet now Dagmar was blindingly livid and had no idea why.

But if she was going to be livid, she was going to enjoy it.

"So forgive me, Lord Gwenvael, if my idea of a happy life

doesn't involve sitting around waiting for you. Hoping and praying that you're not off doing what seems to come so naturally to you." She walked up to him, pointed her finger in his face. "I have things to do, I'll have you know. I won't be waiting around for you or anyone. And what I sure as hell won't accept is someone else waiting for you in my stead!"

He wrapped his hand around her fist and yanked up, forcing her onto her toes. Her forefinger was still extended and he slid his tongue around the tip. The way he did that, the rough with the gentle, drove her mad some days . . . and most nights.

"Is that what you think I really want? You spread out and waiting for me? No other thought in your head other than how you can please me?"

"That's what every man wants."

"Then every man can find that. I want more." He took her entire finger into his mouth and sucked it, his tongue still playing with the tip, his eyes studying her closely.

She watched him, her stomach twisting into knots, her knees weakening. "You always want more," she told him, panting a little.

He nodded while leisurely drawing her finger from his mouth. "You're right. And so do you. Do you really think you'll be satisfied going back to the life you had? After all this? Pretending to be the good daughter while performing the role of a battle lord in secret?" His voice dropped lower, the huskiness making her nipples ache for his mouth. "Finding a husband and pretending to be a good wife, while at night you dream of me. Cream for me. Long for me. Your hands not nearly able to do what my mouth can."

"Is that all you're offering me, Defiler? Your skills in bed?"

"No." He turned her hand over and stroked his fingers across her palm and up her forearm. Even with her gown covering her skin, she still felt him as if she were completely naked. "I'm offering a partnership."

"A partnership?" she asked, making sure to sound bored. "You mean as in business?"

He sniffed in disdain, his hand still stroking her forearm but now moving up to her shoulder, her neck. "Don't insult me. Business bores me and as dragon I simply take what I want. There are caravans of gold, supplies, and jewels just waiting for me. They're no better than the blond who just ran out of here and equally as satisfying. I have my sights on much bigger prizes than that."

"And you need me for that, do you?"

"For a good game, the right partner is paramount. I can only imagine what we can do together, Beast, both our families underestimating our skills. The world our playpen."

"And if I get bored with the game?" Since after two hundred years she felt confident he wouldn't.

"That won't happen. You're addicted to it as I am. You love the challenge. Your brain turns with the possibilities the idiots of the world offer us. As I've been waiting for you, you've been waiting for me. And we both know it."

"You're awfully confident."

"So are you. And there's no shame with confidence. It's conceit and stupidity that get you killed."

"But if I don't love you—"

"Don't lie to me, Dagmar." Now both his hands were stroking her shoulders, her neck. She frowned as the rash she still had on her neck began to itch a little worse and wondered if it was rude to ask him to scratch it for her.

"Lie to anyone else if you wish. Lie to them, play with them, tell them what they want to hear. But not with me. Never with me. Never again."

She pushed his hands off. "Why?" She stepped away from him. "Because you're so bloody special?"

He followed her, kept pace with her as he always did. "See?

You understand completely. Now, don't fight me. Be a good Beast and come here."

She lifted her skirt and crawled up onto the bed, moving away from him as he placed his hands on the bedding. "Oh, no. Northland women lie down for no one."

"Then you best get into practice."

Gwenvael stepped back off the bed and Dagmar frowned. "Now what are you doing?

"Just thinking . . ."

"Are you in great physical pain, or is that your thinking expression?"

Gods, she was so mean—he adored that.

"I'll need to improvise a bit," he went on.

"Improvise? For what? And why are you locking the door?"

"Privacy. My kin don't understand those simple boundaries." He walked toward one side of the room, keeping his eye on her as he did. She moved back on the bed, watching his every move. He found linen bedsheets in the closet and quickly tore them into strips.

"What are you doing?"

"You should take your spectacles off."

"Why?"

"A simple suggestion." He dumped the strips on the bed, quickly counting them. Stepping back, he examined the bed. "How are we going to do this without bedposts?"

Dagmar stared at him. "What are you talking about?"

He snapped his fingers. "I know." Gwenvael quickly tied the strips end to end. As he did, he explained, "I realize I should prove my love to you. For humans, that usually means killing someone or something, but dragons do that all the time, so it's simply not that special to us."

"Which means?"

"Which means giving you a proper Claiming."

"Proper?"

He finished tying off the strips and went flat on the floor. He laid one end on the bed and tossed the other end across the floor until it came out the other side. Standing, he moved around the bed and pulled the end out, placing it on top of the bedding. "Now this bit is your choice. . . ."

"My choice?"

He loved the sound of confusion and frustration in her voice. It wasn't an easy thing to catch The Beast unawares.

"Now your choices are: you can take your clothes off and submit—I think that's what my grandmother did—or we can go toe-to-toe." He held up his fists in a standard boxing pose, enjoying how she began to laugh, then stopped herself, going back to a haughty frown. "That's what Annwyl did. Or you can make a run for it."

Dagmar's frown grew worse as did her confusion. She looked at the torn sheets on the bed and back at Gwenvael. He raised a brow, and her expression cleared.

And that's when she tried to make a run for it.

How did she get herself into these situations? And why did she insist on enjoying them? But what else could she do when she got to the door, her hands reaching for the lock, only to have Gwenvael grab her around the waist. She slammed her foot against his instep and pushed him back.

"Ow! You viper!"

"I believe that's your mother."

She went for the lock again, but he was right behind her. She dodged under his arms and ran across the room. The dragon was only seconds behind her, so she charged toward the bed, leaping on it and running over it to the other side.

Dagmar ran right into his arms. Physically, she was slow

on her best day, but she'd still never met anyone who moved as fast as the dragons. Especially when they were human.

Gwenvael forced Dagmar into the wall, his impatient hands tearing off her dress, his mouth ravaging hers. She struck at his shoulders with her fists and his shins and knees with her feet. She knew she'd hit something with meaning when he grunted and pulled back. But it only allowed him to turn her around and force her back against the wall.

He pressed his body into hers, holding her in place while he finished ripping the dress and shift from her body. She groaned when he licked the back of her neck and yelped when he nipped her shoulder blade.

His hand slipped between her thighs, two of his fingers sliding inside her. Dagmar's body trembled and she took hold of the other hand pressed to her shoulder. She brought it to her mouth, kissing it, licking his fingers until his hand relaxed. That's when she bit down on the flesh between his thumb and forefinger.

Gwenvael cried out and scrambled away, releasing her. He tried to pull his hand away, but she wouldn't let go, smiling around the flesh she'd dug her teeth into.

"Unleash me, woman!"

Her smile grew, much to his annoyance.

Gwenvael reached for her with his free hand, but she kept stepping back or moving to the side. Anything to keep out of his reach.

He scowled, staring at his hand. "Is that blood?"

She nodded happily.

"Crazy female," he muttered. "Beast, you are!"

Dagmar shrugged, enjoying herself entirely too much. Who had time for this sort of violent silliness? There were plans to make, supplies to arrange for, messages to be sent. There were always important things to do, and this was not one of them. And yet, she was having so much fun. Did it really matter if every once in a while she had a little fun that didn't involve the manipulation of others and the eventual peace or war of her people? Was it wrong to take a little time for herself and the dragon she adored? That she loved?

She did love him. She knew that now, with her teeth dug into his flesh and the taste of his blood filling her mouth. She loved Gwenvael the Defiler with all her hard, unsympathetic, uncaring heart. And the fact that she was causing him great discomfort but he had yet to punch her in the face, told her he loved her, too.

It would never be a normal union, not with them. He'd never think to bring her flowers or arrange a romantic dinner in their room. And he'd always flirt with others if it got them to smile or got him what he wanted.

Yet what Dagmar knew she could count on was that Gwenvael would always be loyal to her, would always protect her, would always make her laugh, would always treat her as if she mattered, and would never play the games on her that they would always play on others. And she felt confident about all this because she knew that mixed in with his love for her was a little bit of fear.

In the end, their loyalty and allegiance would be to their families and their people. But their devotion would be to each other.

Well . . . and, of course, her dogs. But he could find that out later.

A drop of blood splashed on the floor and Gwenvael cried out, "I bleed! Death comes for me!"

Dagmar didn't release her grip on his hand, but she rolled her eyes in disgust. It was all the distraction he needed, his free hand reaching out and taking firm hold of her breast. His thumb and forefinger gripped the nipple, applying pressure and twisting lightly.

Gwenvael licked his lips, his teasing fingers making Dagmar groan and her body writhe.

"Bring those pretty tits over here, Lady Dagmar."

She did, moving closer without him exerting any force at all.

"Good lass." He slid his arm under her rear, lifting her up so he could wrap his mouth around her breast. He sucked hard while his tongue teased the tip, making it painfully hard.

She wrapped her arms around his neck and her legs around his waist, her body quaking as he continued to suck on her breast. The wonderful feel of his mouth against her had Dagmar nearing climax. Her body shook until she finally released her grip on his hand so her head could fall back against her shoulders and she could groan in desperate need.

"Ha, ha!" he cheered, her breast falling from his mouth and his wounded hand raised in the air. "So easy, Lady Dagmar."

He carried her to the end of the bed. She put up a fight, but he kept his valuable bits away from her mouth this time. He spun her toward the bed and pushed her down on it.

"Now I can't promise you this won't hurt, but I will promise to make it worth it."

Before she could even get back to her feet, he had the torn sheets tied to her wrists. If she pulled with one arm, she nearly tore the other from its socket.

"Ingenious," she sneered.

"Isn't it?" He rested back on his heels for a moment. "I won't say that I don't trust you, but I don't trust these legs of yours. They're sly."

"What does that mean?"

He answered by tying the rest of the torn sheets around her ankles and then to the legs of the bed.

"Now that's simply perfect."

"Do you ever get tired of patting yourself on the back?"

"No!" He pushed her flat against the bed. "Don't move. I need a few minutes to examine my canvas."

The sound of that worried her. "Your what?"

"You're moving."

"With good reason."

He leaned in and asked, "Do you want me inside you or not?"

"No," she told him flatly.

"Forgot who I'm dealing with," he muttered.

"Clearly."

"Never ask the hard questions first," he said, sliding two of his fingers inside her. She was already wet and ready, his fingers moving in and out of her only made her needy and a bit desperate.

He stroked her for what felt like ages, his other hand occasionally brushing against her clitoris as a reminder of what she really needed.

When her hips pushed back against each thrust and she moaned into the bedding, he stopped.

"Now, my Lady Dagmar . . . Do you want me inside you or not?"

"Yes," she hissed between clenched teeth.

"Good. Then don't move. This is very precise work."

She rolled her eyes yet again and wondered what the hell he was doing back there.

She felt heat first and thought it was quite rude of him to burn her without permission. Were there not rules for this sort of thing among their kind?

Then the pain became worse and she couldn't explain where it came from. She felt it all over, from the heels of her feet to the top of her head. Unsure of what the hell he was doing but trusting him as always, she gritted her teeth, trying to hold in her cries.

His fingers brushed against her sex and a cry slipped past her lips as she climaxed, her hands gripping the bedding and her body shuddering from the intensity of it.

Gwenvael entered her with one strong push, burying himself to the hilt until she felt his hips and pelvis slam into her rear. The pain of his skin against hers startled another cry out of her, but as he ruthlessly took her, her cries became louder, more intense. At first it was the pain alone, but then the pleasure returned, combining into some wonderfully messy burst of passion that had her tearing at the bedcovers and sobbing into them. Nothing had ever felt like this. So indescribably intense and overwhelming.

If he knew he caused her pain as well as pleasure, he never showed it, taking her harder and harder as they went. She felt his big hands dig into her hair and pull her head back, turning her just enough so he could kiss her.

Her tongue stroked his, bold and demanding. She hid nothing from him when they were like this. Both of them stripped down to their most elemental.

It was right that it should be like this. Raw and brutal and intense. Because he'd just marked her as his own. She was his now, as he was hers. And nothing would ever change that.

Gwenvael had meant everything he'd said to her. They were partners now. Mates. They would stand together against whatever life had to throw at them, doing what they could to protect those they cared about.

She came again, her cries pouring into his mouth. He felt her clench around him and he couldn't hold back. He came inside her, the hand gripping her hair tightening, his hips pushing against her so he knew she could feel what he'd done to her.

And what he'd done to her was made her his.

It took several minutes for him to get his breath and full control of his limbs back. When he did, he slowly pulled out of her, his cock partially hard and more than ready for another go. But he knew that Dagmar needed a short nap before they could begin again.

The snoring was kind of a dead giveaway.

Chapter 35

Morfyd held the newest red gown up in front of her and debated if it was too much. Too bold? For her anyway? She'd begun to hate these impromptu family feasts. But this would be the first time she'd go to one and not have to hide her feelings toward Brastias from anyone. Even her mother and father.

The thought terrified her, but she was determined not to back down now. He loved her and she loved him; nothing else mattered. And she would keep telling herself that until this whole nightmare was over!

"I need your help," Dagmar said as she walked into her room without knocking.

"What's wrong?"

"Other than being in love with your idiot brother? Dog-slobber rash."

"Dog slob . . . ?" *No. Probably best not to ask.* "Let me see."

Dagmar stepped in front of her and Morfyd realized the Northlander had been telling the truth. She did love Gwenvael—she could see it in those cold grey eyes. Morfyd might even feel sorry for her, if Dagmar wasn't such a plotting little cow. They were perfect together, Dagmar and Gwenvael. And even better, Dagmar was perfect for Annwyl. The human queen needed a good politician by her side, and that was Dagmar.

Morfyd laid her gown aside and leaned in closely to examine Dagmar's rash. After a few minutes of staring, she stepped back. "Where did you get this?" And she was unable to keep the terseness out of her voice.

"A dog—"

"Don't mess me about," Morfyd snapped. "Did my mother give you this?" Oh, and she better not have!

"Did your mother give me a rash?" Dagmar asked dryly. "Well . . . We've never been that close, she and I."

"It's not a rash, and we both know it."

Dagmar studied her for a moment. "We do?"

"It's the Chain of Beathag."

"Which is . . . what? Exactly?"

Morfyd took a step back. "You really don't know?" Dagmar shook her head. "And my mother didn't give it to you?" Another head shake. "Oh . . . oh, my."

"How bad is it?" Dagmar asked calmly. "Am I dying?"

"What?"

"If your mother's involved, I'm assuming I'm dying."

"You're not dying." She grabbed Dagmar's arm and pulled her in front of the mirror. "This is not a rash. The red marks are from you scratching it, but the brown marks are similar to the Chain of Beathag. A gift of great power from the dragon gods. It extends the natural life of the wearer by five or six hundred years."

"Oh." Dagmar stared down at her chest. "That was very nice of him."

"Of who?"

"Nannulf."

Morfyd blinked. "The war god? *That* was the dog you were talking about?" Dagmar shrugged, nodded. "When did you see him?"

"This morning. He and Eir came to visit me."

"Eir? Do you mean Eirianwen?" The barbarian got to call the dragon goddess of war Eir? How was that fair? "You don't even worship the gods."

"I know. But he's a canine and I'm good with canines."

Dagmar was so matter of fact about it all. Talking to gods, getting hundreds of years added on to her life, falling in love . . . Did anything faze this human? Did anything— *anything!*—bother her?

"Your face is getting red," Dagmar noted.

"Yes. I'm sure it is."

"Is something wrong?"

"Wrong?" She threw up her hands. "Well . . . in the next ten or twenty minutes, I'll need to go downstairs and kowtow to that bitch mother of mine in the hopes that she'll give Brastias the Chain of Beathag so we can live happily together for the next few centuries. And you, *you* who worships no one but yourself, gets it because a dog who's a god likes you."

"He's more wolf than dog."

"Shut up!" Morfyd covered her mouth with her hand, horrified with herself. "Oh, Dagmar. I'm sorry. Oh, that was rude. And uncalled for. I don't know what came over me."

"I do. It's called parents." She smiled and winked, making Morfyd feel worse because she was being so sweet about it all. "You really don't think Rhiannon will give Brastias this . . ."

"Chain of Beathag. And she'll give it to him," Morfyd admitted. "I know she will. But she'll make me crawl to get it."

"Morfyd, after meeting your mother and getting to know her, I'm forced to agree with you." Morfyd finally laughed. "That being said, I wouldn't worry too much about your pride. We all tolerate things for those we love. And I'm sure your Brastias is quite worth it all."

"He truly is."

"Then you will endure. For we all endure when we're in love." She was talking about herself now. How she'd have to "endure" Gwenvael. And endure she would, Morfyd was sure of that. *Poor thing.*

"But," Dagmar went on, "before you run off to do any of that, perhaps you can give me something for the pain."

"Pain? From the rash?"

"No. That's merely itchy. I need something for the pain of this . . ."

Morfyd's eyes widened at the sight Dagmar presented to her. The Northlander's back to her and her dress lifted up above her waist so Morfyd could see . . . *everything*.

"Uh . . . oh . . . Dagmar." It was taking everything— *absolutely everything!*—not to laugh. "Um . . . congratulations?"

"Instead of feeding me shit and telling me it's bread, why don't you get some bloody ointment before I start screaming."

"Absolutely. I'm sure I have . . ." She covered her mouth, choked back laughter—barely. "Something."

Gwenvael stared down at the surcoat he'd put on over his chain mail, once again trying to remember whom he'd wiped from the face of the earth for this.

Then he realized it would be mostly family tonight, so would it really matter? He thought not and fitted his belt around his waist.

A brief knock at his door and he looked up. "Enter."

Annwyl and Morfyd walked into the room. They stared at him, both of them looking beautiful in their gowns, Annwyl's a deep forest green and Morfyd's a bright and bold red.

They stood and stared at him. Perhaps it was a glare. It was something.

"What?" he asked when they didn't say anything for entirely too long.

Annwyl put her hands on her hips. "You marked her *ass*?"

* * *

Dagmar dodged Fal's busy hands once again and cut through the crowd in the Great Hall. Yet, she couldn't be too angry with the dragon. She'd never experienced such male interest before—it was rather intoxicating.

As was Bercelak's wine.

Now *this* her father would consider real wine. None of that weak Southlander wine, but a hearty, rich, take-the-rust-off-your-shield wine. Between that and Morfyd's ointment, Dagmar was feeling very little pain.

Stopping, she stared at Queen Annwyl. Desperation in her face, the queen mouthed, "Help. Me."

Rolling her eyes, Dagmar walked over and tapped Éibhear on the shoulder. "You have to put her down now," she explained—yet again—when he looked at her.

"I don't want to." He hugged Annwyl tighter, making the queen gasp. "We almost lost her. I was unhappy about that. *I hated being unhappy!*"

"I know. I know. But you're crushing her." She pointed at the ground. "Down. You must put her down."

With an adorable pout, the blue-haired dragon shook his head. "No."

"All right. But I have a concern. About Izzy."

"I already told my brothers and now I'm telling you . . . I don't care about Izzy except as a niece. She's a very spoiled, annoying niece."

"I absolutely understand that and told the same thing to Gwenvael. But, as you know, I have twelve brothers. And when I see one of them dragging one of the servant girls off behind the stables, I worry. And when I saw Celyn doing the same thing—"

"What?" He immediately dropped Annwyl and, thankfully, the queen had her balance back well enough to manage not falling on her ass. "Where?"

"I saw them going out that way." She pointed toward the other end of the Great Hall. "She seemed a little unsure."

"Damn him!" Éibhear took off after Izzy, and Dagmar motioned to one of the servants for another chalice of wine.

"Thank you." Annwyl adjusted her dress by grabbing her breasts and moving them around, then took the chalice the servant held out for her. "I do love him but once he gets hold of you, he's like a wild monkey."

"I've noticed."

The queen took a deep sip of her wine and asked, "And if Izzy is really behind the stables—"

"She's over there somewhere." She waved toward a group of giggling young females. "I will say Celyn tried, but Izzy completely blew him off."

Laughing, the women saluted each other with their chalices and took several more sips.

Morfyd rushed up to them a few moments later. "We have a problem. And stop drinking that wine," she snatched the chalice from Annwyl. "You're still breastfeeding!"

"So what? The healer said I could."

"That healer is human and humans are idiots. No offense, Dagmar."

Dagmar shrugged and drank more of her wine.

"I'll not have you risk my niece and nephew until they're weaned off those udders."

"Everyone needs to stop calling them that!"

"Now more importantly, there seems to be a rumor going around that you're undead and unholy. Lord Craddock has been trying to stir up the other human baron lords."

Without a word, Annwyl began to walk off and Morfyd grabbed the back of her dress, yanking the monarch to their side. "Don't you dare go over there and tell that man you're undead!"

"Please let me go over there and say it! *Please!*"

"No. Tell her, Dagmar. Tell her it's a horrible idea."

"Well . . ."

"Well? What do you mean well?"

"My suggestion?" She motioned the two women closer with a tilt of her head. "Don't *say* you're the undead. That's too obvious and can be used against you with the other monarchs. But if he *fears* you're the undead that could definitely work to your advantage."

"That's brilliant."

"I know."

"It is," Annwyl agreed. "But I have no idea how to do that."

"Leave it to me." Dagmar shot back the rest of her wine, straightened her shoulders, and tossed her hair back. "By the time I'm done, he'll be too terrified to stir up anything with anyone."

Gwenvael pursed his lips and thought about relieving some of the pressure, but Fearghus walking over distracted him.

"Why did Dagmar convince that idiot Craddock that Annwyl might be or might *not* be undead?" Fearghus asked while handing Gwenvael a pint.

Ruminating on that for a moment, Gwenvael finally answered, "I have no idea. But I'm absolutely positive it was done for a good reason."

"That I know. I was simply curious." Fearghus exhaled and went on. "I haven't had a chance, but . . . when everything was going on with Annwyl and the babes, you stood by me. I wanted to thank you for that."

"Was there ever a moment you thought I wouldn't stand by you?"

"Actually . . . no. Which surprised me more." They chuckled, and Fearghus added, "But thanks all the same, brother."

"No thanks needed." When there was moaning from under his foot, Gwenvael pressed down harder.

"Are you planning to let Fal up some time tonight?" Fearghus asked.

Gwenvael glared at his cousin, annoyed Fal was getting blood on his favorite pair of boots. "He was grabby hands again with my Dagmar." Gwenvael leaned over and snarled at the dragon under his foot. "I've told him again and again that's not a good idea."

"Apparently he's not listening."

"He will if I snap his neck."

"But then we'll never hear the end of it from Mum."

Briec found Talaith outside, past the Garbhán Isle gates. She sat on a boulder and stared up at the sky. The moon wasn't yet full, but it still surrounded her in a soft glow.

"There you are. I was looking for you."

"Everything all right?" she asked, still staring up at the sky.

"Well, let's see . . . My brilliant and beautiful sister is suddenly in love with some lowly human. Keita isn't speaking to anyone. Annwyl is convinced her daughter hates her while Fearghus is convinced his son is plotting to kill him while he sleeps. I found my mother and father acting like animals in the war room—yet again. But that pales in comparison to finding my father—a dragon considered one of the greatest warriors of our time, mind you—telling his grandchildren, 'Goo, goo, gaa, gaa,' when he thought no one was looking. And to top the evening off, Gwenvael has Claimed Dagmar as his own for eternity by marking her ass, which he keeps slapping periodically as the night goes on."

Talaith's head fell forward as she laughed hysterically.

"She is brilliantly livid, if I do say so myself. And if I were him, I'd be afraid to go to sleep tonight," Briec continued.

"Your family is amazing."

"That's a nice way of putting it."

Briec sat behind her, pulling her in between his legs until she could rest her back against his chest. He wrapped his arms around her, enjoying that there was just enough room for the both of them.

"Don't you want to come inside and dance with me for a bit?"

"I will. Soon."

Leaning in close, he pressed his lips to her throat. As she often did, Talaith moved her head to the side, allowing him better access. He gently nipped her skin, working his way down to her shoulder, while his hands slid down her arms. His brutal lust for her always surprised him. He'd thought it would wane over time, but it had grown steadily day by day as she had grown and changed over time, becoming more confident and comfortable in her new life.

He slid his hands down her arms and onto her thighs. She had such delightfully strong thighs, he always enjoyed running his hands over them, dragging his fingers up under her gown so he could touch her smooth skin. He brushed against the leather ties that held her sheathed dagger, his cock hardening more knowing it was there, knowing that when he took her again tonight— as he'd done for most of the afternoon—it would still be there in easy reach, making her even more deliciously dangerous.

Briec continued to travel up her thighs, but when her hands grabbed his, he let her have control, wanting to see what she'd do.

Talaith drew his hands up farther, close to her sex. But she didn't stop there, she kept moving until she reached her stomach. She pressed his hands against her belly, sighing contentedly when he smoothed his fingers across it.

He adored how soft her skin was. How her entire body reacted to his merest touch. How . . . how . . .

Gods.

Briec pulled away from Talaith's neck and looked down at her. Her smile was soft and content, her eyes dreamy.

It had been years since Briec had studied the ways of a Dragonmage, but he still had some skills. And that's why she'd told him like this, knowing he'd understand without her having to say a word.

Emotions he'd never felt before ripped through him, making him feel slightly drunk and extremely panicked. He knew there were all sorts of things a dragon would say to a dragoness at a time like this, but Talaith was no dragoness. And that's what worried him.

"I can't lose you," he said simply.

Her brown gaze turned to him in surprise. "What are you talking about?"

"What Annwyl went through. If Eirianwen hadn't stepped in, brought her back, Fearghus would have lost her. I can't lose you. I won't. You mean everything to me, Talaith."

"Sssh." She turned in his arms, rising up on her knees, her hands framing his face. "It'll be all right."

"You don't know that."

"I do. I know. This isn't Rhydderch Hael using my body for his experiments as he did with Annwyl. This is different. I'm different. I have strength Annwyl doesn't have. Powers that will protect me, and are already moving into place to protect the child. Our child."

"Are you sure? I won't allow myself to be miserable, Lady Difficult."

"Because it's all about you, Lord Arrogant." Her grin was wide and bright. She wanted this child. "Trust me. I'll not say I won't be as happy or as miserable as any other woman full with child, but what happened to Annwyl won't happen to me. The hard part is over now. The walls have been broken, gods of every type and pantheon roam through the worlds freely, and what was once unthinkable . . . will one day be quite common."

"I don't care about one day. I care about you."

"I know." She kissed him, her mouth soft against his. "Your love and faith in me is why I know I'll be fine. That we'll be fine."

"And what of Izzy?"

"We tell her nothing."

He pulled back, startled. "Talaith."

"You know what she'll do if we tell her." Yes. Briec knew. He knew his daughter would change her plans to leave with the Eighteenth Legion because she'd fear leaving her mother's side. She'd want to be here for Talaith, even if it meant giving up what she wanted. "I won't have that hanging over my head, Briec, or have her resent me because of it. She'll learn about all this soon enough, just not yet."

"If you're sure."

She sighed, frustrated, and leaned back. "Must you question me?" she suddenly barked, irrationally annoyed in his opinion.

"I'll question you if I want! And is this how it's going to be from now until you are blessed with having *my* offspring? One moody-cow moment after another?"

"Oh, trust well, Lord Arrogant, that I plan on making your life a living hell."

"Who says you don't already?"

"I haven't even begun!"

"Uncaring wench!"

"Difficult bastard!"

Then they were kissing, their mouths fused, their tongues teasing and stroking while they ripped each other's clothes off.

And that's how Briec knew Talaith spoke true—everything would be just fine.

* * *

Dagmar slammed a small jar of ointment on the desk and bent over it, giving Gwenvael complete access to her ass.

"Get to work," she ordered.

"I'll need a basin and cloth. Don't forget my lecture on hygiene."

"That is *not* what this is for, you disgusting bastard. It still hurts."

"Sorry about that."

"No, you're not."

"No. I'm not. Especially when I saw Fal sniffing around you yet again."

"Fal's a boy. I'd never be interested in him."

"So me, Briec, and Fearghus didn't need to throw him off the top of the building?"

Dagmar straightened. "You did what?"

"He's unclear on boundaries. And don't look at me like that. He's still alive."

Dismissing it all with a wave, she walked to the bed and removed her dress and her shift. She lay across the bedding, face down. And, like the royal she was, Dagmar waited for him to do as she bid.

Taking her foot, Gwenvael slowly rolled her over onto her back. She winced and glared. "What are you doing?"

He carefully bent her legs back until they touched her chest. "I bet if you don't move it doesn't hurt."

"So?"

Gwenvael pushed her bent legs apart and settled in between, his face by her pussy. "Guess you better not move then."

Panting, she shook her head. "Don't."

"Too late. I have to have you. Have to taste you. But you have to keep still. No squirming, writhing, or anything else."

He licked his lips. "No matter what I do to this sweet little pussy—don't move."

Her hands gripped the bedding. "You're a bastard."

"And you love me for it, don't you?"

"Reason help me, but I do."

Gwenvael smiled, happier than he'd ever been before. "And I love you, Beast. Now, remember," he teased, enjoying how she couldn't help but squirm anyway, "don't move."

Keita the Viper walked past the rows of fighting, training dragons and into the heart of Anubail Mountain, the underground fortress of the warrior dragons. It was here that the greatest Dragonwarriors of the Southland were born. Royal or low born, it didn't matter once you crossed the threshold and dared to enter.

As she passed, all stopped to watch her. She recognized a few of the males, but none had left an indelible mark in her life. None had been unforgettable.

She walked into the main cavern. The dragon she'd come to see stood in the middle of a rune-covered circle made of refined steel and trained hard with a long staff. Ignoring those who stared at her, Keita moved into that training circle and went down on one knee, her head bowed.

The staff swung over her head, missing her by less than an inch. Even as she felt it go by, she didn't move, she didn't cringe—she simply waited.

The staff slammed into the floor and one long talon tapped patiently. Still, Keita didn't move.

"Well, well, well. If it isn't her mighty ladyship. The Princess Keita herself. And what are you doin' here, little princess?"

Keita went back on her haunches, her front claws planted firmly on the floor. "I need your help, Elestren."

"My help?" the low-born female asked. "For what?"

"To teach me to fight. To kill."

"We all know how to kill, little princess. It's in our blood."

"I want to learn to fight like you. To be able to take on any dragon that challenges me, whether I'm in this form or my human one."

Elestren began laughing. *"You?"* She laughed harder. "The pretty little princess wants to learn to fight like me?" She stepped closer. "You want scars like mine, too? They don't go away, you know? Once the cuts go past the scales, they're permanent. Even on your human form. Sure you want them? You with your male pets and pretty gowns? Sure that's what you want?"

What she wanted was to never feel as weak and helpless as she had with that barbarian, Ragnar. He'd used her in his games and she'd never forgive that, nor would she ever let it happen again with him or anyone else. She was no mere prize to be won or lost, no bargaining chip to be used against her bitch mother. She was Keita the Viper—and she'd do whatever necessary to make sure she truly deserved that name.

Keita looked the warrior in the eyes. "It's what I want."

Elestren regarded her closely and nodded. "I believe it is." The dark green dragoness walked over to the altar against the far wall. "When we fly into battle, we call on the war goddess Eirianwen. You want to stay here and train with me, whether you fight with our armies or not, you'll dedicate your life to her, just as I've done."

Keita strode to the altar without hesitation and took the dagger handed to her. Holding her claw over the thick marble, she slid the blade across her palm. Her blood mingled with the thousands of Dragonwarriors who had come before her, including her father.

"I dedicate my life and the lives of those I kill to the mighty Eirianwen," she intoned solemnly.

Elestren took her dagger back. "I'll show you where you'll

be sleeping—alone, if you have any sense—and tomorrow we'll begin."

Keita turned to the dragoness. "Thank you, cousin."

"Don't thank me yet." Elestren eyed her coldly. "I'm going to enjoy making you bleed, little princess."

Watching her cousin walk away, Keita asked, "Is this still about when I called you fat ass? Isn't it time you got over that?"

And when Keita ducked the long staff that flew at her head, she knew she'd at least proven her reflexes were quick.

Chapter 36

Izzy made it to the front gates before she turned around and saw them all standing there, watching her go. There were few who could say they had not one but two queens bidding them farewell before they went off to war. Plus Izzy's father, grandfather, and uncles were out there too, the dragon necklace they'd had made for her from the steel of their favorite weapons hanging under her padded shirt and against her heart. But it was her mum that caused more tears to well up in Izzy's throat, knowing it would be months before she again saw the woman who'd risked everything for her.

Izzy gave one last wave and quickly walked through the gates. When she knew they could no longer see her, she took off running, forcing her tears back as she didn't want anyone in her unit to see she'd been crying.

The troops were gathering in the west fields, and she'd been grateful her family said good-bye to her here rather than in front of everyone else. She'd bet that was her father's smart idea.

She was nearly to the field, able to see horses, banners, and rallying troops through the trees, when she heard her name called.

She stopped and spun around to find Éibhear standing there.

"I see you said good-bye to everyone."

She chuckled, wiping the wetness from her face with the sleeve of her shirt. "You know how me and Mum are."

"I do."

She smiled at him. "Coming to kiss me good-bye then?"

There went that tic she'd begun to notice. It was in his right cheek and she'd caught sight of it for the first time at the last feast when he abruptly walked over to her and said, "I thought you were behind the bloody—oh, forget it!" And just as abruptly walked away.

"No," he ground out, the tic worsening. "I've come to *say* good-bye."

"You could have done that back there."

He let out a sigh. "You're right. Sorry I bothered."

She watched him turn, heading back to Garbhán Isle. Cranky and rude as always, he was. What was it about her that irritated him so? He was so nice to everyone else.

She bit her lip a moment before she said, "They say you're going to the north with Grandmum's armies."

He stopped but didn't turn around. "I am."

"Will you miss me at all?"

He let out another sigh, more aggravated than the last. "Of course I will." He faced her again. "I'm your uncle and I'll miss you."

"Gwenvael's my uncle. Fearghus. You're *not* my uncle, Éibhear."

"Izzy—"

"You'll never be my uncle."

"I'm not talking about this anymore."

"The way Celyn *isn't* my cousin."

His silver eyes glinted in the early-morning suns and he snapped, "Going to play that game now are you, princess?"

"He likes me."

"For now. Until he gets what he wants and gets bored."

"He's nice and he's too terrified of Briec to be cruel."

"But if you're in love with him—"

"I'm not."

He tried to hide it, but she knew she saw relief on that infinitely beautiful face. "At least you're going to be smart about it," he muttered.

"He'll never have my heart, Éibhear."

"Good—"

"Not like you do."

"Izzy . . ." He began to back away from her. "Stop."

"Go to the north, Éibhear. Go wherever you want. It won't make a bit of difference. Because when the time is right . . . You'll be mine."

"That's it. You're a spoiled brat and impossible to deal with."

"But you love me anyway."

"No, Izzy. I don't. Get it into your thick head already. You're my brother's daughter and that means something with my kin. But, at the end of the day, you're not my problem. Still, try not to get yourself killed, eh?"

Hurt, but not willing to show it, she said, "I'll try to avoid that."

He nodded at her and walked off.

"And don't worry," she told his back. "I wasn't planning on waiting for you."

"Good. You shouldn't."

"I've always felt my virginity should go to someone who actually *earns* it."

And that's when Éibhear tripped over his own feet and went head first into the trunk of a rather large tree.

"*Gods dammit!*" he roared, gripping his head.

Not inclined to wait around, Izzy quickly spun on her heel and ran to meet with her already moving troops.

Dagmar quickly crawled to the edge of the ridge and lifted her large spectacles to her face. "Dammit! We missed it."

"Mhhmm?"

Gwenvael's arm went around her waist and he began kissing her lower back. "This is your fault," she accused, trying to ignore the feel of his mouth against her bare skin.

"Probably." He moved lower. "But do you really mind?"

"Yes!" she lied.

"Liar."

His tongue began to trace the lines of his Claiming mark. Dagmar's eyes crossed and she lowered the extra spectacles before she dropped them.

"You make the worst spy," she accused.

They'd come up there to watch Baron Lord Craddock's wife entertain herself with one of Annwyl's soldiers. Yet Dagmar had been overwhelmingly delighted when it turned out her liaison was with a local pig farmer who, she'd heard from Morfyd, had a strange affection for his merchandise and rarely bathed.

Unfortunately when things began to turn interesting between the farmer and her ladyship and strange snorting sounds began to be used—by both—Gwenvael had completely distracted her . . . several times.

How was she to get anything done when he kept doing that to her?

"Don't blame me because you can't keep quiet." He kissed and licked his way up her back. "I think it was that last scream that frightened them off. Now aren't you sorry I didn't gag you as I suggested?"

"If you gag me, I won't be able to scream for help."

He nipped her shoulder and dug his hand into her hair,

turning her head so he could take her mouth. His kiss was long and lingering, and she relaxed into it, letting him take what he wanted from her.

Pleasure and happiness—at one time she'd never dared to hope for these. Now she had more than she knew what to do with.

He rolled her to her back, his hands sliding up her sides and to her arms. As if time didn't matter, his kiss went on and on while his fingers gently stroked her skin. It wasn't until her arms were pinned over her head that he pulled from their kiss and softly asked, "So what were you and Fearghus talking about earlier?"

Quickly forgetting about the Craddocks and their bitter, unhappy lives, Dagmar sighed. "Nothing much."

He entered her slowly, Dagmar's body arching into his while he planted tiny kisses against her jaw and throat.

"My lovely Dagmar," he murmured. "Such an excellent little liar."

Dagmar's squeal of protest rang out and she kicked and tried to pull her arms away, but Gwenvael refused to release her as he mercilessly tickled her.

"Stop! Stop!"

He did. "What were you talking about?"

"Baron Lord Craddock." She squealed again, kicked harder. "Let me go! You can't do this to me!"

"But I am!" he gasped out. "And I have to say I do enjoy it this way. Every time I tickle you, like right . . . here!"

"Stop!"

"Your pussy squeezes me so hard." He groaned. "Gods that feels good."

"Stop! Stop!"

He took his time, but he stopped. "Tell me."

"I'm not lying, you rude bastard. We were talking about

Craddock. Rumor is he's raising an army near the South-land coast."

"And?"

"And what?" She squealed when he tickled her again and spit out the rest when he stopped, "All right! All right! Fearghus wants us to go and find out what really is happening on Craddock's territory. Arrange a truce if we can, plan for war if we can't. But with the wife's obvious indiscretions in play, I hope a war with Craddock will be unnecessary."

Gwenvael frowned. "Fearghus wants me to go as well?"

"He thinks we're an excellent team. Figures I can handle the court and you can handle the merchants and get information from the working girls—which had better be all you get from them."

Using his free hand, he touched his cheek. "And risk this pretty face by upsetting the love of my life? Never." He chuckled when she only smirked at him. "Now . . . Is this the first time you two have discussed this little trip of goodwill?"

"Yes." His fingers went at her again and she screamed, "No! No!"

"Well?"

"We talked about it two weeks ago."

"That was around the time I was certain you and Annwyl were up to something. I'd wondered how you'd talked Fearghus into sending that little gift to your father."

"I don't know what you mean."

At this point she was quite aware she was goading him, but when he took her with those long powerful strokes, making her come again and again while tickling her beyond reason, she didn't really care.

Letting out one last shudder, Gwenvael rolled off Dagmar and smiled. "Conniving cow."

She laughed. "I was wondering why you hadn't said anything."

"Why would I? I love watching you work. My brothers don't know what to make of you. And that's just high entertainment for me."

They looked at each other, both breathing hard, exhausted to their bones, and Gwenvael studied her. Dagmar's hair, saturated with sweat, stuck to her forehead and her eyes blinked hard as she tried to focus on his face without her spectacles. He understood now that her mind would never stop turning, never stop planning—and she'd never be happy with a simple life at court.

"I love you, Dagmar. Every plotting, conniving inch of you."

Her cheeks turned a lovely shade of red, but her expression didn't change. She'd never show that he'd embarrassed her with his direct words. Words he would never speak to any other.

"And I love you," she returned simply, the words as unadorned and perfect as she was.

Gwenvael opened his arms and Dagmar moved over, collapsing into them. He stroked his hands down her sweat-covered back, his fingers sliding against the lines of her brand. He did that often, happy and grateful that she wore his mark.

He sighed contentedly and kissed her. "Do you realize that the entire world is at our disposal, Beast?"

"Of course I realize that." Could she sound haughtier? Then he realized that she actually could sound *much* haughtier. "But we're not supposed to say it out loud. Instead we're supposed to silently recognize the fact and use it to our will until we get everything we want."

Gwenvael sat up and pulled Dagmar onto his lap. His hand cupped her cheek and chin as he looked into her eyes so she could know that every word he spoke—to her—was the absolute truth. "I have everything I want, Dagmar. Everything I could ever want."

Her smile was pure pleasure even as her cheeks reddened more. "Then what's the point of the game if we have everything we could want?"

Gwenvael watched as Lady Craddock stumbled from the bushes, quickly smoothing back her hair and making sure her gown was back in place. Tragically for her, the biggest mistake she'd made was *not* that she hadn't cleaned off the mud-crusted, man-sized palm prints on the back of her dress. Nor was it her eagerness to bring war to the people she should be trying to protect. No, Lady Craddock's biggest mistake was to focus cruel gossip on the twins. Spreading rumors and lies about the twins being unholy or the products of dark gods had drawn Dagmar's wrath quicker than anything else could have. Now both royal husband and wife would have to pay the price. And pay they would—later.

"The point?" He kept one arm around Dagmar's waist while he reached into the basket of food and wine Fannie had sent them off with. "The point is entertainment. And do you know what the best part of that entertainment is, my love?"

"No, but I'm sure you'll tell me in excruciating de . . . what is that?"

With a wide grin, Gwenvael held up the small set of cuffs and collar he'd snuck into the basket. "What do you think?"

Outraged but laughing, Dagmar desperately tried to wiggle out of his grasp.

"The best part, my sweet Dagmar"—he pinned her to the ground and leered into her smiling face—"is that they'll never see us coming."

Epilogue

Sigmar Reinholdt stood in front of all his men, his sons right by his side.

And, no more than several hundred feet across from him, was Jökull himself. Plus the twenty thousand troops Jökull had to Sigmar's ten thousand.

Sigmar knew they'd most likely lose today. The troops Jökull had were made up of murderers and scum. The kind of troops bought with great money, but only held as long as the money lasted. Sigmar would never lower himself to buy anyone's loyalty. His troops would fight by his side because they were loyal to him.

His biggest worry at the moment was that Jökull's men could get past him and get to the fortress. But he had plans for that as well. Unpleasant plans but everyone knew what was expected should the word come. They'd all rather die by their own hands, than become slaves to Jökull.

"I really thought she'd come through for us, Da," his eldest murmured beside him.

"She tried. I know she did." And he was grateful she wasn't here. The thought of losing his only daughter, even by her own hand, would have distracted him from important matters right in front of him.

Jökull sat tall on his horse, looking smug and ready.

"Do you surrender, brother?" he yelled across the distance

between them. As part of the Code, Jökull had to ask for surrender before any kind of massacre could take place.

"No true Reinholdt would ever surrender," Sigmar replied . . . also part of the Code.

It used to always amuse him when Dagmar would complain, "That Code has to be the most contradictory load of horse crap I've ever read."

"No true Reinholdt would ever think we would!" Sigmar added, his men cheering and raising their swords or shields in agreement. "Come, brother. The suns are rising. Let's waste no more time."

But Jökull wasn't listening to him. He and several of his men were staring off, watching a lone rider tear down the space between the two armies. The horse was big and black, like something coughed up from the pit of one of the hells. And his rider?

A woman.

The men on both sides were so surprised, no one catcalled or spoke. They simply watched her as she raced closer to him and Jökull.

She saw the banners and pulled the beast she rode to a stop.

"You The Reinholdt?" she asked.

Sigmar had never seen a woman like her before. She wore her long hair tied back by a leather thong and had on a sleeveless chain-mail shirt, chain-mail leggings, and leather boots. She had swords strapped to her back and a shield hanging from her horse. She was scarred and branded on both her forearms, and although partially covered by her gauntlets, he could still see parts of a dragon image burned into her flesh.

And though she was armed to the teeth, she wore no full armor, nor any colors.

"I be Sigmar."

She pulled a letter from under her saddle. "This is from your daughter."

He took it and opened the expensive parchment. It was short but to the point.

> Father—
> *As a Northlander, we all knew what I'd do.*
>
> Dagmar

"Who's Jökull?" the woman asked.

"I'm Jökull, wench." Jökull leaned over the pummel of his saddle, leering at the woman. "And who are you?"

She turned her horse and smiled at him. "I'm Annwyl." Then with a speed Sigmar had never seen before, she ripped one of the swords from its sheath and threw it. The weapon flipped end over end until it slammed full force into the middle of Jökull's head, yanking him back off his horse and into the men behind him.

She looked over her shoulder at Sigmar. "I can only stay today. Have to get back to my twins and my mate before he comes looking for me—which won't be good for you. Oh! And I'm supposed to bring someone named Canute with me when I return. Dagmar said for you not to argue about it. But my troops will stay." She nodded in the direction she'd come and he saw those troops marching over the ridge. "That's five legions your daughter negotiated out of me. She's good, warlord. And once we get this all cleaned up for you, she'll be home to see you." She smiled. "She has a very big surprise for you." She snapped her fingers. "And I'm supposed to send a very big hello to . . . uh . . . Eymund?"

Sigmar's eldest nodded at the woman.

"From Gwenvael."

His son's shoulders slumped and his brothers chuckled beside him.

Then Annwyl the Bloody, Queen of Dark Plains, faced the confused and panicked troops of Jökull.

"I want my sword back," she announced to them, pulling her second sword from its sheath. "Now who's gonna stop me from getting it?"

His eldest leaned in close and reminded Sigmar, "I guess Cousin Uddo was right all those years ago, eh, Da?"

"What?"

"When he'd called her Beast." His son grinned and motioned to the mad bitch riding flat out into Jökull's troops with her sword raised. The mad bitch his daughter had sent to them. "I think, unfortunately for poor Uncle Jökull, Uddo was bang on."

It started slow, deep in his chest, but burst out of him. Great, powerful laughter, his troops joining in as Annwyl's legions swarmed over Jökull's hired troops.

"Get in there, men!" Sigmar finally ordered, swinging his ax off his shoulder. "Anyone not in our colors or Annwyl's—dies!"

He raised his ax high, knowing there was only one war cry that would mean anything to himself or his men on this day. "For The Beast!" he bellowed.

And as one, her kinsmen yelled back, *"For The Beast!"*

Did you miss the first two books in
G.A. Aiken's fabulous dragon series?
The magic begins with
DRAGON ACTUALLY . . .

Dragon Actually

It's not always easy being a female warrior with a nickname like Annwyl the Bloody. Men tend to either cower in fear—a lot—or else salute. It's true that Annwyl has a knack for decapitating legions of her ruthless brother's soldiers without pausing for breath. But just once it would be nice to be able to really talk to a man, the way she can talk to Fearghus the Destroyer . . .

Too bad that Fearghus is a dragon, of the large, scaly, and deadly type. With him, Annwyl feels safe—a far cry from the feelings aroused by the hard-bodied, arrogant knight Fearghus has arranged to help train her for battle. With her days spent fighting a man who fills her with fierce, heady desire, and her nights spent in the company of a magical creature who could smite a village just by exhaling, Annwyl is sure life couldn't get any stranger. She's wrong . . .

[And just wait until you meet the rest of the family . . .]

"Hold, knight." She stared at him, taking a deep breath to still her rapidly beating heart. *By the gods, he's beautiful.* And Annwyl didn't trust him as far as she could throw him. Which wasn't far. He had to be the biggest man she'd ever seen. All of it hard-packed muscle that radiated power and strength.

She tightened her grip on her sword. "I know you."

"And I know you."

Annwyl frowned. "Who are you?"

"Who are *you*?"

Her eyes narrowed. "You kissed me."

"And I believe *you* kissed *me*."

Annwyl's rage grew, her patience for games waning greatly. "Perhaps you failed to realize that I have a blade to your throat, knight."

"And perhaps you failed to realize"—he knocked her blade away, placing the tip of his own against her throat—"that I'm not some weak-willed toady who slaves for your brother, Annwyl the Bloody of the Dark Plains."

Annwyl glanced down at the sword and back at the man holding it. "Who the hell are you?"

"The dragon sent me." He lowered his blade. "And he was right. You are too slow. You'll never defeat Lorcan."

Her rage welled up and she slashed at him with her blade. But it wasn't one of her well-trained maneuvers. It felt awkward and messy. He blocked her easily, slamming her to the ground.

Her teeth rattled in her head. Good thing her wound had already healed, otherwise Morfyd would be sewing it up once again.

The knight stood over her. "You can do better than that, can't you?" She stared up at him and he smiled. "Or maybe not. Guess we'll just have to see."

He wandered off. Annwyl knew he expected her to follow. And, for some unknown reason, she did.

She found him by the stream that ran through the glen. It took all her strength to walk up to him. She really wanted to run back into the dragon's lair and hide under his massive wings. She wasn't afraid of this man. It was something else. Something far more dangerous.

As she approached, he turned and smiled. And Annwyl felt her stomach clench. Actually, the clenching might have been a bit lower.

She'd never known a man who made her so . . . well . . . nervous. And she'd lived on Garbhán Isle since the age of ten; all she'd ever known were men who made it their business to make women nervous, if not downright terrified.

"Well," she demanded coldly.

He moved to stand in front of her, his gorgeous smile teasing her. "Desperate are we?"

Annwyl shook her head and stepped away from him. "I thought you said something about training me for battle, knight." *For the dragon*. She would only do this because the dragon asked her to. And she would damn well make sure he knew it, too.

"Aye, I did, Annwyl the Bloody."

"Do stop calling me that."

"You should be proud of that name. From what I understand, you earned it."

"My brother also called me dung heap. I'm sure he thought I earned that too, but I'd rather no one call me that."

"Fair enough."

"And do you have a name?" He opened his mouth to say something but she stopped him. "You know what? I don't want to know."

"Really?"

"It will make beating the hell out of you so much easier."

She wanted to throw him off. Make him uneasy. But his smile beamed like a bright ray of sunlight in the darkened glen. "A challenge. I like that." He growled the last sentence, and it slithered all the way down to her toes. Part of her wanted to panic over that statement, since it frightened her more than the dragon himself. But she didn't have time. Not with the blade flashing past her head, forcing her to duck and unsheathe her own sword.

He watched her move. Drank her in. And when she took off her shirt and continued to fight in just leather leggings, boots, and the cloth that bound her breasts down, he had to constantly remind himself of why he now helped her. To train her to be a better fighter. Nothing more or less. It was *not* so he could lick the tender spot between her shoulder and throat.

Annwyl, though, turned out to be a damn good fighter. Strong. Powerful. Highly aggressive. She listened to direction well and picked up combat skills quickly. But her anger definitely remained her main weakness. Anytime he blocked one of her faster blows, anytime he moved too quickly for her to make contact, and, especially, anytime he touched her, the girl flew into a rage. An all-consuming rage. And although he knew the soldiers of Lorcan's army would easily fall to her blade, her brother was different. He knew of that man's reputation as a warrior and, as Annwyl now stood, she didn't stand a chance.

Her fear of Lorcan would stop her from making the killing blow. Her rage would make her vulnerable. The mere thought of her getting killed sent a cold wave of fear through him.

Yet if he could teach her to control her rage, she could turn it into her greatest ally. Use it to destroy any and all who dare challenge her.

The shifting sun and deepening shadows told him that the hour grew late. The expression on her face told him that exhaustion would claim her soon, although she'd never admit it. At least not to him. But he knew what would push her over the edge. He grabbed her ass.

Annwyl screeched and swung around. He knocked her blade from her hand and threw her on her back.

"How many times, exactly, do I have to tell you that your anger leaves you exposed and open to attack?"

She raised herself on her elbows. "You grabbed me," she accused. "Again!"

He leaned down so they were nose to nose. "Yes I did. And I enjoyed every second of it."

Her fist flashed out, aiming for his face. But he caught her hand, his fingers brushing across hers. "Of course, if you learned to control your rage I'd never get near you." He brought her fingers to his lips and kissed them gently. "But until that time comes, I guess your ass belongs to me."

She bared her teeth, and he didn't try to hide his smile. How could he when he knew how it irritated her so? "I think we've practiced enough for the day. At least I have. And the dragon now has a scouting party for his dinner. But I'll be back tomorrow. Be ready, Annwyl the Bloody. This won't get any easier."

About a Dragon

For Nolwenn witch Talaith, a bad day begins with being dragged from bed by an angry mob intent on her crispy end and culminates in rescue by—wait for it—a silver-maned dragon. Existence as a hated outcast is nothing new for a woman with such powerful secrets. The dragon, though? A tad unusual. This one has a human form to die for, and knows it. According to dragon law, Talaith is now his property, for pleasure . . . or otherwise. But if Lord Arrogance thinks she's the kind of damsel to acquiesce without a word, he's in for a surprise . . .

Is the woman never silent? Briec the Mighty knew the moment he laid eyes on Talaith that she would be his, but he'd counted on tongue-lashings of an altogether different sort. It's embarrassing, really, that it isn't this outspoken female's Magicks that have the realm's greatest dragon in her thrall. No, Briec has been spellbound by something altogether different—and if he doesn't tread carefully, what he doesn't know about human women could well be the undoing of his entire race . . .

They dragged her from bed before the two suns even rose over the Caffyn Mountains. She fought as best she could, but the noose they'd wrapped around her throat cut off her ability to breathe, weakening her. And they bound her hands tightly with coarse rope because they feared she'd cast a spell on them. She had none to cast, but what really annoyed her was her inability to get the dagger still tied to her thigh.

Of course, only she would get an entire town to try and kill her. *Nice one, idiot.*

Strong men threw the end of the rope over a sturdy branch and slowly pulled her off her feet. They didn't want her to die too quickly. They wanted to watch her hang for awhile, and it looked like they'd prepared a pyre for a good, old-fashioned witch burning.

Lovely.

The man she called husband screamed at her. He screamed how she was a witch. How she was evil. How they all knew the truth about her and now she would pay. If she weren't fighting for her life, she'd roll her eyes in annoyance.

But what truly galled her . . . what set her teeth absolutely on edge—other than choking to death—was that the goddess who sent her here all those years ago was the same one leaving her to die.

She thought the evil bitch would at least protect her until

she finally accomplished what she needed her to do. What she'd been training to do since she was sixteen.

But Talaith, Daughter of Haldane, had learned long ago that no one was to be trusted. No one would ever protect her. No one would ever do anything but use her. Eventually she'd learned to trust no one but herself.

Of course a few allies might have helped you this day, Talaith.

She coughed and squirmed in her bonds, praying her neck would finally just break. She would definitely rather not die by burning. Talaith never considered flame a witch's best friend.

As she wondered what it would take to snap her neck using her own body weight, she saw him.

He stood out like a jewel among pigs. Her arrogant, handsome knight, still in his chain mail with the bright red surcoat over it, but without the black cape he wore that shielded part of his face and hair from her sight. She wasn't sure if it were her imagination or if her impending death had made her sight untrustworthy, but he had—*silver?*—yes. He had glossy silver hair that reached past his knees. But it wasn't the silver hair of an old man. This beauty couldn't be more than thirty winters. At most.

Gods, and he was a beauty. The most beautiful thing Talaith had ever seen. Well, at least she'd leave this world with something pretty for her last vision.

He walked up to one of the townsfolk and motioned toward her.

"She is a witch, m'lord!" a woman—whose child Talaith saved from a poisonous snakebite the year before—screamed. "She's in league with demons and the dark gods."

She wished. At least the dark gods protected their own.

The knight stared at her for several moments. If she could, she wouldn't have been too proud to beg for mercy. But, even if she could speak, she wouldn't bother. Those cold violet eyes of his told her it would have done no good anyway.

If only you'd fucked him like you wanted to, he might feel slightly obligated to help you. But you had to be a hard bitch.

Of course, according to her husband, she was always a hard bitch.

With a bored sigh, her knight turned and walked away, disappearing into the surrounding woods.

Typical. Even a brave knight wouldn't help her. Every day her life grew more and more pathetic.

"Die, witch! Die!" *How lovely.* Her own "dear" husband started up that endearing chant. The bastard. She'd meet him on the other side when his time came and she'd make sure he suffered for eternity.

The noose tightened a bit and she felt more of her life slip away while they continued to pile extra wood around the stake.

Funny how one's mind plays tricks when so close to dying.

For instance, if she didn't know better, she'd swear that was a giant silver dragon ambling out of the forest. An enormous, amazing creature, with a silver mane of hair that gleamed in the morning sunshine and nearly swept the shaking ground at its feet. Two massive white horns sat atop its head and a long tail, with what looked to be a dagger-sharp tip, swung lazily behind him.

Silently, he stood behind the townspeople. So focused on her, they were completely unaware of his presence. *Who knew I could be so fascinating as to distract an entire town?* Of course, they could also be ignoring the dragon because it was simply a figment of her imagination. A dream of a grand rescue that would never come.

Her fantasy dragon leaned forward and nudged Julius the baker with the tip of his snout. Julius glanced behind him, nodded and turned back to her. Then he froze where he stood . . . just before he pissed himself. That's when his wife glanced at him and behind him. She screamed, grabbed her son, who had been seconds away from throwing a rather large rock at Talaith, and ran. Soon after, the rest of the townsfolk caught sight of her fantasy dragon, screamed and bolted away.

She frowned. Perhaps she still had enough of her power so she could conjure the image of the beast, but somehow she doubted it.

The dragon shot out a few flames at the retreating humans, but nothing to do any real harm. Finally, it stared at her for several moments, turned and walked off.

Unbelievable. Even my rescue fantasies are disasters.

But as she wondered if her afterlife would be as pathetic as her current life, the dragon's tail whipped out. The tip cut through the rope that hung her from the tree, and she dropped.

Expecting her ass to hit the unforgiving ground at any moment, she tensed in surprise as the tail wrapped itself around her body and held her.

Now that the noose was not so tight, her senses slowly came back to her. That's when she realized a tail really did have her. A tail attached to an enormous dragon casually walking through the forest. She tried to move out of its grasp, but the tail pinned her arms—with her still bound wrists—against her body. And her noose still tight enough she couldn't call for help.

Of course, who would she call? Her husband? Probably not. Lord Hamish, ruler of these lands? If she had the strength, she would have laughed at that.

No. It looked as if she was going to be the breakfast of a monster.

As the dragon made it into a clearing and suddenly took to the air—with her still wrapped up in its tail—Talaith had only one thought . . .

Typical.